SUMMER OF LOVE

Jessie Penwarden is the only daughter of the vicar of Abbot's Cove, on the Cornish coast. Her parents have wrapped her in cotton wool since her brother's death during the Second World War, but when Jessie and her friend Rita Levant meet some boys at a summer dance Jessie falls in love for the first time. Riding on the back of Will Tremayne's motorbike seems incredibly glamorous, though she daren't tell her father she is falling in love with a biker boy. Meanwhile Rita's reckless nature leads her into trouble, and the Penwarden family soon has greater things to worry about than Jessie's blossoming romance.

SUMMER OF LOVE

SUMMER OF LOVE

by

Rachel Moore

Magna Large Print Books
Long Preston, North Yorkshire,
BD23 4ND, England.

British Library Cataloguing in Publication Data.

Moore, Rachel
    Summer of love.

    A catalogue record of this book is
    available from the British Library

    ISBN   978-0-7505-3361-4

First published in Great Britain in 2010 by Allison & Busby Ltd.

Copyright © 2010 by Rachel Moore

Cover illustration by arrangement with Allison & Busby Ltd.

The moral right of the author has been asserted

Published in Large Print 2011 by arrangement with
Allison & Busby Ltd.

Magna Large Print is an imprint of Library Magna Books Ltd.

Printed and bound in Great Britain by
T.J. (International) Ltd., Cornwall, PL28 8RW

CHAPTER ONE

There wasn't a breath of wind on the moors on that August Saturday afternoon. The air was heavy and still, fragrant with the scents of clover and heather and wild thyme, and the silence was only broken by the stultifying drone of bees. The two girls lay on their backs, eyes closed, as if seeing which one could merge in with nature for the longest time. It was only when the drone of bees gradually became something louder and slightly more intrusive that Jessie Penwarden drew in her breath and sat up so fast that it made her head swim.

'For goodness' sake, Jessie, don't get your knickers in a twist, it's only one of the planes from over Penzance way, not one of those Luftwaffes or whatever they call them,' her friend Rita said lazily. 'The war's been over for three years, and the Jerries are our friends now, remember?'

'Tell that to my dad,' Jessie muttered, feeling her heartbeat begin to relax. 'He's never forgiven them for shooting down Adam, and he never will.'

Rita sat up as well now, looking at her friend a bit uneasily. 'I thought your dad was in the business of forgiveness, being a vicar. Isn't that what he's supposed to preach every Sunday?'

'Of course, but it's pretty hard to do so when your only son's plane was been shot out of the sky in the last few weeks of the war when everybody expected him to be coming home to a hero's welcome,' Jessie retorted, unable to keep the bitterness out of her voice.

She knew she shouldn't take on so. It was a long time ago now, and the small community of Abbot's Cove in the far south-west of Cornwall had finally recovered from the effects of the second world war, like the rest of the country. Even though food was still rationed and women still carried on making do and mending as the government had instructed them to do during six long years of war, of course her dad preached forgiveness in public.

It was only at home, within the privacy of their own four walls, that he sometimes ranted over the unfairness and futility of it all, and it was times like those that Jessie and her mother knew it was best to leave him alone until he had got over it. Especially now, when it was coming up to what would have been Adam's birthday, and that was always the worst of times.

Jessie shook the bracken out of her long brown hair now, knowing that she had been up on the moors for long enough, and that the hot sun was starting to make her fair skin prickle. She just wished the unexpected sound of that plane hadn't revived so many memories in an instant.

She had still been a gawky kid when they got the news of Adam, still growing into her adolescence and all that it entailed, including viewing everything so melodramatically.

At seventeen, she should be able to accept that bad things happened in wartime. They weren't the only family, even in a small place like Abbot's Cove, to have lost someone. But that didn't make their own loss any easier to bear, and her brother Adam had always been a hero to her. Being four years her senior, she had looked up to him, and he had treated her as indulgently as he would an adoring pet. He had loved flying, and it was a cruel fate that had made him lose his life at eighteen, doing what he loved best.

And she still missed him, she thought, with a tiny sob that she tried to hide from her more practical friend.

'Come on,' Rita Levant said now. 'I promised Mum I'd fetch her a new library book this afternoon and she'll be wondering where I've got to all this time.'

'How do you know what she wants?' Jessie said, trying to show interest, while her imagination was still taking her to places she didn't really want to go.

Rita shrugged. 'Well, she can't get out of the house in her wheelchair to fetch them for herself, and as long as it's a love story she doesn't mind.'

Guiltily, Jessie brought her thoughts round to what her friend was saying.

'It must be hard for you, Rita, having to look after her so much.'

'Not really,' Rita said cheerfully. 'I've always had to do it, so I just get on with it. You'd do the same if it was your mum.'

They had reached the edge of the moors now, and below them lay the small, sprawling community of Abbot's Cove, surrounded and protected by the high cliffs of the rugged south-west coast

11

of Cornwall. Even though she had lived here all her life, the sight of it never failed to stir Jessie's romantic heart. From here, high up on the moors, the small straggle of cottages always made her think of a Hollywood version of toytown, the church where her father preached every Sunday standing out like a beacon from the rest of the buildings. Curving away from the village was the cove of golden sand, and farther along the coast the crumbling, almost vanished remains of what had reputedly been a monastery centuries ago, from where their village had got its name.

The ghosts of the monastery had virtually passed into legend now, but they always provided good tales to tell in local pubs in return for a glass of beer from unwitting visitors who found their way to the quaint rural community of Abbot's Cove. Beyond the beach on that lovely summer afternoon the blue sea sparkled and glittered in the sunshine, so calm and beautiful it was almost impossible to imagine that so short a time ago people lived in fear of what the next day's news would bring, or which family would be receiving the telegram they all dreaded.

Once they reached the outskirts of the village Jessie spoke quickly to Rita before she really descended into misery. 'See you at the dance tonight?'

'Hope so, providing Mum's OK, fingers crossed. Those boys from Penzance we met last time said they might come again, and I'm not missing the chance of seeing them, so TTFN.'

She waltzed away, her fair hair, as long as Jessie's, bouncing on her shoulders. Jessie felt a

12

twist of envy for her cheerfulness, and admired her for it too. With all her troubles, her disabled mother, and her drunk of a father, Rita always looked on the bright side, while years ago their old English teacher had told Jessie she was far too sensitive, and she should stop taking on the worries of the world, fretting over other people's problems that she couldn't solve.

Growing up, she thought she had done that, until Adam had been killed. It had knocked all the stuffing out of her, even though she had probably been a fool to think her handsome brother had been invincible. Older and wiser now, and far more cynical, she admitted, she made a concentrated effort not to worry about anything so much. It was just that sometimes, like hearing the unexpected sound of that plane today, she was jolted into knowing she was still the same sensitive girl she had always been, and that was something that would never change.

By the time she reached the old vicarage, after passing the time of day with acquaintances she had known all her life, she had recovered from her brief melancholy, and was wondering how anyone could ever want to leave Abbot's Cove. On days like these, when the fruits and blossoms of summer were still in full bloom in country gardens, Cornwall could be a blissful place to live, and days when the winter storms and raging seas could change the whole area into a dangerous, alien place, were farthest from anyone's thoughts.

'I'm home,' she called out as soon as she entered the large kitchen where her mother was

13

inevitably preparing food. The smell of baking could usually lead Jessie to her mother's whereabouts, she thought with a smile.

Ellen Penwarden looked up with a smile, wiping her forehead with a floury hand. Still youthful at forty-three years old and often having to deal with a frequently irascible husband, she rarely lost the look of serenity on her face. Even after the shock of Adam's death, Ellen had been the steadying influence that had held the family together.

'How's Rita today?' Ellen said, as she always did.

'Same as ever,' her daughter replied automatically. 'I don't know how she copes sometimes, and her dad's not much use, is he?'

Ellen continued rolling out pastry. 'That's not a very charitable thing to say, my love. I'm not sure your father would like to hear it.'

Jessie felt her eyebrows rise. That was a laugh. Considering he was a vicar, her father was hardly the most charitable of men. His views were rigid and unrelenting, and he had the kind of voice that dared anyone to contradict what he was saying, whether in or out of the pulpit. The only time Jessie had ever seen him nearly fall apart was when Adam died, and even then, he had seemed unable to share his grief with his womenfolk. It had been a terrible time for all of them, she conceded, but it was her mother who had kept the family's faith alive, not her dad, and she was sure he would never like to be reminded of that, or even to admit how much his own faith had faltered then. As a fourteen-year-old girl at the time, it was more sharply etched in her memory than she wished it to be.

'Well, everybody knows Mr Levant spends most of his evenings at the pub, instead of giving Rita a hand,' she went on, more defensive of all that her friend had to do than condemning the man out of hand.

'I daresay they're comfortable with their lives, Jessie, and everyone deals with problems in their own way. None of us knows what goes on behind closed doors in other people's lives, and if Mr Levant has to drown his sorrows in a glass of beer now and then, it's his business. Besides, I've never heard Rita complain. She's always bright and cheerful.'

'She wouldn't complain, would she? Sometimes, I swear that girl's turning into a saint,' Jessie said, not so much censuring her friend as suddenly angry with the thought that she could never live up to such expectations herself. And it was hardly now and then that Zach Levant drowned his sorrows in his beer. The whole village was aware of him rolling home singing bawdy songs every night. No wonder her own father disapproved of him so much, Jessie thought, with a momentary sympathy for his efforts to convert the village. If Thomas Penwarden had his way, the whole blessed lot of them would turn into a community of saints!

'And this is your best friend you're talking about?' Ellen said mildly, in reply to her daughter's comment.

Jessie started to laugh. 'Oh well, perhaps it takes an ordinary sinner to appreciate a saint,'

15

she said lightly, knowing she would never dare to say such a thing in her father's hearing. 'Anyway, Mum, we're going to the dance tonight. Dad won't object, will he?'

'I'd say it's a bit late to be asking for his approval, since you seem to have already made up your mind. Just be careful, and remember who you are.'

Halfway up the stairs to her bedroom, Jessie thought it was an odd thing for her mother to say. How could she ever forget who she was! The entire village knew who Jessie Penwarden was. She was the daughter of the vicar, whose son had been killed during the war, and who had protected his only daughter like some precious object ever since.

She was alternately comforted and madly irritated at the thought. She was a young woman now, and she didn't need to be cosseted like a child, although she often thought her father was never going to see her as anything less.

Sometimes there was a kind of recklessness inside her that wanted to break out from the safe and comfortable life she undoubtedly had. They weren't rich, of course. God knew vicars didn't earn great salaries, but they were settled, with a decent roof over their heads, and her father's job was a job for life. She should be happy, and, mostly, she was. She had friends she had known all her life, friends she had grown up with in this small community, especially Rita, her best friend, with whom she shared all her secrets, and who probably knew her as well as she knew herself.

Except for the one little devil Jessie kept inside

16

– that just sometimes she wished she was anything but a vicar's daughter in a tiny Cornish community, and could be something else – *anything* else.

But as soon as such a thought crept into her mind it was followed immediately by a sense of guilt, and she always squashed it at once. The only time it was revived so much that it wouldn't go away was when she was in her bed at night, and let herself dream of what might have been, and what could still be, with a bit of courage. Maybe she could have been a singer. She sang in the choir at church and sometimes took the solo parts. She knew she didn't have a strong voice but people called it a sweet voice, and maybe she could have been on the stage, or in films or musicals. How fantastic would that have been!

As Jessie heard a door bang downstairs she heard the gruff tones of her father's voice as he greeted her mother, and she gave a soft sigh and put the daydreams aside. Instead, she sat in front of her dressing table mirror, brushing out the tangles and the bits of bracken from her long hair, and wondered if those boys from Penzance really would turn up at the village dance tonight. She wouldn't blame them if they didn't. They had only arrived last time because it was probably a novelty to come roaring down here on their motorbikes to see what the hayseeds living out in the sticks were doing.

She felt her heart begin to beat a little faster all the same. There were three of them: a blacksmith with grimy fingernails; an apprentice stonemason; and the third one worked for a small delivery firm. Rita had fancied the blacksmith, despite his unkempt appearance, but Jessie had been more attracted to the third young man. His name was Will Tremayne. He was tall and muscular, with dark brown hair and blue eyes that almost matched the colour of her own.

Oh yes, she remembered the boys from Penzance, she thought dreamily.

But there was no time to be letting her thoughts roam in that direction, as she heard her father's voice rise even more. It was always the same on Saturday evenings. Even without the memory of Adam's birthday in September, Thomas Penwarden had his Sunday sermon to prepare, which he always chose to leave until the last minute, so he could bring in any topical allusions to what he called 'goings-on' in the village. Heaven help the young person who had got into any scrapes that reached his ears, Jessie thought sympathetically, and thanked God it had never been her!

At the same moment she was annoyed with the thought that she might become far too timid because of her father's influence. If he knew she was dreaming about seeing Will Tremayne again, for instance, he'd probably stop her going to the dance at all, even though it was run and overseen by the Ladies' Committee, and was therefore deemed to be respectable. Good Lord, during the war, they had even had the occasional influx of GIs turning up, and that *would* have given her dad something to get het up about if he'd known how many village girls had sneaked a quick kiss outside on moonlit evenings. Jessie hadn't been allowed to go to the dances then, so she'd never had the chance to know any of the glamorous GIs. But she'd heard about the things that went on, however exaggerated they might have been. And she was red-blooded enough to envy them too!

'If only we'd been born a few years earlier, we might have become GI brides ourselves,' the schoolgirl Jessie had said to Rita at the time, complaining at the injustice of it all.

'No, we wouldn't. You'd have had your dad down on you like a ton of bricks at the very thought, and he'd never have let you go off to the other side of the world with a Yank. And I'd still be here, looking after my mum.'

'Haven't you ever been curious to see America?' Jessie had asked.

Rita had sniffed. 'No, thanks very much. Anyway, you know what they say about Yanks. They're only after one thing.'

Jessie had shivered at the thought. They had still been naive enough to be unsure exactly what the one thing *was* that the Yanks wanted, but it was more than a hazy idea that it must be something slightly wicked. They hadn't yet left the restraints of school behind, and they were as innocent of anything to do with sex as when they were infants. It was the older girls at the school who had finally enlightened them.

'Well, I'm not doing anything like *that* with a boy,' Jessie had said, shocked at one of the older girl's graphic descriptions.

Her name was Dorothy Glyn. She was in the class above Jessie and Rita, and therefore far more knowledgeable about such matters. Besides

19

which, she lived in Penzance, and the town girls felt themselves far superior to the Abbot's Cove girls...

Dorothy had scoffed at her innocence. 'You'll have to if you get married and have babies. Where do you think they come from, ninny, and how do you think they get there?'

'I'm not doing it either,' Rita had declared. 'I'm probably going to be a nun, and then I won't have to, and Jessie can have her thing sewn up if she wants to.'

Which started them both giggling helplessly, imagining Rita as an unlikely nun, and some strange hospital doctor attempting to sew up Jessie's thing while she stubbornly refused to unlock her tightly crossed legs.

For some reason that long-ago conversation came into Jessie's head as she thought about going to the dance that evening. Not that either of them ever had any intention of letting a boy go all the way – or even part of the way, since even now they weren't too sure just how far that was. They were still both as dumb as each other in that respect, she thought resentfully. If only she had had an older sister instead of a brother, she might have been able to ask her about it. And then she was reminded of Adam again, and she squashed such shameful thoughts immediately.

In any case there was the family supper to get through before she could think of getting ready for the dance, and she quickly realised her father was in one of his bad moods. She practically had to assure him that going to a dance was not

20

tantamount to the forbidden passions of Sodom and Gomorrah – without mentioning such explosive words, of course – and that if the Ladies' Committee didn't approve of it and kept their beady eyes on everyone, they would have stopped it long ago.

Sometimes, Jessie felt as though she had to tiptoe around her father to go anywhere. It was a wonder he'd ever agreed to her working in the local chemist's shop, with the various potions and medicines that the chemist-cum-dispenser made up especially for village folk along with the regular medicines for dyspepsia and headaches. Thomas didn't agree with doctoring, and he was suspicious of any medicines that weren't natural remedies. Anything else was akin to witches' brews, according to him. He believed in time and prayer to heal ailments, and God would do the rest. If you weren't meant to recover from whatever ailed you, then it was God's will and you had to abide by it. As for these newfangled antibiotics, he simply didn't understand them and refused to discuss them.

But tonight it was the monthly dance and the implications of young men and women being in close contact with one another, despite the chaperones of the Ladies' Committee, that was getting his dander up. Jessie often wondered if it was like this in the towns, or if such narrow-mindedness was confined to insular communities like Abbot's Cove.

'You know I'm going with Rita, Dad, and we'll be perfectly all right together,' she told him as patiently as she could, considering she was seeth-

21

ing inside at still being treated as a child. For heaven's sake, girls as young as herself had been leaving home and becoming independent and doing all kinds of men's jobs during the war.

He gave a derisive snort, looking more like a Victorian father now than a man living near the middle of the twentieth century. 'I'm not sure that's such a recommendation, knowing what a disgrace to the community the father is.'

'That's not fair, Dad! You can't condemn Rita because of her father, and she's always been a good daughter, looking after her mother the way she does. You can't deny the truth of that, can you?'

'Don't talk to me about truth, miss, and I'll thank you not to speak to me in that manner. You're still a minor in this house, and don't you forget it.'

As his voice rose, she could see his face getting darker, but she had had to defend her friend, and it wasn't fair to condemn Rita because of her father's weakness. Apparently tomorrow's sermon wasn't going too well, she thought cynically. It was always the same on Saturday nights. But as usual her mother's calm voice intervened and managed to soothe ruffled tempers.

'Thomas, we both know that Jessie will be going to the dance and will come to no harm, so if you two have quite finished this pointless argument I hope you're both going to sample the apple and blackberry pie I made this afternoon. *If* it's not too much trouble, my dears, or have I been wasting my time?'

One sure thing about the vicar was that he

could always be relied upon to give in to the needs of his well-rounded stomach, and nor was he slow in complimenting his wife for another fine pie and the topping that went with it.

'I can't take the credit for a tin of evaporated milk,' Ellen replied crisply. 'But if you've finished, Jessie and I will take the dishes to the kitchen and you can go back to working on your sermon, which I suspect isn't finished yet.'

He gave her a grudging smile. 'How well you know me, my dear. Very well, I'll leave you womenfolk to your duties, and, Jessica, be sure to be home by ten-thirty and not a minute later,' he added as a passing shot.

She fumed again. He knew how she hated being called Jessica, and she always saw it as a barb when he did so, just to annoy her. If she hadn't been brought up to respect her elders and to honour her mother and father as the commandments decreed, she'd have said he was a bully.

'He doesn't mean to upset you, love,' her mother said as they started on the washing-up. 'He can't help being concerned for you, and he's always extra tetchy at this time of year. It's just his way.'

'I know, but it's not my fault that Adam was killed, and I don't have to be wrapped in cotton wool for the rest of my life because of it, do I?' she burst out.

Ellen's hands were stilled in the sudsy water for a moment, before she spoke evenly again. 'I'll forget you said that, Jessie. I don't want to fall out with you, so if you're planning on going to the

23

dance this evening, you had better leave the rest of this to me, and go and get yourself ready.'

As Jessie mumbled an apology and got out of the kitchen as quickly as she could, she knew, of course, that it hadn't been the right thing to do to mention Adam like that. They had all been devastated when they learnt that her brother's plane had been blown out of the sky with no chance of any survivors. Jessie the schoolgirl had fully expected her brother to come home from the war as the family hero, and she and her mother had wept uncontrollably for days when the news came, while Thomas had retreated into himself, shutting himself away in his study or in the church, and hardly saying a word to anyone. It had been a horrible time, and there were still days when the memories came back to haunt all of them, but, young as she was, she knew she was right in thinking that you couldn't let it rule your life.

She held her head up high as she went up the stairs to her bedroom to get ready for the evening. Adam was gone, and she was a young woman of seventeen now. She was no longer a child, and she had the right to blossom as any normal young woman should, and not be held back by a dogmatic parent with his head and his ideas still in the past. With that thought brimming in her mind, she got down to the more important business of washing herself all over, dabbing talcum powder in her armpits, and changing into a soft blue flowered frock, a precious pair of nylon stockings, and white shoes.

Finally, she applied a touch of pink lipstick to

her mouth and stood back to judge the effect, not quite willing to admit that the tingling sensation running through her now was due to wondering what effect her appearance might have on a certain Will Tremayne.

CHAPTER TWO

Jessie Penwarden wasn't the only person with her heart set on going out that evening. Away on the outskirts of Penzance in the cottage he shared with his mother, Will Tremayne was another, but the fact that there was a dance at Abbot's Cove was only one of the reasons he was keen to go. Penzance might seem like the bright lights to people living down in the sticks, but truth to tell, if you didn't go into the town itself, there wasn't much to do.

It had been different while there was a war on, he thought, a little guiltily. The Yanks had been here, billeted with various people in the town and cheering everybody up with their sweets and chocolate and gum for the kids, and God knew what else for the local girls, and there was plenty of activity in preparing for an invasion that never came. Despite all the rationing and the propaganda about being careful who you spoke to in case they were German spies, which caused more excitement among the local lads than fear, there was always plenty of community spirit then too, with everybody doing their bit, as Mr Churchill kept telling them.

When they first came, some of the Yanks had called Cornwall the back of beyond, and they had certainly livened the place up. Three years on, now that the town had returned to normal, it all seemed a bit dead. Will's dad had gone off years ago, allegedly with some French tart, or so the rumours went, leaving him and his mother, Doris, to fend for themselves. Getting his first job as a motorcycle courier with a local delivery firm had made him feel a hell of a fellow, even though Doris hated what she called the death machines.

But it had brought in a weekly wage when they most needed it, and coupled with his mother's laundry work for some of the nobs in the area, it allowed them to keep the cottage and to live a respectable life. Besides, as he'd told her, he was now part of the Motorcycle Despatch Group, a self-styled title he and his pals had given themselves. It also gave them a bit of status to offset the fact that what they enjoyed most was racing around the countryside at speed and seeing which one of them could outdo the other. In his mind, Will fancied himself as one of the elite motorcycle despatch riders who had done dangerous work behind enemy lines during the war.

'You be careful now, Will, and mind how you go on that death machine,' his mother told him, as she always did, when he was finally ready to leave home that evening – just as if he was still a kid instead of nearing his twentieth birthday, he thought with an impatient sigh.

'Don't worry about me, Mum. I know what I'm doing, otherwise Mr Spencer wouldn't have employed me, would he?'

It was always the best argument, especially knowing that old Spencer was rather sweet on his mum, and she was flattered by it as well – two facts that seemed slightly laughable to Will.

27

Besides, it was obviously going nowhere, considering that his dad was still alive – at least, as far as they knew.

'Well, Jim Spencer was always a good judge of character, I'll say that,' Doris agreed, with no idea that her son silently chuckled at the way her cheeks went somewhat pinker as she said it. But he gave her shoulders a quick squeeze all the same, knowing that she only wanted the best for him.

But he had no more time to spare on what his mum and old Spencer might think about each other. Tonight he was going to have some fun, and into his mind then came the image of a girl with long, dark brown hair and startling blue eyes that he'd met at the last Abbot's Cove dance, a month ago. He tried to remember her name – Jessie something, that was it. He wondered vaguely if she'd be there that night – and then turned his thoughts more importantly to the sound of his pals' motorbikes as they stopped outside his cottage, revving up their engines as aggressively as some latter-day dinosaurs out for the kill. Local folk might tut-tut at what they considered sheer thoughtlessness at disrupting the peace of the countryside, but it was still music to Will's ears.

'Come on, Will, we haven't got all night,' he heard Des Greenaway bellow above the sound of the engines. He blew his mum a kiss before she had the chance to complain, and went out of the cottage to join the others.

He felt puffed up immediately. A fine bunch of fellows they looked, sitting astride their bikes like avenging angels – or something. More like devils, as far as Des and Ronnie Hill were concerned, he thought, hiding a grin. Neither of them had a great reputation when it came to girls, and they weren't above a bit of pilfering when it suited them, either, but they'd always played fair with Will, and that was what mattered.

He remembered something he'd heard his dad once say to his mum, in the dim and distant past when his dad had bothered to come home at all. It was about some lad who'd got a girl into trouble, before Will had really been old enough to know what kind of trouble that meant. He knew it now, of course. You couldn't go through the war years without seeing the way some of the local girls flirted with the Yanks, and how one or two of them had mysteriously disappeared from the town, supposedly to stay with a relative or to get a job in another part of the county. By now, Will and everyone else knew what that meant. He'd never wanted to think of his dad as a rogue, but it had slowly dawned on him that that was exactly what he was.

'Boys will be boys, Doris, and girls should be grateful,' his dad had said, with the kind of laugh that implied he thought himself a hell of a bloke who could charm any female he wanted. It was a pity Will hadn't been mature enough to know that being a hell of a bloke also meant he didn't think twice about leaving his family for his French tart. If he'd been old enough he'd have punched his dad's lights out. But that chance had gone, and Will was older and wiser now – and harder too – since his dad had left him and his mum to fend for themselves.

He knew damn well that Des Greenaway and Ronnie Hill were certainly followers of his dad's kind of thinking, and if they sometimes thought Will was just trailing along in their wake, it suited him to let them think that way for now. Fact was, there were no other bikers around the area and it was good to feel part of a group. If he also felt superior to the other two, that was something he wasn't letting on, either.

As for the girls the trio were hoping to meet that night at the dance, he had no doubt which one of them he fancied. The brown-haired girl who had caught his eyes last time was still upper-most in his thoughts as the bikers careered their way over the top of the moors and down the country lanes towards Abbot's Cove. There had been a sprinkling of rain earlier, and their outer clothes were well splattered by the time they neared the village hall.

'This is the life, eh, boys?' Ronnie Hill yelled back to the others. 'Nobody to answer to but ourselves.'

'Amen to that,' Will shouted back, as the wind tore at his face, stung his eyes and carried the words away. 'For now, anyway.'

Maybe someday in the future he'd find himself a wife and settle down, and be the kind of man his father never was. But not yet. The war years were behind them, and now was for having fun, and there was still a kind of recklessness in having come through it all unscathed, even for those who'd been too young to really get caught up in it at all.

Jessie Penwarden and her friend Rita Levant linked arms and strolled towards the village hall that evening, anticipating what the dance might bring. The small shower of rain earlier had scented the spring flowers in cottage gardens, and an earthy smell emanated all around them that was refreshing after the heat of the day. Then the two girls gave a scream as three motorbikes suddenly slewed to a halt alongside them, scattering dirt and leaves, and making them rub away the muddy mess on their summer dresses in a fury.

'What do you think you're doing, you idiots?' Rita yelled out.

'Same as you, girls, going to the dance,' Des said with a leering smile. 'Who fancies the first one with me?'

'Get lost, you twerps,' Jessie retorted. 'Come on, Rita, let's go inside.'

She had already begun rubbing at the soft fabric of her dress too hard, and instead of brushing away the mud she had managed to smear it into the material, leaving a few ugly streaks.

'Look at my dress! My mother spent hours making it for me, and she'll kill me when she sees it in this state.'

Upset and furious, she felt close to tears. She hadn't even confided in Rita how much she had been looking forward to this evening, letting her imagination run away with her. In her dreams she had been floating around the dance floor in the arms of a certain Will Tremayne, and she had seen the dawn of love in his eyes. Instead of which ... instead of which, the two bikers with him were sitting back on their machines and sniggering at the plight of the two girls, and Will was doing nothing about it all. No apology, no sign of regret, nothing. Well, if that was the kind of bloke he was, she was glad she'd found it out quickly, before she really fell for him. Then he got off his bike and fumbled for something in his pocket. Seconds later he handed her a folded hanky.

'Here, take this to clean off the worst of it. I'm sure there's somebody in the cloakroom to help you, and I don't need it back.'

He was so embarrassed she didn't have the heart to refuse his offer. She took the handkerchief silently, and Rita marched her inside the hall, while they heard Will's mates laughing at him and calling him a right little knight in shining armour. Jessie didn't care. It had been a sweet gesture, and she clutched the hanky tightly as they made their way inside and straight to the cloakroom.

'Good heavens, Jessie, what's happened to you?' One of the overseeing Ladies' Committee said at once as the girls went inside.

'I got splashed, Mrs Price,' Jessie muttered. 'Can you help me get the marks off my dress before Mum sees it?'

The woman's eyes softened from their usual sternness. As the wife of the chemist who Jessie worked for, she seemed to think she had to keep an eye on the girl, despite the company she kept. She and Chem, as she always called him, had no children, but if they did, she would have liked a daughter to turn out like Jessie Penwarden.

'Come along then, my dear. You're a good girl,

Jessie. There should be more like you, always concerned about your parents' opinion.'

'That's probably aimed at me,' Rita whispered, giving a dig in the ribs. 'Like father, like daughter.'

'Don't be daft. You're nothing like him. You don't drink, for one thing.'

Perhaps she shouldn't have mentioned Zach Levant's drinking, but everybody knew about it anyway. Before she could apologise to Rita, Mrs Price led them both to the washbasin and dampened Will Tremayne's clean hanky with a bit of soap and water. Jessie watched her dab at the marks on her dress, feeling suddenly weird, as if she was in a kind of trance. This was Will's hanky, part of his life, and he was sharing it with her. What a daft thing to think. She swallowed, wondering if she should have eaten more supper, because she was feeling decidedly light-headed, and the dance hadn't even begun yet. It must be excitement, that was all.

'Are you all right?' she heard Rita say urgently.

'Of course I am. It's just very hot in here, that's all.'

'It'll be even hotter in the hall,' Mrs Price observed. 'There's plenty of Miss Hope's lemonade for sale, proceeds to the church funds, of course, so if you girls feel in the slightest bit unwell, you be sure to drink a glass or two.'

'Old trout does a fine job in touting for church funds,' Rita whispered when Mrs Price had finished doing what she could with Jessie's dress, and left her to dry out. 'I reckon she fancies your dad.'

Jessie burst out laughing, and her world turned the right way up again. The thought of the prim and proper Mrs Price, with her regimented grey marcel-waved hair and parchment skin, fancying Jessie's roly-poly of a father, was enough to make anybody laugh! Even more so was the thought of her dad's eyes ever straying from her mum and the pulpit he held so dear.

'Never in a million years, but thanks for that, Rita. It's the best thing I've heard tonight,' she said, still chuckling at such an unlikely pairing.

'Well, thank goodness something's cheered you up. I thought that little episode outside was going to finish the evening good and proper. At least she did a good job with your dress, Jess. Your mum will never know.'

She would know, though. She'd know that Will Tremayne was capable of doing a chivalrous act, and that he was nothing like the two farm yokels he rode around with. He was special.

By the time the dress was dry enough for them to make their appearance in the hall, it was to find it crowded, and the music was blaring out from the gramophone player. Predictably, there was going to be a selection of old-time dances, a few waltzes and quicksteps, and some so-called party dances, including some excuse-mes. As far as any of the dances the Yanks had brought over to towns and cities that were more progressive than here, Abbot's Cove had stood firmly still and didn't hold with any of them – at least, not as far as the Ladies' Committee was concerned.

But she wasn't going to think of any of them now. Some people were already dancing to a military two-step, but on either side of the hall there was the usual row of boys on one side and girls on the other. Jessie could see Will and his mates, huddled together on the far side of the hall and giggling over something.

Rita nudged her friend. 'That Des is a bit of a rough diamond, but he's a smasher too, isn't he?' she whispered.

'I suppose he's good-looking in an Errol Flynn kind of way, but I don't like him,' Jessie replied.

'Well, that's because you've only got eyes for that other one. Anyway, that suits me. We don't both want to fancy the same boy.'

Jessie was about to say she didn't really fancy anyone, even though it wasn't strictly true, when the music stopped, and it was announced that the next dance was going to be a ladies' excuse-me waltz.

'Choose your partners, girls, and see how long you can hold on to him before someone else claims him,' the arch voice of Miss Hope rang out.

'Come on,' Rita said. 'This is our chance. Those three will sit there all night unless we jerk them into action. Let's see what they're made of.'

Before Jessie could argue, Rita had grabbed her arm and was steering her across the hall to confront the three bikers.

'You can't refuse to have this dance with us, so on your feet, boys,' she said breezily, holding her hand out to a grinning Des, while his mate Ronnie egged him on.

'May I have the pleasure?' Jessie mumbled to Will, her face a fiery red, but determined to do it right if she was going to do it at all.

35

'I'm not much good, but if you're willing to risk it, so am I,' he said, standing up at once.

She hadn't realised quite how tall he was. He was right, too. He wasn't much good at the waltz, but neither was she, and somehow they stumbled their way around the hall. She felt shivery inside, just knowing that his arm was around her waist and she was literally in his arms. When he trod on her toe she leant against him to keep her balance for a moment, and it was the sweetest feeling to be aware of the thud of his heartbeats against her own. Was this how it felt to fall in love, she wondered? And did he feel it too?

She realised they hadn't spoken since they began dancing, except for the occasional apology from one or other of them. It was absurd, and yet somehow it was also just right, because despite the dumpiness of their movements she still felt as though she was floating on air, knowing she had dreamt of this all this week. She was seventeen years old, and at this moment she felt as young and naive as a newly hatched chick. She was sensing life for the very first time... The idyll was suddenly broken as she heard a female voice right in her ear.

'Excuse me.'

She was pushed out of the way by the other dancers as a girl in a bright yellow dress elbowed her way into Will's arms for the remainder of the dance. Jessie stood there undecided for a moment, feeling ridiculously bereft. Rita and Des were hovering near, and Rita hissed in her ear.

'Excuse her back, you idiot. Don't let her get him.'

It seemed a pretty daft thing to do so quickly, but as if propelled by a force she didn't know she possessed, Jessie fought her way back to where Will and the girl were making an ungainly show of themselves, and she tapped the girl firmly on the shoulder.

'Excuse me. My partner, I think.'

'Thank goodness for that,' Will said in some relief. 'That one had two left feet. You're a guardian angel.'

Jessie laughed in embarrassment. 'I wouldn't say that. I just thought we made quite a good dance partnership, that's all.'

'So will you dance a few more with me? I need somebody to teach me the steps. After this one, I'll buy you some lemonade if you agree.'

She looked up into his face, knowing her own must be flushed, and wondered if he had any idea just how much she was attracted to him.

'Well, I don't need a bribe to teach you a few dance steps, but a glass of lemonade would be nice,' she said demurely.

They walked to the refreshment table together, and there was no sign of Rita anywhere. Not that it mattered. Rita was perfectly capable of looking after herself. They found some chairs, and now that she had Will all to herself, she wanted to learn more about him, and it seemed he wanted the same of her.

'Phew!' he said, whistling softly. 'I've never been out with a vicar's daughter before.'

'You're not going out with one now,' Jessie said. 'It's only a village dance.'

'We could put that right. How about if I come

down next Saturday and take you for a spin on the bike? You could show me these old abbey ruins I've heard about.'

'Maybe. I'd probably have to meet you at Rita's place near the end of the village, since it wouldn't go down too well with my dad if you turned up on a motorbike.'

As if by magic, Rita appeared at her side right then, accompanied by the other two boys. Her cheeks were flushed, her lipstick smudged, and it didn't take two guesses to know what had been going on. For a moment Jessie was almost envious, wishing she was as easy-going as her friend, but with a background like hers, she knew she was always going to be taking the cautious approach to life. But Rita wasn't going to have it all her own way. While the other boys went to fetch some lemonade, she spoke quickly.

'Will's taking me out on the bike next Saturday, and I said I'd meet him at your place, all right?'

'Couldn't be better, since the boys are coming down next Saturday as well. We can all start out together, even if we don't stay together, if you see what I mean,' she added with a wink.

'You just be careful,' Jessie felt obliged to say, and hating herself the minute she'd said it for sounding like one of her dad's committee ladies.

Rita flung an arm affectionately around her shoulders.

'And you just be reckless for once!' she whispered in her ear.

By the end of the evening, Jessie was feeling on top of the world. She had a boy of her own, and she had a date for next Saturday. In bed that night, she wrote the words in her diary, together with Will's name, and she stared at them for long moments afterwards, her mind milling around.

A few years ago other girls her age had been to war, or done dangerous war work, had met GIs and got married and been whisked away to America to live a life of luxury with none of the deprivations the war had imposed here. Girls her age had really lived a full and sometimes dangerous life ... while a girl like her, living in a backwater with a father who was almost Victorian in his attitudes, was getting excited over her very first date with a boy.

She wondered what her brother would have thought of Will Tremayne. Adam's image came into her mind, as it still did so easily, her young, handsome, daredevil brother, who had somehow managed to defy what their father might have wanted for him, because he was a hero, and had died because of it. She knew instantly that Adam would have approved. He would have liked Will, who lived with his mother but had the kind of civvy job that meant he wasn't tied to a desk or something mundane.

Yes, Adam would have approved, and with a small sigh Jessie closed the diary and put it in her bedside drawer beneath her underwear.

At church next day she knew Rita would be sitting in a pew near the back, accompanying her mother in her wheelchair. Whether or not Zach Levant would put in an appearance always depended on how much he'd had to drink at the local pub the night before, and whether or not his head and his legs could stand it. Jessie and her mother always attended, no matter what the weather, and only illness could keep either one of them away. Jessie glanced around as she heard the squeak of the wheelchair, and smiled at her best friend, the special smile that spoke of shared secrets.

The little church at Abbot's Cove wasn't big enough or grand enough to boast an organ, but as always Miss Hope played valiantly on the upright piano, and the congregation sang the hymns lustily and loudly, and then settled down to listen to, or sleep through, Vicar Penwarden's sermon. It was always something of a relief when it was over, the last hymn had been sung, and they could all spill out into the sunlit August morning.

'I want a word with Rita, Mum,' Jessie said. 'So I'll see you at home.'

'Don't be too long, then,' Ellen replied. 'You know your father doesn't like to be kept waiting for his Sunday dinner.'

Mrs Levant was already talking to some friends when Jessie caught up with her and Rita, and she drew her friend aside.

'Are we going for a walk on the moors this afternoon, or do you want to go for a bike ride?'

They always spent their weekends together, but it dawned on her that her friend wasn't looking as eager as usual. Rita usually looked forward to getting out of the house on Sunday afternoons, since it was the one time her dad was always there, usually sprawled out in an armchair and snoring like the clappers, but at least his presence was there to keep her mum company.

'I'm already going out, Jess, but not with you,'

she said uneasily. 'Look, I'm sorry, kid, but after we parted company last night Des said he'd be coming down on his motorbike again, without that boring mate Ronnie of his always hanging around. We're going for a ride somewhere.'

'Oh, I see.'

'You don't mind, do you? It's not as if we're joined at the hip like Siamese twins, is it?' Rita said, trying to make a joke of it.

'Of course I don't mind,' Jessie said, knowing damn well that she did. She minded very much, especially at the thought of Rita going off with that oaf Des. It would be different next week when they were all together. There was safety in numbers and all that. Without knowing why, she knew she wouldn't trust Des Greenaway farther than she could throw him.

'Good,' Rita said with relief. 'I might still say I've been out with you, though, Jess, in case anybody asks.'

Her mother called out to her then and the time for chatting was over. But if those last words told Jessie that even Rita thought it wasn't the best idea to be seen out on her own with the likes of Des Greenaway, it just underlined her own unease about the whole thing. Then she shrugged. She wasn't Rita's keeper, and Rita was savvy enough to take care of herself, for goodness' sake.

'Are you and Rita going out this afternoon?' Ellen Penwarden asked when they returned to the house, where the smell of the slow-roasting Sunday dinner was filling the vicarage with a succulent aroma.

'We're probably going up to the moors, or

41

maybe take a walk along the cliffs for a change,' Jessie said, hoping with a weird stab of foreboding that this was the only little white lie she was going to tell on her friend's behalf.

'That's nice,' Ellen said absently. 'Don't go too near the edge, that's all,' she added as she always did.

'Oh Mum, we know those cliffs like the back of our hands,' Jessie said. 'Maybe I'll bring you back some sea pinks – but if we change our minds and go down to the cove I'll look for some fossils to add to your collection.'

Listening to herself, she felt a momentary panic. One little white lie always seemed to attach itself to another, elaborating and embellishing the first one. Rita was so much better at this than she was. It wasn't in her nature to lie, but here she was, making all sorts of plans that weren't going to come true ... except that, come hell or high water, she knew she was going to bring back *something* for her mother that afternoon, if only to alleviate her conscience.

That was one of the penalties – or maybe the penance – for being a vicar's daughter, she thought ruefully.

CHAPTER THREE

Mondays were always the busiest days at the chemist's shop in the village. From the number of folk who appeared with their prescriptions for their cough medicines or stomach settlers, Jessie guessed that the doctor's surgery was probably just as busy after the weekend.

Then there were those who didn't want to bother the doctor at all, and the shop was always crowded with folk who just came in for a gossip and something that the chemist could prescribe for them, as though this was the natural place for such a gathering.

Harold Price was a jovial chemist, far more so than his eagle-eyed wife Vera, who could always guess when a body came into the shop requesting something she shouldn't, or the things that she needed, and putting two and two together. Many a young married woman's family had been the last to know when there was a baby expected, and many an older woman's family the last to know that she was on the change, but Vera Price was inevitably the first. Harold attended to the needs of his customers diligently, while his wife fancied herself as keeper of the village morals.

Jessie enjoyed working there. It was as though the whole spectrum of human life came through the chemist's doors, she once told Harold.

'I couldn't have put it better myself,' he'd said,

43

beaming at having such an intelligent and imaginative girl working for him. She was a sight more so than her friend, Rita. But Harold was a generous enough soul to think that just because the other girl had a drunkard and a loudmouth of a father, it didn't have to rub off on his daughter. Besides, the mother was a gentle soul, and it was sad enough for her to be afflicted with such a boor of a husband without censuring the daughter for being a bit flighty. At least she was always cheerful.

'You're in a pensive mood today, Mr Price,' Jessie said, in a rare quiet spell on that Monday morning, when he'd failed to answer one of her questions. 'You'll be mixing up the pill bottles in the dispensary if you're not careful.'

The man laughed at her teasing. 'That's one thing I'll never do, my dear. Imagine handing out a bottle of laxative pills instead of dyspepsia ones! I dread to think of the outcome.'

Jessie giggled at his unconscious pun, while his wife, coming in from the back of the shop in time to hear the last remarks, frowned at such frivolity.

'To listen to the two of you, anyone would think this was a music hall instead of a respectable establishment.'

Behind his wife's back, Harold rolled his eyes at Jessie. Heaven help anyone who got on the wrong side of Vera Price, she couldn't help thinking, and then turned her thoughts to other things as the shop door tinkled and several customers came in to keep her busy. She smiled and chatted as she dealt with those wanting sticking plasters or cotton wool or calling for their prescriptions to be made up while they passed the time of day with their neighbours.

Every now and then, though, her thoughts strayed to the coming weekend. There was no dance this week but she'd be seeing Will on Saturday afternoon. It was enough to make her nerves quiver with something she couldn't altogether understand, a kind of lovely and shivery feeling at the same time.

She wondered vaguely how Rita had got on going out with Des the previous afternoon. Jessie had done exactly what she said she was going to do, taken a walk up on the moors and found some sea pinks near the cliff edge, and then walked down to the cove and searched for some fossils for her mother. At least that much had gone according to plan, and no lies had been told.

Rita Levant worked in a little haberdashery and gift shop bordering the sandy curve of the cove. They sold all kinds of Cornish bric-a-brac that attracted the visitors who came down here from upcountry to discover and explore the quaint little Cornish hideaways, now that travel was becoming popular again, three years after the war ended.

The trains took them to Penzance, and little branch lines and buses took them even further west. With petrol more available now, motorcars and even the occasional charabanc found their way as far as Abbot's Cove and even down to Land's End, that great outcrop of rock from where there was nothing but the Atlantic Ocean all the way to America.

The winter of 1947 had been a terrible one for the whole country, and even Cornwall had been frozen solid for several months, but now the country was looking as verdant and beautiful as ever, and visitors were flocking to see these folk who lived at the far end of the country and were as much of a mystery to city folk as alien beings.

'I don't know why anybody would pay good money for something like this when you can pick them up on any beach for yourself,' Rita commented, as she dusted a box of shells on that Monday morning.

'London folk can't go to a beach and pick up shells, that's why, nor any of the ornaments made from polished Cornish stone,' Fay Yendle said. 'You get on with your work, girl, and don't question the whys and wherefores. Just remember that the more folk buy, the more likely we are to stay in business.'

'There's not much doubt about that, since we're the only shop selling this stuff,' Rita said with a small sniff.

'Well, thank your stars that the tourists seem to like it, then,' Fay retorted. She eyed the girl quizzically. 'I don't know what's the matter with you, Rita. You've been in a bad mood ever since you arrived. Go and make us a cup of tea, my dear, and cheer up. That sour face is not going to sell anything today.'

Rita flounced off to the little back room, half-filled the kettle with water and stuck it on the gas ring, banging two cups and saucers on to a tray with a force that was near to anarchy. But it wasn't fair to take out her feelings on a couple of

46

pieces of china. What she really felt like doing was dunking her head and the rest of her body beneath the waters of the cove and washing away all the bad memories of yesterday.

She caught her breath between her teeth. How could she have been such a fool to listen to Des Greenaway's coaxing voice and let herself do things she knew were wrong, just because he knew exactly how to go about it, arousing her passions? And there was no one around except themselves...

But when had it all turned so bad, so that there was no going back?

She couldn't get the ugly images out of her head now, no matter how hard she tried. Des was a big, handsome fellow in a rough sort of way, his skin weather-beaten from being out in all kinds of weather at the smithy, his hands rough and calloused, hurting her tender flesh. And his voice ... his oh, so persuasive voice, exciting her, scaring her, but ultimately winning her over...

'Come on, kid, you're not going to deny me a little feel, are you? Just a little feel, sweetheart. I bet it's not the first time.'

Oh, but it was, but the shame of it was that she couldn't bear to let him think she was such an innocent...

'Of course not. I wasn't born yesterday,' she'd said with a nervous giggle.

And then they were lying down among the bracken and the long grass, and he was prising her legs apart with those short, probing fingers, finding her moist and ready, but still not prepared for the sudden piercing way his fingers were going to hurt her, nor the sudden invasion

47

of her body.

She felt her face flame as she gasped out, but by then it was too late, because his fingers were followed by something else as he lay across her so heavily, pinning her down so that she couldn't move, couldn't get away from him, and no amount of sobbing in her throat or pleas for him to stop was going to help her now. It was as if he *couldn't* stop, not until the thing was done, and she felt the gush of something hot and fluid inside her.

She lay there stunned as he lay even heavier on her, his body spent, his breath coming in panting rasps, and then at last he rolled away from her, and she clamped her legs together as tight as they could go, pulling down her clothes, and turning her face away from him in shame. She caught the whiff of smoke and tobacco, and realised he had lit up a Woodbine. It was the way they did it in the movies, she thought, almost hysterically, and it was supposed to be smart and sophisticated, but this was nothing like a movie. This was sordid and nasty, and she wished she was anywhere but here. She wished she could turn back the clock and that today had never happened.

'You don't need to worry, kid,' he said eventually. 'Nothing can happen the first time. It'll be better next time, though, when you're not so tensed up.'

His words seemed to explode inside her head, and without warning she lashed out at him, lashing blows down on his face and head, and knocking the cigarette out of his mouth as she began spluttering angrily.

'There's never going to be a next time, you bastard,' she screamed, uncaring that there might be passers-by who would hear her swearing. 'I never want to see you again after what you did to me, you hear?'

'All right, all *right!* Good God Almighty, what a fuss to make after a bit of rutting. You've made me drop my fag now, so what are you trying to do – set the bracken alight?'

Rita stared at him speechlessly. Any feelings she had ever harboured for him were stone cold now. He had no idea what he had done to her, mentally, at least. He only thought about his precious cigarette.

'I want to go home, and you'll have to take me, since I can't walk all that way looking like this,' she said, scrambling to her feet and smothering another sob as she saw how soiled her clothes were. There was blood and dirt and something else that she didn't care to think about. She scraped up a final bit of dignity. 'If you don't take me right now, I'll report you to the police for what you've done to me.'

'Well, there's no need to take on like that,' Des Greenaway said, eyeing her warily now. 'Come on, get back on the bike and we'll call it a day. And like I said, there's nothing to worry about. Nothing'll happen the first time.'

It was only later, much later, that Rita began to think seriously about those last words.

She heard the sound of a kettle whistling, and brought her thoughts back abruptly to the present, here in the little back room of Fay Yendle's gift shop. She blinked back the angry tears, knowing only too well what a fool she had been. No self-respecting girl let a boy go all the way. Jessie would never have done so. Jessie had a damn sight more self-control than she did. Jessie was her best friend who shared all her secrets, but this was a secret Rita knew she couldn't share with her. Jessie would be shocked and upset, staring at her with those big, soft blue eyes of hers and making her feel even dirtier than she did already.

'What on earth are you doing with that tea, Rita?' she heard Mrs Yendle call out. 'My throat's parched, and if it will cheer you up you can slip along to the baker's and buy us each a fruit bun to go with it.'

Rita flinched. It was doing no good to brood on it, and what was done was done, however shamed it made her feel. Even a good sluice down in the tin bath in the scullery while her dad was out at the pub hadn't made her feel any better, because no matter how hard she scrubbed herself, she could still feel the imprint of Des Greenaway's fingers on her – and more.

Desperately, she tried to push the whole episode out of her mind and left the shop to walk along to the baker's. She had to pass the chemist's shop on the way, and for a moment she paused to look through the window. There was Jessie, as bright and perky as ever, smiling with the customers, and looking so bloody spotless in her white over-all. Rita cursed herself for feeling so resentful at that moment. It wasn't her friend's fault that they were born in very different circumstances – and had to live with the consequences. Nor could Rita blame her drunk of a father for what she had done this time, she reminded herself. This was down to her, and nobody else.

Jessie caught sight of her and waved out, and Rita waved back automatically, pulling a face and blowing out her cheeks behind the back of the large woman Jessie was serving. It was her usual style, after all. Rita, the joker, the brash one...

They met after work for a few minutes before going their separate ways. Jessie wasn't exactly put out that Rita had gone off with Des Greenaway yesterday instead of their usual walks or bike rides, but she was determined not to let it show if she was.

'You'll get me shot if Mrs Price catches you making faces at her customers,' Jessie greeted her, grinning at the memory all the same. 'What were you doing, playing truant?'

As she said it, for a moment she felt a flash of their old carefree schooldays when those who dared to play truant had been thought such daredevils. Even Rita hadn't done that, tempted though she might have been. She laughed now, and if Jessie hadn't been so intent on watching the clouds of butterflies on the buddleia bush in a nearby garden she might have noticed the strained note in Rita's voice.

'I was buying buns for our tea break. Mrs Yendle thought I needed cheering up.'

Jessie laughed. 'That'll be the day! You're the one who cheers up everybody else. Anyway, I can't hang about for long after work tonight, Rita, because Mum's making toad-in-the-hole for supper. But I'm dying to hear about your date

51

with your blacksmith yesterday.'

'It was all right,' Rita said cautiously. 'We didn't do much, and I can't say I'm as keen on riding on the back of a motorbike as I thought I'd be. It's not all that comfortable and the wind can make your eyes smart. I shan't be doing it again.' She ignored the irony in her words.

'I'll remember that, then,' Jessie said, unaware of any hidden meaning behind what her friend said. 'See you soon, Rita.'

'Yes. See you soon,' Rita echoed mechanically.

After work, Jessie walked back to the vicarage feeling a touch lighter than before. It wasn't that she wanted her friend to be disillusioned with her blacksmith, but for the life of her she couldn't take to him – or his friend, whose name she couldn't even remember. It was a pity Will Tremayne had them for friends, because they would probably keep coming to the monthly dance as a trio, and she would much prefer it if he came on his own. Her heart did a little skip of pleasure as she thought it – because she would be seeing him next weekend too, even though his mates would probably be with him.

So she was being a dog in the manger to resent Rita having her private moments with Des, when she wanted to do the same with Will. Anyway, she thought dreamily, she was going out on Will's motorbike next Saturday, and she didn't care if it did make her eyes smart when the wind blew. Just as long as she was with him. She knew you had to wrap your arms around the rider, just to keep on the machine, and that was something else to take her breath away...

'What's the matter with you tonight, girl?' Thomas Penwarden said testily over supper that evening. 'That's the second time I've asked you to pass me the salt, and you're sitting there looking into space as if your head is somewhere in the clouds.'

'Sorry, Dad,' Jessie said hastily. 'I was just thinking about something Mrs Price said to me today, that's all.'

'Oh? And what was that?'

Talk about pushing yourself into a corner, thought Jessie frantically. It had been the first thing to come into her head, and right now, her head was totally empty of anything the blessed woman had ever said to her. Trust her father to be interested in any of Vera Price's comments, though, since they were two of a kind in many ways. She thought furiously.

'Well, you know how Mr Price likes to have a bit of a joke with his customers, and Mrs Price said it was sometimes more like a music hall than a respectable establishment.'

Vicar Penwarden nodded in approval. 'She was probably right. There's a time and place for jollity, and when folk have come straight from the doctor's surgery for their medicines, the last thing they want is for any tomfoolery.'

'Don't you think that sometimes it's exactly what they do want, to take their minds off their troubles?' Jessie said.

She hadn't meant it as a rebuke to her father's comment, but she might have known he'd take it that way.

'A person's medical details are private, and I hope you don't make light of folks' problems, or discuss them out of turn, Jessica.'

She gave a sigh as her mother protested that she was sure Jessie didn't do anything of the sort.

'Of course I don't, Dad. I was only thinking, that's all. I do have a right to think for myself, I suppose?'

For a moment she thought she was about to get another tongue-lashing. It was absurd, when she was practically a grown woman, to be treated in this way. But her mother intervened before anything else could be said.

'If you two are going to start an argument, then please do it elsewhere and not at the supper table,' Ellen said crisply. 'I haven't spent all afternoon making you both a nice supper, to say nothing of baking rock cakes for the Tuesday afternoon Mothers' Meeting, to listen to the pair of you wrangling.'

'I'm sorry, Mum, and this is a lovely toad-in-the-hole, especially with Dad's runner beans,' Jessie said quickly. 'They're really tasty this year, Dad.'

If there was one thing that would appease her father more than anything, it was a bit of praise for his skills in his little garden plot. You just had to know how to handle him, Jessie thought with a sense of relief as she saw his frown lift. Her mother could do it far easier than she could, but she'd had more years of practice at it. And after all, his pride in his family and his flock were what mattered most of all to him, even though, as a man of the cloth, he wouldn't thank her for calling it pride. She knew all of that, and she loved him because of it all, or in spite of it, so she forgave him his bombastic ways – most of the time.

As for daydreaming about Will Tremayne, such dreams were private and best kept to herself.

It seemed an interminably long week until Saturday came around again. By then, Rita seemed to have returned to her usual cheerful self, although she still said she had changed her mind about going out on the motorbikes with the bikers, citing her mother having caught a summer cold and needing her at home that afternoon.

'That's a shame,' Jessie said sympathetically when they parted company after work finished in the middle of the day. 'Why can't your dad look after her for once?'

Rita snorted. 'He's going fishing with some of his drinking pals. You know what that means. There won't be any fish caught, but there'll be plenty of empty bottles of beer thrown overboard when they're out in their boat. Enjoy yourself, Jessie – and don't do anything I wouldn't do,' she added teasingly.

'That gives me plenty of leeway, doesn't it?' Jessie said, teasing her back.

It was only when they had parted company, and Rita had more or less flounced away, that Jessie realised how strained she had looked at that last moment, and wished she had asked her a bit more about what had happened on her date with Des. But it was too lovely a day to bother her head about it for long. Besides which, she had to

55

get ready to meet Will, and with Rita staying indoors for the afternoon now, at least there was no likelihood of anyone querying why the two girls weren't spending the afternoon together.

She felt a tingle in her veins every time she thought about it. Not that she wasn't going anywhere with Rita – but that she and Will would finally be able to spend time alone. Providing those other blessed bikers didn't turn up as well, she thought anxiously. Somehow she didn't think Will wanted that either.

She left the house and walked quickly through the village until she reached Rita's cottage, paying a token visit inside to say hello to her mother. She didn't look or sound as though she had a cold, but by now, Jessie's insides were jumping so much with anticipation, she hardly took much notice other than to pay lip service in passing the time of day.

'I told our Rita she doesn't need to stay in with me if you two had other plans,' Mrs Levant said fondly, 'but she's a good girl to her mother.'

'Don't make me blush, Mum,' Rita muttered, 'and you know I promised to clean those kitchen cupboards for you today.'

So that was her excuse. And she must really have gone off that bloke if cleaning kitchen cupboards was preferable to spending an afternoon with him. But there was no time for talking as Jessie heard the chug chug of a motorbike, and she bade a hasty goodbye to them and walked quickly to the end of the lane.

Will sat astride his motorbike, gently revving the engine and master of his machine. Thankfully there was no sign of his usual companions.

'I wasn't sure you'd come,' he greeted her, his smile telling her he was glad that she had. 'Hop on the back, tuck your skirt around your knees and hold on tight. If the wind gets in your eyes, press your face against my shoulders.'

Was there ever a more exciting prospect, Jessie thought! But before she got completely carried away by the thrill of it all, she had to ask.

'Where are your friends?'

'Don't know. We don't want to wait for them, do we?'

'No thanks!'

'Good. So how far do you want to go?'

She hoped there wasn't a different meaning behind those words. Respectable girls didn't go all the way ... but girls in love could sometimes get carried away and forget their inhibitions. All the popular magazines told you so – the ones her father never approved of her reading, where there were occasional letters sent in by readers who had done the unforgivable and were now regretting their folly. It was the same in some of Mrs Levant's library love stories, which Rita read as well, and often reported on significant passages to Jessie.

'Well, are we going somewhere or aren't we?' she heard Will say more impatiently. 'Or do you just want a mystery tour?'

She gulped. 'If you've really never been to the ruins of the old abbey as you said, let's start there,' she said.

'You're not afraid of ghosts either, then?' he said with a grin as she climbed up on the bike

57

behind him and wrapped her arms around him. She could feel the warmth of his body and the tingles were back again.

'I'm not afraid of anything,' she said, more boldly than she felt, since all of this was more daring to her than he might imagine. Living and working in Penzance as he did, he was practically a man of the world compared with her insular upbringing in Abbot's Cove, and as the motorbike started up and she felt the breeze lift her hair, she felt a kind of recklessness in her soul.

Sweet sixteen and never been kissed had nothing on her. Well, actually, she was sweet seventeen and never been kissed ... except by her dad, and that didn't count.

'The old abbey it is, then,' Will said, and the next moment she felt as though she was soaring into the unknown as the bike gathered speed, and she was clinging on to Will's back in a perfectly legitimate way, and resting her cheek against the roughness of his jacket.

It was only a few miles to the old abbey from which Abbot's Cove had got its name, and yet as they covered the distance, putting the village and the community behind them, Jessie began to feel as if she was in a different world. She had been to the abbey ruins many times before: with Rita on their bicycles; with her brother, who had teased her and frightened her to death with his spooky tales; with a group of school friends on a school history trip; but never with a young man of her own before.

As the words came into her head, she felt her heart give a little flip. Will wasn't really her young man – not yet, anyway – but she hoped with all her heart that he was going to be ... and that he was thinking of her as his girl.

She felt the bike slow down and realised they had almost reached their destination. Ahead of them the gaunt turrets and arches of the ruins glittered in the sunlight, enhanced by the various minerals in the stones. To anyone with a fanciful nature, like most young and impressionable Cornish girls of Jessie's age, they were either welcoming or menacing, like a thousand eyes watching these interlopers in a once sacred place. She shook off the feeling, quite sure that someone like Will, practical and manly, would have no truck with such ideas, and would probably think her a madwoman if she voiced them.

They got off the bike and left it outside the main walls as they began to walk inside what was left of the site, overgrown with grass and bracken and wild flowers now, and probably home to numerous small animals and insects.

'So what do you think those ancient monks would think to see their old abbey in ruins, and people just visiting it as a curiosity or to have picnics? I wonder if they'd be offended, or glad it had just disintegrated with age. At least they should be thankful or glad that the Jerries weren't the ones to bomb it out of existence,' Will said, startling her with his perception after her recent thoughts.

'Do you think they know?' Jessie said nervously.

He laughed. 'I don't know. Do you?'

She gave a small shiver despite the heat of the sun. 'I'm sure my dad would have his own ideas

59

about that, but I think walls and stones can absorb something of the people who once lived inside them. And now you'll think I'm crazy,' she added, feeling her face go hot with embarrassment.

'No, I don't,' he said, and she felt his hand squeeze hers as they wandered through the maze of ruins. 'I think you're smashing.'

'So what do you think they would have made of us?' she asked hurriedly.

'Who?'

'The monks.' She reminded him of what they had been talking about, suddenly nervous at the way he was looking at her.

She was so bloody naive, she thought, in a burst of anger against herself and her upbringing, and the almost puritanical ways of her dad. Rita would be handling this so much better than she was. Rita would be bold and breezy, puffed up at being out with a good-looking boy and knowing exactly the right things to say. While she was practically overcome with nerves every time Will looked at her in a certain way – the way he was looking at her now.

'The Jerries did once drop a bomb near here,' she went on quickly, averting her eyes from him. 'It could have flattened what was left of this place, but instead it exploded harmlessly into the sea. Do you think that was God preserving what was left of the old abbey? My dad said it was, but he would, of course. The local newspaper said it was probably just the pilot dropping off the rest of his load before he went home to Germany. You probably read about it, but I mean, what is there to bomb down here, except the moors and a lot of old ruins? Much farther west and he'd have been at Land's End and out in the Atlantic Ocean.'

She knew she was talking too fast. Making an idiot of herself, when she had wanted this afternoon to be so perfect. She felt the start of ridiculous and annoying tears prickle on her eyelashes, and she dashed them away before Will could see them. By now, he'd be regretting he'd ever asked her out, jabbering away like that.

'You're more than smashing,' he said in a voice that was huskier than before. 'You're gorgeous, and you think a lot. I like a girl who's got more inside her head than air bubbles.'

She turned her head slowly to look at him. Silhouetted against the sunlight in one of the old stone arches, he had a sort of halo around his head. Like an angel, she thought foolishly, and then stopped such blasphemous thoughts in this place. She took a deep breath.

'Thank you. I'm sure my parents thank you too,' she said, almost primly.

Will laughed, moving out of the sunlight's halo, and he was no longer some ethereal being, but a living, breathing, exciting young man.

'To hell with your parents – begging his vicarship's pardon,' he said teasingly. 'It's your approval I want – not theirs. Not yet, anyway.'

Jessie caught her breath, not quite knowing what he meant by that. It could mean anything, or nothing. He caught her hand and pulled her down beside him on the soft carpet of grass inside the confines of the ruins.

61

'You know damn well I like you, don't you, Jessie? I like you more than any girl I've ever met. And I think you must like me a bit too, or you'd never have agreed to come out with me. Would you?'

He was caressing her hand now, and the mere touch of his fingers made her feel peculiarly weak. She nodded, too overwhelmed by the unexpected surge of feeling inside her to speak.

'Right now what I want more than anything is to kiss you,' Will went on, still in that odd, husky voice. 'But I'm not sure I want to risk having my face slapped by a vicar's daughter.'

She gave a choked laugh, and then it was almost as though someone else was saying the words.

'Well, why don't you forget that I'm a vicar's daughter and take a chance?' she said.

It must be the heat that was making her feel a little light-headed, as if she was acting a part in a film. The stones in the ruined walls held in the heat of the day, making it almost oppressive. And all this ... was it just play-acting? But then she knew just how real it was as Will pulled her into his arms and she felt the touch of his lips on hers.

It was the lightest of touches at first, and it could have meant anything – or nothing at all. She hoped desperately in her heart that this wasn't just a shallow encounter, and that it was the beginning of something very real. She was in love for the first time in her life, and something deep and very basic inside her told her that she wanted it to be the one and only time.

CHAPTER FOUR

The sound of voices made the two people in the ruins of the old abbey draw apart and sit up hastily. A small group of dedicated walkers had begun prodding and poking inside the abbey walls, studying leaflets about the place, and taking little notice of what looked like a young courting couple enjoying the afternoon sunshine on the grass.

'I bet the monks wouldn't be too keen on the likes of some of them,' Will whispered. 'There's not a religious bone between them, I'll bet. What do you think they are – amateur archaeologists or something?'

His words brought Jessie back to earth with a bump.

'I don't know. Perhaps. They sound like strangers, anyway.'

She felt stupid, making small talk when they had just shared a kiss. But that was all it was, she reminded herself. Rita wouldn't have turned a hair at what had just happened, while she was naive and *stupid*, when she wanted to appear so worldly. But if she had, Will may not have wanted to take her out at all. She was utterly confused, and increasingly angry with herself for analysing every little thing instead of enjoying the moment.

'I've upset you, haven't I?' Will said, when the strangers had moved out of earshot. 'I'm sorry,

Jessie. I thought you liked me too.'

'I did. I do! It's just ... oh, damn and blast it. Put it down to being a vicar's daughter – if that makes any sense.'

Miserably, she thought he'd back off for good now. He'd be thinking of her as a real goody two-shoes, too timid to even take a kiss at face value, when all her instincts were telling her that what she wanted more than ever right now was to do it again – and again.

She heard him give a small laugh. 'You make a lot of sense to me, and I like you more than any girl I've ever met – and before you go reading anything about that, I haven't met that many! It's nice to know a girl with standards, and I knew from the start that you weren't the flighty sort. It doesn't bother me at all, and it just makes me want to get to know you more.'

While he was speaking, Jessie's face had broken into a smile, and somehow she couldn't stop smiling now, because he was saying all the right things, and she knew in her heart that they were sincere. He wasn't like those other bikers, who she wouldn't trust an inch. She would certainly never have come out here on her own with one of them, and for a fleeting moment she hoped Rita had been sensible enough not to spend too much time alone with that Des Greenaway. But she only spared Rita that one fleeting moment, because Will had picked a few buttercups and was holding them under her chin to see if the sun's reflection would show whether or not she liked butter.

'That's an old wives' tale,' Jessie said, laughing

outright now.

'I daresay it is. Either that or it's just an excuse for a chap to get close to a pretty girl's face,' he teased.

'Do you need an excuse, then?' she said, oddly breathless.

'I don't know. Do I?'

He didn't wait for an answer, and then he was kissing her again, and she was kissing him back, and this time there were no inhibitions between them, and she finally emerged from the circle of his arms, flushed and breathless.

'Well!' was all she could say.

'Well indeed, Miss Vicar's Daughter!'

She laughed self-consciously. 'I think we can dispel the implications of that title for good, at least between us.'

'Gladly,' Will said. 'But maybe we've been here long enough, and since we've no longer got the place to ourselves, do you want to go for another ride? We could go down to Land's End if you like.'

'You won't believe this but I've never been there,' she confessed. 'Rita and I were going to cycle there once, but she got a puncture before we'd got very far, so we had to walk our bikes home again.'

'My God, you know how to live life to the full in Abbot's Cove, don't you? You've really got to see the Atlantic breakers on the cliffs at Land's End, so we'll go there this afternoon and I'll treat you to a cream tea in a café before taking you back. How does that sound?'

A young man treating his girl to a cream tea in a café sounded marvellous and sophisticated.

Already she felt as if she *was* his girl. At least she was pretty sure he didn't have a string of them. He wasn't that type of boy. He was too honest and open, and she would have trusted him with her life.

Hanging on to his back on the rear seat of the motorbike over rough ground a while later, she hoped grimly that wasn't exactly what she *was* doing. But they survived it all and she was duly awestruck at the great rolling breakers of the Atlantic crashing into the Land's End cliffs, where they could even feel the chill of the spray from so high above. She ventured as near to the edge as she dared, knowing that the next landfall was three thousand miles across that vast ocean to America, because the wooden signpost told them so.

Jessie had a sudden insight into the feelings of all those GIs who had come to Britain during the war, and whose homes were so many thousands of miles away. No wonder so many of them had been homesick and welcomed the company of local families, to say nothing of the local girls!

'What are you thinking about so pensively?' Will Tremayne asked her, having to shout above the sound of the wind and waves.

'American GIs,' she answered without thinking.

'Well, that's flattering, I must say,' he replied with a grin.

Jessie felt her face go hot. 'I didn't mean I knew any of them. I was only a kid when they came here, and we didn't really see very many so they were a bit of a novelty to us. I was just trying to imagine how they must have felt, being sent to

66

England, and especially to a place like Abbot's Cove, after living in glamorous places like New York – or even Hollywood! They must have thought they were coming to somewhere out of the Dark Ages!'

Will laughed. 'You are funny, but that's one of the things I like about you, Jessie. You care about people and you take account of their feelings.'

As she blushed even harder at the compliment, he went on, 'Anyway, not all of them would have come from big cities. I bet some of them came from tiny places no bigger than Abbot's Cove, and coming to England, courtesy of their war department, was the biggest adventure of their lives.'

'Courtesy of Adolph Hitler, you mean,' Jessie retorted.

The sunlight dipped a little as a cloud crossed over the sun, and she felt unaccountably sad for all those GIs who had never come back from the fighting, and never crossed the sea again for the journey home. Just like her brother, who had never had the chance to grow up and marry and have a family of his own.

'Hey, where've you gone now?' she heard Will say. 'One minute you were smiling, and now you've gone all closed up on me.'

'Sorry. Just thinking, that's all,' she said, and it wasn't just the wind and the salt spray that was making her shiver. She lightened her voice with a determined effort. 'Look, there's a café just back there, and did somebody say something about a cream tea, or did I imagine it?'

'You didn't imagine it,' Will said, clearly

relieved to see that her mood had changed again. He didn't know what had caused her sudden bleak look, but he admired her tremendously for the deep-thinking girl that she obviously was. In fact, it was far more than admiration that he felt for her, but it was too soon to let her know how strong his feelings were becoming. Far too soon.

They walked to the café holding hands loosely, and were served their cream tea by a large, homespun woman in a coverall apron, and they both had to stifle their giggles at the way she balanced plates on one arm and dished them out as though they were a deck of playing cards.

By the time they had taken a more leisurely ride back to Abbot's Cove, Jessie knew this was the best afternoon of her life so far. And then her heart jolted as Will asked her out again the following Saturday, this time to the cinema in Penzance.

'I'm not sure I could. It might be difficult, and it's not that my parents object to me going to the pictures or anything, in case that's what you were thinking,' she said, suddenly defensive.

'I wasn't. But why would it be difficult?' he demanded.

'Well, I'm hardly likely to go to Penzance on my own to go to the pictures, am I? I could ask Rita to come as well, but you probably wouldn't be too keen on that, would you?'

'It wasn't what I had in mind,' Will said dryly. 'Can't you just say you're meeting an old friend in Penzance? You do have other friends, I take it?'

Jessie bristled at once. 'Of course I do. Some of the girls I went to school with live between here and Penzance. I could always say I was seeing one of them, I suppose.'

'There you are, then. Let's say I meet you off the bus around six o'clock, and I'll take you home on the bike afterwards.'

'And how am I going to explain that? No, I'd have to catch the last bus back, and I can't say any more than that. I'll try to make it, but if I'm not on the bus, you'll know why.'

She wasn't at all sure that he did know why. Nor why it was so against her nature to keep telling all these lies. If her father didn't have the vocation that he did, it might not have bothered her so much, but living with someone who regarded himself as one step short of sainthood had literally put the fear of the Almighty in her about lying. But she had already done so, and maybe she was already damned... She took a deep breath, and looked at Will, trying hard to preserve her dignity.

'You must think I'm being an idiot, but I live a different life from yours. We're all a product of our environment, aren't we? That's one of my dad's pet phrases, by the way. I haven't suddenly swallowed a dictionary. But if you want to change your mind about seeing me again, I'll understand, truly.'

He caught hold of her hand. 'Who said anything about changing my mind about seeing you again? If you like, I'll come to your house and ask your father formally if I can take you out.'

'Good Lord, don't do that!' Jessie said in a fright, until she saw that he was laughing at her now.

69

'I won't, if you promise to get the bus to Penzance next Saturday and come to the pictures with me.'

She gave in. She wanted to, anyway, and there was no way she wanted to let him get away. She liked him too much for that. Liked ... or fancied ... or loved ... and now she had something special to look forward to next week. All she had to do was filter in the name of one of her old school friends to her mother from time to time, mention that she had happened to see her, and they had arranged to go to the pictures in Penzance next Saturday. Her mother wouldn't object to that, and Ellen could find a way to get round her father. Jessie hoped it would be as easy as it sounded. She was seventeen, for heaven's sake, not a child! And Queen Victoria was dead.

Jessie was getting impatient with Rita's funny mood all the next week. Not funny ha-ha, but funny peculiar. Jessie suspected it could be because her bloke hadn't turned out to be quite the charmer she had expected. Charmer he definitely was not! But Rita had seemed to like him, and now she didn't even want to talk about him anymore.

'Well, I want to ask you a favour,' Jessie said at last, when it looked as if she was not going to get any more information out of her friend, no matter how she tried. 'If you happen to meet my mother in the village and she mentions Dorothy Glyn, don't sound surprised. I know we haven't seen her for ages, but I told my mother I'd seen her recently, and now I'm supposed to be going to the pictures with her in Penzance next Saturday.'

Rita's eyes opened wider. 'Crikey. So what are you really doing?'

Jessie spoke crisply. 'I really am going to the pictures, just not with Dorothy, that's all.'

In the small silence that followed, Rita started to grin.

'My God, you're meeting *him*, aren't you? That Will chap. Well, well, and you're telling little white lies to your dear mama! You're not so different from the rest of us after all, are you, angel face?' She oozed sarcasm now.

'What does that mean? And why are you being so nasty all of a sudden? I don't know what's got into you lately. I'll tell you all about it – providing you can get all that vinegar out of your tongue.'

Rita shrugged. 'Sorry, I know I asked for that. But are you sure you know what you're doing?'

'Why wouldn't I? Will's not some kind of monster.'

'I hope not. You can never tell, though, can you? He could be a sheep in wolf's clothing. Some of them are.'

'Well, don't judge all of them by the bad one or two,' Jessie said, still unaware why Rita sounded so bitter, and dying to ask her if it had something to do with her blacksmith. But of course it did. There was no other explanation. She tucked her arm through her friend's as they walked down to the cove at the end of their day's work, and she could feel the tension in Rita's body.

'Why don't you tell me what happened between you and that other one?' she said. 'I know some-

71

thing did, and you've been scratchy ever since. He didn't try it on, did he?'

Rita disentangled herself as a stray dog came trotting up to them, barking and wagging its tail as if he'd seen a long-lost friend. Rita bent to stroke him, avoiding any answer. Whether or not she would have said anything to Jessie right then, the moment was gone as she picked up a stick and threw it for the dog to race after and bring it back to her, tail wagging even more furiously.

'Let's take him down on the sand,' she said. 'He looks ready for a game.'

She ran ahead while Jessie followed more slowly, her eyes narrowing. Something had definitely gone on between Rita and Des Greenaway, but if Rita decided to keep it to herself, so be it. It wouldn't last long, anyway, and one thing was for sure: it had shaken Rita's confidence in a way Jessie had never seen before. But Rita's secrets were always bursting to be told, and there was only ever one person she told them to, so Jessie knew she'd find out in the end, whatever it was.

It was easier than she thought to mention to her mother that she had seen her old school friend Dorothy again, and was going to the cinema with her in Penzance the following Saturday. Ellen nodded approvingly.

'I remember Dorothy. A quiet girl with long plaits. She came here for tea with several other school friends once, didn't she? What is she doing now?'

'Oh, I think she said she's working in a grocer's shop,' Jessie said hastily, inventing quickly. That

72

was the worst of lying, even little white lies. One always led to another, and then another ... and she avoided her mother's eyes as Ellen went on about how Dorothy probably didn't have the plaits anymore, and must be quite the young lady by now, and trying to remember the names of some of Jessie's other school friends.

'Anyway, it's all right, isn't it, Mum?' she went on desperately.

She almost wished she would say no, then it would relieve her of living out the lie. But of course, she didn't really want her to say no, because it would mean she couldn't see Will Tremayne again, and her heart gave that treacherous little leap whenever she thought of him.

'Of course it's all right, my dear,' Ellen said.

So, late on Saturday afternoon, after ages deciding what to wear and fumbling with the money in her purse for the fare, Jessie wore a cool white dress and stockings, and her best shoes and crochet gloves, and caught the village bus to Penzance. She alighted to find Will waiting for her. This was a different Will from the one in the biker clothes, she registered with a little pleased shock. He wore tidy clothes and his hair was brushed down, and his shoes shone. He looked as though he was going to meet his girl ... and Jessie was all fingers and thumbs as he helped her down from the bus.

'I'm glad you came,' he said simply.

'So am I.'

'I've been telling my mother about you,' he said easily, startling her as they began to walk.

'Have you? What about me?'

He laughed. 'Don't looked so scared. I just told her I was walking out with the prettiest girl for miles, that's all.'

It was flattering and scary at the same time, because there was no way she was ready to tell her parents about Will. Not now, if ever. Her dad would have a blue fit if a motorbike came roaring up to the vicarage. In his eyes bikers were nothing short of aliens.

But she wasn't going to think of him now. They were nearing the cinema, and she felt excitement take hold of her. Everyone knew that courting couples went for the back row, where they could hold hands and have a cuddle and even a kiss or two under cover of the darkness. If that was what Will intended, she certainly wasn't about to object! He paid for two tickets, and the usherette shone her torch and showed them into the back row without even asking. They obviously looked like a real courting couple.

They settled into their seats as the newsreel came on. The Olympic Games had been held in London in August, after the previous two had been abandoned because of the war, but it had little pomp and no special stadiums built due to post-war austerity, and few people of Jessie's acquaintance had taken much interest in it.

The next news item mentioned that Queen Wilhelmina of the Netherlands had abdicated in favour of her daughter, Juliana. Jessie vaguely recalled the name of the queen from school history lessons. Three years before the outbreak of war, one of Britain's own kings, Edward VIII, had also abdicated in favour of his brother, the present

King George VI. It was odd how royalty could do such things, thought Jessie, although in Edward's case it had been forced upon him because of his carrying on with an American divorcee.

Jessie had been very young at the time, but her brother had explained it all to his wide-eyed sister, and she could still remember how her father had been so volatile over the disgrace of it all. Imagine an ordinary person deciding they didn't want to be married anymore and abdicating – that was what they did, of course, except that it was called divorce. She didn't know anybody who was divorced, and it seemed a bad thing to do, when you had once promised to love and cherish someone until death did them part – and in the sight of God too. She gave a sudden shiver, and felt Will's arm around her shoulders.

'Don't worry, once they get through all this news stuff, the film will be starting soon,' he said. 'I hope you're going to enjoy it, Jessie.'

She snuggled up against him, thinking that no matter what film it was, she was already enjoying the closeness of being here with him. There were several other couples in the back row, all of them oblivious to anybody else except one another, and she mentally found herself registering how much, or how little, she was going to tell Rita about it tomorrow.

Minutes later the film started, and to Jessie's horror she realised it was a war film. She hadn't even thought to ask. She'd been so excited by the thought of going to the flicks with Will, it hadn't seemed that important. If she'd thought about it at all, she'd imagined they would be seeing some nice, romantic picture, with the hero and heroine going off into the sunset at the end of it all. Instead of which, she had to sit through an all-action film with men shooting and killing each other, and worse still, watching planes being shot down out of the sky in flames. After an hour, she began to feel as if she couldn't breathe, and the pleasure of cuddling up to Will was fast losing its thrill. At one particularly savage scene, she simply turned her face into his jacket and couldn't watch.

'Hey, are you all right?' he whispered. He had been so wrapped up in the 'boys' own' action, he hadn't noticed Jessie's reaction, but now he was suddenly aware of the shallowness of her breathing.

'I don't know,' she said in a strangled voice.

'Come on, let's get out of here,' he said releasing her from his hold. 'We'll get some fish and chips and eat them on the beach before you go home.'

She didn't argue. If he expected her to say they should stay and watch the rest of the film because he had paid for it, she didn't care. She just wanted to get out of there, with its far too vivid reminders of what had happened to Adam.

A short while later they were sitting on the sands eating fish and chips in newspaper, with the tang of salt and vinegar in their nostrils and on their fingers.

'I don't know what happened back there,' Will said finally, when she seemed to have recovered. 'But maybe we'd better give the pictures a miss next Saturday. We'll go somewhere else instead, and you can choose.'

'I can't see you next Saturday,' she said, too abruptly.

He didn't say anything for a minute, and then shrugged. 'Oh well, whatever you say, but I thought we'd had a good time last week and today.'

'It was the best time,' she said quickly. 'I'm sorry, Will, I didn't mean to say it like that. It's just that next Saturday is – *was* – my brother's birthday, and I need to be at home.'

'Was?' he said, picking up on the word at once.

She had no choice then but to tell him about Adam, and the way he had died, and how the war film had upset her so much. And with the telling, all the pain of losing her adored brother came rushing back. It wasn't easy telling a virtual stranger – because Will was still that, compared to all her growing-up years with Adam – how much she still missed him every day.

'At least you had a brother,' Will said cryptically.

'What's that supposed to mean?' Jessie said, hurt at such crassness.

He apologised swiftly. 'I didn't mean it like that. But since we're swopping life stories, you might as well know that I was one of twins. Despite my size now, we were both very sickly at birth and it was touch and go which one of us was going to survive the first couple of hours. I was the lucky one, but in one of my father's less than savoury moods, he once shouted at me that it was a pity the wrong one lived. I always wondered if the doctor concentrated on saving me so much that my brother was the one to suffer for it, and I've carried the guilt of it around with me ever since. So now you know I'm not the kind of tough guy you see at the pictures.'

As he made a kind of tortured attempt at a joke, the shock of his words temporarily took away all Jessie's feelings of self-pity over Adam.

'You can't feel guilty over an accident of birth,' she exclaimed. 'It's not your fault you were the stronger twin – and you had to be some sort of tough little guy to have survived at all.'

'Thanks for that. So shall we both stop soul-searching now and talk about something else? You say you can't see me on what would have been your brother's birthday, and I guess I can understand that. So how about the Saturday after that? Will there be a village dance that week?'

'It's the week after. But that's two weeks away.'

She hoped that didn't sound too forward, but it obviously wasn't, because Will agreed with her. 'I've got things to do at home tomorrow, but how about on Sunday week, then? Are you allowed out on Sundays, or is it all Bible readings and whatever else vicars' daughters do on Sundays?'

She laughed shakily. 'Well, I'm not on a leash, and of course I'm allowed out once morning church is over, though I think it's best if I meet you at the end of the village again. Will that do?'

His smile said anything would do, as long as he could see her again. Jessie felt her nerves tingle at the look in his eyes. It was so warm it was almost embarrassing, that look...

They finished their fish and chips, crunched up the newspaper and tossed it into a waste-paper bin at the end of the beach. Walking back to the bus stop, at ease with one another now, Jessie wished that this evening could never end, but of course it had to. Evenings like this, still mellow and balmy with the tail end of a Cornish summer even though it was early September now, were never meant to end, she thought dreamily.

And then the bus arrived, and there was no more time for dreaming. If she had expected a quick kiss goodbye, she didn't get it. Instead there was a squeeze of her hand, and then she was getting on to the bus and handing over her return ticket, and as the bus moved off, Will's image receded into the background. And she turned back to face the surprised eyes of a middle-aged woman from the village whom she recognised slightly, and found herself eternally thankful that she hadn't been caught in a clinch with a boy.

'My cousin,' she commented airily, as if it was any of the woman's business. The woman merely nodded and carried on talking to her companion, while Jessie could have kicked herself, wondering why she had just told another idiotic and un-necessary lie.

CHAPTER FIVE

On Sunday afternoon, Jessie cycled to Rita's house, and after she had said hello to Rita's mother and registered the volcanic sound of her father's snoring from the armchair in the sitting room, she asked Rita if she was coming out for a ride.

'You go, love. You've been looking real peaky this last couple of days,' Mary Levant said before Rita could answer. 'Some fresh air will do you good, and I'll be all right with my love stories.'

Jessie thought fleetingly that it was just as well she had them. She doubted if there was much romantic love coming her way from the bawdy man with his mouth gaping open, and the belt buckle of his trousers undone for comfort. She immediately blanked out such thoughts, since the last thing she wanted to think about was the drunken Zach Levant making love to his poor wife!

'Are you sure, Mum?' Rita said, oddly listless. 'If you want me to stay with you, I will.'

'I've told you. Now go,' her mother said with a laugh. 'I'm going to sit outside in the back garden, so I can get a bit of peace and quiet,' she added meaningfully.

The two girls cycled out of Abbot's Cove and towards the old abbey ruins. The place had a special meaning for Jessie now, because it was where Will had first kissed her. She knew she was in a kind of seventh heaven about it all, as bad as one of the soppy heroines in Mrs Levant's love stories, but she couldn't help it. She had never been in love before, and she was seeing everything through the proverbial rose-coloured glasses.

'Let's stop here for a while. You haven't even asked what happened when I went to the flicks with Will. Aren't you curious?' Jessie said, knowing how unusual it was for Rita not to demand to know every detail.

'All right,' Rita said, almost flinging her bike down on the grass, and flopping down after it. 'So what happened with your wonder boy? Did he vow undying love to you and ask you to marry him?'

She sounded so sarcastic that Jessie's eyes opened wide. 'Good Lord, Rita, of course not. What's up? I know there's something eating you, so why don't you tell me? You're not ill, are you?'

'No, I'm not ill,' she snapped.

'Well, what is it, then? I'm getting worried now. You're being very odd and secretive lately. Your mum has noticed it too, and if you can't tell me, who can you tell?'

'There's nothing to tell. Just leave me alone.'

Jessie sat up on the grass, staring down at her friend quizzically, completely bewildered by this attitude. Rita snorted.

'Oh, stop looking at me with those cow eyes, can't you? All right, I'll tell you. If you must know, I'm late.'

'Late for what?'

Rita rolled over in the grass, away from Jessie, a

picture of impatience.

'What do you think, dummy? Not late *for* anything, just late!'

'Oh, your *monthlies*. Is that all? Well, you've been a few days late or early before, haven't you? I don't know why it should be anything to get so het up about,' Jessie said, almost annoyed that she had been made to feel so concerned over what was probably nothing at all.

'Yes, but it's never meant anything before,' Rita said, mumbling so much that Jessie could hardly hear her.

'There's no need for it to mean anything now, is there?'

Later, Jessie knew she must have been feeling extra dumb today, or else it was because she was still eagerly counting the days until she saw Will again, because it was only when Rita turned towards her with stricken eyes that the penny finally dropped. Her eyes opened even wider with shock.

'Rita, you didn't do anything stupid with that Des, did you? Don't tell me you let him go all the way!'

'He said nothing could happen the first time, and I believed him – and before you ask, it wasn't anything like the books and pictures tell you. It was horrible and I hope I never see him again.' She took a deep breath, and then it all came out in a rush. 'But then I found this old medical book of Mum's – and it frightened me to death. It says it's an old wives' tale that nothing can happen the first time, and now I'm terrified that I could be in the family way, Jess. My dad will kill me if it's

82

true, and God knows what the shame of it will do to Mum. So now you know.'

She was shaking all over by the time she finished talking, and Jessie hardly knew what to say. The fact that Rita had been so wanton and so stupid as to let the revolting Des Greenaway go all the way was secondary now to the implications of what could happen, so she said the only practical thing that came into her head, her voice more stilted than it had ever been with her friend before. But neither of them had had to face this situation before.

'You can't be very late. It was only a couple of weeks ago. You're worrying over nothing.'

'That's all right for you to say,' Rita almost grated. 'But my little friend should have arrived four days ago, and it hasn't.'

'Four days is nothing.'

'It is, when I've been such a fool!'

As neither of them could think of a single thing to say right then, Rita gave a sudden harsh laugh.

'Anyway, you were right, as usual, and I suppose I feel a millionth of an atom better for having told you. Nobody else knows, mind, and I know I can trust you to keep it to yourself.'

'Of course you can, idiot, and I won't mind betting that pretty soon you'll be wondering what you were so het up about. Just hold on to that fact, and try to act normally, or your mum will really think you're ill.'

'I'll try.'

'And ... was it really so awful?' Jessie said hesitantly, hardly knowing why she was asking, but needing to know.

'Horrible. And I don't want to talk about it anymore. So tell me about your date with wonder boy,' Rita said, making a great effort even though she was still consumed by what had happened, and what might be happening inside her. The thought that something that was still only a speck could actually turn into a baby ... especially one that had half of that awful Des Greenaway in it ... no, she wouldn't think of it. She *wouldn't* think of it.

She tried to show an interest in what Jessie was telling her about her chap. Lucky Jessie. They said the sun always shone on the righteous, and it was certainly shining on Jessie right now. She tried to be glad for her friend, and she was glad. She was very glad, and if only she didn't have this great gnawing fear inside her, she would have spent the afternoon teasing her about it.

Will Tremayne had been toying with the idea of getting a small car for some time, and the idea was gathering strength now. He had some money saved up, and if he didn't have quite enough he'd pay the rest on the knock. In any case, he would have to keep his motorbike because the small delivery firm he worked for paid him to be a courier, and he doubted if old Spencer would agree to pay mileage for using a car instead. But with a car he'd be able to take his mother out occasionally, and it would be easier to see the girl at Abbot's Cove. Her father could hardly object to a presentable young man turning up to see her in a car, either, he thought, his imagination surging ahead.

The merest thought of Jessie set his heart beating faster. He had been out with girls before, but never one he couldn't stop thinking about, night and day. Even his mother had noticed there was something different about him, especially when he'd got so smartened up just to go to the pictures.

'So what's her name, Will?' she asked smilingly, when he paused in digging the garden he'd promised to do for her that Sunday afternoon.

'Whose name?'

Doris Tremayne laughed good-naturedly as she watched her good-looking son wipe the sweat on his brow and lean on his spade. He was a catch for any girl, she was thinking, and that wasn't just a mother's bias.

'Oh, come on, don't you think I know the signs? You told me you've met a girl, and I won't pry, but can't you even tell me her name?'

Will grinned back. 'All right, it's Jessie. And before you start hearing wedding bells, I've only known her a few weeks.'

Doris said nothing as he got on with his work. She went inside to make him a cool drink. She hardly needed to ask any more. With a mother's intuition, to say nothing of her Cornish insight, as sure as she had heard him say the words out loud, she could hear his thoughts. *And she's the one*.

Her face softened. She hoped he would have more luck with his future than she had had with his father. Although it hadn't been all bad, and she couldn't deny that the first heady years of their marriage had been wonderful. It had started to go wrong when she had lost Will's twin brother so soon after birth, of course, and for some reason her husband had blamed her for it. But as Will grew into a boy, that blame had turned on him. It wasn't fair, of course, but nothing in life was totally fair. And then the war had started, and she knew damn well that while she had doted on their boy, trying to compensate for his father's lack of affection for him, Ted was turning to other female attractions.

If only the war hadn't happened, she sighed, like so many others did, then maybe they would still be a family, instead of Ted going off with that floozie of his. In her idle moments, when she could be bothered to care, Doris wondered what had become of them. She no longer had any love for him, and the French tart was welcome to him, but she would always wonder. You didn't share a life with a man for all those years and not be curious about what had become of him. She stopped her meandering thoughts and took the glass of lemonade out to the garden where Will was working.

'So are you seeing her again?' she asked casually, picking up the conversation from where it had been left off.

Will laughed, plunging the spade into the garden and taking the glass from his mother to take a long draught.

'Not until next Sunday. And just to titillate your nosiness a bit more, she's a vicar's daughter, so I have to mind my Ps and Qs.'

'She'll have no worries there,' Doris said. 'You were brought up decently, my lad. Any girl should consider herself lucky to have such a polite young man courting her.'

'There you are, then,' Will said, handing her the empty glass and returning to his digging.

He didn't know why her words irritated him – except that they hardly sounded like the character of a wild young biker, and for that, Jessie's father would no doubt be thankful! But nor did it say anything about the passion inside him whenever he thought of her, passion that he had never felt before, which he knew had to be kept under control. No way was he going to turn out like his father, but that didn't mean he couldn't feel the healthy desires any young chap did for the girl of his dreams, and Jessie Penwarden was certainly that. He knew it in his soul ... and bloody hell, if that wasn't a phrase to make her daddy approve of him, he didn't know what was!

'I'm packing it in for a while, Mum,' he said eventually. 'I'll get those plants in for you after supper. It'll be best to water them in once the sun has gone down a bit, and I need to wash off some of the earth and dust.'

And to rid himself of some of the unexpected and pleasurably lustful feelings that had suddenly filled his head and his loins...

Jessie had easily put the small incident on the bus on Saturday night behind her, too busy thinking about her next meeting with Will. She dreamt of him all the following week. In her dreams time was already moving swiftly ahead, the way the scenes in a movie did. This year, next year, some-time ... and she stalwartly refused to think of never. She dreamt of going steady in a proper and formal way, of her mother approving and her father finally accepting that Will was a thoroughly decent young man to court his daughter. In time that courtship would become a betrothal, and then it would be Vicar Penwarden himself who would marry his only daughter and the man she loved. They would live happily ever after... And there the dreams ended, because she had no idea where or when it would happen. It was simply enough, for now, to have such dreams.

But dreams had to be put aside as the week wore on, because, apart from Rita's momentous confession, the tension in the Penwarden house became ever more tense as the day of Adam's birthday approached. It was always a bad day for them all. Jessie couldn't even remember when or how it had been decreed that they would spend it in mourning for their lost boy. It had just happened.

Her father always refused to come out of his study at all until mid morning. As far as his womenfolk knew, he simply spent it in private grieving, and if his wife always suspected she could smell strong spirits on his breath for the rest of the day, she was wise enough not to mention it. She and Jessie tiptoed around the house, doing the ordinary chores, and preparing the special supper they always had in honour of Adam. His favourite meal was meat and potato pie with onion gravy, plus a good helping of roasted parsnips and garden peas which Thomas picked from his own vegetable patch.

The rituals were always the same too. They

would say their usual grace at the table before the meal, and Ellen would have lit special candles for Adam and placed them in the vicarage window. And woe betide anyone who came calling for Vicar Penwarden's help or advice on any pretext whatsoever on this day of all days, because they would get short shrift.

During the afternoon the three of them would have been to the churchyard, where they would say a prayer over Adam's grave, and leave some of his favourite woodland flowers in a vase. Thomas would contemplate silently for a while before they all went home, and then they wouldn't see him for the rest of the day, much to his womenfolk's relief.

'It's really hard on the nerves, hoping that nobody will come to the vicarage while we're so preoccupied. I find myself praying that nobody's died on that day or wants to arrange a christening or a burial,' Jessie had once confided in Rita.

'Other people don't realise it's a special day for our family, and if that's not enough we have to go through it all again on the day Adam died, so we have to experience it all twice over. Just as if we don't think of him every day, anyway,' she added, in case Rita thought she didn't.

'Well, if you want my opinion, I think it's ghoulish,' Rita had replied, ever blunt. 'I can imagine your dad wanting to do the pious thing, but I thought your mum could have talked him out of all this ritual by now. It's not as if you're ever going to forget him, is it?'

Of course, Rita was right, but it would take a stronger woman than either Jessie or her mother to stand up to Thomas and say so, especially when he was in one of his fiercest moods. They had decided long ago that it was better to put up with his ways and go along with them for the sake of harmony. It was only one day after all – well, two days, really. Privately, Jessie wondered uneasily if losing Adam had shaken her father's faith and that this was his way of atoning for it. He had taken his son's death harder than any of them, almost to the point of madness, but no amount of grief or sorrow could bring him back, and life had to go on. It might be a cliché, but it was true, all the same.

She had awoken on that Saturday morning in much the same frame of mind as usual on this day, almost dreading to go downstairs and face her mother, who would have taken a tray of toast and tea into Thomas's study for him to eat alone.

Sometimes Jessie thought it should be bread and water, the way they allegedly treated prisoners, to allow him to do proper penance for something that was none of his doing, but for which he seemed to take so much blame. Just as if his caring God would take away his only son for any misdeeds Vicar Penwarden might have done in the past.

'How long is this going to go on, Mum?' she asked Ellen. 'None of us will forget Adam, but we can't grieve for ever, can we?'

'Don't let your father hear you say such things,' her mother said sharply. 'I daresay in time the pain will lessen, but he does feel things so strongly. You know that, Jessie. It's part of the burden a vicar has to bear.'

'Well, it seems a pretty unnecessary one to me,' Jessie muttered. 'I thought it was only God who took the world's ills on His shoulders.'

Ellen sighed. 'I don't want to fall out with you, Jessica, especially not today. You're young and thoughtless at times, and you speak before you think, but perhaps when you have children of your own you'll understand.'

'I'm sorry, Mum,' she said, instantly contrite. She gave her mother a quick hug to show that she meant no ill, and turned away to hide the stinging tears in her eyes.

Didn't they know how much she loved and missed her brother too? Didn't they remember what a hero she had always thought him, even before he joined the air force and looked so handsome in his uniform? But this wasn't the time to get too emotional, or they would both end up weeping. This was simply a day they had to get through, and abide by the manner in which Thomas wanted to honour it. And days didn't last for ever. There was always another one tomorrow.

So the day of Adam's birthday passed with its usual family rituals. Sometimes Jessie found it hard to imagine her brother being older now, being twenty-one and a man, perhaps courting some nice girl from the village, even thinking about getting engaged sometime in the future. She knew her father would think twenty-one was far too early for a young man to tie himself down, even with the prospect of a long engagement. In Thomas Penwarden's eyes, between twenty-five and thirty was a good age for a man to be married.

It was accepted that a girl could be engaged a bit younger, a thought that sent Jessie's thoughts soaring off in another direction, when she should still be thinking about her brother's life, the way her parents were undoubtedly doing. She stirred restlessly at the supper table. Supper was over now, and her mother usually spent the rest of the evening knitting or mending, while Thomas disappeared in his study to finish his sermon for tomorrow – or whatever else he did in there when he was in such a sombre mood. Heaven help them all tomorrow, Jessie thought fervently, if they had to sit through one of his most melancholy and interminable ones.

'Mum, would you mind if I went out to get a bit of fresh air?' she said abruptly. 'I just want to walk and think. Don't worry. I'm not going to do anything frivolous.'

'It's all right, my dear,' Ellen said putting down her knitting for a moment. 'I know this day is never easy for you, any more than it is for me.'

'No, it's not, and I don't wish to be disrespectful, Mum, so don't be angry, but I'd have thought a man of his calling would have been able to accept that it was God's will to take Adam from us.'

She'd never dared to say it quite so openly before, and she wasn't sure how her mother would react, but Ellen merely looked sorrowful.

'I'm not angry with you, my dear, but your father is a man who is still grieving for his son, as well as being a vicar. I'm sure he'll come to terms with it in his own way. Meanwhile, yes, you go out for an hour. Go and see Rita if you want to.'

Jessie was glad to escape. She put on her coat and shoes and left the house quietly. The last thing she intended to do was to see Rita. The thought of listening to any more of her pointless bleating about what she had done wrong, and what the consequences might be, was more than Jessie could take after the day she had had. It had been even more exhausting than usual, added to which, she had a sudden irrational fear for her father. Sometimes he retreated so far into his own thoughts that neither she nor her mother had any chance of reaching him, or knowing what he really felt.

By the time she reached the curving sandy cove, the sun was low in the sky and the sea had lost its clear daylight beauty. Now, it looked glassy and eerie as she walked down on to the sand. But it suited her mood. She was thankful that there weren't too many people about this evening, and that she hadn't seen anybody she knew. The evening was turning chilly with the first hint of autumn in the air, and there was a soft breeze blowing in from the sea. But she was so wrapped up in her emotions, she hardly felt it.

She sat on a rock, staring unseeingly at the waves, and thinking again, as she had when she was at Land's End with Will, how empty and lonely that vast ocean must be, and how many miles it was to America. How brave those early explorers must have been in their sailing ships, with no idea where they were going, and what dangers they might meet at the other end. Just as brave as all those young men in the second world war, flying in their flimsy planes to face an enemy whose sole intent was to blow them out of the sky.

Jessie shivered as the unwelcome thought came into her mind, reminding her instantly of Adam, and this awful day that had just passed. Family birthdays used to be such joyful affairs, but not this one, not anymore. Perhaps it hadn't been such a good idea to come here after all, all alone with thoughts that would only get gloomier and sadder. She should have been at home, keeping her mother company, bolstering one another up and sharing their sorrows.

She jerked up her head as she heard a sound to break the stillness, and her heart began to beat faster. It was definitely the sound of motorbike engines, and she had specifically told Will why she couldn't see him today. She hadn't thought he'd be so insensitive as to ignore her reasons, and as she turned around to face him she realised it wasn't Will at all. It was those other two ... and they were getting off their bikes now and walking down the sandy cove towards her.

'Well, well, if it isn't little Jessie,' Des Greenaway said with a leer. 'It must be our lucky day, Ron. Are you looking for company, darling?'

Jessie scrambled off her rock. Her heart was in her mouth. There was no one else in sight, and it was already dusk. Knowing what Des had done to Rita, she couldn't deny that these two scared her. In fact, she had never been so scared in her life before.

'I'm just going home,' she said stiffly.

They were alongside her before she could move out of the way, and Des's hand was suddenly fixed firmly on her arm and pressing into her skin. She felt her flesh being twisted, and she bit her lip, determined not to cry out loud.

'Oh, come on, what's your hurry? You've got plenty of time to be friendly, haven't you? You and that friend of yours seemed to be as thick as thieves, so where is she tonight?'

Ronnie had seemed to be the more silent of the two, but at Des's words, Jessie heard him give a small chuckle. *He knew*, she thought, horrified, and it made the whole episode all the more shameful to think that these two might have been discussing what Des had done to Rita. She felt a sudden blind fury on her friend's behalf, and as if the thought gave her some strength she didn't know she had, she wrenched her arm out of Des's grip and gave him an almighty shove.

Unprepared, he lost his balance and cannoned straight into Ronnie, and the two of them fell down in a heap. Without waiting for anything more, Jessie started to run as fast as she could on the yielding sand, wanting to get as far away from them as possible.

'Bitch!'

She heard Des yell after her, echoed by the two of them laughing as they scrambled to their feet in a flurry of sand, but she wasn't hanging about for anything more. She fled back in the direction of the vicarage and safety, her breath tight in her chest, a stitch in her side, knowing that her fate might so easily have been the same as Rita's.

By the time she reached home she was sobbing, and she slipped indoors as quietly as she could, calling out to her mother that she was having an early night. Since it was such a bad day for the family she knew Ellen wouldn't question it. It was an extra worse day for her now, with the memory of Adam's birthday being even more ruined. She would never forgive Des Greenaway for that.

CHAPTER SIX

On Sunday afternoon, Jessie walked through the village to the end of the lane where Rita lived. She had had a restless night, still shaken from the encounter at the cove. She was even unsure, now, how she was feeling about seeing Will again. He was nothing like his two friends, but they *were* his friends, and who knew what blokes got up to or discussed when they were together? The thought that Will might even know what had happened between Des Greenaway and Rita was something else to make her uncomfortable. All this week she had been looking forward so eagerly to this afternoon, and now the pleasure of it was spoilt.

She half-wondered if she should call for Rita and suggest they spent the afternoon together instead, but how foolish was that? Will was expecting to see her alone, and until last night it had been all Jessie could think about too. In any case, she thought, with her usual burst of spirit, he was nothing like those other two. She trusted him.

She caught sight of Rita inside her house and waved to her. Rita knew Jessie's plans, and as she hurried on towards the end of the lane, she waited for the familiar sound of a motorbike engine. When it didn't come, she began to get uneasy. Surely he hadn't forgotten?

Another thought occurred to her, sending her

heart plummeting. Surely his mates hadn't got to him and told him what had happened last night at the cove, and what a little simpleton the vicar's daughter was? Surely it hadn't been enough to make him go off her? Jessie couldn't bear to think it of him.

She strained her eyes in the direction of Penzance, but there was no sign of a motorbike coming her way. Her pride asserted itself, and she stuck her chin in the air in a gesture of defiance. She would give him a little while longer, and then she would go back to Rita's. All the same, her eyes blurred and she had to bite her lips hard, because she had really believed Will liked her, and she didn't want to think that he was so shallow.

In the distance she could see the dust thrown up by a small motor car chugging this way. She didn't think anything of it until it began to slow down towards her. She assumed it would be visitors about to ask the way to Land's End or St Ives, and prepared to answer their questions. Then the car stopped, the driver's door opened and as a figure got out, her jaw dropped.

'Will!' she stuttered. 'I thought I was seeing things!'

He laughed self-consciously. 'She's a little beauty, isn't she?' he said, patting the bonnet of the car affectionately. 'Not strictly a hundred per cent perfect, and she needs a bit of attention, but nothing that a mechanical chap can't put right.'

'Is it yours?' Jessie said.

'Not yet. I've got her for a trial run this afternoon, and if I'm happy with the performance, I'm going to talk terms with the owner. I should be able to get her for a reasonable price, considering the work that needs doing. But what do you think?'

Jessie didn't know what to think. Nobody of her acquaintance owned a car just for pleasure. Shopkeepers and furniture removers and builders' merchants who delivered goods obviously had cars or vans, but it seemed as if Will was going up in the world if he could afford to buy a private car!

'Come on, Jessie, get in,' Will coaxed. 'I don't want to stay parked at the side of the road all day, attracting attention.'

Considering there was nobody else in sight, it didn't seem likely. But, as he came round to the passenger side of the car and opened the door for her, she was filled with a sudden sense of excitement. She slid inside, and the smell of the leather was warm and sensual. As he joined her in the driving seat, she gave a little laugh.

'It's like being enclosed in a little world of our own, isn't it?' she said without thinking, and then blushed in case he thought that was a provocative thing to say. And *damn* those other two, she thought furiously, for putting such a thought into her head.

Will laughed back, clearly delighted at her remark. 'That's just what it is, and you know what they say: "The world's our oyster" – whatever that means. So where do you want to go today, my lady? We can go anywhere you like.'

'Are you sure it's not going to break down?' she said, remembering he'd said the car needed some work done on it.

He shook his head. 'The mechanics are sound.

It's just the paintwork that needs touching up, and it could do with a spot of welding on a couple of rust patches. Don't worry, we won't break down.'

'You sound very knowledgeable considering you've only got it on trial!'

'Ah, but I know the car. It belongs to a chap at work, and I've seen how he looks after it. I've been thinking about getting a car for some time, so this wasn't a hasty decision. So what do you say? Are we going to sit here discussing cars, or are we going off into the wide blue yonder?'

The phrase reminded her uncomfortably of Adam and his flimsy plane. Will was so excited over the car that he hadn't yet asked her how yesterday went. She knew he would do so eventually, just as she knew she was going to tell him about the unexpected and unwanted meeting with Des and Ronnie last night. But all that could wait.

'Well, I've never been to St Ives...' she began.

'Then St Ives it is, and by the way, what have you done to your arm?' he added, seeing the marks where Des Greenaway had twisted it last night.

Jessie flinched. 'It's nothing. I bumped into the corner of my dressing table,' she said quickly.

Thankfully, he didn't question it, and the next minute he had got out of the car again, and cranked up the engine with the starting handle. It gave her a small fright when the engine sprang into life while he was still outside, but as soon as he took control of the steering wheel and they were on their way, she began to relax. And, after all, it was so much better to be driving along in a car and feeling a bit like royalty than to be clutching on to someone's back or dear life on the back of a motorbike.

It was strange to think she had never been to St Ives, which wasn't so many miles away, but it was on the north coast of the county, while they were on the south. Will drove right around the peninsula, and to Jessie it was like entering a new and unknown world to be driving through villages and hamlets with names such as Sennen and Zennor and St Just. Her own village of Abbot's Cove might as well have been on the other side of the world for all she knew of these places, and it emphasised again how very insular they were.

In the sunlight the gaunt, crumbling chimneys of long-forgotten tin mines loomed up out of the moors like brooding sentinels. As children, Jessie and Rita had always thought of them in that fanciful way, as if they were the guardians of these ancient moors and the people who lived in the far south-west of the country. She smiled at such childish ideas now, but they still charmed her all the same.

When they came to the hill overlooking St Ives Bay, Will stopped the car, and they stepped outside to breathe in the fresh sea breezes and to get their first glimpse of the town far below. The sea glittered in the sunlight; small pleasure craft nestled in the harbour; fishermen leant lazily on the quay, exchanging yarns; and the raucous sound of seabirds filled the air.

'Oh, it's so pretty,' she exclaimed, 'and a lot larger than Abbot's Cove.'

'Isn't everywhere?' Will said with a laugh. 'Do

you want to get nearer to take a proper look?'

Jessie shook her head. 'Not yet. I'd like to just sit on the grass and absorb it all if you don't mind.'

'Suits me. There's nothing I'd like more than to sit on the grass with my girl on a Sunday afternoon and let the rest of the world take care of itself.'

It thrilled her to hear him call her his girl. She sat down on the warm mossy ground with her face turned towards the picturesque scene spread out below them, while he sprawled beside her, a blade of grass between his teeth. A small silence fell between them, and after a few minutes, knowing he was watching her, she felt almost compelled to ask him what he was thinking.

'Two things,' he told her. 'One is how pretty you are and what the hell you're doing out with a dull chap like me. And two – I was wondering how yesterday went for you, and if you want to talk about it. Tell me to shut up and mind my own business if you like, but I kept thinking about you yesterday after you told me about your brother.'

Jessie didn't say anything for a minute, aware that her heart was beating more loudly at his words. She wondered if he could hear it, but probably not, with all the noise that the seabirds were making.

'Well, firstly,' she said at last, 'nobody could ever accuse you of being dull, so if you were fishing for a compliment, you've got one. And secondly, it was the same as usual yesterday, with my dad wrapped up in his own misery, and my mother and I trying to make the best of it. I don't know how long he'll go on tormenting himself like this. At some stage in your life, you just have to let the pain go, don't you?'

Will leant across and kissed her. It was no more than a kiss of sympathy; there was no one around to witness it, and she felt comforted by it. She was tempted to forget the rest of it and not burden Will with what had happened at the cove at all, but the words rushed out before she could stop them.

'Actually, something else happened to upset me even more. And now that I've started saying it, I wish I hadn't. Forget I said anything, Will.'

He sat up, and she automatically did the same.

'Well, you can't stop now. What happened to upset you even more? I don't believe it could be anything so bad, but whatever you want to tell me, I would never betray a confidence, Jessie.'

And she would never betray Rita's, she found herself thinking. But what happened last night had nothing to do with what Rita had told her. In any case, she had to say something now, and she took a deep breath.

'The house had become so stifling that I felt in need of some fresh air in the evening, so I walked down to the cove and sat on a rock, just thinking about Adam and so many things. The sun was going down and it was getting dusk when I heard the sound of a motorbike. For a minute I thought it was you – and I was angry to think you had ignored what I said about yesterday being special.'

'It wasn't me, and I certainly hadn't ignored it.'

'I know, and I'm sorry for doubting you,' Jessie said quickly. 'It was those other two bikers, the ones you were with at the dance the first time we met.'

'Go on,' Will said, his voice ominously quiet.

She suddenly glared at him. 'I don't know how you could ever be friends with such oafs, Will. They're pigs, both of them, and that Des made horrible suggestions to me. He grabbed my arm, and that's really what these marks are. I managed to push him hard, and he and Ronnie Hill went crashing to the ground. It would have been funny if I wasn't so scared that they'd follow me, but thankfully they didn't, and I ran back home through the lanes as fast as I could.'

She was shaking by the time she finished telling him, and when she dared to look at him again she could see the fury in his face.

'The bastards,' he ground out. 'Sorry about the language, Jessie, but I can assure you they're no real friends of mine. The only thing we have in common is our bikes, and if I decide to buy the car I'll only be using mine for work in future. This has made me even more determined to go ahead with it now. But are you sure they didn't hurt you, apart from twisting your arm?'

'Quite sure. It was just a rotten end to a rotten day.'

Jessie swallowed hard, hoping he didn't think she was making too much of all this. Nothing had really happened, after all, and she had just been in a vulnerable state on that particular day. Some girls probably wouldn't have made so much fuss, and just had a bit of fun with their flirting. Girls like Rita – and look where that had got her!

She felt Will's arms go around her, holding her tight.

'We're not all the same, Jessie,' he said, just as though he was reading her thoughts, 'and if it'll put your mind at rest I doubt that I'll be seeing much more of Des and Ronnie.'

'It's not up to me who you see,' Jessie mumbled, embarrassed now at putting him in this position.

'If it means upsetting you this much, then I think it is. It won't break my heart not to see them again, anyway, so let's forget about them and just enjoy the afternoon.'

He squeezed her to his side, and then he spoke softly again.

'And by the way, it would break my heart not to see *you* again.'

The words took her so much by surprise that she twisted her head to look at him. His face was so close to hers that it was almost inevitable that it would end up in a kiss, and this time it was a longer, lingering kiss. They only broke apart when they heard the sound of giggling and realised they were no longer alone. There were other courting couples finding the dips and hollows in the grass where they could relish the scents of the sea and glorious air, enjoying the spectacular views of the pretty town below.

'So will you be coming to the dance next week?' Jessie said, momentarily lost for something sensible to say.

Will laughed, tracing the curve of her cheek with his finger and making her shiver at the sensuous touch. 'Of course, if you'll promise to have every dance with me.'

'Won't that look a bit obvious?' she said, teasing.

'That's what I want, so that everybody will know that you're my girl.'

Everybody, including the entire Ladies' Committee... But why not? She wasn't doing anything wrong, and what did she have to hide?

'Let's be obvious, then!' she said, feeling reckless.

After an hour, when the sun became too hot to be comfortable, they got back in the car and Will drove back by the more direct route across the county to Penzance and down to the village.

'I'm definitely getting the feel of this car now, and I'll see what price I can get it for when I see my mate at work tomorrow,' Will said. He glanced at Jessie. 'Would you like to come to my house for ten minutes? We've got to pass it on the way, and I know my mother would be tickled to meet you. I've been so cagey about you that I'm not sure she thinks you exist.'

'Well, my parents have no idea about you at all, but that's mostly because my dad thinks I'm too young to have a young man. I think he'd like to keep me wrapped in cotton wool for the rest of my life.'

'And what a waste that would be. Anyway, what do you say? Straight back to Abbot's Cove or stopping at my house?'

It never occurred to Jessie to wonder if his mother was going to be there at all. She trusted him in a way she would never have trusted his two biker friends. It also meant something when a young man wanted to introduce his girl to his mother. She agreed, feeling somewhat breathless, and they eventually arrived at the neat little cottage just outside the town.

Will's mother was listening to some music on the wireless and embroidering a table runner when they went inside. She looked up in surprise when they entered, and then she nodded as she saw her son's companion.

'So you're the secret Will's been hiding!' Doris exclaimed with a welcoming smile. 'Come and sit down, my dear. It's such a hot day I daresay you'll be glad of a cold drink.'

She suggested they take the drinks into the back garden where Will showed Jessie the plants he'd planted recently, and between them he and his mother put Jessie at ease at once. It made her wonder why her own household couldn't be as free and easy as this one. Perhaps it was because there was no older man here to hamper proceedings, Jessie thought guiltily. Dropping in so casually was never approved by Vicar Penwarden, unless it was by someone recently bereaved. Any other visitors always had to mean an occasion, planned beforehand. Jessie liked Will's mother enormously, and by the time they left she was promising to come and visit her again.

'She's so nice,' Jessie told him enthusiastically, 'but don't expect me to return the compliment and invite you home. Not yet, at any rate. I shall have to feel my way first.'

'Just as long as we can go on seeing one another, that's fine by me,' Will replied easily.

It was fine by Jessie too. In fact, she realised she felt happier than she had been for a long time. Yesterday's sadness was in the past, and she had her own future ahead. If that was selfish, she was very sure that Adam wouldn't have thought so. He would have wanted her to be happy.

'Why the secret smile?' Will said.

'I was thinking how my brother would have approved of you,' she told him honestly. 'I hadn't realised how alike you are, but it's true.'

'Then I shall take that as a great compliment. Now, do I drive you all the way home or leave you at the end of the lane?'

'End of the lane, please. I want to call on Rita before I go home, if only to salve my conscience. She's been a bit off colour lately, so I want to check that she's all right.'

'Proper little Florence Nightingale, aren't you?' Will said with a grin. 'Did you ever think about being a nurse?'

Jessie laughed. 'No, but you can't help getting involved with other people's problems when you work in a chemist's shop!'

'I'll see you at the dance next Saturday, then. By then, I should be the proper owner of this car, so there'll be no more splashing your frocks from motorbike wheels when the weather's bad.'

He remembered. It made Jessie's heart glow to know it. Remembering every little detail of each time they had been together was something that was second nature to her. In any case she recorded it all in her diary. But you didn't think boys remembered things in the same way. The fact that Will did was something that made him even more special to her.

When he stopped the car at the end of the lane, he glanced around to see that nobody was around, and then he pulled Jessie towards him to give her a last kiss. It was cosy and intimate in the soft leather interior, and she felt flushed when she stood outside, watching the car recede towards Penzance again until she could see the dust from his wheels no more.

She hummed a tune beneath her breath as she walked along to Rita's house. When she reached it she could see her friend sitting with a book in the window seat of her bedroom. She was waving frantically, and Jessie waved back. She was going to see her, anyway, but she gave a small sigh now, hoping that nothing more had gone wrong.

There was never any need to be formal here, any more than there was at Will's house, and Jessie went inside after a brief knock on the door, saying a cheery hello to Mrs Levant and ignoring the inert figure in the armchair.

'Go on up, Jessie love,' Mrs Levant said. 'Perhaps you can put a smile on her face. She's in a right old stew today and nothing I do is right for her.'

It didn't sound too good, and after the lovely afternoon Jessie and Will had spent, the last thing Jessie wanted was to have her happiness deflated. But it was too late now. She was here, and she went up to Rita's bedroom and flopped down on her bed.

'What's up? Your mum says she can't do anything right for you today.'

Rita scowled. 'What do you think is up? The

same as yesterday and the day before and the day before that, of course!'

'Nothing's happened yet, then?'

'God, you're quick to catch on, aren't you?' she said sarcastically.

'Don't blame me for it, Rita! I didn't go off with that horrible bloke.'

'Keep your voice down, can't you? I don't want Mum to hear us. And shut the door a minute. I've got something important to ask you.'

Jessie had a strong feeling that she wasn't going to like this, but she did as she was instructed and closed the bedroom door before sitting back on the bed, with Rita sitting beside her now.

'What is it?'

'You've got to help me, Jess,' she said, her voice shaking. 'I'm convinced there's something growing inside me, and you know what I mean by that. I can't even say it aloud now.'

'You *don't* know for sure, Rita, and you need to give it more time before you start panicking. If you're still worried, you'll have to see Doctor Charles.'

'I couldn't do that!'

'You'd have to see him eventually, if it was what you suspect – which I'm sure it's not!'

Rita's face was stricken now. 'Oh, God, Jessie, how could I have been so stupid? But you've *got* to help me.'

'I don't know how. If you're thinking of finding some backstreet woman to do something about it, you can forget it. Girls have bled to death taking that risk. Tell me you're not thinking of anything so foolish, Rita,' she finished urgently.

It was also against all the Church's teachings, and Jessie had been too steeped in that at home to even consider it. But now was obviously not the right time to go all religious about it to Rita.

'I wasn't thinking of anything like that,' Rita said, ashen-faced now.

'What then?'

Rita fiddled with the tassels on the end of her bedspread and looked away from Jessie when she answered.

'Well, you work at the chemist's, and people come in for all sorts of things that Mr Price makes up for them in the dispensary.'

Jessie's heart jumped. 'You surely don't expect me to ask him to make up something for *this*, Rita! You don't even know if it's necessary yet!'

'Oh, don't get on your high horse before you hear what I've got to say. I've been having another look in Mum's medical books, and it says that only if a woman's life is in danger from having a child – or if the child has died inside her – then in those circumstances it might be necessary to give her some medicine to bring it on early.'

'I can't believe this,' Jessie said, jumping to her feet. 'However you dress it up, you're talking about killing a baby, Rita. Even if what you fear is true, your life isn't in danger, and there's nothing dead inside you!'

'There might be!' She swallowed hard. 'Anyway, how about this: couldn't you ask old Price, in a hypothetical way – if that's the right word – what a woman could take in these circumstances? You could say we saw something about it at the pictures. If we could find it out, we could go to Penzance or farther afield, and get some medicine made up by a chemist well away from Abbot's Cove. I'm desperate, Jess.'

'You're mad!' Jessie said flatly.

'No, just desperate,' she said again. She clutched Jessie's hands. 'Please, Jess, do this for me. I'll never ask for anything ever again, I promise.'

At that moment she sounded so much like the Rita of their infant days, pleading to borrow something of Jessie's and promising never to ask for anything ever again, that it twisted Jessie's heart.

'That's all very well, but I don't know how I could possibly get around to broaching the subject,' she muttered.

'But you'll try, won't you? I knew you would. Oh, Jess, you're the best!' Rita said, close to tears.

She didn't feel like the best as she went home a short while later. This afternoon with Will had begun and ended so joyously until she called in to see Rita. Now, she felt soiled, as if some of Rita's shame was rubbing off on her. And so it was. By agreeing to do as Rita asked, she was going to be her unwilling accomplice in something that Jessie knew was wicked and against everything her father had taught her. She had no idea what she was going to say to Mr Price. Rita seemed to have worked it all out, but it wasn't Rita who was going to put the question to him. Between them, she and Rita had concocted the story of a girl in a Hollywood picture who was in a similar sort of plight and had begged her doctor to help her. He had refused, naturally, but the tale that Jessie had to make sound convincing

112

was that the two girls had been curious as to what sort of medicine could be so powerful as to bring on a miscarriage.

Jessie shuddered every time she thought about it. She couldn't use that word, of course, because young unmarried girls weren't supposed to know about such things, so that was another stumbling block. What exactly was she supposed to say? But she had promised Rita, and she wouldn't break that promise, however painful it was going to be. And she knew she had to do it soon.

CHAPTER SEVEN

Jessie kept tossing and turning all night, worrying about how she could possibly do what Rita asked. While they ate breakfast, her mother commented on how pale she looked, and at the dark rings beneath her eyes.

'Are you feeling all right, my dear? If you're not well, perhaps you should see Doctor Charles for a tonic.'

'I'm fine, Mum. I've got a bit of a headache, that's all.'

As her mother spoke, for a moment it had been tempting to agree to what she said and ask the doctor if he thought she needed a tonic. It would be so easy, then, to ask him the question – hypothetically – that she was so reluctant to ask the chemist, knowing that he wouldn't betray a confidence. Doctors didn't do that, did they?

But the thought of repeating the story she and Rita had invented to their kindly old doctor, who had brought her into the world, was something Jessie knew she simply couldn't do. No, it had to be Mr Price or nobody. He was always discreet too. He had to be, in his business, Jessie thought, desperately trying to make the best of it.

Mondays were definitely not the best of days to try to discuss something so personal. In any case Vera Price was always fussing about, acting more like the dispenser than Harold himself at times.

114

She was such a know-it-all, she would have the answers to the problem, but Vera would be the last person Jessie would ask, knowing how she kowtowed to the vicar. Jessie didn't care to imagine what would happen if she reported to him what his daughter was enquiring about!

No, it would have to be Tuesday afternoon when there was usually a lull in the shop, and when Vera usually went to Penzance on the bus to do some shopping. Tuesday afternoons were more relaxed on both counts. About three o'clock she made a pot of tea for Harold and herself, and they retired into the small dispensary for the welcome refreshment. By now, Jessie was a bag of nerves, but, gritting her teeth, she knew it was now or never.

She spoke as casually as she could, despite the fact that her heart was thumping and her palms were damp as she gripped her teacup.

'Mr Price, there's a question that's been bothering me and Rita recently, and I said you'd probably know the answer.'

She saw him almost physically preen himself and she plunged on wildly.

'The last time we went to the pictures there was a woman in the film who was going to have a baby, but for some reason it was vital to her health that she didn't have it. It was something to do with some illness. The doctor gave her some medicine and it did whatever was needed. What kind of medicine could be so powerful that it would take a baby away?'

Oh, God, was he looking at her suspiciously now? Did he suspect that she wasn't talking about some woman in a film, but about Rita?

115

'Well, at least it was responsible of the film-makers not to mention any such medicine that might put ideas into gullible women's heads. It's not the kind of information that should be bandied about,' the chemist said sternly.

'Yes, but what could it be?' Jessie persisted, wondering if this was all she was going to get for her trouble after all.

Harold Price cleared his throat. 'I'm not sure I should be talking to you about this, Jessie. You've always taken an interest in the dispensing business and I know you're a sensible girl and are merely eager for knowledge. But it's not the kind of thing I care to discuss with a young girl.'

She bit her lips hard. If only he knew how deeply personal this was for her best friend...

'I understand,' she murmured. 'But I really would like to know, Mr Price.'

After a few seconds he sighed, and Jessie knew instinctively that he was fighting with his feelings that he shouldn't be telling her these things, and his constant need to air his knowledge.

'Very well, then. What a doctor would do in these circumstances is to give the woman a douche. You know what that is, so I won't elaborate. It may contain carbolic acid or even plain soap and water, which would bring about the ... er ... expulsion. Or he may give her an irritant such as quinine in the form of pills or medicine. There are even home remedies such as taking large doses of castor oil or Beecham's Pills or Epsom salts. Sadly, there are many ways of bringing about an abortion, my dear, and I think we've had quite enough of this conversation now.'

'Thank you, Mr Price. That was very enlightening,' Jessie said, knowing that as he had warmed to his tale he had given her plenty of information. The next thing would be to pass it on to Rita as soon as possible.

As the shop bell rang out she fled thankfully out of the dispensary and into the main part of the shop, leaving him to drink his tea and look after her thoughtfully as he wiped his brow.

As soon as she had finished work that evening, she walked down towards the cove and Yendle's haberdashery and gift shop. Rita was still serving a customer with some ribbons, and as soon as she was done she came outside, looking decidedly more cheerful than she had done recently. Before Jessie could say anything, Rita had whisked her away from the shop, squeezing her arm tightly.

'You were right, Jessie,' she said, almost hysterically. 'You were always cleverer than me, telling me not to worry. I had the cramps when I got up this morning, and I knew my little friend had arrived at last, so I can put the whole rotten affair behind me now.'

Jessie looked at her with a mixture of relief and horror. 'Thank goodness!' she stuttered.

'Well, you could sound a bit more pleased for me,' Rita said, laughing. 'Although you never doubted it, did you? I always said you had a sixth sense about things, and now I know you have. So there's no need to say anything to old man Price after all, which will please you.'

She took a proper look at Jessie's face then, and

117

her smile faded.

'Oh, my God, you've already said something, haven't you? Oh Jess, I'm really sorry. I know how you hated the thought of telling lies. What did the old goat say?'

'The old goat was none too pleased at having to go into detail about it,' Jessie said in annoyance. 'And I was less than pleased at having to broach the subject at all. I felt a real fool, Rita, and if you weren't my best friend I'd never have done such a thing for you.'

Rita looked crestfallen now. 'Well, I can promise you it will never be necessary again.' She gave a cracked laugh as she realised the extent of what she had asked her friend to do. She squeezed her arm. 'Do you remember what you said when those older girls first told us what you had to do to have babies, Jess? You were going to have your thing sewn up, remember? It's a pity I hadn't taken your advice and had the same thing done to mine!' she went on, trying to put a smile back on Jessie's face.

'It's a bit late for that now, as far as you're concerned,' Jessie said, with the ghost of a smile as she remembered.

'And how do you feel about it now?' Rita said slyly as they began to walk back through the village. 'Now that you've got your biker boy and shared a few kisses I've no doubt, don't you ever feel differently about you know what?'

'Not differently enough to get myself in the same situation as you did,' Jessie said, shaking her off. 'And he's got a car now. If I'd had the chance to tell you that on Sunday, you'd have known already. I don't have to go on the back of a motorbike when we go out anymore.'

'Well, that's nice for you. I don't suppose we'll be seeing so much of each other at weekends anymore, then.'

She sounded jealous and resentful, which was a bit rich, thought Jessie, considering what she had just done for her.

They had come to the point where they went their separate ways, and for the first time there was an awkwardness between them. Knowing one another all their lives and growing up together through their schooldays, there had been the usual childish squabbles between them, but nothing as fundamental as this.

'I shan't be seeing Will all the time,' Jessie said at last. 'And we can hardly miss one another in a place as small as Abbot's Cove, can we?'

'Hardly. I'll be seeing you around, then,' Rita said, and turned on her heels to walk away.

It might have sounded like a compromise to save face, but as Jessie walked quickly home to the vicarage, she had a hollow feeling in her stomach, as though something precious had somehow been lost. During the evening she tried not to dwell on the feeling, and to take an interest in her mother's ideas for fund-raising for the war widows in the Abbot's Cove area and beyond. There were still many who needed help, and those who wouldn't accept charity at any price, but Ellen was the most tactful of women, and Jessie admired her tremendously for it.

After supper, the vicar, as usual, left his women-folk to spend the rest of the evening in his study.

There were often visitors needing his assistance on one matter or another, and they were encouraged to use a side door for the purpose of church or ministering affairs, rather than disturbing the rest of the family.

It was nearly nine o'clock when Ellen was making some cocoa for herself and Jessie, and preparing to take some refreshments on a tray to her husband, when Vicar Penwarden suddenly appeared in the room, his face colourless and grim, as if he had just suffered a great shock.

'What is it, my dear?' Ellen said quickly, instantly wondering if there had been news of one of his parishioners having had a terrible accident. There had been such heartbreaking tragedies over the years, and she couldn't help the possibilities spinning through her mind. Living so close to the sea and the cliffs, there was always danger. In the past, several children had wandered too close to the edge and plunged over to their deaths. The sea had been rough today too, and there would have been fishermen out in the bay at the mercy of the waves.

'Jessica, come to my study at once,' the vicar said, his voice like thunder. 'And you will please accompany her, Ellen.'

Jessie's heart jumped. Whatever it was, she knew the next few moments were not going to be pleasant. And yet she still didn't connect anything in her mind until she followed her mother into the study and saw the set faces of the two people sitting stiffly on Vicar Penwarden's upright chairs.

The chemist, Harold Price, looked as though he wished himself anywhere but here, while his wife, Vera, had her lips fixed in such a hard, tight line that they almost disappeared into her cheeks.

'What's happened?' Ellen said in bewilderment.

Thomas spoke harshly. 'I would like you to sit down, my dear. You, Jessica, will remain standing.'

By now, Jessie's lips and throat were so dry she could hardly swallow. Her legs shook so much she would dearly like to sit down as well, but she knew better than to disagree with her father's commands.

'Now then, Mr Price,' Thomas said, addressing the unfortunate chemist, 'will you please repeat what you told your wife earlier this evening, and what has since been reported to me?'

One glance at Vera Price's face told Jessie that there would be no reprieve from whatever she imagined to be the truth of the tale she and Rita had concocted. But what had *she* concocted from it? It had been an innocent question, no more – at least, in the way she had asked it. A thirst for knowledge – and that was something her father had always encouraged in his children.

Harold cleared his throat noisily. 'It's difficult to remember the exact words that were used.'

'Please try, Harold,' Vera said icily, forcing him to continue.

'Well, Jessica told me she had seen a film in which there was some medical problem with one of the characters, and it had made her curious. She wanted to have my expert opinion on what methods could be used to bring about an ... an... abortion,' he finally managed, almost whispering the word.

His wife tut-tutted at his inadequacy. 'What my husband means is that the girl made up some cock and bull story about seeing such a disgraceful film, when the truth of the matter must seem blindingly obvious, even to my husband!'

If the other three people in the study noticed how disparagingly she spoke of her husband, nobody seemed to care. By now, all eyes were on Jessie, and Ellen's hand had gone to her throat.

'Jessie, what is Mrs Price saying?' she croaked.

Thomas thumped his hand on his desk in a fury, making them all jump.

'Isn't it obvious what she's saying, woman? Why would any young girl ask such a question without a reason for it? Jessica has been guilty of the sin of fornication and this is the result. Now, she wants to further compound her sins by going against God's will and trying to rid herself of the issue.'

As her father's tirade went on, Jessie's knees finally gave way, and she sank to the floor for a few moments, only to drag herself upright as quickly as she could, rather than have the assumption made that she was trying to atone for her sins. The sins that she wasn't guilty of...

'It's not true!' she gasped wildly. 'None of it is true.'

'Are you denying that you asked my husband these questions?' Vera Price snapped before the vicar could get a word in.

'No, I'm not, but it was for a purely innocent reason. It had nothing to do with myself!'

As if they were all the participants in a play, the

woman seemed somehow to have taken centre stage, while the others remained silent. She was judge and jury all rolled into one, Jessie thought wildly, as the horror of what was happening was seeping into her brain.

'And can you deny that Mrs Brevill of the Tuesday Club saw you getting on to a bus in Penzance a while ago, and that you were saying goodbye to a young man who you told her was your cousin?'

'Jessica doesn't have a cousin in Penzance,' Ellen said faintly. 'Although she did say she was going to the cinema with her old school friend, Dorothy.'

'So that's probably how she got the idea of the ridiculous story about a character in a film having a medical problem, when it was really a shameful problem of her own,' Vera went on, as triumphantly as though she had just solved a crime.

'You've got it all wrong,' Jessie almost wept.

Vicar Penwarden had clearly had enough of the chemist's wife taking over the proceedings now. He lifted his hand for silence, and because everyone in Abbot's Cove was so used to obeying him, Vera clamped her lips together again. Then, the only sounds in the study were the ticking of the grandfather clock in the corner, the uneasy shuffling of Harold Price's feet as he realised what he had unleashed, and Jessie's uneven breathing.

Thomas spoke loudly. 'Before we go any further and turn this meeting into an inquisition, I am going to ask my daughter one question. She

123

has been brought up in a God-fearing house, so I expect to have an honest and truthful answer, and for that reason I will not ask her to put her hand on the Bible.'

'I will do so gladly, if you wish it, Dad,' Jessie said shrilly. 'I've got nothing to hide!'

'Be quiet, miss. I think you've got plenty to hide if what Mrs Price has said about your meeting with a young man in Penzance is proven. But that is a matter to be dealt with among your family in private. What concerns all of us here, and will obviously affect your future in the community, is whether or not you are the person in the story you told Mr Price.'

Before anything more could be said, Ellen put her hand on his arm, finding it as rigid as iron, as was his entire body.

'I beg you, Thomas, take a moment to calm yourself. Whatever we are about to hear, Jessica is our daughter and deserves our love and support.'

'Even if she was prepared to go against all the Church's teachings, and commit the most appalling of sins in destroying an unborn life?'

'I was *not!*' Jessie found herself screaming. 'I was not the woman concerned with such a thing, and nor would I ever be so wicked.'

'Then who was?' Vera demanded, suspicion building in her eyes.

'*I told you.* It was nothing more than a hypo-thetical question. My parents brought up Adam and myself to have a thirst for knowledge, and the only reason I wanted to know was out of a natural curiosity.'

'Manners, please, Jessie,' Ellen said severely,

out of long habit.

Manners! To the old trout who was accusing her of something she would never have done, and for which trying to help a friend had got her into this mess! But even as she thought it in a fury, Jessie knew that no matter what happened, she would never betray Rita.

'Will you all please calm down and let me deal with this?' Vicar Penwarden thundered now, silencing them all. He turned to his daughter again.

'Now then, Jessica, we have all heard what Mr Price has to say, and I presume you are not going to deny that you asked him for this information, no matter what the reason?'

'Yes, I did,' she said sullenly.

'So I will ask you this one question. Did you require this information from Mr Price because you wanted it for your own personal needs?'

'No, I did not!'

Even as she raged back at her father in a way she had never done before, she could see the anguish in his eyes at even having this conversation with her, especially in front of members of his congregation. He had his pride, and whatever it was doing to her, Jessie knew that he would feel he was also losing status in their eyes.

'But you cannot deny that you have been seeing a young man who you pretended was your cousin, Jessica,' Vera Price put in. 'You told Mrs Brevill a blatant lie.'

The implication was obvious. If the girl could tell a lie about one thing she could easily tell a lie about another. Jessie turned her frantic gaze on her.

'Why are you doing this to me? Why are you so determined to make me out to be so wicked? You and your so-called pious friends are nothing but evil-minded gossips in this village.'

Ellen put her hand on her daughter's arm. 'That's enough, Jessica. You will apologise to Mrs Price this instant.'

Jessica wrenched away from her mother, her eyes blazing.

'I'll do no such thing. I'll do something else instead, and if you and my father and anyone else cannot take my word for what I'm about to do, then damn you all to hell.'

Thomas Penwarden reeled at hearing such blasphemy from his daughter, but before he had any idea of what she intended, she had pulled the heavy family Bible down from its shelf and laid it on his desk.

She put both hands over the Bible and gazed at it steadily. Remembering her father's ugly words, she spoke as strongly as she could manage, considering that she was shaking all over. She knew her face must be scarlet with embarrassment, but it had to be said.

'I swear by Almighty God that I am not guilty of the sin of fornication. I have never lain with a man, and nor have I ever been in need of the kind of information I asked Mr Price for.'

She touched her fingers to her lips and then pressed them gently back onto the Bible before removing them. Then she stared intently at the chemist and his wife, then at each of her parents in turn.

'If that is not enough to satisfy you,' she said, more dignified now, 'then shame on all of you for refusing to take the word of someone prepared to swear on the Holy Book.'

The first sound to break the uneasy silence was Harold Price, constantly clearing his throat as usual.

'I think it is time we left, Mrs Price,' he said, addressing her in a ridiculously formal manner. 'These good folk need to deal with family matters in their own way, and I can only offer my sincere regret in this misunderstanding, and in bringing this matter to your parents' attention.'

He looked directly at Jessie. 'I'm truly sorry, my dear, and if you want to take a day off tomorrow, please do so.'

'You mean she's not sacked?' his wife put in sharply. 'Chem, please think what you're saying.'

'I have done enough thinking, and enough damage too,' he told her, more assertive than usual. 'Jessie has always been a good and conscientious worker, and nothing I've heard here tonight has done anything to change my wish for her to continue being so. So we will bid you all goodnight.'

It was obvious he couldn't get out of the vicarage quickly enough now, and Jessie guessed that Vera would be getting a good slice of tongue pie from him, and a good thing too. She hardly dared look at her father, who by now had slumped down in his chair behind his desk, his gaze on the Bible that was still in front of him. The Bible in which he believed implicitly.

Ellen spoke to him quickly. 'I think we all need

127

that cocoa now, and perhaps a tot of brandy to go with it wouldn't go amiss, my dear. Shall Jessie and I leave you while we see to it?'

Thomas nodded without speaking, and Jessie escaped thankfully with her mother. It had been such a terrible evening, and brought about so unexpectedly, simply because Harold Price hadn't been able to resist telling his wife what he and Jessie had discussed. She hadn't anticipated that. Vera was such a do-gooder, and such a crony of her father's, that she would have seen it as her duty to come storming up here to repeat it all. How noble ... and how cruel.

But at least it was over now, and no real harm done. But her relief suffered a jolt a short while later. Her father decided to remain alone in his study with his cocoa and however much medicinal brandy he decided to take with it, while Jessie and her mother drank theirs in the parlour.

'So how long have you been seeing a young man, Jessica?' Ellen said, in a voice that dared her to deny it.

'Not very long. He came to the dance with some friends and we got talking,' Jessie said jerkily.

'And is he the boy you were seen with at the bus stop in Penzance by Mrs Brevill, who you said was your cousin? Or is there more than one?'

'Of course not!'

'So where does Dorothy Glyn come into all this?' Ellen persisted. 'I assume it must be the evening you were meant to be going to the cinema with her, so did you actually do so? And no more lies, please, Jessica.'

It would be so easy to say yes, and that she just

128

happened to see Will later, or even that she didn't really know him and he'd just helped her on to the bus. So easy ... and so deceitful. She felt her head droop, knowing she couldn't do it.

'I haven't seen Dorothy for ages, and it was Will Tremayne who I went to the cinema with. He's very nice and respectful, and I know you'd approve of him if you got to know him.'

Neither of them had heard Thomas come out of his study until they were suddenly aware of him standing in the doorway, his face as black as thunder.

'Am I hearing correctly? How long have you been consorting with some young man behind my back?' he roared.

Jessie flinched. 'Dad, I'm seventeen years old, and lots of girls my age have got boyfriends.'

'I don't care what other girls do. You're still a minor until you're twenty-one, and while you live under my roof you'll do as I say, young lady. And there'll be no more dances for you, either. I shall have serious words with Vera Price and the Ladies' Committee to make sure they keep a careful check on just what goes on there and even whether they should continue.'

Jessie gasped. 'You can't keep me confined like a child, Dad, and you can't stop the dances, either.'

But she knew he could, and he would, if he was so inclined. Shocked and humiliated by all that had happened now, she scraped back her chair, ignoring her mother's remonstrations, and said she was going to bed.

'At least I can have some privacy there,' she

129

said furiously. She slammed out of the room, uncaring that her father was shouting after her. But despite all her bravado, her eyes were blinded by tears before she even reached her bedroom. And in the midst of it all, she wondered despairingly how she was ever going to see Will again.

CHAPTER EIGHT

Out of habit Jessie recorded the upsetting evening in her diary, holding back none of her fury at Vera Price's spitefulness in reporting something that had been said in confidence. She had never written down what Rita had asked her to do, nor about her friend's fears, and she didn't intend to do so now. Seeing the words written down would have made her own part in the deceit all the more shameful. But Vera had completely misunderstood her reasons for speaking to the chemist, and it was Jessie who was paying the price.

The diary page became damp with tears, because there were more things at stake now. It was like throwing a pebble in a pond and watching the ripples inexorably spread out. In doing what she had for Rita, she had somehow ruined everything for herself. She couldn't even go to the dance on Saturday night and she would never be allowed to see Will again ... and she had no idea how she was going to let him know.

She took a last shuddering breath as she heard clumping footsteps coming upstairs, and she quickly pushed the diary into her drawer and turned out her light. Almost cowering beneath the bedclothes for fear her father was going to come into the room and rant at her again, she heard him close his own bedroom door, and she wilted. As she did so, her feelings gradually changed to

131

anger at being treated this way.

Despite what Rita had been going through these last weeks, she found herself envying her friend. Rita's home life was so free and easy, compared with Jessie's own. Rita's mother was disabled, but she could still smile and encourage her daughter to go out whenever she liked, and had no problems with whatever company she kept. She trusted her daughter – however misguided that might be in the circumstances... Rita's father was a layabout and a drunk and a bit of a buffoon in the village, but there was a lot of love in that household. Jessie was quite sure that if Rita mentioned a certain young man as being special, he would be welcomed and not treated with suspicion. As the thoughts whirled through her mind Jessie knew the anger could just as quickly descend into self-pity, and she pulled the bedcovers over her head like a child afraid of monsters in the night and tried to make her mind a blank.

By morning she had made a decision. If she couldn't go to the dance, then Rita would have to let Will know that there had been a family problem, and that she was unable to see him that night. She had no intention of shutting him out of her life completely, but for now, that would have to do. Unable to stay in bed any longer, she got up far earlier than usual, but Ellen was already in the kitchen and she looked at her daughter in surprise.

'I thought Mr Price said you could take the day off today,' she said.

Jessie looked at her unblinkingly. 'I've got no

reason to hide away, and I prefer to be at the shop than to stay in the house,' she added pointedly.

'You know your father only wants the best for you, Jessie,' her mother said unhappily.

'By wrapping me up in cotton wool as if I'm some precious object? I'm flesh and blood, Mum, a normal girl, and he shouldn't treat me like this.'

Ellen's voice became steelier. 'I think we both know that because of what happened last night he's seeing you rather differently. We both accept that your discussion with Mr Price was innocent, but you have lied to us, Jessica. You have been seeing a young man behind our backs, and it has obviously happened more than once.'

Jessie pushed her plate away, no longer having any appetite for the jam and toast that Ellen had set in front of her.

'What if it has?' she said angrily. 'I'm not a nun, and I don't intend to act like one just because Dad's such a pillar of the church.'

Ellen's face was as white as her daughter's now. 'I'm thankful he's already gone out and hasn't heard you say such things. Isn't it enough that we've lost Adam without him having to face the fact that you are becoming so rebellious?'

'That's not fair!' Jessie said, jumping up from her chair now, the tears starting again. 'You can't blame me for what happened to Adam, nor make him out to be such a saint, because he wasn't, and I won't listen to any more of this.'

She rushed out of the room, grabbing her coat on the way and ignoring her mother's angry calls. She felt so distressed that she needed to walk around for a while before reaching the chemist's shop and Vera's inevitable hostility. In any case, she was far too early and the shop wouldn't be open yet. The one thing she knew Vera wouldn't have dared to do was to insist that her husband fired her, for the whole village would want to know the reason.

She found herself walking towards the churchyard and then her heart began beating painfully fast as she saw her father contemplating Adam's headstone. She made to turn away, but she was too late.

'Jessica,' he called out.

She had no option but to join him, not knowing what to say to him or how he would behave towards her. She could see the sorrow in his eyes – but was it for her, or for his lost favourite? She stood by his side, stubborn and silent.

'There were some harsh things said last night,' he said finally. 'I came here this morning, as I often do, to try to imagine what Adam would have made of it all. Young as he was, he had seen more of the world than I ever had. He was a young man in tune with modern ways, while I am not and nor do I wish to be.'

'We still have to move with the times,' Jessie muttered.

'That may be so, but nor should we forget the values of the past which shaped the people that we are,' he said sharply.

'So what has Adam told you?' she asked, not meaning to be blasphemous or sarcastic, but finding this conversation unbearable.

Thomas's sorrowful gaze was on her now.

'More to the point, what do you suppose he would be telling you if he were here now? Don't you think a wise older brother would be advising you about the things that an old-fashioned father felt difficult to say?'

'I think it's dangerous to live so much in the past that you can't appreciate the good things about the present,' Jessie told him, her eyes flashing. 'I loved Adam as much as you and Mum, but he's gone, and we all have to get on with our lives.'

She turned and walked quickly away from him, knowing she had never spoken to him in such a way before and that he would never forgive her. She would doubtless be in for another lecture that evening, but for once she didn't care. What *had* she done wrong, for heaven's sake? Nothing, except to try to help a friend – and to tell a few little white lies. She certainly hadn't been guilty of the sin of *fornication*, as he had accused her.

She had been walking so fast that she had to slow down eventually because of the stitch in her side, and before she realised it she had come right down to the cove. The waves were gentle this morning, washing and cleansing the sand. Jessie wished all her troubles could be washed away as easily.

There were still ten minutes to go before most of the shops in the village opened for business, but the door to Yendle's haberdashery and gift shop was already ajar, and she could see Rita strolling down towards it as if she didn't have a care in the world. As soon as Rita caught sight of Jessie she joined her at the cove, her feet slipping and sliding on the soft sand.

'You look like hell,' she said cheerfully. 'What's up?'

Jessie looked at her speechlessly for a minute, unable to summon up the words. Rita had no idea of the chaos that had occurred through Jessie asking Harold Price for the answer to Rita's problem. She didn't know that Vicar Penwarden had virtually forbidden Jessie to see Will Tremayne again. As far as Rita knew, her problem was solved and would be as quickly forgotten.

'Jessie, what's happened?' she said again, when her friend didn't reply to her question. 'Are you ill?'

'No, I'm not ill. I wish it was something as simple as that.'

'Well, are you going to tell me, only Mrs Yendle's already got the shop open and she'll be in a bad mood if I don't get there soon. If it's going to take too long to tell me what's wrong, let's meet down here after work and you can tell me then. And for goodness' sake, cheer up. You'll be putting all your customers off if they see you with such a gloomy face. Whatever it is, it can't be that bad!'

She gave a quick wave and scurried back to the gift shop, leaving Jessie feeling more resentful than she ever had towards her. Rita had done some madcap things in the past, and there had been times when Jessie had had to pick up the pieces, but never anything like this. And how quickly Rita could brush all the trouble aside, leaving Jessie the one to brood over what had happened.

Jessie arrived at the chemist's shop with seconds to spare. Harold Price looked at her in surprise but with guarded admiration too.

'I didn't expect to see you today, Jessie. I told you to take the day off if you wanted to, didn't I?'

'I'd rather be at work, thank you. That's all right, isn't it?'

'It's more than all right. In fact, I want to apologise for the way things turned out. I know we talked in confidence, and I should never have mentioned any of it to Vera. Somehow it just seemed to snowball, the way these things do,' he went on, seemingly unable to leave the topic alone.

'Well, it's over now, and I'd prefer it if we could just forget it ever happened and treat this as an ordinary day,' Jessie said in a strangled voice.

She didn't relish the moment when Vera would come into the shop as she usually did halfway through the morning, but by then the day had resumed its normality. Customers still wanted their prescriptions filled and to purchase their stomach medicines and indigestion pills, and they had no idea of the turmoil that had been raging inside their helpful assistant's head for the past twenty-four hours – it still could be, if she let it.

But at last the interminable day came to an end, with little more than silent glares from Vera, to which Jessie gave her unflinching looks in return. Nothing was mentioned about last night's episode. Jessie had been determined not to give the woman any excuse to call her insolent, but nor did she go out of her way to be anything but

137

icily polite if it was necessary to speak to her at all.

Rita was already waiting for her at the cove, tossing pebbles into the sea, still looking as though nothing ever bothered her for long. Which was just about right, Jessie thought resentfully. And Rita still had no idea of what she had put her friend through last night.

'You don't look any more cheerful than you did this morning,' Rita greeted her. 'Are you going to tell me what's wrong? You and Will haven't had a fight, have you?'

'You don't have any idea, do you?' Jessie said.

Rita shrugged. 'Not unless you tell me. I bet he tried something on last time you saw him and you got all prissy with him,' she added with a snigger.

'For goodness' sake, Rita, is that all you ever think of?' Jessie snapped. 'It's got nothing to do with Will, and everything to do with you!'

Rita's eyes opened wide. 'With me! What have I done?'

'Well, for a start you persuaded me to ask Mr Price if he knew how a woman could bring about an abortion – and before you say anything, that's *exactly* what it was.'

'Well, now you know it's not necessary, and you might look a bit glad for me,' she said, and then the penny dropped. 'Oh God, Jessie, I know how you hated the idea.'

'I'd not only done what you asked, but Harold had blabbed to dear Vera, and the next thing I knew the two of them were in my dad's study, and I was being accused of trying to find out the messy details on my own account.'

Rita looked stricken. 'You don't mean they thought you were the one?'

'Of course I do. Are you stupid?' Jessie said bitterly. 'How do you think I felt, with my own father accusing me of *fornication* – which is how he put it, of course. And Mum stood there looking tearful and shocked, while I had to defend myself over something I hadn't done.

'And before you ask,' she went on, anticipating the next question, 'no, I didn't mention your name, and I stuck to the story, even though I had to swear on the Bible that I had never been with a boy.'

'Oh God, Jessie, I'm so sorry,' Rita croaked. 'You know I never meant to get you into trouble.'

'There's more,' Jessie went on grimly, not letting her get off the hook so easily. 'Mrs Brevill saw me with Will when I was getting on the bus in Penzance and like an idiot I told her he was my cousin. She knows Mrs Price, so that was reported to her as well, and now my dad thinks I've been sneaking about with boys all the time, and he's forbidden me to go to the dance on Saturday night. There's no way I can let Will know, so you'll have to tell him what's happened.'

She paused for breath and Rita looked at her uneasily.

'Not all of it?' she asked uneasily.

Jessie's eyes were wrathful now. 'Don't worry, you needn't tell him how we cooked up that pack of lies to save your skin. No, just tell him that there's been some trouble at home and I'm not allowed to go to the dance, but that I'll see him in the same place as last week on Sunday afternoon.'

The words were out of her mouth before she could stop them. But why not? she thought defiantly. It was the middle of the twentieth century and she shouldn't be treated as if she was some kind of chattel.

'I'm really sorry, Jess,' Rita said, more meekly now. 'But do you think it's wise to see Will on Sunday? Wouldn't it be better to wait a while?'

'Until he's gone off me, you mean, or I end up as some bitter, loveless old crone? No, my father isn't going to rule my life. He tried to rule my brother's, and if the war hadn't come along, Adam would probably have been coerced into entering the Church just to please Dad. Instead of which—' Her voice broke, and then strengthened again. 'I was too young to see how he tried to manipulate Adam, but I can see it now, and it's not going to happen to me.'

'Gosh, Jess, I've never heard you talk like this before, nor to stand up for yourself where your dad's concerned.'

'Well, you're hearing it now. So are you going to do as I say?'

'Of course I am. As for Will, I doubt that he'll stay at the dance for long if you're not there. It's obvious that he's only got eyes for you.'

If Jessie felt mollified at hearing that, she was also bitterly disappointed that she wouldn't be there to see Will herself. But she knew better than to defy her father by going out on Saturday night. Proper explanations – such as she was prepared to give without betraying Rita – would have to wait until Sunday.

On Wednesday evenings Vicar Penwarden ran a junior Bible class at the church, and Jessie was relieved when he left the house after supper. The atmosphere at home was cooler than usual, but hopefully they could put last night's episode behind them, Jessie thought as she helped her mother wash up the supper dishes. Later, such hopes were short-lived when Ellen produced something from the sideboard drawer and placed it on the table between them, and Jessie's heart sank as she saw the familiar blue cover of her diary.

'I saw this when I put some of your ironed underwear in your dressing table drawer, Jessica. I would not normally have opened it or read any of it, but in view of what happened last night I overcame my scruples. I think you owe me an explanation.'

'Has Dad seen it?' was all Jessie could stammer.

Ellen's face softened slightly. 'No, and at present I would rather he didn't. He has been really unwell ever since last night's events. I'm worried about him, and I don't want to upset him any more than is necessary. So, Jessie? Who is this boy you have been seeing? I want the truth now.'

Jessie took a deep breath. 'I told you last night, Mum, his name is Will Tremayne and he lives just outside Penzance. He works as a motorcycle courier for a delivery firm in Penzance, but he's just bought a small car so that he can take his mother out. And me,' she added, since Ellen would have seen the entry in her diary about the day they went to St Ives.

The memory of that lovely day overwhelmed her for a moment, culminating in the visit to Will's home to meet his mother. She realised she had also mentioned that in the diary, so at least her mother knew she hadn't lied about Mrs Tremayne's existence. And she couldn't bear to have the sweet memories spoilt.

'They're really good people, Mum,' she said desperately. 'If Dad wasn't the way he is, I'd have mentioned Will before, but he seems to want to keep me on a leash for ever. Doesn't he ever want me to get married and have children of my own?'

'I hope you haven't been discussing any such thing with this young man,' Ellen said sharply.

'Of course not. I've only known him a few weeks, but with some people you just know they're somehow special, don't you? Didn't you know that when you first met Dad?'

They had never spoken of such intimate things before, and as Jessie felt her face flush, she realised her mother's embarrassment too. It shouldn't be this way, she thought. If she had been brought up in a free and easy household like Rita's, she was sure she could have discussed anything with her mother instead of feeling so repressed about such a normal part of growing up.

'We're discussing you and this boy,' Ellen said.

'I wish you could meet him and see for yourself, but I suppose that's out of the question,' she replied sullenly.

'I think it would be unwise for the present. Jessie, we don't want to stop you growing up, just

142

that we ask you to take things slowly. You're still very young and you can understand your father wanting to protect you. You're all we have left, my dear.'

The stark reminder made Jessie's throat choke. 'Adam was still young when he died and he never had the chance to do the normal things in life, did he? By now, if he hadn't been blown out of the sky, he might have been married and had a child of his own. But I shouldn't be made to live in his shadow!'

She wasn't sure how the conversation had got around to Adam, nor how her mother was going to react to that remark. But perhaps she was finally seeing her daughter as the young woman that she was, instead of the child her father still wanted her to be, because after a moment Ellen handed her diary back to her.

'All we ask is that you respect your family and respect yourself. Now put this away and we'll say no more about it.'

It was inevitable that Sunday morning's church sermon was going to be pointed towards the evils of mankind. Jessie sat through it all, fuming that she and Rita had unwittingly been the cause of Vicar Penwarden's heavy-handed attempt to make Abbot's Cove the purest village in Christendom. She knew he had spent all last evening perfecting the words he was going to say, while she had spent the hours trying to imagine what Rita was saying to Will and how he had reacted when she wasn't at the dance. She couldn't wait for the morning service to end when she could

143

catch up with her friend, who seemed to be avoiding her. But eventually she grabbed Rita's arm and pulled her to one side where they couldn't be overheard.

'What did Will say?' she asked at once.

Rita gave a heavy sigh. 'Look, Jess, I'm sorry, but I didn't go last night. I was in two minds about it and then I couldn't face it in case Des was there.'

'What? So Will doesn't know why I wasn't there either?'

'Well, I'm sorry,' Rita said again, 'but I did have more important things on my mind than sorting out your love life!'

'I doubt that I've even got one now. Thanks for nothing!'

'I'm sure he'll turn up this afternoon, anyway, Jess, and you can explain it to him then. Don't tell him all of it, mind,' she added with a grin. 'You won't, will you?'

'There's nothing to tell, is there?' Jessie said, angrier at her airy-fairy dismissal of it all than she could say.

She left her and went to join her mother, upset that Will would have expected to see her at the dance with no idea why she wasn't there.

'Are you seeing Rita this afternoon?' Ellen said.

'Of course, if that's all right.'

It was another lie, but Jessie was determined to see Will again, to explain as much as she felt able. She wouldn't tell him everything that had happened because it was far too embarrassing, but she desperately wanted him to know how much she had wanted to see him, and what a rotten evening she had spent instead, imagining some other girl in his arms. Even if he wasn't inclined to ask someone to dance, there were always the ladies' choices, and the excuse-mes when girls could invite whoever they liked, and Will was a very good-looking boy. The best-looking boy, she amended with a little glow in her heart.

Early that afternoon she cycled through the village and left her bicycle outside Rita's gate. Nobody would question it, since it had been left there often enough when the two girls were together. Then she walked to the end of the lane, straining her eyes in the direction of Penzance in the hope of seeing a car coming this way – or even a motorbike, she thought despairingly as the time went on and there was no sign of him.

It hadn't really been that long, but at last the familiar sight of the car he had driven before came into sight and stopped alongside her. Without getting out, Will leant across and opened the passenger door, and she slid inside.

'I thought you weren't coming,' she said breathlessly.

'I wanted to see you anyway, so I took a chance that you'd be here,' he replied.

She gulped. Something was wrong and she didn't know what it was. But she didn't have a Cornish sixth sense for nothing, and whatever it was, she sensed that it was more than the fact that she wasn't at the dance last night. Or perhaps it was simply that. Perhaps he had found someone else more to his liking and was deciding how to tell her. Perhaps she was too much of a small-time village girl and he wasn't so keen on courting a vicar's daughter, and preferred someone from the town, like himself. She opened her mouth to say something – anything, since the silence between them seemed to go on and on, even though it was only seconds before he started driving the car again.

'I need to talk to you, Jessie, but I can't stay long. I thought we'd just drive away from the village, then park along the cliffs and go for a walk. What do you say?'

'It sounds fine to me,' she mumbled.

She was right. He didn't want to stay with her very long, and he was going to say he didn't want to see her again. Her entire body seemed to be falling apart at the certainty. She liked him so much. She more than liked him. She knew she loved him, and even though people said first love didn't always last, she had had the strongest feeling that this was a love that would last for ever. The only thing was, love was no good at all if it was only one-sided.

They drove in silence and although they were physically close enough to touch it was as though they were no longer together, she thought, consumed with misery. This should have been such a happy day, but even the sun seemed to have deserted them now, and a band of cloud had descended, bringing the first hint of an autumn chill in the air. She was glad she had worn a light jacket over her summer dress, but it was more than the air that was chilling her now.

They reached the cliffs and Will stopped the car and got out. Jessie followed suit, still mute and summoning up the courage to face what was coming with as much dignity as possible. After the week she'd just had, she knew she should be able to face anything, but Will had been the one thing she had clung on to all this time. Without him...

As she shivered, he tucked her hand in his arm and told her they had better walk fast as it was decidedly chilly now. The wind was blowing in from the sea and, far below, the waves were pewter grey, choppy and angry.

'Perhaps this wasn't such a good idea. If you have to go quite soon, perhaps you could have said all you wanted to say inside the car,' she murmured, not sure how long she wanted to prolong the suspense. 'And before you start, Will, I'm sorry I wasn't there last night.'

'I wasn't there, either.'

She looked at him sharply. His face was set and she knew at once that something was badly wrong. Perhaps she had been mistaken after all. Perhaps he wasn't breaking up with her. Perhaps it was something to do with his mother ... or perhaps his father had turned up again out of the blue. The thoughts flew wildly around her head. Despite her anxiety for him, a touch of guilty relief swept through her. Whatever it was, perhaps it wasn't anything to do with her after all.

'Do you want to tell me why?' she asked, almost timidly. 'I know you weren't so keen on going there with your friends, and they'd probably have jeered at you for preferring to meet me.'

'It wasn't that. They didn't go, either. They couldn't. Not Des, anyway.'

He spoke jerkily, and Jessie had a horrible

feeling that was almost a presentiment.

'Why not?' she whispered. 'What's happened to him, Will?'

'He's dead.'

The words were carried away on the wind, and Jessie looked at him in horror as he tried to hide the great, unmanly tears that were wrenched out of him.

CHAPTER NINE

As if his legs wouldn't hold him up any longer, Will sat down abruptly on the short springy turf above the cliffs, and Jessie immediately sat beside him, clinging on to his arm. Whatever else she had expected, it had never been this. She didn't know what to say, and then Will took a deep breath and brushed his hands across his eyes.

'Sorry. It was just saying it out loud. My mother says that the more I say it the more real it will become, but it hasn't worked yet.'

Jessie spoke carefully. 'She's right about that, Will. I had to keep saying it aloud after Adam died to try to make myself believe it. It's always impossible to take in, especially when it happens to someone young.'

Will nodded, yet it was as if he was hardly taking in what she was saying. 'But you expect bad things to happen in a war. You don't expect it to happen when you're doing your everyday work.'

'Do you want to tell me what happened?'

Of course he did, or why would he have come? She felt enormous sympathy for him, since he was clearly finding it difficult to come to terms with it at all. A woman could know the release of weeping all night, but she supposed a man could only feel shame and embarrassment at showing his feelings so openly. It was all wrong, but that was the way it was.

Will finally drew a deep breath and began to talk. 'You know he was a blacksmith. He was shoeing a horse at the smithy when something startled the animal and it kicked out violently. You can imagine the impact from a large horse wearing a metal horseshoe. Its hoof struck Des on the temple and laid him right out. He came round after a while and just seemed a bit groggy, but his eyes wouldn't focus properly so his boss sent him home. He should have seen a doctor, but I doubt if it would have done any good, because after he'd gone to bed that night he never woke up again. The verdict was that he'd got a blood clot on the brain and it killed him.'

'Oh, good Lord, how terrible,' Jessie said, totally shocked now. The fact that she had never liked Des Greenaway was immaterial. All that mattered was the fact that a young man had been killed in such a horrible way. It had clearly affected Will deeply, and as if following her thoughts he continued talking.

'My mother and Des's mother were old friends from their schooldays. Mum was very cut up when she heard about it, and she's spent the last few nights sleeping at their house but she's back home now. Both she and Des's mum hated motorbikes, and they both thought he'd come to grief on his bike at some stage because he was so reckless on it. Anyway, it's given Mum the jitters and she needs me there, so I can't stay away too long, Jess. And now you know the reason why I couldn't see you last night, and why I can't stay today.'

'I do understand, and of course you'll want to

150

be with your mum. I'm so sorry about Des, Will.'

He looked at her properly then. 'You said you didn't go to the dance either. Do I want to know the reason why, Jess? You haven't gone off me already, have you?' he said, trying to make a joke of it when she could see that he didn't feel in the least like joking, any more than she did.

'Of course I haven't gone off you. I asked Rita to tell you that my dad had put his foot down, only she didn't go, either, so it was all a bit of a mess, wasn't it?' she said carefully.

'I knew something was up as soon as I saw you. Well, now you know what a softie I can be, so why don't you tell me your troubles?'

'I'm not sure this is the right time.'

'Well, I think it is, if only to take my mind off what's happened to Des for a few minutes.'

'That's just the problem,' Jessie said slowly. 'I'm afraid Des is very much involved.'

She hadn't intended to mention him at all. She wasn't going to tell him about Rita and the stupid plan they had cooked up between them that had led to the awful scene at the vicarage. She never meant to betray Rita, and she hadn't promised her anything. But somehow, here in the open air, with no one around them and only the seagulls wheeling above with their mournful sounds adding to the misery of this day, it seemed inevitable that she was going to tell him everything. It was somehow cleansing to have no more secrets between them.

She spared him nothing, not even Rita's description of how hateful the encounter with Des had been.

151

'He didn't force himself on her, well, not at first. Not until it was too late,' she said bitterly. 'I know she seems a bit flighty and all that, Will, but she'd never done such a thing before, and she was terrified that she was going to be in the family way. By the time she found out that she wasn't, I had already spoken to Mr Price, and you know the rest.'

'So the chemist's wife assumed that you needed the information for yourself, and she sounds a right old harridan. But your father believed it too? Christ, it must have been awful for you, sweetheart.'

She was shaking so much that she hardly noticed the endearment or the cursing. 'Someone had seen us together so they knew I had been out with a boy, and I felt compelled to swear on the Bible in front of them that I had never done – well, you know what, without me having to spell it out. It was horrible and humiliating, but it was the only way I knew my father would believe me.'

She was hot with embarrassment herself now, and then she felt Will's arms go around her, holding her close. Holding her tight in a way she had begun to believe he would never hold her again.

'Oh, God, I'm so sorry you had to go through all that, Jessie. I always knew Des was a bit on the rough side, but I never thought he'd go that far.'

She didn't remind him of the time she had been so scared when the other two bikers had cornered her at the cove. He'd had enough to deal with without adding to it. She stayed close in his arms,

152

more than thankful that there were no barriers between them that they couldn't overcome.

'I wish I could stay longer,' he said regretfully, 'but I really do need to get back home today, Jess. Mum's in quite a state, as you can imagine, but at least she's relieved that I've got the car now, except for work.'

'You bought it, then,' Jessie murmured unnecessarily.

'Well, it's partly on the never-never, but it shouldn't take me long to pay it off. But all this business with your father has made me think we should get things on a proper footing. It seems pretty mean that you had to bear all this on your own, so why don't I call and see him sometime? It's a bit old-fashioned to ask if I can start courting his daughter, but he seems an old-fashioned sort of chap.'

Jessie shook her head vigorously. 'Not yet, please, Will! Let me talk it over with my mother first. You're right about him, though. He's an old-fashioned sort of chap all right,' she added wryly.

She gave a small smile for the first time that day, wondering how her prim and proper father would react at being called a chap of any kind. As Will saw her smile he hugged her closer, and then his lips were on hers and he was kissing her as if his life depended on it, and all her nerve ends were alive again and she was kissing him back...

'You don't know how much I needed that,' he finally whispered against her mouth, 'just to feel you warm and alive in my arms and to remember that normal life does go on, no matter what.'

It was so much an echo of what Jessie believed

that she could only lean against him, feeling the beat of his heart against her own and rejoicing in it.

By the time they decided reluctantly that it was time to go, they walked back to the car with their arms entwined.

The clouds had miraculously lifted, and it was like an omen that the sun had come out again to warm them. There was no doubt in Jessie's mind now that despite the terrible events of the past week she had found her destiny. Those events had involved other people, not them, and she was convinced that nothing was going to separate them now.

When they reached the lane at the end of the village again, Will brought a piece of paper out of his pocket.

'This is my address. I'm not sure when I'll be able to see you again, Jessie, because I know this next week is going to be busy and, of course, Ronnie and I will be going to the funeral sometime soon. Look Jess, please write to me and let me know how things are for you at home, and when you think it would be a good time for me to meet your parents.'

'All right,' she said, and then he leant over and kissed her again, uncaring whether or not there were any onlookers.

Then she got out of the car and watched until the car was out of sight, overwhelmed all over again at what he had told her about Des Greenaway. The one thing that neither of them had discussed, and which she knew she was going to

154

have to do, was how to tell Rita.

But it was now or never, she thought grimly as she knocked at the front door of the Levant house and then went inside. As usual, Rita's father was snoring loudly in his chair, and Mrs Levant gave Jessie a cheery smile.

'Just listen to him driving them home, Jessie love. You'd think he'd never had a night's sleep in his life before, wouldn't you?'

Jessie smiled back. She had never been more thankful that this friendly woman had no idea of the trauma that her daughter had been going through lately, and that she would be unlikely to hear of the disaster that had befallen Des Greenaway, because it would be the last thing that Rita would be telling her. Jessie was sure she would never have mentioned him to her mother, either. As for the news of one young man's tragic death being reported in a local newspaper, it might never even appear down here in Abbot's Cove. The town of Penzance was not so many miles away from the insular village, but it might as well have been a world away for anything the two communities had in common.

'Is Rita around?' she asked Mrs Levant.

'She's in the back garden feeding the chickens on the dinner scraps. I don't know why her father got those blessed birds, and I swear they'll be ancient old hens before they produce any eggs,' she said with an indulgent laugh.

No matter what Zach Levant did, his wife forgave him. It was one of the things that mystified Jessie and made her oddly envious of the kind of free and easy life the Levants had, compared with her own. But as far as Zach and his wife were concerned, well, she supposed that was what love did. She put them out of her mind and went out to the back garden where Rita was throwing the scraps to three scrawny-looking birds in the chicken coop. She looked at Jessie with a small frown between her eyebrows as she straightened up.

'Don't tell me he didn't turn up. Have you been waiting for him all this time?' she said by way of greeting.

'He did turn up, but he couldn't stay, and I need to talk to you, Rita.'

'What's on your mind? I can see something's happened. He hasn't given you the old heave-ho, I hope.'

There were neighbours in the next-door garden who could overhear every word that was said, and this definitely wasn't the place to tell Rita her news.

'Look, the sun's out again now, so let's ride our bikes to the top of the moors,' Jessie said desperately.

'Crikey, this sounds serious. All right, but wait until I get my jacket and I'll tell Mum I'm going out.'

There were some things that couldn't decently be told over a chicken coop either, while three mottled hens were squawking away, pecking and fighting over scraps. Some things needed the space and freshness of the open air, and it wasn't until they had reached the top of the moors, thrown down their bicycles and were perched on an old granite cromlech as they caught their breaths that Jessie felt able to tell her friend what had happened to Des.

She knew Rita hadn't cared for him in the way she cared for Will. She knew Des had done a terrible thing to Rita, and that it was something that could never be reversed. For all that, Rita had been attracted to him in the first place, she had been flattered that he had asked her out, and when she learnt what had happened to him she went white and looked as if she was going to faint.

'Dear Lord, Jess, that's terrible,' she said hoarsely.

'I know it is, and I'm sorry I had to tell you, but I didn't expect you to take it quite so badly,' she said uneasily.

'You don't understand.' She was almost gasping now. 'You don't know how many times I wished him dead, and now it's happened. You know what they say about wishes, don't you? I brought this on, Jess. I made it happen.'

'Don't be so stupid. You didn't make it happen. It was an accident.'

Rita shook her head so hard her hair swung around her head and over her face. 'Things happen for a purpose, and I wished this on him, I know I did. This was justice for what he did to me, but I never meant my wishes to be taken seriously. I never thought they could be.'

Jessie caught hold of her shoulders and shook her. 'They *can't*. Listen to yourself, Rita. You're supposed to be the practical one, and common sense should tell you that you didn't make this happen. You're not a witch, for pity's sake! Some-

157

thing startled the horse Des was shoeing and made him kick out, so it was nothing more than a terrible accident. You've got to believe that or you'll go mad, so don't start blaming yourself.'

Jessie was becoming more alarmed by the minute by the wild look in Rita's eyes, but gradually her shaking stopped and the colour returned to her cheeks. When she finally spoke, it was as if she was trying to convince herself.

'I suppose you're right. You can't wish things on people, even though some of the old women in the village think you can. I've never been one of them, and I don't intend to start now.'

'Remember that, then, or you'll end up as crazy as some of them!'

Rita gave a small shrug. 'You don't believe in their old herbal potions that are supposed to help you find your true love, then? One of the old standing stones on the moors that has a hole in the middle is supposed to let you see him if you circle around it three times at midnight.'

Jessie looked at her uneasily. 'Where have you been getting all that nonsense from? My dad would be furious if he thought I was listening to such heathen rubbish.'

'Well, I suppose a vicar has to believe every word of the Bible, but Mum's got some old Cornish folklore books about the ancient stones on the moors, and it's not all rubbish. Even this one that we're sitting on has probably got a history behind it.'

Jessie jumped down. 'Well, if it does I don't want to know. Besides, I know my true love already without looking through some stupid hole in a stone. Honestly, Rita, I thought you had more sense.'

Rita's face was red with fury now. 'Oh well, if that's what you think of me, I might as well go home.'

She picked up her bicycle and made to ride off, and then she stopped, looking back at Jessie with stricken eyes.

'Oh, cripes, Jessie, how could I have forgotten what we came up here to talk about? I really am sorry about Des. It's such an awful thing to happen to anybody,' she conceded.

'I know. I'm sorry too,' Jessie said with a shiver, wishing she didn't keep imagining what had happened quite so vividly. 'But there's nothing we can do about it. We don't know where he lived or when the funeral is, and I doubt that either of us would want to be there in any case.'

Rita shook her head rapidly. 'Not likely. Do you?'

'Of course I don't.'

Truth to tell, Jessie was relieved. Some of Rita's ideas were just too weird, and she didn't want to have to defend her own father, either. Besides, how could anybody disbelieve what the Bible said? She hadn't been brought up that way.

She felt very sober when she and Rita parted company. Hearing of Des Greenaway's death had somehow brought back all the emotions she had felt on hearing the news of her brother's death. There was no similarity between the two events, and Adam had been doing his duty for king and country, but Jessie knew that for Des's mother the pain would have been every bit as acute as

159

her own mother's had been.

Did Des have a family besides his mother? She had no idea. Did he have a father who would be experiencing the grief as well, or would his mother have to bear it all alone? Was there a young sister to wonder in bewilderment how this could happen, the way she had felt when Adam died? She realised how little she knew of him, and nor had she wanted to at the time when he had been so hateful to her and Rita, but all that was farthest from her mind now. Now he was merely another young man who had been killed in a horrible way and she could only feel sadness for him.

She reached home and put her bicycle away, still upset by what Will had told her and having to repeat it all to Rita. She wanted to go and hide herself away in her bedroom and not have to speak to anyone. Once there, she prowled around the room at a loss to know what to do next. She was still trembling, and she began to realise it was exactly the way she had been after Adam. It was the same sense of loss and meaning in anything, the same anxiety about the fragility of life, and the feeling of being thrust back into long-forgotten childish fears about death and darkness and the unknown.

She didn't want to feel this way about Des Greenaway. She *didn't*, but somehow she couldn't seem to separate it all in her mind. Adam and Des Greenaway ... and then a sudden stab of anger caught her unawares. How *dare* she couple them together, in however small a way? They were so different in every way, and it insulted her brother's

160

memory to be reacting like this.

From elsewhere in the house, her mother's voice jerked her into movement and she sat up so quickly it made her head swim.

'Jessie, is that you? Can you come downstairs a minute, please?'

Now what? Jessie wondered. Had she been found guilty of some other misdemeanour that her father had discovered? Remembering the easy atmosphere of the Levant house, she felt resentful that her own was so regimented, and that it depended so much on Vicar Penwarden's moods. She went downstairs to find her mother in the sitting room. To Jessie's relief she was smiling.

'I've just had a telephone call from one of my old school friends who I haven't heard from for years. She moved to Sussex before the war to work as a children's nanny, and later married a motor mechanic. She's coming to Cornwall to visit her relatives in Penzance and wants to come and see me.'

'That's nice,' Jessie said automatically, her mind still revolving far too much around what had happened to Des Greenaway to show any great enthusiasm about a woman she didn't know.

Her mother looked at her sharply.

'What's wrong? I can tell by your face you're upset about something, Jessie. Has something happened? Is Rita's mother all right?'

Jessie swallowed hard. Of course something had happened, but it had happened to someone she hadn't liked, and to someone her mother didn't know. Because she was her father's daughter and had been brought up on what he preached, she knew she should feel compassion for the terrible accident that had happened to Des, and so she did, but for the life of her she still couldn't feel any liking for him. But nor did she have any of Rita's wild thoughts that because you wished somebody dead – even if it wasn't really meant – then it would happen.

She shivered, and felt her mother catch hold of her arm and steer her to a chair. The next thing she knew she was being handed a glass of water. She took a long drink without thinking, and the shock of the cold water running down her throat made her shiver even more.

'Now why don't you tell me what's wrong?' Ellen said quietly. 'I know that what happened earlier this week was unfortunate and that your father went off the deep end as usual, but we both know you were innocent of what that silly Mrs Price had said, and you shouldn't let it fester in your mind, my dear.'

'I haven't. It's not that. I've just heard that someone I knew slightly has died and it made me think of Adam. I'm sorry, but I just couldn't help it.'

'It's not that boy who you wrote about in your diary, is it?' Ellen said.

'It was his friend. Someone I'd seen at the dance a few times.'

Whatever she and Rita had thought of Des, he had been Will's friend. Without warning Jessie burst into tears. She was horrified at herself for letting Des Greenaway's death affect her like this, but it had and she couldn't do anything to stop it.

162

It was bringing back too many painful memories of the dark days when they had heard of Adam's death. That was when the nightmares had begun, tormenting her with images she didn't want but couldn't fight. She hadn't told anyone about them, not her mother and certainly not her father, who would probably say she was temporarily possessed by the Devil, and that with God's help it would pass in time.

She hadn't wanted his platitudes and his strong beliefs then, and she didn't want them now. She didn't want to hear tales of hereafters and the dear departed having gone to a better place. In her tortured mind then, as now, the dear and not-so-dear departed had died an untimely death and were gone for ever.

She had never expected Will's news to affect her this way and she realised the breath was very tight in her chest and she was gasping now. She was vaguely aware that Ellen was reaching for the telephone and speaking rapidly to someone at the other end. Then she came back to Jessie and was holding her hands tightly.

'I've asked the doctor to call round to see you, Jessie, and no arguments, please. You've clearly had a shock and you look very pale, so it won't hurt for Doctor Charles to take a look at you.'

'I don't need a doctor,' Jessie said feebly. 'I'll be all right in a minute.'

'You'll stay right where you are, my dear. I don't want you being ill when Olive comes.'

Jessie looked at her blankly. For the life of her she couldn't remember anyone called Olive. She wondered briefly if this was how it felt to be going mad, when names meant nothing to her anymore.

'I told you about my old school friend just now,' Ellen went on, trying to keep her interested and hoping she would lose the lost, dead look in her eyes that was frightening Ellen far more than she would let on.

Thomas should be here, she thought, in a moment's rage. If only he hadn't gone off, heaven knows where, tending to one of his village flock, when he was needed here with one of his own. She bit her lip, knowing the thought was probably unworthy of a vicar's wife, and that Thomas would be giving comfort where it was needed, but she wasn't thinking of herself as a vicar's wife at this moment. She was simply a mother anxious for the welfare of her child.

The doorbell rang and she flew to answer it. At least this was one of the advantages of being a vicar's wife, she thought now, in a reversal of her earlier annoyance. Despite it being Sunday, the doctor would always come, sure that she wouldn't be wasting his time. But it wasn't the doctor. It was Rita Levant.

'Is Jessie in, Mrs Penwarden?' the girl said. 'I was a bit worried about her earlier. We'd heard some bad news.'

Ellen drew her inside. 'What is this all about, Rita? I know someone has died, but I don't know who it is. It's got Jessie in a terrible state and I've sent for the doctor. Is it one of your old school friends?'

Rita shifted from one foot to the other. She didn't know how much Jessie might have said about Des Greenaway, but now she knew Jessie hadn't given the whole thing away and she didn't know how much to reveal. She should never have come, but she was here now, and she couldn't just back out of the house.

'It's just someone we met at one of the dances,' she mumbled. 'He had a bad accident and then he died. We didn't know him very well at all, but he was young, and it always seems so much more terrible a thing when it happens to somebody young.'

Oh God, she was floundering, her voice rising in panic, knowing she would be reminding Jessie's mother that they had already gone through the trauma of hearing about someone dying young in their own family.

'Look, I won't stay if you're waiting for the doctor, Mrs Penwarden. Tell Jessie I'll see her tomorrow, will you?'

She turned and practically ran down the vicarage path, almost bumping into Doctor Charles who was coming the other way. With a muttered apology, she raced away from the house and down to the cove where she could cool off and give herself time to think. It was only then that she registered that the doctor was going to see Jessie. She honestly couldn't think why Jessie had been so upset about Des Greenaway. She'd hated him as much as Rita had, and he'd been the cause of all their problems recently. Well, *her* problems really, she thought guiltily, only it had been Jessie who'd got caught up in it all, with that busybody Vera Price getting the wrong end of the stick.

She wished more than anything in the world

that she'd never set eyes on Des Greenaway, but her thoughts quickly veered away from all that, knowing where wishes could get you. Besides, if they hadn't met Des and his mates, Jessie would never have met Will Tremayne, and at least things seemed to be going well for her there. She stayed at the cove until she had calmed down. By then it was well past mid afternoon, and she had almost persuaded herself that when she saw Jessie tomorrow, the first shock would be over, and they could get back to the way they were before. Ever optimistic, Rita certainly hoped it would be so.

CHAPTER TEN

Thomas Penwarden came home a few minutes after the doctor had left to find his wife looking worried.

'What's happened now?' he said with a frown. 'Is it Jessie again?'

After what she had just heard, Ellen was irked at the assumption that their daughter was the cause of her anxiety, however true it might be.

'Jessie is not feeling well. Someone she knew slightly has died in an accident. She seems to be associating it with Adam's death and it's hit her very hard. Even though it's Sunday I sent for the doctor and he's given her a sedative to calm her down.'

Thomas's face was a picture. 'Why in heaven's name should she be thinking about Adam after all this time?' He hastily revised his words. 'What I mean is, of course we still think about him, but she's young and she shouldn't harbour thoughts of death after all this time. It's not healthy.'

'Thomas, someone she knew has died. Isn't it natural that she should be upset, and to be remembering how she felt when we heard about her brother?'

'I'll speak to her.'

'I wish you wouldn't. Not yet, anyway. She's resting in her room, and you know how you always antagonise her.'

He stared at her for a long moment before he spoke.

'Is that how you see the relationship I have with my daughter, Ellen?'

'Yes. I'm afraid it is.'

He turned on his heel and strode away from her, leaving her troubled, and realising that she hadn't yet told him about the impending visit of her old friend next week. That would be something else to goad him into a bad frame of mind, she thought, wondering just how he had ever changed so dramatically from the eager and energetic young vicar she had married. But she didn't have to look very far back to know that. She knew his seriousness had developed gradually over time as he took on more and more responsibility, but it had been that day, three years ago when the telegram had arrived, and they realised they had lost their beloved son, when all their lives had changed for ever. Her eyes welled with tears then, knowing that it wasn't only Jessie who grieved for their boy, and wishing with all her heart that Thomas could share that grief more openly, instead of bottling it up inside himself.

He knocked on the door of Jessie's bedroom gently, and heard a mumbled reply from the other side of the door. He couldn't tell whether she told him to come in or not, but he did it anyway. Jessie was lying flat on top of her bed, eyes wide open and staring vacantly at the ceiling.

'Jessie, my dear,' Thomas said, moving towards the bed. 'Your mother has just told me about your friend, and I'm very sorry. Would you like us to say a prayer together for her?'

He could never have envisaged the response his words evoked. One minute Jessie seemed to be out of this world altogether, and the next, she was sitting upright on her bed, arms wrapped tightly around her knees, her face a furious red, her eyes blazing at him.

'No, I do *not* want to say a prayer, thank you, and what makes you think my friend was a *girl*, anyway?'

Thomas was so startled that he took a step backwards. 'Who was it, then?' he demanded.

Jessie gave a shuddering breath.

'Dad, I'm not a child, as I keep reminding you. I do know boys as well as girls. There were plenty of them in my class at school! This person who died wasn't one of them, and I didn't know him very well. He was just somebody who had been to the local dances a few times, that's all. I didn't even like him, but it was a terrible shock to hear what had happened to him. I certainly don't want to *pray* for him.'

Thomas's eyes flashed at this tirade. 'We should all pray for our enemies, Jessica.'

'I didn't say he was my enemy. Just that I didn't like him much,' she muttered.

Her head drooped, remembering how much more terrible this whole episode might have been. She was sorry for what had happened to Des, and she wouldn't have wanted it to happen to anybody, but supposing Rita had been carrying his child as they had so feared for a while? How much more terrible for her would it have been now, with nobody to come forward and do

169

the right thing by her?

She became aware that her father was sitting on the side of her bed now and that his arms had gone around her. It was such an unexpected gesture from a man who didn't find demonstrations of affection easy that her eyes prickled at once. She could smell the rough wool cloth of his jacket, and she found herself leaning against him and weeping silently.

'It was so terrible, Dad,' she almost gasped as she relayed what Will had told her. 'I can't be a hypocrite and pretend that I liked him in any way, but for it to happen like that to a young man is just unbearable.'

'And it made you think about Adam all over again,' Thomas stated.

'I think of him often,' she said.

'Do you think I don't?' she heard Thomas say. 'There's never a day goes by without something reminding me of him. But we have to go on, Jessie, and we have to believe that this – all of it – was God's will. It's the only way to survive whatever is destined for us.'

She broke away from him, looking deep into his eyes and acknowledging the pain there. She was stunned at hearing him speak so freely to her in a way he so rarely did, but she was angry too.

'So do you really think your caring God had destined for Adam to be blown out of the sky from the day he was born? Or that Des Greenaway was destined to be struck on the head by an animal he was shoeing and then to die from a brain clot? Is that how God works? To give sons to mothers and then snatch them away when it

170

pleases Him?'

Oh Lord, she knew she had gone too far now. She could see it by the stricken look on her father's face, when she was denying everything that was meaningful to him. But she couldn't help it. She refused to believe that such sorrow had been endlessly preordained. If that were so, what was the point of living at all, if you were destined to die whenever some higher order had already decreed it?

'Would it help if you were to go to this boy's funeral, my dear?' he said, to her complete astonishment.

She looked at him warily. 'I don't know. Would you allow it?'

'I think you have proved to me that you are indeed no longer a child, and have far deeper thoughts in your head than even you realised. Of course I would allow it, Jessie. I think it would be the right thing to do, so get in touch with whoever you need to and see to it. I'll leave it entirely up to you.'

Impulsively she hugged him, and then they both turned away in embarrassment. If she thought it a little sad that father and daughter should feel such awkwardness she refused to dwell on it.

'Come downstairs whenever you're ready, my dear,' Thomas said as he left the bedroom, 'and if you need me to help in any way, please let me know.'

She didn't. The person she needed to get in touch with was Will, and Rita too. They should both go, if only as a gesture of support for Will – and for Ronnie Hill, who would also be feeling

171

devastated at the death of his friend. And in a weird kind of way, maybe by attending this young man's funeral, she would also be saying goodbye to Adam in a way they were never able to do properly.

She leapt out of bed and washed her face to wipe away the traces of tears, then ran downstairs, suddenly energised at knowing what she had to do. Her parents were talking quietly in the sitting room now, and they stopped speaking at once as she entered the room.

'I'm going to see Rita,' she announced. 'She knew Des Greenaway a little too, and I think she would want to go to his funeral as well. And then...' she took a deep breath, 'and then I'm going to suggest that we cycle over to Will Tremayne's house to find out what the arrangements are.'

'Who is this Will Tremayne?' Thomas said at once.

Ellen put her hand over his. 'He's a friend of the dead boy, Thomas, and he's the one they need to contact.'

Her eyes dared him to say anything more, and for once he conceded with a small incline of his head. Neither Jessie nor her mother was under any illusions that his usual rigid attitude had really changed, but for now it was enough, and Jessie left the house, feeling slightly better at having decided on doing something positive, and cycled quickly towards Rita's house.

'You're not serious?' Rita exploded, when they had gone into the back garden and Jessie explained why she had come. 'You really think I'd consider going to that lout's funeral and have to listen to some pious words said about how sad it all is, knowing what he did to me?'

'I know all about that, Rita, and you'd better keep quiet if you don't want your mother and the neighbours to hear you,' Jessie hissed. 'I want to do it for Will – and for Ronnie too. He was harmless enough, wasn't he? And I reckon he'll be feeling pretty bad right now. As for Des, well, he'll never hurt you again, will he? Can't you show the smallest bit of compassion?'

'My God, you really are your father's daughter, aren't you?' Rita said bitterly. 'I always said you'd turn into a saint before you're done.'

'I'm anything but that. I intend to go to the funeral, anyway, for Will's sake. I'm going over to his house now, to see what the arrangements are. Are you coming with me or not?'

Rita didn't miss the way her friend's mouth was trembling. She wasn't given to as much intuition as Jessie, but sometimes she saw what she wasn't meant to see.

'How much has all this to do with Adam?' she said.

Jessie flinched, and her voice was tight and strained when she answered. 'A lot. None of us had the chance to say goodbye to Adam properly. We couldn't even see him after ... well, *after* ... and it made things even worse than they already were. Des's friends and family have got that, at least.'

When Rita finally saw she was serious, she reluctantly agreed.

'It's a bit late in the day to be calling on people who aren't expecting us, but if you think Will's mother won't object, I suppose we'd better do it. What made you think of going to the funeral, anyway?'

'My dad, if you must know.'

'Blimey, now I've heard everything,' Rita said dryly.

Will Tremayne was polishing his car in the road outside his house when he heard the whirr of bicycle wheels and then saw the flash of summer dresses out of the corner of his eye. He looked up to see two girls slewing to a halt beside him on their bikes, and his smile widened as he recognised them.

'What are you two doing here? It's a bit far for a bike ride, isn't it?'

His words included them both, but it was to Jessie that he looked, and he couldn't hide the relief in his face. It had been a pretty horrible few days lately, and he was thankful for anything that stopped him thinking about what had happened to Des.

'Oh, we're used to it,' Jessie replied, 'and we wanted to come and see you about something in particular.'

Will wiped his hands on a rag as he recognised the seriousness behind the words. And it may have been just the wind in Jessie's face that was making her eyes a bit red, but he fancied he could tell by the puffiness beneath them that she had been crying.

'You'd better come inside, then. Mum will be

174

glad to see you, Jessie. She's been a bit gloomy after spending so much time with Des's mother, and I know the sight of you will cheer her up. You too, Rita,' he added as an afterthought.

They followed him indoors, and he called out to his mother that they had visitors while he went to wash his hands and tidy himself up, as he called it. Jessie wouldn't have cared if he'd stayed exactly as he was in his working clothes. The mere sight of him had steadied her nerves, and she and Rita were welcomed by Mrs Tremayne.

'We're just about to have our tea, and you girls are welcome to share it,' she said generously.

'Oh, I'm sorry, we didn't mean to come just at teatime,' Jessie said in embarrassment, seeing now that the table was already laid. Her own mother was very particular about not turning up uninvited at someone's house at mealtimes, but Mrs Tremayne waved her objections aside.

'Nonsense. I'll put the kettle on, and it's only a few fish paste sandwiches and my cherry fruit-cake, so of course you can join us. Will and me will both be glad of the company.' They could hardly refuse, so the girls sat down while she got on with her preparations.

'It's good to see you again, Jessie, and to meet you, Rita,' Mrs Tremayne said when they were all sitting down together at the table a short while later. 'We've both been a bit downcast recently, and you know the reason why. Poor young Des. It was a terrible thing to happen, and he was always such a good boy to his mother.'

Rita choked over her fish paste sandwich at that, and Jessie glared at her.

'We didn't know Des very well, Mrs Tremayne,' she said hastily. 'In fact we only knew him from the few times he came to the dances in Abbot's Cove. But we thought it might be a friendly gesture if we attended his funeral, if you think it would be all right. That's what we've come to see Will about...'

Her voice trailed away. She hadn't intended to be talking about this with Will's mother. She had wanted to talk to him privately, and to know what he thought of the idea, and if he absolutely hated the thought of her and Rita turning up, when he knew what they had thought about Des. Would he even think they were crowing over the fact that he was dead? Such a thought hadn't occurred to her before, but it was occurring to her now, and she prayed that he wouldn't think badly of her.

'It's Jessie's idea, Mrs Tremayne,' Rita said quickly. 'Her father's a vicar so she always takes such things to heart.'

She knew it was a daft thing to say, but Will picked up on it at once.

'Does your father approve of this, Jess?' he asked.

'Yes he does, rather to my surprise.'

'Well then,' Will went on, after a glance at his mother. 'The funeral's been arranged for Wednesday afternoon at St Barnaby's church, so if you two want to ride over here by two o'clock, you can come in the car with Mum and me.'

'We'll have to get the time off work first,' Rita said quickly, and Jessie could see that she was already regretting the decision.

'Don't worry about that. In the circumstances

I'm sure it will be all right, so we'll see you here on Wednesday,' Jessie said.

She carried on eating, her heart beating somewhat faster. It was hardly a date. You couldn't call going to a funeral with a boy a proper date but they would be going in Will's car and spending the afternoon together. It was *almost* a date ... and she shouldn't be thinking that way now, either. She tried to concentrate on the general conversation around the tea table, and not to be so very aware that it was Will sitting opposite her, and Will's eyes that were looking at her most of the time with that special look of his that was for her alone. Shutting everyone else out. Shutting out the grisly thought of why she and Rita were here...

'We'll have to be going soon,' she said reluctantly, when Mrs Tremayne had refused to allow them to help with the washing-up. She had just realised that her parents had no idea where she was, and that she hadn't told them she wouldn't be home for tea.

Will walked outside with them. The sun was getting lower in the sky now, and they would want to get home before dark. It was too much to expect that he would kiss her goodbye, thought Jessie, and she wouldn't have wanted him to, with his mother watching from the doorway. He just gave her that extra special smile she knew so well.

'I'm really glad you came today,' he said. 'It's done Mum a lot of good to have somebody else to talk to besides me. We were starting to get on one another's nerves, both trying to be cheerful and to avoid the subject that's uppermost in both our minds. But you've made it a lot easier by saying you'll come with us on Wednesday.'

They said goodbye, and the girls didn't say anything for a few minutes as they began the ride back to Abbot's Cove, and then Rita burst out.

'Well, I'm glad they're pleased. I'm not so sure I am, after all.'

'Why not?' Jessie said. 'You can't back out now, Rita.'

'I could always say I couldn't get the afternoon off,' she hedged. 'Mrs Yendle might not agree to it, anyway.'

'You know that's not true,' Jessie said, starting to get annoyed. 'What's put this in your mind, anyway? You're not scared of going to a funeral, are you?'

'Aren't you? Have you ever been to one before?'

Jessie glanced at her and her bike wheels wobbled on the uneven road surface as she did so. No, she hadn't been to a funeral before, either. She had been so hysterical at the time that they hadn't allowed her to go to Adam's, and the thought of the actual mechanics of it all was something she was trying to put out of her mind. But Rita was looking less than confident now.

'We'll be all right,' Jessie said quickly. 'We'll be together, and it's only a few hours out of our lives, Rita. We can spare Des that much, can't we?'

She wasn't feeling quite so noble when she reached home to face the wrath of her mother. By then, her father had gone to church for the evening service and it was Ellen who berated Jessie for going off the way she had.

'You missed your tea as well, and you know how your father likes us all to sit down for Sunday tea together,' Ellen finished.

'It's all right, Mum,' she said when she could get a word in. 'Rita and I cycled over to Will's house to ask about the other boy's funeral, and his mother asked us to stay for tea. It was all very proper.'

'Without a prior invitation? I must say it seems a very loose sort of household when people can just drop in unannounced.'

'It's not like that at all. I know everybody needs a blessed appointment here, but Mrs Tremayne is a very nice lady, and Rita and I are joining them for Des's funeral on Wednesday afternoon, unless Dad can find something to object about in that!'

She was defiant and upset. This had been a horrible day until the friendliness of Will and his mother, and now it was all being spoilt again. She knew people had to make appointments to see the vicar for formal occasions, but sometimes it felt as though she was living in a straitjacket of a house where nothing was ever done spontaneously. As always she had a fleeting thought of how things might have been different if Adam were still here. Or maybe not. It was something they would never know.

She was aware that her mother was looking at her silently now, and the silence unnerved her.

'Do you really feel so tied down by your father's calling, Jessie?' Ellen finally said.

'Sometimes,' she muttered. 'But the worst of it is that he still treats me like a child, when I left childhood behind me long ago.'

'No matter how old you are, you'll always be his child, and mine too, Jessie. That's a fact of life that we can't change, and nor would we want to, my love.'

Jessie felt a rush of sympathy for her mother then, because if she felt tied down by the restrictions that a vicarage life put on her, how much more so did her mother, who must have once been a free and easy young girl like herself? Presumably.

'I'm sorry, Mum. But you do think it will be all right about my going with Rita to this funeral, don't you? Dad suggested it after all.' She didn't mention Will and his mother again, and was relieved to see Ellen nod.

'I'm sure he'll think it admirable, dear. And if you're feeling a little worried about it all, then think of it as merely being a way of saying goodbye to a friend.'

That was that, then. The irony of her mother's words wasn't lost on Jessie, but they had to go through with it now. There were no objections to their having time off from either Harold Price or Mrs Yendle, so there could be no more excuses. If Jessie had the jitters every time she thought about what was going to happen on the day, she guessed that Rita probably felt a hundred times worse. Rita was still reluctant about going at all, but Jessie was almost fierce in her insistence that they had to do this. She repeated what her mother had said.

'Saying goodbye to a friend! That's a laugh, isn't it?' Rita said sarcastically. 'He was certainly no friend of mine! Do you really want me to be such a hypocrite, Jess?'

'Well, no, but who knows what he might have been if he'd lived? We only saw the bad side of him, and according to Mrs Tremayne he was a good son to his mother. She wouldn't lie about that, would she?'

She listened to herself, being very much her father's daughter again, but she had to do this, to boost Rita's flagging spirits. It obviously worked, because Rita agreed to be ready when Jessie turned up early on Wednesday afternoon. When the time came they both wore suitably sober dresses, and took their regular church hats and gloves in their bicycle carriers for when they tidied themselves up after the bike ride to Will's house.

'It will all be over soon,' Jessie reassured the still nervous Rita when they arrived. 'Imagine yourself somewhere else if you must.'

'That's easy for you to say. I don't have your imagination,' she muttered.

Jessie wished she didn't have it either, because the images of what was to happen had already been re-enacted in her mind over and over again. But the sight of Will and his mother put her more at ease, and eventually the four of them took the short drive to St Barnaby's church in Will's car, and the ordeal had begun.

'I've never seen you in a hat before,' Will whispered to her as they filed into the church. 'It suits you – brings out the colour of your eyes.'

It was just a silly little harmless remark in a day that was destined to be full of solemnity and

181

tears, and it warmed her heart. And there were tears in plenty. There were so many people their own age that she had never seen before, including a red-eyed Ronnie Hill with a group of young men dressed in their usual biker clothes for the occasion to give their mate a good send-off. Jessie wondered briefly what her father would have made of this, but somehow it all seemed perfectly right. Then they all rose for the arrival of the coffin containing Des Greenaway's body, followed by Des's weeping mother, surrounded by older family members like a protective wall around her.

It was hard to take her eyes away from the coffin, and even harder to believe that the boy she and Rita had so despised was dead and silent inside it. Despite her resolve, she felt her own tears bubbling up for a life so cut short, the way Adam's had been. No one deserved this, whatever the circumstances. She smothered a sob, and amazingly, she felt Rita's hand press her arm, and it was Rita who whispered to her to hold on. Right then, Rita was the strong one, while she was consumed with memories of her brother and all that she had lost. But she might have known that all Rita's bravado wasn't going to last.

Later, when Des had been laid to rest in the churchyard and all the appropriate words had been said over him, they went back to his mother's house for a cup of tea and a sandwich. The girls would much rather have gone home, but they were obliged to stay until Will and his mother decided to leave. And naturally, Mrs Tremayne wanted to be with her old friend a little longer. Ronnie Hill and some of the bikers had also come back for what they irreverently called the bunfight, and a little later Ronnie came over to her and Rita.

'I didn't expect to see you here,' he said briefly.

'It was the least we could do,' Jessie murmured, seeing that Rita wasn't in the mood to make false platitudes to Des's friend. She was very thankful when he nodded and moved on, knowing that Rita could hardly bear to look at him. By now she was quite pale at having to listen to all the kind words being said about Des, and she clutched at Jessie's arm.

'Can't we get out of here yet?' she said desperately. 'We've done our duty and I can't stand much more of this.'

'Stay there, and I'll see what Will says.' She wove in and out of the mourners until she reached his side, and edged him away from where his mother was still in conversation with Mrs Greenaway.

'How long are we going to stay, Will? I don't want to hurry you, but I really think Rita's had all she can take.'

'Mum's just saying goodbye,' he said, to her relief. 'One of Mrs Greenaway's cousins is going to stay with her for a few days, so that lets Mum off the hook. I rather think she's had enough too. So if you're ready, we'll go.'

It was a huge relief to be back in the car and on their way back to Will's house again. The atmosphere had visibly changed between them now, and the relief that this day was over was palpable. For the two girls, at least, there was a limit to how long you could go on making false remarks about somebody you had never liked, and pretend to

183

have been one of his friends. But in an odd way this day had also given Jessie a new feeling of respect for her father. How many hundreds of times must he have said the same words as the St Barnaby's vicar over someone he'd been called upon to bury? And how many times must it have brought back to him the painful memories at having been obliged to do this most fundamental task for his own son – or what remained of him.

'So I definitely won't be able to see you on Sunday?' Will said just before they left to go home.

'No, I can't, Will. We've got one of Mum's friends coming to visit,' Jessie said, remembering.

'I'll come down one night in the week, then, if you like. How about next Wednesday? We could go for a drive or a walk, whatever you like.'

'That would be lovely. And Will ... call for me at the vicarage. You can't miss it. It's at the end of the village, next to the church.'

'Are you sure about that?' he said.

'I'm sure.'

CHAPTER ELEVEN

'Crikey, you're taking a chance, aren't you?' Rita said, as soon as they were on their way back to Abbot's Cove. 'What do you think your dad's going to say when he sees a young bloke in a car calling for you at the vicarage?'

'With any luck he'll be out at his junior Bible class by the time Will gets there next Wednesday. In any case, it's about time he realises I've got a life of my own.'

She hoped she sounded braver than she felt. At the time it had seemed a perfectly reasonable thing to say. But Rita wouldn't leave it alone.

'How about the neighbours? There'll be plenty of net curtains twitching behind cottage windows when they see a strange car turning up at the vicarage. You know how nosy people are around here. Remember how it was when the Yanks found their way here during the war? They were like Pied Pipers as far as the kids were concerned, always after them for gum and chocolate. And the older girls did all right too, lucky devils.'

Jessie ignored that remark. 'They should find something else to do with their time than to keep notes on who turns up at the vicarage,' she said angrily. 'Will's not a Yank, anyway. He's a perfectly ordinary Cornish boy, and for all anybody knows, he could easily be calling on my dad for some kind of service.'

'If you say so,' Rita said with a grin, as they freewheeled down the slope in the road, then leant over their handlebars to pedal harder up the other side.

Jessie clamped her lips shut. *Ordinary* was the last way she would really describe Will Tremayne. He might be perfect, though. Perfect for her. And not so much a boy, either, she thought, her face feeling hotter as she remembered the way she had been pressed against him when he had kissed her. There had been no doubting the passion in him, and in her too, she admitted. She had thought Rita a fool to get carried away by Des Greenaway, but she knew how easy it could have been for her to do the same with Will. How easy it could still be...

'What's on your mind now?' Rita said, breaking into her thoughts as they reached the brow of the hill and the village came into view. They paused for a moment, drinking in the scene of the quaint little cluster of cottages far below, the church standing tall like a beacon, the sea shining like a sapphire jewel.

'I was still thinking about Des,' Jessie said, pushing everything else aside. 'Whatever his faults, he didn't deserve to die like he did. I'm glad we went today, Rita. I know he did the dirty on you, but I feel better for having shown a bit of respect.'

It was the wrong word to use, of course. Rita snapped at her, whizzing past her on her bike on the long straight part of the road as they neared the Levant cottage.

'That's the last thing I'd have called it. As far as I'm concerned it was more likely a bit of satisfaction on seeing him firmly planted, and I don't care what your precious dad would have made of that bit of blasphemy!'

'Oh, I'm sure he'd have forgiven you,' Jessie called back as she cycled on by. 'That's his job.'

She couldn't hear what Rita yelled at her after that, because the wind had sprung up again. It was making her eyes smart, and the real meaning of this day was only just beginning to hit her. Whatever Rita's motives for being at Des's funeral, Jessie had secretly thought of it as a bit of personal exorcism, helping to disperse some of the agony of her brother's death, and the fact that they had never been able to hold a proper burial service for him.

Well, there *had* been one, of course, but it was for what was left of him, not the whole person, and that had always horrified the young, impressionable girl she had been then. It had been the cause of so many nightmares as she had been unable to stop imagining the mortuary people trying to piece whatever they could find of Adam's broken body together so that his father could bury him. It had horrified her then and it horrified her now.

She reached home and put her bike away, desperately trying to shake off the unwanted images that had haunted her all this time. She really thought she had conquered them, but after all her hopes, today had simply brought them all back. She wondered how many other thousands of grieving people had the same kind of images after that dreadful war. It didn't help to think of them. It never had. In this kind of nightmare, you

187

were always alone.

She would have preferred not to see anyone right now, but her mother was waiting for her in the sitting room, and immediately wanted to know how the day had gone.

'It was a funeral, Mum,' she said flatly. 'You must know how it was.'

'And you kept thinking of Adam. Did it help?'

The question made Jessie realise that her mother was as intuitive as she was. Well, why shouldn't she be? She was a Cornish woman too, and even though they lived in a house where omens and signs were not part of Vicar Penwarden's parochial thinking, and frowned on as being the devil's work, you couldn't change what was inborn in you. She was glad that for all her mother's sensible appearance and attention to all that was required of a vicar's wife, there was still that free spirit inside her that discounted nothing under heaven.

'I suppose it helped, sort of,' she murmured. She took a deep breath, because it was time to shake off the gloom of the day instead of bringing it home with her to depress her mother as well.

'Mum, Will is going to come down here next Wednesday to take me for a drive or a walk, and I've told him to come straight to the vicarage. I hope that was all right. You know all about him now, so I didn't think you'd mind.'

'And you know your father will be out,' Ellen said dryly. Then she smiled. 'Of course it's all right. I shall look forward to meeting him. And before that you can help me think what we're going to offer Olive and Mark for tea on Sunday.'

188

It took a few seconds for Jessie to guess that Mark was Olive's husband. She didn't know either of them, but the thought of their visit had certainly put a sparkle in her mother's eyes. It gave Jessie a glimpse of the girl she must have been when she and Olive had been school friends together.

'What was she like?' she asked curiously.

'I've been looking out some old photos which will give us both a laugh,' Ellen said. 'She was a very pretty girl and we all envied her her looks. She was a bit like Diana Dors, really, although she wasn't around then.'

'A blonde bombshell, you mean,' Jessie said with a grin.

'You'd better not let your father hear you say such things, but I think Olive liked to model herself on some of the early film stars. I always felt a bit in her shadow, but even though we were only twelve when her family moved away, we were great friends all the same.'

'But you must have seen her since then.'

It was the most Jessie had ever heard about her mother's schooldays, not that she had ever asked her about them. 'You didn't, did you?'

Ellen shook her head. 'That's the sad thing, really. We always vowed to stay friends for ever and we wrote for a while after she left Cornwall, but it soon dropped off. I heard in a roundabout way that she'd got married, and we exchanged Christmas cards for a few years, but that's about it. I always wished we'd kept in touch like we always promised, but we never did.'

'I hope you'll still like each other, then,' Jessie

189

said unthinkingly, and then went on hastily. 'Can I see the photos, Mum?'

She wanted to prolong these moments. It was all helping to take away the difficult day she had just gone through. Besides, if she was to meet this wonderful Olive who she had never heard about before, it was as well to know something about her. Her mother's early years were a bit of a surprise too. She had always assumed her to be a rather serious girl, a bit of a swot, in fact, and to have had serious friends at school. But this Olive sounded anything but that, even as young as she was then.

Ellen went to the sideboard and took out a packet of photos. They were old and some of them were creased, and several of them were photos of a very large school class where you couldn't make out the features of everybody. But there were also several photos of two laughing girls leaning on a sea wall and pulling faces at the camera.

'So this is you at twelve years old?' Jessie exclaimed.

'Yes. A bit different then, wasn't I?'

'You certainly look happy, and so does Olive. I see what you mean about her looks, though. She was really pretty. Do you know if she's got any children?'

Ellen frowned. 'I honestly don't know. It's ridiculous to think that we were as close as sisters at that age, yet I don't know anything more about her life after she went to Sussex and met her motor mechanic. I'm sure I told her when you and Adam were born, though. It seemed that when she left Cornwall she never wanted to come back and she cut off most of her old contacts. I suppose she fancied the bright lights – and she certainly got plenty of that on the south coast during the war!'

'She's a real woman of mystery, then,' Jessie said, wondering if there was any intrigue in all this. If so, her dad wouldn't be at all pleased if there was a femme fatale coming to visit. And she was letting her imagination run away with her again. But at least it kept her mind off the events of today, and when she went to bed that night she found herself starting to weave an imaginary life around the glamorous Olive, who had a faint look of Diana Dors.

When Sunday arrived she was in a high state of anticipation at meeting her mum's old friend, while Ellen was getting ever more nervous, having finally realised they would probably have nothing in common anymore, other than a few photographs of long-ago schooldays. Those undying twelve-year-old vows to always stay in touch had disappeared like will-o'-the-wisp. A few letters and Christmas cards over the years didn't amount to very much, and they didn't even exist anymore. But even though she admitted that she really had always felt in Olive's shadow, Ellen reminded herself that she was the vicar's wife now, and as such, she had some status in Abbot's Cove.

Thomas had shut himself in his study preparing for the evening service when they heard the car draw up outside. Jessie tried not to peer outside too obviously, remembering what Rita had said about net curtains twitching. But it was a swish car all right, and would put Will's boneshaker in the shade. She wondered how many folk had watched its progress through the village until it arrived at the vicarage.

'They're here, Mum,' she said excitedly.

Ellen's hand shook slightly as she filled the kettle. After the drive from Penzance, the first thing they would want was a cup of tea, and she put on a bright smile and went into the sitting room to welcome her guests, telling Jessie to go and fetch her father.

When the visitors entered, the room was immediately filled with the scent of violets. It wasn't the normal delicate scent of wild violets found in the hedgerows and the woods around there. This was an overpowering smell and it made Thomas wrinkle his nose as he came through and took in the sight of the glamorous fair-haired woman hugging his wife.

'You don't look very different, Ells,' Olive exclaimed generously, using a nickname Jessie and her dad had never heard before. 'And this must be Thomas – or do we have to call you Vicar?' she finished with a tinkling laugh.

'Thomas will do,' he said with a tight smile.

Olive turned at once and drew her companion into the circle. 'And this is my Mark,' she announced. 'I always told you I'd find myself a handsome one, didn't I, Ells? And a clever one too. Mark's got his own garage now so we're doing very nicely, thank you.'

'Well done,' Ellen said, slightly bemused at how effusive she was. Though she shouldn't have been.

192

It was no different from the way Olive had always been – except that the accent was different now. The soft Cornish lilt had gone, and she spoke far quicker, seemingly wanting to say everything at once. Maybe that was how it was on the other side of the country – and she didn't miss the hint of snobbishness in Olive's words either.

The kettle began to sing, and Ellen remembered her manners.

'Look, why don't you all sit down and I'll make us a pot of tea. And you haven't really met Jessie yet, have you?'

She escaped to the kitchen, wondering again what on earth she had in common with this rather coarse woman in the too-loud satin blouse and tight skirt and the tangle of faded fair curls. The husband, Mark, had hardly said a word as yet, and she guessed he didn't get much of a chance, anyway. She made the tea, and took in the plate of cakes and little sandwiches into the sitting room. At once, she could sense that the atmosphere had gone icy cold.

'I thought we might take a stroll around the village after tea, if you feel like it, Olive,' she said desperately, seeing that Thomas and Jessie had stony faces now and seemed to be staring nowhere.

'I don't think we'll have time, will we, Mark?' she said quickly. 'We won't bother with anything to eat either, thanks, Ells. We've got a few more folk to see in Penzance, and in any case, these shoes aren't made for walking.'

Ellen automatically glanced down at Olive's well-shod feet and was immediately conscious of her own worn house shoes.

'I was asking about your boy,' Olive went on brightly, nodding towards the photo of Adam on the mantelpiece. 'He's quite a looker in his uniform, and even in civvies I bet he's got all the girls swooning over him.'

Ellen gasped, realising now why Thomas and Jessie had been struck dumb by this insensitive woman. But how could she have known? It wasn't fair to blame her for being so brash, and so very unlike the smiling young girl with whom Ellen had shared so many childhood secrets. But even as she tried to find the words, it was Jessie who came out with them.

'My brother Adam was shot down and killed during the war,' she said brutally.

Mark cleared his throat and then spoke up. 'That's bloody bad luck,' he said, to be hushed up at once by his wife.

'Oops, sorry about the language, Vicar,' she said with a nervous laugh. 'And I'm sorry to hear about your loss, Ells. It must have been dreadful for you.'

'It was,' she managed to reply, and as nobody seemed to know what to say next, she tried to salvage what was turning into an ordeal. 'What about you and Mark? Do you have children?'

Olive shook her head, sending the fair curls bouncing on her shoulders as she accepted the cup of tea that Jessie was handing out and again waved aside the offer of any food.

'We never wanted kids, and knowing what happened to so many other people's we were always glad we never had them. We put all our energies into getting a nice little house for ourselves, and into Mark's business, of course. In a way we did all right out of old Hitler, with so many bomb sites just ready for redevelopment on the south coast, and the bit of lolly that Mark's old granny left him when she popped it. I was always glad I made the move out of here, and I must say that I never realised how small everything was until I came back – or so backward, compared with the rest of the country.'

Jessie carried on handing round tea, hardly daring to look at either of her parents as Olive prattled on. It wasn't her place to defend her family or her birthplace, but was this terrible woman totally unaware of how her words were affecting this family who were still grieving over losing their beloved Adam?

The telephone rang in Thomas's study, and he stood up stiffly, saying he would take his tea into the study and bidding the visitors goodbye, since he would probably be occupied for some time on church business. Lucky Thomas, thought Ellen, not blaming him one bit. She had never expected to feel this way, but she sincerely hoped this visit would be over very soon.

As Olive sipped her tea she was appraising Jessie now.

'You're quite a looker too, Jessie. You could do more for yourself than living in this backwater. If you ever want to leave Abbot's Cove, you could come and stay with us for a bit and find yourself a nice little job. Mark's got plenty of contacts and he'll give you his card with our address on it.'

'No thanks,' Jessie said, uncaring whether it

sounded rude or not. 'I can't imagine anything worse than living in a city, or living away from Mum and Dad and all my friends. I'm perfectly happy where I am, and I would hate to turn into something I'm not.'

'Oh well, the offer's there.'

Olive glanced at Mark, who was fidgeting in his chair now, as if finally realising they had outstayed their welcome and that things weren't going too well. Jessie and her mother gave a collective sigh of relief when they had gone, and the first thing they did was to open the doors and windows wide to release the strong scent of violets, and then they were hugging one another wordlessly.

'It was awful, Rita,' Jessie told her the following day when they met down at the cove after work. 'Mum had been so looking forward to seeing her old friend, but she was like a cartoon figure. She put on this silly voice that she forgot every now and then, and her husband hardly said a word. The last straw was when she said what she did about Adam, though. It was just awful,' she repeated.

She skimmed a pebble into the sea, watching it dance across the water, sending ripples out in an ever widening circle, and thinking that this was just how such an innocent thing as Olive's visit had affected all of them. Once it began, you had no idea where it was going to end. 'What did she say about him, then?'

Jessie flinched and told herself to stop being so fanciful and to concentrate on what Rita had said. She'd come here to unload it all on Rita, so she might as well do it.

'Well, first of all, she didn't know he'd been killed, so I suppose you could forgive her about that, if only she hadn't twittered on about him being a looker and having all the girls swooning over him.'

'Cripes, I bet your dad went wild about that, didn't he?'

'That's putting it mildly. He wasn't exactly pleased, though he didn't say an awful lot,' Jessie said, frowning. 'It was hurtful more than anything else, though, even though the stupid woman had no idea what she was saying, but I think Mum went right off her at that moment. Which was a shame, because she'd been really looking forward to her visit, and I know she was disappointed to see how Olive had changed. I felt really sorry for her.'

'Well, what did she expect, if the last time they saw each other was when they were twelve? Nobody stays the same, do they? I bet your mum doesn't look anything like she did at that age.'

Jessie shrugged. 'I don't want to talk about it anymore. I'm just glad it's over and we can all get back to being ourselves again.'

'Living out in the sticks, you mean.'

'Why not? It's where we belong.'

But was it really all over? What she didn't tell Rita was the ongoing effect it was having on her father. She had expected him to be his usual ranting self once Olive and Mark had gone, and to keep reminding his wife how foolish she had been to think everything would be exactly the same as it had always been. She had expected the vicar to have a good old grouse about Olive and then be done with it. But ever since last night he seemed to have retreated into himself, and she didn't need to be a clairvoyant to know it had been Olive's unfortunate reference to Adam that had started it. She couldn't have known, but it had stirred up all the anguish of that terrible time for all of them. Lord knows what the church sermon must have been like for the unsuspecting folk of Abbot's Cove last night. Her mum had got on with the normal household routines and today Jessie had gone to work as usual, but her father had left the house very early that morning and when she went home at midday her mother had seen no sign of him.

'He'll be at the church again,' Ellen had said, but with less conviction in her voice than usual. 'We know it's the place he always goes for sustenance and when something needs to be thought out, and I'm sure he'll be his old self by this evening. He needs to do things in his own time, Jessie.'

Remembering that little conversation at the cove now, Jessie certainly hoped so, but there was no use brooding on it. It was far better to think of something cheerful and positive, like seeing Will on Wednesday evening. Unconsciously she drew in her breath, and Rita latched on to it at once.

'What are you thinking about now?'

'Just Will,' Jessie said, glad she had something to smile about at last.

'What did your dad say about him coming to the vicarage?'

Jessie got up from the rock on which she had been sitting for too long. The days were already starting to get shorter, and the sun was getting lower in the sky. As the year went on, there wouldn't be many days when it would be so comfortable here in the early evening, especially if winter weather set in and turned the placid sea into a raging torrent. Far out to sea now she could see a boat of sorts on the horizon. It was too far away to make out how big it was. Was it a seagoing ship taking rich people on some exotic holiday now that travel was opening up again after the war? Who were they, and what were their stories? Or was it a working ship with the crew feeling bone-weary after many hours fighting the elements and longing for dry land and home? She knew she was thinking of anything rather than answer her friend's question, but she might have known she couldn't avoid it for ever.

'*Jessie*, you have told him, haven't you?'

'I'll do it tonight,' she said, striding away from Rita as fast as she could, considering how her feet were slipping and sliding on the sand.

'Best of luck, then,' Rita said as they parted company. 'I reckon you're going to need it.'

It was absurd to feel so nervous about telling her father something that would be perfectly natural in any other household. But hers wasn't any other household, and there was never any knowing what mood Vicar Penwarden was going to be in. Sometimes Jessie thought irreverently that he was in totally the wrong business. He took on

199

other people's problems too deeply, absorbing them as if they were his own, and suffering because of it. Outwardly he could be bombastic and unforgiving at times, but Ellen had always known that this was all a front to hide the inner man, and Jessie had gradually come to realise it too. So no, she hadn't yet told him that Will Tremayne was coming to call for her on Wednesday evening, and that it would be virtually a way of saying he was courting Vicar Penwarden's daughter. Or should that be *asking?*

'Mum, I'm home,' she called out, when there was no sign of her mother in the kitchen, which was unusual at this time of day. There was no welcoming smell of cooking, either, and no kettle simmering on the stove.

She didn't feel any alarm. Just like her father, her mother was often called out to tend some neighbour who had had a fall or was in need of help, or to deal with some small village crisis. It wasn't only the vicar who was on call whenever he was needed, and Jessie had become quite used to sharing her parents over the years with the needs of the community.

Neither of them seemed to be home now, so she filled the kettle herself. By the time her parents came home they would at least have a pot of tea ready for them, and she was quite happy to make herself a sandwich for now. In any case, it was rather nice to have the place to herself. This must be how it was when you were married and preparing a meal for your husband on his return home from work, she thought dreamily.

She gave a small giggle, knowing she was letting

her thoughts fly way too far ahead, but doing nothing to stop them. There was nothing wrong with dreaming, and right now she was dreaming it was her and Will in a place of their own. It wouldn't be a great rambling place like this, of course. Rather, a neat little cottage just big enough for two, and later on, perhaps there would be one or two more little people to fill it with laughter...

She felt a shiver of pleasure, just thinking about it. Herself and Will, blissfully living out their happy ever after, with a brace of babies who would be mirror images of themselves...

As the kettle began to sing, it reminded her of that old song... *Tea for two, and two for tea... Me for you and you for me...*

And the sweetest line of all – *a boy for you, a girl for me ... oh, can't you see how happy we could be...* The words probably weren't quite right, but the sentiments were, thought Jessie!

Her fantasy was brought to an abrupt end by the sound of the telephone. Reluctantly, wishing she could hold on to the delicious dreams a little while longer, she went to answer it, putting on her best vicar's daughter's voice as she did so. And as she listened to the rapidly speaking voice at the other end, her expression instantly changed from happy to total shock.

She stammered a reply, her head spinning, and just had the presence of mind to turn off the gas under the kettle before she was flying out of the house, grabbing her bicycle and hurtling through the village towards the high cliffs beyond Abbot's Cove.

CHAPTER TWELVE

Jessie had a stitch in her side and a sawing pain in her chest by the time she saw the crowd of people ahead of her. She had no idea who had made the telephone call, although someone must have rushed back to the village to alert her. She couldn't make out what was happening and she desperately needed to catch her breath. She slid off her bike and bent low over the handlebars for a moment before she had to face the inevitable. Though quite what the inevitable was, she still didn't know. The man's voice had just rattled out the news that there had been an accident at the lower part of the cliff face and that her father had been hurt, and she should come as quickly as she could ... but she had to pause a minute to get her breath back or she was going to pass out here and now.

Someone was calling her name, and she turned her head sharply to see Rita toiling up behind her, her bicycle wheels skewing crazily from side to side as she coped with the slope towards the cliffs.

'What's going on up there?' Rita yelled. 'Mum said she saw you through the window pedalling like fury, and you looked like death.'

It was an unfortunate word to use, since Jessie had no idea yet what had happened to her father. She gulped, and swallowed back the fear in her throat.

'I had a phone call to say Dad's been hurt and that's all I know. I've got to get up there to find out, Rita.'

'Let's get going, then,' Rita said at once.

They pedalled on together. It gave Jessie a smidgin of comfort to know Rita was with her. But not for long. Not when she saw the group of people bending low over somebody stretched out on the short turf at the top of the cliffs, and heard the sound of somebody sobbing. She registered that Doctor Charles was kneeling beside the prone figure on the ground, but she tore her gaze away and grabbed her mother's shaking arms.

'Mum!' she gasped, flinging her bike away from her. 'What's happened?'

It was her father, of course. It had to be her father. She had known it from the moment the telephone call came, even before she heard the voice, something had told her. Maybe it should have told her last night when he had seemed so remote ... and today when she hadn't seen him at all ... and then finding the house empty when she got home from work ... the staccato thoughts flew through her head as sharp as needles.

Ellen took a shuddering breath. 'It seems he slipped and fell down the cliff a little way. Fortunately, some bramble bushes broke his fall, but his arm is all twisted, and Doctor Charles thinks it's broken. He also thinks...' she had a job to put it into words '...he also says he may have had a small heart attack and that's what caused him to fall. He doesn't want to move him until the ambulance arrives to take him to hospital.'

In the same instant as Jessie was taking in all

203

that her mother was saying she realised she was avoiding her eyes. Something else was wrong. Something even worse than a broken arm and a small heart attack ... something that would be against all his beliefs, unless that man was feeling the kind of desperate anguish that would drive the sanest person to do something wicked...

'Crikey, Jess,' she heard Rita say in a hushed voice alongside her. 'You don't think he's going to snuff it, do you?'

'Don't be stupid!' Jessie said, rounding on her at once. 'That's the last thing Mum wants to hear right now. Keep your daft opinions to yourself.'

She pushed past her friend and went forward to where the small crowd was still surrounding her father. Ellen had gone back to him now and was kneeling beside the doctor, both trying to encourage her husband to keep still and try not to move. Thomas's face was grey and drawn, and he was in obvious pain from his arm, and Jessie felt increasingly fearful as the doctor tried to reassure him that the ambulance would be here very soon.

Everyone knew it wouldn't be here very quickly, since it had to come from Penzance, but it had been ordered before Jessie had had the phone call at the vicarage. Heaven knew how long it had been before someone had thought to contact her, though, so she prayed that it was on its way. She felt, literally, as though her heart was in her mouth as she saw her normally strong father lying there so helpless, and knowing that in any other circumstances, he would absolutely hate to be surrounded by all these gawping parishioners, however well meaning. He was covered with someone's jacket and Jessie knew how he would hate all this fuss. He was so used to being in charge, orating from the pulpit in his own dictatorial manner, and now he was at the mercy of his own weakness.

'Can't we give him some privacy?' Ellen choked out. The doctor was evidently thinking the same thing as he asked for some space around his patient, and at once the crowds moved back a little.

'Ellen, my dear,' Thomas said in a weak voice, putting out his good hand to grasp hers as best he could. 'I'm sorry. It wasn't meant to be like this.'

Both she and Jessie had leant forward to catch the mumbled words, but his hand slid from his wife's hold and she gave a gasp. The doctor pushed her aside and took hold of his pulse. After a minute or two he gave a satisfied nod.

'Don't be alarmed, he's simply fainted, which is probably a good thing.'

Jessie felt briefly relieved. At least Thomas wouldn't be feeling any pain while he was unconscious, nor be struggling to sit up or insisting that he was all right, which he would assuredly be doing as soon as he got a little of his strength back. Far better for him to lie perfectly still until the ambulance arrived.

By now some of the villagers had begun to disperse, thankfully so, as far as Jessie and Ellen were concerned. Rita edged forward and asked Jessie if she would be going to the hospital with her parents.

'Of course I will,' she almost snapped. 'Did you expect me to go home and behave as if nothing had happened?'

'I was just going to say that when the ambulance arrives I'll ask somebody to bring your bike to my house until you can collect it.'

Jessie bit her lip. 'Sorry. I didn't mean to bite your head off. That would be good, Rita. Thanks.'

In so short a while, her whole world had frighteningly changed. Less than an hour ago she had been humming a little song at home, thinking of Will, anticipating the delightful time they would have together on Wednesday evening, and now, where would she be? Where would any of them be? The prospect looming ahead of her now was of spending time in a hospital ward with her mother, and praying that her father would get over this and return home, as fit and strong as ever. She swallowed a choking sob, wondering where this was going to leave any of them, and wishing with all her heart that Adam was here to be the strong one.

Her eyes closed tightly for a moment as his image came into her mind, young and smiling, so proud of his air force uniform and having realised his ambition to fly. On the heels of his image came a sudden and unexpected burst of anger, that some madman in another country had robbed them all of Adam's strength when they most needed him. A son shouldn't die before his father, and a father should have his son to rely on in his old age.

Not that Thomas was old by any means! But if today was proving his frailty it was also starting to put the trembling questions in Jessie's mind as to what would become of her and her mother if the worst should happen. She didn't want such questions to fill her mind, but nor could she stop them.

'Are you all right, Jessie?' she heard Rita say.

'I've got to be, haven't I?' she said huskily. In truth, she was wishing she was anywhere but here. Wishing everybody would go away and that she could turn back the clock a few hours before any of this had happened. Better still, to turn it back to before that horrible friend of her mother's had come to stir up painful memories in all their minds.

It seemed an age before they heard the trundling noise of the ambulance coming their way over the moorland turf. The ground was thankfully still baked hard by the summer sun and gave purchase to the vehicle's wheels. Two men in hospital attendants' coats got out and moved swiftly towards Thomas, kneeling beside him to hear the doctor's brisk words. It all floated over Jessie's head. She could no more have repeated what was being said than fly to the moon. But in a relatively short time now, her father was lifted onto a stretcher and placed in the back of the ambulance, and she and her mother were scrambling in after him. He was still mercifully unconscious, but by now an oxygen mask had been placed over his face, making him appear even more ashen than before.

The last thing Jessie saw before she grasped her mother's hand as the ambulance began moving carefully away towards the main road, before speeding on its way to Penzance, was Rita's frightened face. She wished she could have given her a reassuring smile, but she had never felt less like smiling, and her face felt frozen. But after a few moments the attendant sitting beside her father gave the two women a reassuring smile.

'Don't you worry none, my dears. I've seen far worse than this come through with flying colours. Had a drop too much to drink and took a purler over the cliff, did he?' he joked, trying to lighten the atmosphere.

Ellen seemed incapable of replying to that, and Jessie spoke quickly.

'My father is the vicar of Abbot's Cove,' she said, and then she stopped abruptly. It sounded so pompous. She hardly knew how to go on, nor did she want to elevate her father to some godly being when the man was only trying to be kind. Besides, did vicars never drink a little too much or go the way of ordinary mortals?

'Sorry, love, but that proves it, then,' the attendant said cheerfully. 'He'll have God on his side, for certain sure,' he added, and turned back to his patient.

Jessie could feel her mother shaking beside her and prayed that she wouldn't fall to pieces. Ellen was almost as private a person as Thomas, and would already be hating herself for weeping in public. Then Jessie realised that her mother wasn't weeping. She was trying hard to stifle her laughter. Even as the realisation startled her, Ellen whispered in her ear.

'He'd love to hear that, wouldn't he? Having God on his side, I mean. Can't you just imagine him preening? But let's hope that it's so for all our sakes.'

Jessie didn't know what to say. It almost

seemed as though her mother was mocking her father's rigid beliefs, and right now such a thing would be in the poorest taste. But then she saw the tortured look in Ellen's eyes as the laughter faded, and she knew that it was no more than a way of dealing with a situation that was beyond anything they could have imagined happening.

It was a relief when they reached the hospital. Outside the darkened windows of the ambulance they would have passed Will's house on the way, and Jessie wondered fleetingly if Mrs Tremayne had been at home, seeing the vehicle go by with its blue light flashing, and idly wondering what unfortunate person was its occupant. Jessie drew a shuddering breath, unable again to resist the shaming thought of what would become of them if the worst happened ... and then she felt her mother's hand holding on tightly to hers.

'He'd want us to pray for him, Jess,' she said more softly. 'We don't have to do it out loud, but just pray inside your heart for his recovery.'

She was so brave, so strong. She might seem at times to be the rather meek wife of the vicar, always in his shadow, but she was strong all the same, thought Jessie. And she wasn't going to let her mother down now. She nodded mutely, closed her eyes and let the prayer for her father fill her mind.

Everything seemed to be taken out of their hands from then on. Thomas was taken away to some remote part of the hospital where they were going to do whatever was needed for him, and Jessie and her mother were shown into a room where small groups of people sat huddled together. None of them spoke to anyone else, all confined in their own little world of anxiety, waiting for news of someone they loved. All these people, scared of the outcome, of the moment when a nurse or a doctor would appear with grave faces and tell them what they most feared. Or, hopefully, with smiling faces to reassure them that all was going to be well. All of them praying as she and Ellen were praying.

Her father would be proud of them, Jessie thought, with a small burst of something inside her that she couldn't explain. It wasn't pride, or mockery, or even respect. It was just a kind of acceptance of what he stood for, and how it helped. Oh yes, it definitely helped, even for non-believers who suddenly became the most ardent believers in such times as these.

By the time someone came to speak to them they were stiff with sitting, and most of the other people in the room had gone. They looked up expectantly when the nurse came towards them. Was it good news that it was only a nurse and not a doctor? Jessie couldn't tell, but then the nurse smiled, and the flood of relief that she felt was so strong it almost made her weep.

'Do you have news for us?' she heard her mother say huskily.

'Yes, and it's good news, Mrs Penwarden. Your husband has had his broken arm put in plaster now. The doctor says he definitely had a small heart attack so he'll need to stay here for a few weeks until we can assess his recovery fully. He's been sedated so he won't be conscious for a while but you can both come to see him shortly. Then

210

I suggest you go home and return in the morning.'

The relief was almost as much of a shock as if the nurse had said something terrible. Jessie realised how tightly she was clinging to her mother's hand at that moment, and Ellen gradually released her daughter's grip on her. There was almost a transformation in Ellen's face now. It seemed to glow for a moment, as if with some inner peace, and if Jessie had ever doubted the power of prayer, she felt as though she was seeing all of it portrayed in her mother's face.

She wondered briefly if Adam had been watching over him all this time, and dashed the fanciful thought away. It was the effect of the hospital, with all its repellant smells along with the brisk manners of its staff. And such humbling moments couldn't last for ever. All they were anxious about now was seeing that Thomas was settled and safe, and as the nurse led them along to the ward Jessie's heart was beating fast in her chest. She had never seen her father ill before, and she steeled herself for the frightening sight that met their eyes.

He was still so pale, with various tubes attached to him, a monitor recording his heartbeat, and still the oxygen mask over his face. His right arm was in plaster now, and this was going to curtail many of his activities for a time. But at least he was alive, and while Jessie hesitated from going right up to him, Ellen went swiftly to his side and knelt down beside the bed. Even though he was sedated and couldn't hear her, she whispered close to his ear.

Jessie didn't know what her mother said, and in any case it was a very private moment. She felt a lump in her throat, seeing her mother stroke her father's face so gently, and then bend to kiss his cheek. Finally, she went forward and did the same, even though they were not normally an especially kissing family. Situations changed everything, though.

There was no point in staying too long, since Thomas would be out of it for a long while yet, so at last they left the room, being assured that they could come back as soon as they wished in the morning. And several hours since they had arrived at the hospital, they found themselves outside in the cool late-evening air. In such a relatively short time, their whole world had turned topsy-turvy, and for a few moments they were completely disorientated, until Ellen spoke.

'I suppose we should try to catch a bus back home, Jessie.'

'It's too late for that,' she replied. 'The last bus will have gone long ago.'

'Then perhaps we should have stayed in the waiting room until morning,' Ellen said uncertainly. 'I don't think they'd turn us away in the circumstances.'

For the first time Jessie heard the fatigue in her mother's voice. If all of this had been an ordeal for her, how much more would it have been for Ellen, seeing her husband so helpless? She came to a swift decision.

'Look, Mum, we can easily walk to Will Tremayne's house from here. I know his mother wouldn't turn us away, even if we have to sleep on

212

a couple of armchairs in her living room. Dad's being taken good care of now, and it would be far more comfortable than a hospital waiting room, and we could get back here in the morning far quicker than if we were at home. What do you say?'

For a moment Ellen didn't say anything. And then she said, 'I don't think it's a sensible suggestion at all. It would be far too much of an imposition for two strangers to turn up on someone's doorstep at this hour of the night.'

'But I'm not a stranger to them. Mrs Tremayne is a very kindly person, and I've known Will for a while now,' she added, thankful that the darkness hid her blushes at saying these words. 'You were going to meet him yourself on Wednesday, and I know his mother would want to give us some hospitality.'

'I don't know,' Ellen repeated. 'It's not the sort of thing I've ever done.'

'Please, Mum, I know this is the best thing for us, and how else would we get home safely tonight? Neither of us could walk all the way to Abbot's Cove, and besides, what would Dad do in similar circumstances? Wouldn't he be the good Samaritan and never turn anyone away if they were in need?'

She squirmed as she said the words, knowing she was playing with her father's calling to get her own way. But it wasn't only the sudden overwhelming need to see Will again, and to be somewhere safe and warm in a homely atmosphere. It was also the sadness she could sense in Ellen now. The initial drama was over, and Thomas would get well in time, she thought, with her fingers firmly crossed, and it was obvious that Ellen's spirits were wilting. She was the one needing to be looked after now.

'Well, if you're sure,' Ellen finally said, wavering.

It was the only incentive Jessie needed. It was chilly now and neither of them had their outer coats. She tucked her arm inside her mother's, and told her to think instead of the hot drink Mrs Tremayne would be sure to offer them when they reached her house. She prayed it would be so, and that Will and his mother didn't retire early. But somehow she knew in her bones that they would be welcome. She didn't have her Cornish intuition for nothing, and if fate had decided that this was the way her mother and Will's were going to meet, well, you didn't argue with fate.

More than half an hour later they were walking up the path of the Tremayne house. It was cheering to see Will's car standing outside in the road, and to Jessie's relief, there was a light shining out from the uncurtained living room window, while the upstairs was in darkness. Thank goodness for that, at least.

'Jessie, I'm still not sure about this,' Ellen said.

'Well, what else are we going to do? It's a long walk home, Mum, and we're both tired. If you're so worried about it, let's just ask Mrs Tremayne if she knows of any lodgings nearby.'

She thought she knew Will's mother well enough to know what the answer would be to that. But it appeased her mother for the moment, and Jessie

214

knocked boldly on the front door. It was Will who came to answer it, letting out a stream of light onto the path. For a weird moment, seeing him so startled at seeing them, Jessie remembered how it had been not so many years ago, when there would have been shouts of blackout orders and the whole place would have been in darkness. Those days were over for ever, thank the Lord. And then she found her voice, strained and shrill though it was.

'Will, I'm sorry to turn up unexpectedly like this, but could Mum and I come inside for a few minutes, please? We've just taken Dad to hospital and we've missed the last bus home.'

She swallowed as she spoke, and if it wasn't for holding on to Ellen, she would have swayed, and she fought to keep her senses together.

'Of course you can come in, and you must be perished if you've walked all the way from the hospital,' Will exclaimed. 'What's happened, Jessie?'

She could hardly remember anything of the next minutes. Will's mother appeared beside him to see what was going on, and the visitors were quickly ushered inside. Then everything seemed to be said at once, until the Tremaynes knew as much as themselves about what had happened to Vicar Penwarden that night. At some stage, cups of hot cocoa and a plate of biscuits seemed to appear miraculously. Ellen had begun murmuring something about finding lodgings for the night, and Will was offering to drive them back to Abbot's Cove, while his mother said he was going to do no such thing at this hour, and that of course Jessie and her mother must stay here with them.

215

It was suddenly all too much for Ellen. Her hands trembled and she had to put down her cup of cocoa before she spilt it.

'I'm sorry. We've had a shock and it's only just beginning to sink in that Thomas is going to be all right. The doctor assured us of that, but I fear he'll be a very bad patient.' She gave the ghost of a smile. 'In fact, being patient is the last way I'd describe him.'

'He'll give the nurses a dance, that's for sure,' Jessie broke in, thankful to see that the colour was returning to her mother's cheeks and that she could even manage a small joke about her husband. All this time, she had hardly dared look at Will, and had spoken only to his mother. Once she did look at him, she felt her heart turn over at the way he was looking at her. But now wasn't the time for raw love to shine through, and she averted her eyes again, aware that both their mothers were in the room.

Doris Tremayne was bustling about again, asking if they would like a sandwich of cheese and tomato chutney to keep them going until morning.

'Oh no, it's far too much trouble,' Ellen protested, finding her mouth watering all the same.

'Nonsense, my dear. Will and me were just going to have one ourselves, so you'll join us, I'm sure. And then we'll see about some sleeping arrangements for you for the night. It will be makeshift, I'm afraid, but at least you'll be warm and comfortable.'

'You're very kind,' Ellen murmured.

'Well, if a body can't do a good turn for another, then the world's turned into a sorry place, I reckon,' Doris said briskly. 'Now then, Will, you can help me in the kitchen for once while these ladies get their thoughts together after their ordeal.'

It was all a bit dreamlike, Jessie couldn't help thinking. A few hours ago everything had gone on as normal in the Penwarden household and in Abbot's cove. Now, in so short a space of time, she guessed that the whole community was gossiping about what had happened to their vicar, and Jessie was preparing to spend the night under the same roof as Will Tremayne.

Her mouth felt dry, knowing she should be thinking more about her father than such an enticing prospect. Not that there would be anything improper about it, of course, and nor would she want there to be. Well, only *slightly*. Only now and then, when she caught that certain look in Will's eyes when he looked at her, and knew instinctively that he was thinking the same thing. It made her feel all jittery when she picked up her cup to drink her cocoa, and for a very different reason than her mother's agitation. She was angry with herself, knowing this wasn't the time to be thinking of such things. *The sins of the flesh* her dad would call them. But she had never sinned, and she wasn't intending to start now, thank you very much, especially after what had happened to Rita.

Ellen had become adept over the years at dealing with bereaved and sorrowing parishioners. It was part of the role of a vicar's wife that she had taken on gladly, since it was part of her nature to be concerned about other people. However, it was different when it came to your own troubles, as she had discovered when her only son had died. Even then, she had had Thomas's unbearable grief to cope with, and that of Jessie's too. She had hardly had time to worry about her own feelings except in the silent hours of the night.

This was different. Now she was the one left to weep and agonise over Thomas's accident and subsequent heart attack. It was all very well for doctors and nurses to be reassuring, but who knew how much the human body could stand, let alone cope with old sorrows of the mind? She was out of her depth for the first time in her life, and it was Doris Tremayne who spoke to her in a soft and calming voice and made her feel a mite better.

'I've known sorrow of a different kind, Mrs Pen-warden,' she said, 'and eventually we're all given the strength to cope with it. You must know that from your husband's calling. It's a trite thing to say that things always look better in the morning, but I'm sure there's a lot of truth in it. I can offer you a sleeping powder to help you sleep if you think you need it, though.'

'I'd rather not rely on such things, thank you all the same,' Ellen said quickly. 'And you're right. My husband always says that we should face up to whatever God gives us to bear.'

'Then I'm sure He will see you through,' Doris said calmly, taking no offence. 'Now then, you both look exhausted and I'm sure you'll be glad of a night's rest. We have a small box room in which a single bed is always made up, and you're welcome to have it, Mrs Penwarden. I'll put fresh bedding on Will's bed for Jessie, and he can sleep down here on the sofa.'

'We're putting you to far too much trouble!' Jessie burst out, the prospect of actually sleeping in Will's bed overwhelming her.

'No, you're not, my dear. You just finish your sandwich and warm yourselves, and I'll have the rooms ready in a jiffy.'

Again, Jessie hardly dared look at Will. When she did, it was to see the hint of a smile playing around his handsome mouth. Was he imagining her in his bed too? He had always been the perfect gentleman towards her, but she had no doubt that beneath that gentlemanly exterior was a lusty and earthy young man. She felt a surge of something she couldn't explain run through her veins at that moment. She knew she should be thinking about her father and praying for his complete recovery, but right now Vicar Penwarden was farthest from his daughter's thoughts.

CHAPTER THIRTEEN

She knew she wouldn't sleep. How could she, knowing where she was? She had made a token protest at pushing Will out of his bed, but his mother simply said it was less comfortable than the box room bed and that young people were adaptable enough to sleep anywhere these days. It seemed churlish to argue further, and eventually they had all retired for the night. Both Jessie and her mother had been loaned sleeping attire, and Jessie felt lost in the voluminous winceyette of one of Mrs Tremayne's nightgowns.

It buttoned right up to her neck and covered every inch of her with fabric to spare. If there was ever a deterrent to lovemaking, she thought, catching sight of herself in Will's cracked dressing table mirror, this must be it! She squashed the thought immediately as she turned away from the telltale blushes in her reflection and looked around her.

It was a very small bedroom, and the box room was just as small, but she and Ellen were thankful for the hospitality they had been shown. Jessie looked at the pristine sheets and pillow on the narrow bed, and again, she felt her heart begin to beat faster, knowing this was where Will slept every night, and where his head indented that pillow. Was there ever a more emotive place to be when she felt so very vulnerable after all that had been happening?

Determinedly, she slid between the bedcovers, willing away any unclean thoughts that might invade her mind. She remembered her prayers and why she was here. They would help her through ... but once she eventually managed to sleep, she couldn't stop the intoxicating dreams...

She was sinking into the narrow bed that had suddenly become enormous in her dreams, accommodating them both.

'Will, oh Will,' she breathed, entwined in his arms, so exquisitely entwined that it would be hard to tell where one of them began and the other ended. The voluminous nightgown had disappeared, and she could feel the warmth of his skin against hers, stimulating sensations inside her that were new and almost unbearably exciting. Wanting more of them, wanting more of him.

She could feel his mouth on hers, kissing her eyes, her cheeks, her mouth, and then, when she thought the bliss could get no sweeter, his lips were descending lower over her body in such seductively slow and tender movements that she could have fainted with the pleasure of it. They circled her nipples, slow and sensuous and filling her with fire ... and she no longer wanted to faint. She wanted to experience every movement, every tingling sensation that rippled through her body at his every touch.

'You're my perfect angel,' he murmured against her so-willing flesh, 'the only one I ever want in my life, my lovely Jessie, and I never want these moments to end until I have had my fill of you.'

'No more do I,' she breathed again, her eyes closed

in ecstasy as she felt the weight of him covering her. Was this how it felt to be a wanton? This achingly lovely knowledge of another person in a way she had never known before? Passion enveloped them both, and she felt dazedly that this must be how an artist felt, knowing every beautiful inch of the masterpiece he created. She was acutely aware of his shape, his scent, his strength, pulsing against her. In moments now they would no longer be two entities, but one, and she would be part of him, and he of her.

She felt herself opening up for him, her mind filled with a kind of rapture, knowing that she was about to share in the mystical union of a man and a woman for the first time in her life...

Was it that almost biblical expression that entered her dreams at that moment that brought them so crashingly to an end? Forcing her back to reality, to the hot tangle of bedcovers in which she found herself. Her heart thudded furiously in her chest, as if some horror had startled her. It was barely daylight, so maybe it was a noise from the street outside, perhaps the milkman whistling on his early morning rounds as his cart rattled with the sound of milk bottles, or else it was some movement in the house. Whatever it was, she awoke in a state of confusion and shame, her face and body suffused in sweat at knowing what she had been imagining so vividly.

She buried her head beneath the bedcovers as if to try to will away the memory of such an evocative dream before it became an overwhelming desire to remember it all too well, to imprint it indelibly for ever in her senses. In full control of

222

them now, she wondered if she was really a wicked person to have felt so full of lust, even in dreams. Perhaps there was not so much difference between herself and Rita after all, except that Rita had been so much bolder than she was. Or perhaps it was all just a simple reaction to being here in Will's bed, where she had never expected to be in a million years. She forced her heartbeats to slow down, taking long, deep breaths and making herself think rationally.

It had been just a dream, no more. None of it had happened, and it might never happen ... and yet in her soul she knew that one day it would. She knew it as surely as she breathed.

A sudden knock on the bedroom door jerked her out of all other thoughts, whether or not they were prophetic or filled with the newness of desire.

'Who is it?' she said in a small, cracked voice that sounded nothing like her own.

'I've brought you up a cup of tea, dear,' came Doris Tremayne's cheerful voice. 'Can I bring it in?'

'Yes, of course,' Jessie said, desperately hoping she didn't look as dishevelled as she felt. 'You shouldn't have bothered, Mrs Tremayne, really.'

'Now, you just stop protesting, there's a good girl, and we'll get along fine,' said Will's mother briskly. 'It's going to be a lovely day and you'll be wanting to get along to the hospital soon, I daresay. But before then, you and your mother are going to have a hearty breakfast. You'll find the usual at the end of the passage, by the way. Will had it put in for us a while ago so we don't have

223

to go down the garden to the lavvy. There's a small washbasin there, too, where you can tidy yourself. I've brought you a flannel and towel and some soap, so get dressed at your leisure. You'll want to look pretty for your dad later on.'

She put the cup of tea on the dressing table and went out of the room, leaving Jessie thinking numbly that she hadn't given her father a single thought since she had woken up that morning. How *awful* was that! Her mother would probably have tossed and turned all night, worrying about Thomas and praying for his complete recovery, while his daughter had just experienced an erotic dream that had taken her so much by surprise it had knocked every other thought out of her head.

But she wasn't going to allow it to do so! She leapt out of bed, ignoring the cup of tea for the moment. She grabbed the flannel, soap and towel, and sped down the small passage to what Mrs Tremayne called the usual. In the tiny room there was a lavatory with a pull chain, and in the corner was the washbasin she had spoken of, with proper taps and all. Jessie splashed cold water over her face thankfully, washing her armpits and her nether regions, washing away the impurities of her mind, and feeling cleaner in every way once she had finished.

Then she sped as quickly back to her room, closed the door and leant against it, her heart beating fast again. How was she going to face Will after such a dream? She felt as if the knowledge of it all was written in her face for all to see, and she was in a state of total jitters by the time she had dressed in yesterday's clothes, drunk her tea and gone cautiously downstairs.

Ellen was already there, sitting at the breakfast table, while the smell of hot toast and frying eggs wafted towards them. Her mother looked remarkably cool, Jessie thought, almost crossly, as if she hadn't a care in the world. Obviously some of Thomas's faith had rubbed off on her over the years, and she had probably managed to convince herself by now that all would be well.

'Did you manage to sleep all right, my dear?' Ellen asked gently.

'Not too well,' she mumbled. 'I've got a headache now,' she invented, in case her eyes looked puffy and her cheeks over-red.

'Some breakfast will put you right, Jessie,' Mrs Tremayne said, bringing in a tray of food. 'Will sends his apologies for not being here to say goodbye to you, as he had to get off to work early this morning. But if you'd both care to come back for a hot meal this evening, then he'll drive you home, although you'd be quite welcome to stay here another night or two if you prefer.'

'That's very kind of you, Mrs Tremayne,' Ellen said swiftly, 'but we have things to see to at home, and Jessie has to go to work too. Besides, there's a limit as to how long we can wear the same clothes. But we'll be glad to come back here later in the day, and for Will to drive us home.'

Ellen was taking over again, being the efficient vicar's wife in her quiet way as always. Jessie admired her so much, thankful that she could have no idea of the turbulent emotions running through her daughter's head. She was more than

225

thankful, too, that Will had gone to work already. The time and distance between them until later would surely lessen the acute sense of embarrassment she felt whenever she thought of him now.

It wasn't fair! she thought in a sudden rage. She loved him with all her heart, and she was certain that one day their future lay together. One day they would be married and have babies. It was every girl's dream ... and somehow she had spoilt it all by having the kind of dream that she hadn't wanted, nor invited. It had been beautiful while it lasted, more beautiful than her imagination could ever have conjured up, but it was the wrong time and the wrong place, and it shamed her. She was *glad* that she couldn't see him now. Sitting across the breakfast table and making inane small talk over fried eggs and toast would have been impossible.

'Are you all right, Jessie?' Ellen asked her anxiously. 'Yesterday was a shock for us all, but I'm sure that once you've seen your father again you'll be reassured.'

'I'm sure I will,' Jessie replied, knowing that she hadn't been thinking about her father at all. She tried to smile at her mother, wondering what Ellen would think if she knew just where her daughter's thoughts had been going ... this clean-living woman who had surely never had an erotic dream in her life.

But who knew what went on in other people's heads, or thoughts, or dreams? You couldn't control them, and you couldn't invade them. They were private, no matter how shocking they were, and that was the only blessedly good thing to be said about them.

Somehow she ate the breakfast that Will's mother had provided, even though she didn't feel like eating. It was clear that Ellen was doing so much better than she was, and later that morning, when they walked out together in the sunshine on their way to the hospital, she burst out with the question that was brimming in her mind.

'How do you cope with it all, Mum? Last night you were as devastated as I was, and today you seem so calm and so capable. Aren't you still a little bit scared over what might happen to Dad?'

'Of course I am, but I also have faith in God and the doctors that he'll pull through. I hope you have that faith too, Jessie. The more prayers that are said, the more it will help your father. I'm sure folk in Abbot's Cove have been praying for him too.'

'I'm sure you're right,' Jessie said, although all this constant talk of praying was making her feel uncomfortable.

How wonderful it would be if they could turn back the clock to the day before yesterday, when none of this had happened. When her father hadn't gone walking over the cliffs for some inexplicable reason, and slipped over. She wondered just how it had happened. Had he been deep in thought and lost his footing? It wasn't as if the ground had been soft and slippery. Had he suffered the beginnings of the heart attack and felt sick and giddy? She knew some of the symptoms from her work at the chemist's and hearing Mr Price commenting on them. Or had the unthinkable happened, and her father's actions been deliberate? Had her mother's old friend Olive, with her flashy clothes and her thoughtlessness, finally tipped Vicar Penwarden literally over the edge with the agonised memories of the son he had lost?

'Whatever you're thinking, Jessie, it was an accident,' Ellen said, just as if she could read right inside Jessie's mind at that moment. Just as if she was clairvoyant. Or perhaps it was some expression on Jessie's face leading her to wonder what dark thoughts were going through her daughter's head right then.

'I know it was, Mum,' she forced herself to say. 'I'm just thankful that his fall was broken by that bramble bush, or it could have been so much worse.'

'Well, it's true that God works in mysterious ways, my dear, and obviously the good Lord hasn't done with Thomas's services just yet.'

In the circumstances, it was such a jocular remark that it took Jessie by surprise, and then she saw that her mother was smiling almost gaily.

'Oh, cheer up, my love. The sun is shining, and I'm sure your father is giving his orders to the nurses by now. If he's to stay in hospital for a few weeks, we'll be needing to make arrangements about the church, and I've no doubt he'll have decided on some orders for us too.'

She was a marvel, Jessie thought. Circumstances had changed, and so she would adapt with them. She gritted her teeth as they neared the hospital, and told herself she would do her best to adapt too.

Vicar Penwarden wasn't exactly in his usual fine voice by the time they arrived to visit him, but it was as Ellen had predicted. He had been moved to a side ward now, and after a fair night's sleep with his plastered arm stuck out of the bed, plenty of pain relief, plus the assurance that he wasn't about to expire, he had his little team of nurses scurrying around him doing as he asked. Doctors were a different matter, but because of his calling, they were prepared to defer to him as far as was practical, hence the private room.

He looked up expectantly as he saw his women-folk enter the room and he spoke at once, as if to forestall any show of emotion.

'Well, this is a pretty kettle of fish, isn't it?' he greeted them. 'It would have to be my right arm that got broken, so I won't be writing any sermons for a while just yet.'

Ellen ignored any such problems and went straight across to the bed and kissed him on the cheek.

'None of that matters, Thomas, as long as you're going to be all right.'

'Of course I'm going to be all right, and of course it matters. But what's happened to the pair of you? You look as if you haven't slept all night – and are those still the same clothes you were wearing yesterday?'

Jessie moved forward to the bed and answered indignantly.

'Honestly, Dad, is that all you can say to us when we've been so worried about you?'

He inclined his head as he looked at her. 'Well, maybe that was a little harsh, but you knew I'd have my Constant Good Companion looking after me,' he said meaningfully. 'I knew you'd be saying a prayer for me, and I was saying one for the two of you as well. But you don't look at your best, you in particular, Jessica, and we do have standards to keep up.'

Dear Lord, he was impossible! It didn't take long for him to revert to criticising, yet Ellen merely smiled and proceeded to tell him where they had stayed last night. For a moment Jessie expected him to blow up, but the appearance of a nurse hovering over him, and thrusting a thermometer in his mouth while feeling his pulse, had the desired effect. Once the thermometer had been removed, and the nurse had told him all was well, and that the doctor would see him soon, he frowned at his wife and daughter.

'It was very good of these people to accommodate you, Ellen, my dear, although I don't care to think of you imposing yourselves on strangers.'

'They're not strangers, Dad,' Jessie said. 'You would have met Will on Wednesday if you hadn't had your accident, and Mrs Tremayne is a good, churchgoing woman.'

She mentally crossed her fingers as she said it, since she wasn't sure if it was true or not. But she knew it would please her father to think so. It occurred to her just how many little white lies she had been telling lately. Ever since she had met Will Tremayne, in fact ... but it wasn't fair to blame him. It was more like ever since the three young men came roaring down to Abbot's Cove on their motorbikes and all the trouble that had been stirred up with Rita.

'So you haven't been home at all since yesterday?' Thomas went on, starting to look visibly tired now.

'It was too late to catch the last bus, and I was the one who had the idea of going to Mrs Tremayne's. It really saved our bacon, Dad,' Jessie said quickly.

Being a stickler for the good English he always used in his sermons, she knew he wouldn't like the sloppy expression, but it was the only thing she could think of saying right then.

'And it did mean that we could get here early today, Thomas,' Ellen said.

Why did they have to defend themselves all the time? Wasn't it enough that they had worried about him and were here as early as possible to see that he was recovering?

As if he was bored with the whole thing now, Thomas waved his left hand at them. 'Well, I presume you'll be going home today, and Jessie will want to get back to work. I have some instructions for you, Ellen, and the nurse has left a pad and a pencil for you to write them down.'

It was obviously no more than a minor heart attack, thought Jessie a little bitterly, although everyone said the smallest one was said to be a warning. It hadn't taken long for him to start giving orders again, despite the fact that he had to pause to catch his breath now and then. At least the parishioners of Abbot's Cove were going to be spared his dictatorial manner from the pulpit for a while, she thought uncharitably, immediately guilty that it was her own father she was thinking about in such a way. Jessie wondered if all vicars were like him. She hadn't met any others, but she was probably going to do so now.

Her mother had found the pad and pencil and was preparing to take notes. She was so obedient, Jessie thought resentfully, wondering where all this criticism inside herself was coming from. Right now she should be glad that her father was going to recover, and so she was – of course she was – but if she had half-hoped that some ethereal revelation was going to soften his attitude, she was obviously mistaken. You didn't change a person's nature so quickly, no matter what happened to them. And through it all, she knew that her father would have had the utmost faith in whatever God had meant for him. He wasn't meant to die, so he was simply carrying on. You had to respect that, and she did.

Impulsively she bent and kissed his cheek, just as her mother had done. And then she looked into his eyes. She felt her face go hot as, for some reason, the memory of last night's dream swept into her mind. She pushed it away. She didn't want to remember it. She didn't want to associate Will with such a dream, not her sweet, gentlemanly Will...

'Why don't you go and get some fresh air, Jessie?' Thomas said steadily. 'Your mother and I have things to discuss, and it may take a little time, and this is no place for a young girl.'

Didn't young girls get sick and die? What about the brave young girls who had gone to war alongside the young men? What about those who had served as nurses and had seen unspeakable things that no young girl should ever see? So many questions. So

232

many that were impossible to answer. And where was God at such times...?

She found herself stumbling out of the little private room, unsure why she should be getting so upset, nor why all these introspective questions should keep troubling her. Was it all to do with last night and the dream? But it hadn't been real. It was just a dream. She hadn't *actually* lain in a bed with Will Tremayne, arms and bodies entwined – and *fornicated.*

The ugly word that occasionally formed part of one of her father's particularly harsh sermons entered her mind before she could stop it. She gave a small sob, and rushed through the hospital corridors and into the sunlight, breathing in the fragrant air of morning, and knew she could hardly bear to think of Will again. Something terrible had somehow come between them, and he didn't even know it.

If she had been even more foolish and susceptible to omens, she might have imagined that all this was a price she had to pay for her father's recovery. That God – that wise, all-seeing God – had decided that Jessie Penwarden and Will Tremayne were heading towards the kind of situation that Rita Levant had found herself in, and that this was the way to stop it. If she were that foolish...

'Are you unwell, dear?' she heard a voice say as she leant against the hospital wall, and she focused her eyes on the middle-aged woman beside her, armed with a bunch of flowers to take into the hospital for someone she knew.

'I'm just taking a breather, thank you,' she stuttered.

The woman spoke sympathetically. 'Hospitals can make you feel a little faint, can't they? But where would we be without them?'

She moved on without waiting for an answer, and Jessie told herself not to be so stupid. The woman was right. Where would they be without hospitals and the doctors and nurses who made people better? Where would her father be without this one? She steeled herself to go back inside, only to meet her mother coming out to find her.

'The doctor is with your father now, Jessie, so I was sent out of the room while they discussed his progress, though I'm not sure who'll be doing most of the discussing,' Ellen said with a half-smile. 'I must say he looks a little better than I expected this morning, and ready to reorganise his daily routine – at least temporarily. It's obviously going to be a while before he's back in the pulpit. If it was only his broken arm I'm sure he'd insist on it, but the heart attack is an altogether different matter. Even if it was not a serious one, he knows he'll have to take it easy for a while, and he's already resigned to a period of recuperation.'

'That doesn't sound like Dad,' Jessie commented. 'He'll hate having to sit around while other people do his work for him.'

'Then he'll just have to obey orders, won't he?' Ellen said. 'Anyway, once we get back home there are various people I have to contact, including the bishop. For the time being, I have to ask old Mr Jameson to take over your father's duties, but that won't suit the church powers for long, of course.'

'Why not? He's the verger, so why can't he do the job for as long as necessary?'

Ellen sighed. 'Because as soon as the bishop has been informed they will arrange for a temporary vicar to be sent to us. He'll have to live in, and to take over all of your father's duties until he's well enough to do them himself.'

'Live with us, do you mean?' Jessie echoed. 'I don't like the sound of that at all, Mum – and nor will Dad.'

The prospect of a strange vicar person living at the vicarage, and probably clashing with her father on all matters, didn't exactly appeal. Most likely, it would be some older, retired vicar, doing a spell of duty when required, muddling about in her father's study, reorganising his papers and books and sending her father slowly mad...

'You have to remember, Jessie, that we live in a church house, and that if the present incumbent is unwell, we are sent whoever is available to cover his duties. Just be thankful it is no more serious than that.'

'You mean that if Dad had died, we'd be thrown out on the street,' she said baldly.

'I'm sure it wouldn't be quite as brutal as that.'

'But that's what would happen, isn't it?' Jessie persisted.

And just how fast would it have been if her darkest and unworthy thoughts were really true, that the stalwart vicar of Abbot's Cove had tried to end his own life by throwing himself over the cliff? There would have been little respect for him then, and none, by default, for his family.

'It won't happen, Jessica. Your father will get

well, and everything will be as before,' Ellen said calmly. 'Now, let's go inside and find out what the doctor has said.'

Jessie willed the unworthy thoughts out of her head. If her father hadn't gone to pieces when Adam had been killed, what reason was there for him to do so now? Although, young as she had been at the time, she remembered hearing whispered words about delayed shock that could suddenly affect a person years after any actual event. She shivered, and followed her mother back to the hospital room where her father lay back on his pillows, looking more irritated than ill.

'Well, that's it. The damn fool doctor says I must stay here for at least two weeks, on account of my high blood pressure confusing things.'

'You won't do yourself any good by getting angry about it,' Ellen said sharply, knowing how much this had irked him by his language.

'I know that,' he snapped. 'What I need you to do is to get home as soon as possible, and do the things I've asked you to do. You can also let everybody know I'm not at death's door, and that I expect to be back among them as soon as I'm let out of this prison. You don't need to stay here and mollycoddle me. There are enough nurses for that. Just come back tomorrow and let me know everything's been set in motion. That's all I ask, Ellen.'

Only at the last did his voice waver ever so slightly.

'Our plan was to stay here all day,' Ellen said uncertainly. 'Mrs Tremayne said she would give us a hot meal tonight and then her son would drive us home.'

'You don't need to be beholden to these people. I'd rather you got an early bus home and did as I asked.'

As Jessie opened her mouth to protest, her mother put her hand on her arm and gave it a small squeeze.

'If that's what you want, then that's what we'll do, my dear,' she said gently. 'I'll be back tomorrow with all the news.'

'Good,' Thomas said, seemingly pacified. 'But there's no need for you to come as well, Jessie. There are folk in the village needing the chemist's services, and there's nothing you can do here.'

She wanted to say that she'd come with her mother, of course she would. But he was right. What good could they do to be here every day, other than to be the butt of his increasing bad temper? She murmured a reply, and then they both kissed him and left him to get the rest he had been ordered.

'He'll have been given something to help him sleep,' Ellen said positively. 'I could see his eyes starting to droop, and it's better so. Now then, Jess. I'll get the bus, and you had better go to see Mrs Tremayne and tell her what's happening. Stay for Will to bring you home if you like, and I'll let Mr Price know that you'll be back to work tomorrow.'

'But you won't want to be home on your own,' she protested.

'It won't worry me, love. There are times when you don't need anyone else's company, even those you love best, and I've plenty to keep me busy for your father.'

Seeing the way she avoided eye contact now, Jessie realised she really wanted it that way, maybe to have a quiet weep with no one else around. Jessie knew that feeling. She had known it herself when Adam died, and she couldn't begrudge her mother that time of solitude now. She walked with her to the bus stop, gave her a quick hug, and then walked the rest of the way to Will's house, her eyes brimming with unshed tears.

CHAPTER FOURTEEN

Doris Tremayne was a warm and outgoing woman. The minute she saw Jessie walking up the path she knew the reunion with the girl's father hadn't been an altogether happy one. She dreaded what news she was going to hear as she opened the door to Jessie and simply opened her arms to her.

'I'm all right, really,' Jessie finally said.

The tears had dried now and she was sitting in the Tremayne house with the ever ready cup of tea in her hands, having explained that Ellen had felt she needed to go home.

'I'm sure Dad's going to recover, given time,' she went on with a gulp, 'and this is just the reaction to it all. Mum and I were trying so hard to be strong for each other, and now each of us is on our own.'

'You're never on your own, Jessie, dear. We're not such a churchgoing family as yours, but we all turn to prayer when we need it, and I'm sure God gives special favours to the people He values, such as vicars.'

It was a clumsy speech and she said it all without thinking, but it brought a smile to Jessie's lips.

'I'm sure God would value somebody like you, Mrs Tremayne,' she said, and then blushed at being so forward to an older woman.

She felt awkward, wondering what she was going to do here for the rest of the day. It might be better if she got the next bus back to Abbot's Cove and went back to work. Mr Price wouldn't condemn her for being late, and Ellen would surely have called in at the chemist's with the news, so by now the word would have spread that Vicar Penwarden was going to be in hospital for a while.

She cleared her throat, thinking of a way to say as much without appearing ungrateful for the hospitality she and Ellen had been shown here.

'I expect you'll be finding it odd to have idle hands,' Doris went on. 'It's no bother to me if you want to take a stroll around, Jessie, since it's such a fine day. It's a blowy one as well, and I shall be busy washing the sheets and getting them on the line, so you just do whatever you've got a mind to.'

'I'll help if you like.'

'Oh no, you don't want to do that!'

'But I do. You're right, I'm not used to being idle. My father always says idleness is the Devil's way of making a body think of ways of getting into mischief. He has some very strong opinions,' she added lamely.

Doris laughed. 'And they're not always opinions that you share, I daresay, and being a dutiful daughter you probably wouldn't argue with him. But since he's not here, you can be as idle as you like, my dear, so you just choose what you want to do.'

'Then I'll help with the washing,' Jessie said promptly.

'All right, so when you've finished your tea you can help me strip the beds. I don't hold with the old notion of washing on Mondays, ironing on Tuesdays and a thorough house cleaning on Wednesdays. When things need to be done, they get done, and the Devil can go to – well, the devil!' she said with a chuckle.

She was like a breath of fresh air, thought Jessie. She was just what she needed to get over the anxiety of what had happened to her father, and the torment she still suffered over last night's dream. Temporarily, anyway.

But it was more than a little poignant to be taking the sheets and pillowcase off Will's bed, unable to stop remembering ... but in a way it was cathartic too. Stripping the bed helped to strip away everything that had happened between them in the dream, as did helping Will's mum put clean bedding on it and then close the door to the room. Next was the box room where Ellen had slept, and finally Doris's own room. Here was the double bed that had once held Doris and her husband before he ran off with his French tart. Jessie tried not to let her thoughts go in that direction, or the agony it must have brought to Doris and her young son at the time, and made herself think of her help as something she was doing in repayment for this woman's hospitality.

Will came home soon after midday to the extraordinary sight of his mother and Jessie Penwarden struggling to get a double sheet over the washing line in the blustery wind that had sprung up, the two of them laughing like lunatics as the heavy wet cotton repeatedly slapped against their faces and arms.

'Come and help, Will,' Doris gasped. 'The blessed thing got caught in the mangle rollers and we had to yank it out and it's still sopping wet.'

He stared at Jessie, her hair slipping out of its pins, flying about in a wayward manner on her neck and shoulders now, and thought he had never seen anything so beautiful or so desirable. And although she looked startled to see him she was also much more relaxed than she had been last night, despite the effort she and his mother were obviously putting in to control the double sheet.

'Is Jessie your skivvy now?' he said with a grin, not knowing what else to say as he took one end of the sheet and deftly wound it around his arm while he tried to control it and heave it over the line.

'Don't be so rude, Will,' his mother said. 'She offered to help me and we were doing all right until the wind caught the blessed thing.'

It suddenly whipped up a little more fiercely, and this time the end of the wet sheet caught Will full in the face. The two women gave up trying to assist and just stood laughing helplessly as he tried to manoeuvre it back onto the line.

'Give us a hand, Jess,' he yelled. 'This is supposed to be women's work!'

It was enough to make her fold her arms and take a step backwards, her eyes sparkling with mischief.

'Oh, really? Well, since you men always think

yourselves so superior, I thought you'd be able to manage it far better than we could!'

'You tell him, Jess,' Doris said, clearly enjoying the banter between them.

But finally it was done and the lines of freshly laundered bedding billowed in the breeze as they all went indoors. 'What are you doing home so early, anyway?' Doris asked her son.

'There's not much on for me today, so Mr Spencer said I might as well take the rest of the day off rather than hang about the yard. I thought your mother would be here as well.'

'She went home on the bus. There are things she has to do for my dad since he'll be in hospital for a few weeks, but he's on the mend, thank you for asking.'

She didn't mean to be sarcastic, but she was all too aware of how awkward she felt with him now. He didn't know why, and nor did she ever intend telling him, but it had created a small barrier between them all the same.

'Well then,' he said at last, sensing the atmosphere. 'Whenever you want to go, I'll drive you home.'

His mother intervened at once. 'Now Will, where are your manners? We don't have to get rid of Jessie so quickly. She'll stay and have a meal with us later, just as we'd planned.'

'I won't stay if you don't mind, Mrs Tremayne,' Jessie said quickly. 'Mum will be needing me, so now that Will's here, I'd rather go whenever he's ready if it's not putting you out.'

'Of course it's not, my dear,' Doris replied. 'You'll be visiting your dad in hospital now and again, I daresay, and you're welcome to come here any time. We'll be glad to hear he's doing well.'

'Thank you,' she murmured.

She sat beside Will in the car, neither of them saying anything for a while. The last time they had been together it had been so sweet, so companionable, and now she felt as though she was sitting beside a stranger, and it was all her fault. Or rather, all the fault of that stupid dream that she still couldn't get out of her head. Not so much the dream itself, but the embarrassment of it all.

'I can't decide which is the more enticing image,' he said at last, clearly trying to break the ice. 'Thinking of you sleeping in my bed last night while I found it hard to close my eyes on the sofa – or the image of you getting all entangled in a wet sheet this morning!'

'*Don't*, please,' she said tightly.

'So what have I done?' he asked, keeping his eyes straight ahead.

She flinched. 'You haven't done anything. I'm just worried about my dad, that's all, and I can't think of anything else right now.'

'And that's all that's upsetting you?'

'Isn't that enough?' she flared out. 'My dad could have died, falling over that cliff the way he did, and you think I can be bothered with anything else?'

'Well, he didn't die, and by all accounts he's not going to. It was an accident, Jess, and accidents happen. It's not as if he threw himself over, is it?'

When she didn't answer he glanced at her, his eyes widening.

'My God, is that what you think?'

'I don't *know*. I don't want to think it, but I don't know.'

Will drove the car onto the grass verge and turned off the engine. He caught hold of her hands, looking into her troubled eyes.

'Well, you bloody well ought to know. He's your father and you should know him well enough to know he would never do such a thing. He's a vicar, for God's sake.'

'Oh, and you think that makes him different from any other man on the planet when he's got problems?' she said passionately. 'He went through hell when my brother was killed, and I don't think he ever got over it. He may have bottled it up for all these years, but you can't do that for ever, can you? I know he's had it on his mind ever since that awful friend of Mum's came to visit, and who's to say it hadn't tipped him over the edge – literally, as it happens.'

He was angry now. 'I think you're the one who's torturing yourself. Your dad had a heart attack and a fall, and he broke his arm. Why can't you take things at face value instead of looking for hidden meanings all the time?'

'Like in dreams?' she said, before she could stop herself.

'What's that supposed to mean? He's not dead, and if you dreamt that he was, then it proves that dreams are just that and no more. They can't prophesy the future.'

She hadn't realised how fast she was breathing,

nor how tightly she was clinging on to his hands now. She didn't realise it until he leant forward and pressed a soft kiss on her cheek, and imperceptibly she pulled back.

'I think I'd better just take you home,' Will said in a flat voice. 'Don't forget you're welcome at my home at any time, but if I don't see you before, I'll try to come down sometime over the weekend to see how things are.'

'All right. But leave me at Rita's. She's got my bike at her house and I'll ride home from there.'

He drove the rest of the way in silence, and Jessie was filled with misery. He'd be thinking she was some silly kid now, steeped in superstition and omens and the meaning of dreams. He'd probably be wishing he'd never met her at all, and she had brought it all on herself. He couldn't know how disturbed she was about the dream, or his part in it.

They parted without a word and she walked up Rita's path with her heart full. She didn't how it had all happened, but she knew that nothing was ever going to be the same between them again. He probably wouldn't even come to see her at the weekend, and she would have lost him for ever.

She would have preferred to go round the back of the house and collect her bike, but she could hardly do that without letting Mrs Levant know she had taken it. As she glanced in the kitchen window, Rita's mother saw her at once and called out to her to come in.

'How are you, love?' she said at once, swivelling her wheelchair around to greet her as she hovered at the door. 'I know your mum's back, and the word's already gone round the village that your dad's going to be all right, so that's good news, isn't it?'

Jessie nodded numbly. 'It is, Mrs Levant, but I won't stop to chat if you don't mind. I'm on my way home now to see what Mum needs doing. Tell Rita I'm back, won't you?'

She didn't wait for anything more, not wanting to be probed with questions, however kindly meant. She couldn't stop thinking about Will's harsh, sensible words that she should take her dad's fall at face value and not look for hidden meanings. Perhaps she did that far too much. Perhaps she should take life as it came, the way Rita's mother did. The way Rita did.

She cycled home, trying not to catch the glance of any passer-by who would want to know the latest news on her dad. As if she would know any more than her mother did. All she wanted was to be inside the four safe walls of the vicarage and not have to speak to anyone. She flung her bike down in the front garden and rushed inside, slamming the door behind her.

At the sound, Ellen came through from her husband's office with a startled look on her face.

'Good heavens, Jessie, there's no need to knock the door down,' she said. 'And how did you get here so soon? I didn't expect you until much later today.'

It should have been obvious that Ellen was too busy with her own thoughts to realise how callous she sounded. And Jessie was in far too vulnerable a state to take it into account. All she

247

saw was her mother's cross face and the bundle of papers in her hands, and the next minute she had burst into ridiculous, shaming tears. Ellen put down the papers and took her daughter in her arms.

'Hush now, my dear, your dad's going to be all right. It will just take a little time, that's all. There's no need to get so upset.'

Jessie could hardly say that she hadn't been giving her father a second thought at that moment, so she sniffed back the tears noisily.

'I know. It's just coming home and knowing he's not here,' she mumbled. 'Will came home early, by the way, and I just wanted to be here, that's all.'

Ellen spoke more briskly. 'Well, you can go and make us a cup of tea while I finish what I was doing. I'll say one thing for your father. He's always so efficient, and everything's in order in his study. I've already seen the verger about taking over the Sunday services for now, and I'm about to telephone the bishop to see if we should have a temporary replacement from another parish.'

Jessie gave a small smile. 'I'd say you were the efficient one now, Mum.'

'We all are when something needs to be done. Now shoo, Jessie. I'm still parched from being stopped by half the village wanting to know what's happened, so go and make that tea, my lamb.'

She did as she was told. She was a child again, obeying orders. And it was so much easier than being grown-up and having to deal with emotions she didn't fully understand. It was so much easier to revert back to the time when she was a small girl, looking up adoringly at her big brother with his proud boast that he was going to fly aeroplanes one day... The tears almost threatened to choke her again, and she steeled herself, knowing that breaking down wasn't going to do her mother any good at all. They had to be strong for each other now.

She made the tea and took it through to her father's study where her mother was momentarily gazing out of the window, and she knew she was right. They had to be strong for each other. Then Ellen turned around, and for the first time Jessie detected the tiny spark of uncertainty in her face.

'Thanks for doing that, love. I'm still putting off the moment when I speak to the bishop. Silly, isn't it? I know it's got to be done, but once it is, it will seem so final, almost as if we're pushing your father out.'

'But Dad asked you to do this, didn't he?' Jessie said.

'Oh yes. He called it procedure, and you know what he is for doing the right thing.'

'You have to do it, then, don't you?' Jessie said, feeling oddly that she was taking over the initiative.

Ellen smiled, sensing the small reversal in their roles at that moment.

'Of course I do. When I've drunk my tea.'

Before the end of the afternoon, the new order was in place, and the bishop had told Ellen he would be arranging for a temporary vicar to take over Vicar Penwarden's duties in two weeks' time. It would naturally be a living-in position. Even if Thomas was out of hospital by then, he would need to take some time recuperating from the heart attack, to say nothing of having his right arm still in plaster for several more weeks.

Jessie deliberately refused to think about Will. She would be helping her mother arrange the spare room for the unknown vicar, and hoped he wouldn't be too much of a fuddy-duddy. Sometimes, an old, retired vicar was wheeled in as a temporary measure on these occasions, she thought irreverently.

She began to feel in need of some fresh air and with her mother's agreement she went down to the village to inform Mr Price that she'd be back at work the next day. It was nearly closing time at the chemist's shop, and he was fussily sympathetic about her father, and even Vera was less abrasive than usual.

'So I'll be back to work tomorrow, Mr Price,' Jessie finished, unable to listen to their pious remarks for too long. 'Mum will go to see Dad in the afternoon, but there's no point in both of us going, until the weekend, anyway.'

There was something else that was supposed to happen at the weekend, but she tried not to think about that. Family came first.

'I'm sure he's in the best of hands,' Harold said, but by then he was talking to thin air as she went hurriedly out of the shop.

She hadn't expected the general smell of the chemist's shop to remind her so vividly of the hospital, and it had taken her so much by surprise that she had to breathe deeply as she went outside and close her eyes for a few seconds.

'Are you all right, Jessie?' she heard a voice say.

Was everyone in creation going to ask her the same question from now on? she thought in a mild panic. And then she saw that it was Rita, slithering off her bike and peering into her face.

'Of course I am, and thanks for taking my bike to your house. I took it home earlier today,' she said inanely.

'How are things?'

'If by things, you mean my dad, I'm sure you've heard the news on the village grapevine. He's going to be all right, and we're having a spare part staying at the vicarage for a while.'

'Crikey, Jess, don't bite my head off! I only asked if you were all right. So did you stay at the hospital last night?' When Jessie didn't reply immediately, she went on. 'Well, did you or didn't you? I know you didn't come home, because I went to your place to see if you were back. So where did you stay?'

'Look, can we walk down to the cove or are you in a hurry to get home?'

Knowing what Rita's response was likely to be, this was hardly the right place to reveal to Rita exactly where she had spent last night, with people still out and about in the village.

'I can spare ten minutes, but I need to get back to cook our tea. Mum was feeling a bit off colour this morning, and Dad's less than useless in the kitchen.'

Their domestic arrangements were all going over Jessie's head. They hurried on down to the cove, finding it far less welcoming than usual.

251

The wind was gusty, blowing sand into their faces and eyes, and making it feel gritty against their skin. Rita shivered, wrapping her cardigan around her more closely.

'Where did summer go?' she grumbled. 'We could have picked a better spot, so let's make it snappy, shall we? So what did happen last night?'

Jess felt a touch of the devil inside her as she answered. 'I slept in Will's bed.'

It was just as well she hadn't made the bald statement outside the chemist's shop, or Rita's screech would have been heard from one end of the village to the other. As it was, it was partly carried away on a gust of wind as Rita flung down her bike, grabbed Jessie's arms and spun her around to face her, almost knocking each other over on the sliding sand as a result.

'You're kidding!' Rita shrieked.

'No, I'm not. He wasn't in it, of course,' Jessie said, as soon as she could catch her breath.

'So how did it happen? And where was he? Come on, you've got to tell me everything now!'

It sounded far less exciting when she explained that it had been too late to catch the bus home from Penzance, and that she had persuaded her mother to seek hospitality at Will Tremayne's house.

'I can't imagine your mum agreeing to that.'

'She didn't have much choice, unless we walked home, and neither of us could have faced that. So we asked Mrs Tremayne if she knew of anywhere we could stay for the night, and of course, she said we must stay with them.'

Her eyes blurred for a moment, and she couldn't

252

have said whether it was with the memory of that blissful dream, or the sting of the sand in her eyes.

'So what were the sleeping arrangements, then?' Rita persisted, with a gleam in her eyes as she was clearly hoping for something erotic.

Jessie shrugged. 'Nothing like you're thinking. It's not a very big house, but I think they once had an evacuee staying there during the war so there's a bed in the box room, and Mum slept there. Will was turfed out of his room to sleep on the sofa and I had his room. That's all there is to it.'

Rita finally let go of Jessie's arms so fast that she almost stumbled again.

'And I bet you spent the whole night wishing he was there with you!'

'Of course I didn't. We'd just taken my dad to hospital, in case you've forgotten, and I was too worried about what was happening to him to think about anything else.'

Rita picked up her bike again and shook her head slowly as they turned to go back up the cove to the main road again.

'My God, Jess, sometimes I think you're not normal. You'd seen your dad safely into hospital by then and you couldn't do anything more, so don't tell me you didn't spare a single thought to where you were – or hope that Will might come sneaking in at any minute.'

'You're mad,' Jessie said flatly. 'I didn't think any such thing. And even if I had, both our mothers were in the house. I did dream about him, though.'

'I knew it!' Rita said triumphantly. 'I bet it

wasn't the kind of innocent dream you've had about him before, either. Come on, Jess, was it?'

She grinned, giving in. 'Not exactly. But you're not getting anything else out of me, so give up trying.'

Rita hugged her arm. At this rate, she'd be black and blue, Jessie thought.

'I'd say you're pretty normal after all, then,' Rita said.

She was still smiling when she got home again, telling herself she had let things get all out of proportion by fretting over the dream. It was only a dream, brought on by unusual circumstances. It didn't mean she was turning into some kind of vamp. Will had said that dreams couldn't foretell the future. She hoped this one did, though, and she'd be a fool if she thought otherwise.

Ellen had some more news for her.

'I've telephoned the hospital, and your father's more comfortable now, but they're still worried about his blood pressure, so they won't be letting him home for a while. I shall go and see him again tomorrow, but there's no need for you to come until the weekend, Jessie. You'll need to get back to work, and for us to behave as normally as possible.'

Jessie couldn't hide a small feeling of relief that she wasn't expected to go to the hospital every day. It was a place that made people well, but there was an undeniable sense of anxiety about it too. She found herself wondering how many tales it could tell if it could speak, or if hospital walls actually held memories – or was she being completely crazy now? But she soon learnt that it wasn't the only bit of news Ellen had for her.

'The bishop rang me again to give me the name of the man they're sending down to us. He's called Stephen Daley and he told me he was an army padre during the war. The bishop speaks very highly of him, and says he's a likeable and sympathetic person.'

Jessie didn't want to know anything about the man in advance, although it was natural that the bishop would keep them informed. While he was just some nameless person who would be arriving at some vague date, she could cope with it all. But now he had a name. He was real – and Vicar Stephen Daley sounded like a bit of a saint. It didn't make her feel any more comfortable to know he'd been an army padre during the war, either, and she wondered what Ellen thought about that. Might it not make him want to talk about some of his wartime experiences? He might even bring them into his sermons.

It could stir up even more memories that were still painful for her family to face, because of Adam. And she still wasn't completely sure it hadn't been Olive Glyn's brash and thoughtless remarks that had contributed to her father's state of mind before his heart attack. Too many uneasy possibilities kept bubbling over inside her, and she couldn't seem to rid herself of them.

'I wish he hadn't been an army padre,' she burst out. 'Couldn't we have had someone else?'

Ellen looked at her steadily. 'I can see what you're thinking, Jessie, but it may even help your father in some way. He's never been able to talk about Adam properly, but he may be able to open up to this new man.'

'Wouldn't you mind if he did so, when he's managed to shut us out of his real feelings all this time?'

She hadn't meant to say as much, and it seemed to slight her mother more than herself. She bit her lip, seeing Ellen's face tighten.

'Let's just wait and see, shall we, dear? The most important thing is that your father returns home fully recovered. Apart from that, nothing else matters.'

Jessie just managed to restrain herself from saying a pious *Amen*. But somehow she wasn't in the mood for the faint sense of holiness in her mother's reaction right now – and there was one more thing. She knew perfectly well that she wasn't going to like this Vicar Stephen Daley.

CHAPTER FIFTEEN

Will had every intention of driving down to Abbot's Cove as he had promised, in the hope that things had settled down between him and Jessie by then. It wasn't always easy for a chap to know what went on in a girl's head, but he hoped that being apart for a couple of days might have solved whatever bee she had got in her bonnet. But then everything changed.

Late on Saturday morning a small parcel was delivered to the Tremayne house. They couldn't make out the stamps and the smudgy postmark, but his mother's name and address were written in an unfamiliar handwriting that neither of them recognised.

'Perhaps somebody's sending you an early Christmas present,' Will said.

'Well, if they have, I can't imagine who it could be,' Doris replied, searching for scissors to cut the string and open the brown-paper parcel.

And then her face went white and her eyes widened in complete shock and disbelief at the contents. There was a shabby case containing a pair of glasses, a military medal that could have done with a bit of cleaning, an old pocket watch and several well-thumbed books, all wrapped in a man's jersey.

'My God, who's done this?' Will raged now. 'It must be some kind of sick joke to send such rubbish through the post. Give it here, Mum, and I'll throw it all in the dustbin.'

'*No*, don't do that. Can't you see who these things belong to, Will?'

He stared at her, seeing the way her eyes were welling up and he sensed the way her heart seemed to be beating so fast, and then he gasped.

'Not *Dad*,' he said in a cracked voice.

'There's a letter as well,' Doris whispered. 'You'll have to read it to me, Will. I'm too jittery to see it properly.'

She sat down heavily on a chair with the man's jersey clutched in her hands. Will could sense the raw emotion in his normally well-adjusted mother now. Whatever he had felt at the time when his father walked out on them, he knew she was suffering, trying to anticipate the contents of the letter as he drew it out of the envelope. He glanced at the signature first. It wasn't from his father, as he had almost desperately hoped it might be. It was from a woman called Madeleine Dupont. A Frenchwoman.

As he quickly scanned the page, the first thing that spun through his mind was that the woman they always thought of as his dad's French tart clearly had an excellent command of English. The letter was addressed directly to his mother, and after a few moments when he had to get his throat working properly, he read it aloud slowly, although he almost choked at the first few words.

'*To Mrs Tremayne, dear friend,*
Forgive me for addressing you this way but I almost feel that I know you, and your son, since I heard so

much about you over the years from the man we both loved. Yes, I say that frankly and unashamedly. I did love Ted Tremayne with all my heart, and if it is any reassurance at all to you he always regretted the pain he must have caused you both by leaving you.

But, my dear Mrs Tremayne, I must also tell you that Ted has lived in a terrible twilight world for the last few years. He was severely wounded during the war and lost much of his memory as well as other functions which I find too painful and delicate to divulge. I gave up my own work to act as his companion and his nurse for all that time, until the good Lord finally saw fit to end his suffering and take him to his rest.

I lost him two months ago, and it was a blessed release for him. Only now have I found the courage to write to you and send you a few of his belongings. There is nothing else of value. I felt that I owed it to you to let you know what has happened, and if you ever want to reply, or to visit the place where he now lies in peace, I would welcome you and your son wholeheartedly.

Yours in grief,
Madeleine Dupont.'

Will's face was almost black with anger as he finished reading the letter, and he hardly dared look at his mother. When she made no response he finally glanced at her. She sat ashen and motionless and then held out her hand for the letter.

'You don't want to read it,' he said harshly. 'I should burn it together with this other trash.'

Doris shook her head. 'I want to see it, Will.'

259

She read it silently, her throat working as she took in all that she was being told. She had long ago lost any love she had for Ted Tremayne, but it was harder to forget the heady memories of their early years together. And it was clear that this woman had loved him too. It was written in every heartbroken word. She knew Will was watching her anxiously, and she could feel the burning anger in him, plus the simmering resentment for the woman who had taken his father away. But Ted hadn't been forced to go. He had wanted to go to her, more than he'd wanted to stay with them. A young son could forgive many things, but Doris knew he could never forgive that.

'What are you thinking, Mum? What are you going to do? After all this time, it's cruel of her to get in touch like this,' he burst out.

Doris took a shuddering breath. 'No, it's not cruel. She's trying to make amends in her own way. It closes a chapter in all our lives, and I'm not going to do anything.'

'Well, I've certainly got no wish to go and see where he's buried. Leave it to her to put flowers on his grave if she wants to.'

'Will, stop it. He was your father and now he's dead. It's been a shock for both of us, but we should have a little compassion for her too.'

He couldn't let this go. 'He should have been sending you money all this time. There must be money owing to you now. I should see a solicitor and see what's to be done about it. It's not right that she should have everything.'

But he had underestimated his mother. She had

260

been so calm ... but without warning she suddenly began screaming at him, pummelling his chest as he tried to restrain her.

'No, I won't have it, Will! Do you think I want anything of him now? To have his leftovers? And I hardly think she's had an easy time of it, being his companion and his nurse. She doesn't say what horrors they have both been through from the time he was badly wounded. It has probably been a living death for both of them all this time. So what we are going to do is to let sleeping dogs lie. I won't hear of you going to a solicitor, or trying to find out anything more, do you understand me?'

'Yes, *all right*. For God's sake, Mum, you're scaring me now! Sit down and take some deep breaths before you pass out.'

He had never seen her like this before. Whatever else he had thought about doing that day flew out of his head in his concern for her now. He was seriously out of his depth. She looked old and ill and she was shivering violently. He felt helpless and impotent, knowing she needed a doctor – or at the very least another woman to understand her feelings.

'Mum,' he said urgently, 'I'm going to fetch Mrs Greenaway to sit with you and then I'm going to fetch the doctor. You're not to do anything until I get back, do you understand?'

He rushed out of the house without waiting for an answer. His mum had helped Mrs Greenaway when Des had been killed at the farm, and she would be the one to give his mother whatever comfort she could. He had no idea what that might be. They hadn't spoken about Will's father for years, and he didn't know whether or not she still loved him. She might even start to feel relief that she was finally rid of her two-timing husband for ever. And by God, he never wanted to know one way or the other, he thought furiously.

He banged on Mrs Greenaway's door, gasping out the news that his mum needed her, and then tore off to get the doctor. He couldn't think of anything else but the fact that it really was just the two of them now, and his feelings towards the woman who had sent the letter from France were nothing short of murderous.

To his relief Mrs Greenaway said she would come at once, and was prepared to stay with Will's mother as long as she was needed. Which was just as well, since the doctor eventually said she was in danger of a complete collapse and needed rest and care until she recovered from her shock.

'You'll need to go to work on Monday, Will,' the neighbour said firmly, once Doris had been sedated and sent to bed. 'Your mum won't want you muddling up the house here, and I'll be here to look after her and cook your meals. I can stay as long as you like, since there's nobody at home for me to worry about now.'

'I didn't think she still cared about him,' Will muttered, unable to shake off the way the news had affected his mother so badly.

'They had a history, my dear, even before you were born, and that's what she'll be remembering now. She'll remember the happy times, not the bad ones.'

'Well, this French woman's letter should have been enough to make her think of the bad times!' he said angrily. 'It was all her fault.'

Mrs Greenaway shook her head sadly. 'It's never just one person's fault, Will. It takes two to make a marriage, and three to break it. The blame wasn't all on this Dupont woman's side. If you want to blame anything, blame the war. Blame Adolf Hitler. If it hadn't been for the war, your father would never have gone to France, and I'm sure none of this would have happened.'

He realised she was avoiding his eyes as she spoke and he replied sharply.

'But you *do* think it might have happened anyway, don't you? Do you know something I don't, Mrs Greenaway?'

She sighed. 'I only know that men who have a roving eye will always have it wherever they are, and I'm saying nothing more. Now let me get us both a cup of something hot and then you go and tinker with your motorbike or your car or whatever you young lads do, and try to stay calm for your mother's sake, Will.'

He couldn't get anything else out of her, and like an automaton he did as he was told as he tried to get used to the idea that his father was dead. All this time, he realised that in the back of his mind – his stupid, juvenile mind– was the thought that one day his dad would come home again, smiling and youthful, picking his boy up in his arms and swinging him around the way he used to when Will was knee-high to a grasshopper. The teasing old phrase he hadn't thought of in years made the unmanly tears start to his own eyes and he blundered outside to the back garden with his mug of cocoa, where nobody could see his distress.

Was this the way it felt when someone got bad news during the war? When a dreaded yellow telegram came, telling them that a loved one had been wounded or killed in action? But those injuries or deaths had been honourable, the stark, yet dignified words informing wives and mothers and sweethearts what had happened. Letting them hold their heads up high for the heroes their menfolk had been. While his father's death had been mindless and lingering, if he had read between the lines correctly, in a foreign country, cared for by a woman who was his nurse and companion, and nothing more.

For a fleeting moment the image of Jessie Penwarden flashed into his mind, sweet and lovely and wholesome. She had lost someone too. She had told him about her brother Adam who had died a hero's death, blown out of the sky while doing his duty for his country. And it was no solace to Will that his father's injuries, however horrific, had been caused by the same war, because to him there was no comparison.

There had been no noble telegram, no uplifting letter from some unknown commanding officer, nothing, until now. A letter from his dad's French tart with a few pathetic bits of his belongings. It shamed him so much that he knew he simply couldn't face Jessie again until he had got everything straight inside his head. And God knew how long that might take.

The weekend came and went, and Jessie had accompanied her mother to the hospital, where they had been assured that her father was progressing as well as could be expected – that tired old medical phrase that was meant to be reassuring, and told you precisely nothing. Although, if Thomas's irritability from his inactivity and the frustration of having his right arm in plaster so that he was obliged to submit to too many intimacies about his person was anything to go by, he was definitely on the mend.

They had been to church as usual on Sunday morning, and reported to Thomas that the verger had done a good job, declining to mention that there had been several loud snores coming from the rear pews as Mr Jameson droned on and on. Thomas's sermons might be loud and forceful, thought Jessie, but at least his thunderous tones always kept everybody awake.

'This new vicar's probably going to be some old guy who thinks he won the war single-handed,' Jessie commented to Rita when they had a few moments together after church.

'Or he might be some dishy young bloke with film star looks,' Rita went on dreamily.

Jessie sniffed. 'Trust you to think of that. No, he'll be at least forty, if not more. He'll come down here intending to brighten our lives and convert us all, and that won't please Dad if he thinks somebody else is taking his place in the village's affection, I can tell you. It'll probably give him a relapse.'

'Don't be so daft,' Rita said with a giggle. 'Honestly, I don't know what's got into you lately,

Jess. Though I suppose you're pining because you didn't see Will yesterday.'

It wasn't that. At least, she didn't think so. She wasn't so shallow that she was going to fade away because Will Tremayne hadn't been in touch like he said he would. But he'd promised to come down to Abbot's Cove sometime over the weekend and he hadn't arrived yet. If he'd turned up while they were at the hospital, she was sure he'd have waited, or even called to give Rita a message for her, or stuck a note through the vicarage door. No, something must have happened, and she didn't know what. She clung on to that thought, rather than that he had simply got tired of her and had taken the easy way out. Which was exactly what she *was* starting to think. And who could blame him after the chilly way she had behaved the last time they met?

'I think he's definitely gone off me,' Jessie said miserably to Rita when another week had come and gone and the arrival of the temporary vicar was imminent. And still there had been no word from Will.

'Oh well, you know what they say. There are plenty more fish in the sea,' Rita said encouragingly.

'Yes, but Will was *my* fish,' Jessie said, so plaintively that they both began to laugh, until she sobered again. 'You know how much I liked him, Rita, and it was far more than just liking him. I thought he liked me in the same way.'

'Why don't you write to him, then? You could say you were sorry you missed him last Saturday, and that gives him a chance to give himself an alibi if he needs one.'

'Like I said, you've been seeing too many Hollywood pictures again.'

Rita grinned. 'Maybe I have, but why don't you do it anyway?'

'Because I wouldn't know what to say without sounding as if I was chasing him.'

'It seems to me you're both as bad as each other. He didn't turn up for what might be a perfectly good reason, and you're too stubborn to find out why.'

'Perhaps I am. Oh well, maybe I'll give it a few more days, and if I haven't heard anything by then, I'll cycle over to his house to see if everything's all right. Or maybe I won't,' she added defiantly.

As the days passed, she was still undecided about doing just that, but it all went out of her head on Wednesday evening. Her mother had gone out to one of her meetings, and Jessie was in the house alone when she heard the roar of a motorbike in the road outside, loud enough to make her heart stop. It was Will. It had to be Will, though why he had arrived on his bike instead of in the car, she couldn't think. But neither did she care. All she wanted was to see him again, and as she heard footsteps crunching on the gravel outside the front door, she flung it open, a wide smile on her face.

'Good evening to you, miss. I hope I've come to the right place. This is the vicarage, isn't it? I was expecting to see an older lady,' the stranger said with a distinct Irish accent.

Jessie couldn't speak for a moment. The sheer

disappointment that it wasn't Will standing there was briefly tempered by the thought that this was a very personable man, his shock of brown hair ruffled by the breeze. His face was tanned, his eyes very blue, and her dad would have said he was smiling back at her rather too warmly for a stranger.

'Yes, this is the vicarage,' she found herself saying inanely. 'I'm sorry, you were obviously expecting to see my mother. She won't be back until later, and my father's in hospital. I can give my mother a message if you like.'

She didn't need to give him so much information, and she didn't quite know why she had, nor why she seemed to be fumbling for words.

'I'm sorry, I seem to have given you a shock by turning up like this,' he went on more apologetically, 'especially on my usual mode of transport, since most people don't expect to see a vicar on a motorbike.'

'You're not ... good Lord, you're not Vicar Stephen Daley, are you? We weren't expecting you until sometime tomorrow.'

'As sure as God made little fishes, I'm one and the same,' the man said, still smiling. 'But if Mrs Penwarden's not here, I can go and take a look around the church until later, just to get my bearings. I'd like to leave a few things here tonight, but I'll wait until your mother returns, and I'm sure there's a hostelry in the village where I can get some refreshment in the meantime.'

'You don't need to do that, Vicar,' Jessie said quickly, feeling more foolish by the minute at the assumption that she might need a chaperone.

'Please come in and I'll make you some tea. I'm afraid we don't have anything stronger,' she added.

As he followed her inside the house, she couldn't help wondering, a mite hysterically, just how the sedate citizens of Abbot's Cove were going to take to an Irish motorbike-riding vicar who apparently liked a little tipple. But she realised he must have read her mind.

'Don't you worry about that, miss,' he said, a wicked twinkle in his eyes, 'and in case you're thinking I'm going to shock the village folk, I'll remind them that Jesus spent his time with beggars and thieves – and drinkers too, I daresay. And by the way, the name's Stephen.'

'And I'm Jessie,' she murmured, her heart giving a little lurch.

He held out his hand to shake hers. 'I'm very pleased to meet you, Jessie, and I hope we're going to get along very well, although I'm sorry for the unfortunate circumstances that bring me here, of course. How is your father?'

A short while later, Ellen Penwarden came home to the unexpected sight of her daughter and a good-looking young man sitting companionably together in the sitting room, with cups of tea and slices of her home-made fruitcake in front of them. Jessie flushed as she met her mother's eyes.

'Mum, this is our temporary vicar, Stephen Daley. He arrived a while ago just to make himself known to us and to take a look at the village. He'd like to leave a few things here tonight and move in properly tomorrow,' she added, hoping her mother wouldn't think she was being far too forward.

By now Stephen had stood up and was extending his hand to Ellen.

'I must apologise for descending on you like this, Mrs Penwarden, but I was curious to see this village that I've heard so much about from the bishop.'

'It's perfectly all right, Vicar Daley, and I can see that my daughter has been taking care of you.'

'Yes she has, and the name's Stephen, please. In fact, I would prefer it if the community called me Vicar Stephen, or even just Vic. It's what I was used to in the army and it seems less intimidating. I would like your approval, of course, so what do you think?'

Ellen was clearly taken aback and answered cautiously. 'If you think it wise, then, of course, it's your decision. But I must warn you that many of our parishioners are elderly and may not approve.'

'Ah well, if I can get the Lord's message through to some of the war-weary men in the front line, then I'm sure I can win them round,' he said easily. 'But we'll see how it goes, and meanwhile, before I turn up again tomorrow, I thought I'd drop in at the hospital and introduce myself to your husband.'

'You're not going to believe it, Rita,' Jessie said excitedly, having left the house early the next morning in time to forestall Rita before she got to work, and explained the reason why. 'He's not forty, although he's not twenty either. I reckon he's somewhere in between, and by the time he left the house he'd already got Mum eating out of his hand. Although when he turned up on a motorbike I nearly fainted. I don't know what Dad will make of him,' she added with a giggle, 'but I'm dying to find out.'

'It sounds as though you're smitten already,' Rita said in amazement.

'You'd be wrong, then! He's certainly a bit of a charmer and I'm sure people will like his Irish blarney, if that's what you call it. I'm not sure that I could take it for ever, though.'

'Well, you don't have to, do you? Once your dad gets back in harness, he'll be gone. But it was funny, him turning up just like that. I hope you asked him for some identification. I mean, he could have been anybody, couldn't he?'

Jessie tossed her head. 'I think I can spot a bad 'un when I see one, and he's certainly not that.'

Even so, she knew Rita was right. She hadn't asked Stephen for any identification. She had just taken him at face value and, thankfully, she had been right when he had eventually shown her mother the letter of introduction from the bishop, and Ellen had been perfectly satisfied with that.

'Well, that's what I thought about Des Green-away at the time,' Rita went on feelingly, 'and look what he turned out to be.'

'And now he's dead,' Jessie reminded her, 'and thank goodness you weren't left with more than you bargained for.'

Rita stared at her in annoyance. 'How did we get on to this topic of conversation?' she demanded. 'Des is in the past, and although I wouldn't have wished his end on anybody, that's where he'll stay as far as I'm concerned. But now I'm dying to have a look at this Vicar Stephen too. You never know, I might fancy him myself.'

Jessie burst out laughing. 'Oh yes? I can hardly see you as a vicar's wife!'

Rita responded by crossing both hands across her chest in a pious manner.

'I might surprise you one day. I might yet end up doing Good Works.'

'And I might yet see those pigs flying across the sky,' Jessie said dryly, as she so often did when Rita mentioned one of her wild schemes.

She was still thinking the same thing as she turned up for work at the chemist's shop a few minutes later, a smile still playing about her mouth.

'You're looking much brighter this morning, Jessie,' Harold Price greeted her. 'Have you had good news about your father? Is he coming home soon?'

She started. She hadn't given her father too much thought lately, other than to think that the house seemed agreeably quieter without him, and that was hardly the way to think about your own father, she thought guiltily!

'I don't think he'll be home for a few weeks yet, Mr Price,' she said hastily. 'He's progressing well enough, and our new vicar will be moving in with us today, so we'll be having a different kind of sermon on Sunday, I daresay.'

She knew that giving Harold Price the information would be enough to set him up for the rest of the day, knowing he could impart it to anyone who cared to listen. She also managed to hide a smile as she spoke, trying not to imagine the kind of sermon Vicar Stephen, also known as Vic, was going to deliver to the God-fearing residents of Abbot's Cove next Sunday.

CHAPTER SIXTEEN

Thomas Penwarden was not the best of patients. He had always been an active man and he hated having to be idle. Even more, he hated the fact that because of his wretched right arm being in plaster he needed help in his most basic needs. It didn't do anything for his standing in the community, where everyone in Abbot's Cove looked up to him, to hear the nurses commenting cheerfully that he shouldn't be embarrassed, and that they had seen plenty of personals before.

But not *his* personals, he said savagely to himself, not dignifying the words by saying them out loud. He knew by now that he was not supposed to get upset about anything, since it just sent his blood pressure soaring, and made the doctors tut-tut and mutter about keeping him here even longer if he didn't calm down. He had always thought it better to explode in anger than to keep things bottled up, for other people, anyway, he conceded. As far as his son's death was concerned, he had bottled up his grief and anger inside himself for far too long, and he knew it.

He was lying in bed, contemplating the doctor's next visit when he heard the door open. There was no privacy here either, he raged. Private room or public ward, people came and went whenever they pleased. There was really no reason for him to be kept isolated anymore. He'd been told he wasn't in imminent danger now of needing urgent treatment, but thankfully they hadn't moved him yet. He felt guilty even as he thought it, knowing that a man of the cloth should feel able to talk to the other patients in the ward in need of reassurance. It was just that right now he didn't feel up to the job, and maybe he was the one needing reassurance for a change...

'Vicar Penwarden?' he heard a voice say while he was still brooding over what new indignities he was about to be put through.

'Of course I am, unless there's been a miracle overnight,' he said sarcastically, not bothering to look up. 'What do you want now? More tests?'

He heard the visitor cough, and he turned his head sharply. The man wasn't wearing a white hospital coat and he didn't recognise him. And then he unwound the scarf from around his neck and Thomas saw the clerical collar. Before he could gather the questions in his mind, the man strode across to the bed and held out his left hand.

'It's a pleasure to meet you, sir, except that I'm sure we'd both rather it wasn't like this. Vicar Stephen Daley at your service ... literally, as it happens. You'll have seen the letter from the bishop informing you that I'm to take over for you while you're incapacitated.'

'So you're the one he's sent while I'm incarcerated in here, are you?' Thomas said, studying him more intently.

'The very one. I've already met Mrs Penwarden and your delightful daughter, and I wanted to assure you that I'll do my very best to keep everything running smoothly at Abbot's Cove until your happy return.'

All Thomas could think of at that moment was that the man was certainly a smooth talker. A good-looking chap too, and Irish by the sound of it. They weren't all incense-swingers, then, he thought irreverently. The older residents of the village might not take to him, but he had no doubt that the younger ones would. Thomas wasn't sure whether that pleased him or not.

'Are you married?' he said. Not that it really interested him at all, except that he was quite sure Ellen wouldn't want an entire family moving in.

'I'm not, sir, and I have no such intentions at present.'

Thomas grunted. 'Then you'd better sit down and tell me a bit more about yourself. I've nothing else to do but to lie here until they come and tell me I can get up for a few hours, which is all they allow me at present, so since you're here you might as well amuse me for a while. I hear you were an army padre.'

He hadn't meant to say any such thing. It didn't matter a jot to him what the man did before he came here, and he knew at once that he shouldn't have said it, when Stephen Daley latched on to the words at once.

'I was, Vicar, and I spent much of my wartime service in France. I saw plenty of action, or rather the results of it. I did my share of comforting the wounded and writing letters to the bereaved, and such tasks were not altogether easy, as you might imagine.'

Perhaps he thought he was adding to his credentials by telling him this, Thomas thought. He nodded, ready to let the moment pass, but it was too late.

'I understood from the bishop that your family suffered a bereavement during the war too. Your son, I believe. It's always painful when a son goes before his father. It's the wrong way of things, and unfortunately war brings it all home to us. Many's the time I've found it hard to find the right words to say, but if we don't do it, who is there at such times?'

Thomas half-turned his head away. He hadn't expected a sermon and he didn't damn well want it, either. He didn't want some young whipper-snapper telling him solemnly how it felt to be a bereaved father. He knew that only too well. He had nurtured it inside himself for all these years now. But this young man held his interest all the same, he thought unwillingly. There was some-thing almost saintly in his smile – and if that was the airy-fairy thought going around the staid Thomas Penwarden's head, then he'd probably had too many painkillers recently.

'Sometimes it helps to tell a stranger the things that are in our hearts, especially the things we don't want to burden our loved ones with. Don't you find that, Vicar?' Stephen Daley went on quietly. 'I often encountered some resentment from a family when I tried to comfort them, but it's something we learn to deal with. Just like a doctor, you know that a servant of the Lord is always discreet in what he hears, and I assure you that I will not fail you.'

'Are you talking about my parishioners or about me?' Thomas said, wondering how this bit of homespun philosophy had subtly turned to something more personal, unwanted and unwelcome.

Stephen smiled. 'The Lord is always ready to listen to anyone, however great or small, and I consider it a privilege to try to follow his ways. If I'm called upon to help somebody, I'm always ready to listen, too. Even someone such as yourself, if I don't presume too much.'

'I don't know about that, but if you've nothing better to do, and I certainly haven't, you can stay and talk for a while longer,' Thomas found himself saying, albeit grudgingly.

The next time Ellen came to visit her husband she found him less resentful of the new young vicar the bishop had found than she had expected. In fact, his whole demeanour seemed to be more relaxed since Stephen Daley had called to see him. She had thought he'd be his usual irascible self at having to stay in hospital a while longer yet, and fretting that his place in the village was about to be usurped – even more so when she was obliged to let him know that Stephen had turned up on a motorbike in the village, which was not how Abbot's Cove folk expected their vicars to behave!

'Oh well, he's young and he's modern,' Thomas grunted, taking her even more by surprise. 'But I have to admit that he's a thoughtful young man and he's seen more of life and death than any man of his age has a right to see. He may not have been actively fighting during the war, but he knows what suffering is, and I applaud him for the way he's dealt with it.'

'Well, it seems as if he's found a champion,' Ellen said, taken aback. 'I thought you'd be dead against him.'

'I'm not saying I think he's wonderful, but sometimes we can learn something from the young,' he answered enigmatically. 'I wonder what Jessie thinks about him.'

Ellen smiled, thankful to find her husband in a reasonably good mood for a change. 'I don't know that she thinks anything about him, other than that he's pleasant enough. He's clean about the house and his person, and he's already made the acquaintance of a few people in the village without antagonising them.'

'Yes, but what does she *really* think of him, woman?' Thomas asked with a frown. 'I'm not interested in his housecleaning habits. What does Jessie think of him as a person? What do *you* think of him in that respect?'

Ellen looked at him suspiciously now. 'Just what devious idea is going around in your head, Thomas?' she said at last.

He leant back on his hospital pillows. 'Nothing for you to worry your head about, my dear. I'm just glad to hear the new man is fitting in to the community, that's all.'

'Oh yes? He told me he'd been to see you and that you'd had a long talk.'

She hesitated and then reached out and pressed her hand over his. 'He also told me what it was about.'

'Then he had no business to do so. It was said

279

in confidence.'

'It's too late for that now, Thomas, and please don't get that closed look on your face again. Stephen told me how you finally opened up to him about Adam. Why haven't you been able to do the same with me for all these years? Was I so impossible to talk to, my dear, when we had so much grief to share?'

He closed his eyes for a moment, and when he opened them again his words were slow and husky.

'Perhaps because I knew we would hurt one another too much, Ellen. And perhaps that's why it was easier to bare my soul to a stranger than I ever could to you, no matter how much I cared for you.'

But she couldn't mistake the anguish in his eyes. Wordlessly, she held out her arms to him, and a short while later when a nurse looked in to see if he wanted anything, she saw the extraordinary sight of the middle-aged vicar and his wife hugging one another and weeping silently together.

Jessie's feelings were still bruised that Will hadn't got in touch with her as he had promised, but as the days wore on she was also becoming hardened to the fact, and deciding that if he didn't want her, then she wouldn't want him either. She knew it was no more than silly childish bravado that made her feel that way, and she couldn't keep it up all the time, but it was the only way she could save face, instead of constantly going about with her heart on her sleeve.

Besides, she had plenty to keep herself occupied, now that Stephen Daley was in the house, helping her mother with the cleaning and cooking. And after all, it was nice to have another man about the place. He was lively company, with plenty of Irish banter, and not at all the kind of holy Joe that Rita had teased her that he was going to be.

Rita was already swooning over him, of course, Jessie thought with a grin, and she had listened to his first Sunday sermon with something like adoration in her eyes. Most of the village had turned out to inspect him on that first Sunday, and most seemed to like what they saw. He was so confident, but not in an arrogant way, and yet it was clear that he was also anxious over his reception in the village, as the Penwarden women found when they went back to the vicarage after that first Sunday morning.

'Do you think it went all right? Tell me the truth now, ladies. I was keen not to upset anybody, and I knew they'd be comparing me with Vicar Penwarden,' Stephen asked them, when they were sitting down to their Sunday dinner.

'You know very well you did fine, Stephen,' Ellen said with a smile. 'You've got them eating out of your hand already.'

'Well, it doesn't always work that way when they see somebody new coming into a community who's not old and doddery – oh, Lord, not that I mean your husband is old and doddery, Mrs Penwarden!'

'It's all right, Stephen, we know what you mean,' Jessie said with a giggle. 'They're even getting used to your motorbike now, and that's something of a miracle.'

'Talking of that, I was wondering if you'd care to come for a ride on it with me sometime, Jessie. I've been here a few days now and feel I've got to know the lie of the land of the village fairly well, but I'd like to take a look around the countryside, and who knows it better than someone who was born here? I'd especially like to see the ruins of the old abbey. They tell me it's haunted, and that intrigues me.'

Jessie kept her eyes on her dinner plate for a moment, aware that her heart had begun to race painfully fast at the mention of the old abbey. The last time she had been there it had also been on somebody's motorbike. It had been Will's, and it was the place where they had shared their first sweet kiss...

'It sounds like a good idea while the weather's still pleasant,' her mother was saying now. 'I'm going to the hospital again this afternoon, but you're quite at liberty to show Stephen around if you'd prefer, Jessie, and I know your father won't mind since you saw him yesterday.'

There was something in the way she said it. It was nothing tangible, but it was just something. If Jessie had been feeling more imaginative or suspicious, or even put her Cornish intuition to the test, she might almost think it was as though Ellen was encouraging her daughter and the new young vicar to be seen out together. Almost as if Ellen didn't know very well that Jess was pining inside for her sweetheart to get in touch with her again.

'What would Dad have to say about that?' she said, almost insolently.

'I'm sure he wouldn't have any objections,' Ellen said. 'He's taken quite a liking to Stephen.'

The object of their discussion broke in. 'Look here now, ladies, it's up to Jessie to decide. It was only a suggestion, and I can easily find my way around on my own, but it's more fun with two, and it's always interesting to see a place through someone else's eyes.'

'Of course I'll show you around,' she said quickly, before she stopped to think any more deeply.

And maybe it would lay a few ghosts of her own, if there were any there to be laid. The old abbey ruins had always been the happiest of places in her childhood. The place where she and Rita and so many of their school friends had played among the old stones, hiding from one another and pretending to spook one another with ghostly tales, even though they never really found anything threatening about it. It was just childish, shivery fun. It was the place where courting couples met and kissed and fell in love. It was also where three motorcycling boys from Penzance had come chasing two Abbot's Cove girls and where one of them had suffered badly from the lust of a boy who was now dead.

'Are you all right, Jessie? You've gone quite pale,' Ellen said sharply. 'I hope you're not sickening for something, with winter not even upon us yet.'

'I'm fine,' she said with an effort, pushing the bad thoughts away, 'and even if I wasn't, I work in the right place, don't I? Mr Price always insists

283

on dosing me up at the first sign of a sniff or sneeze. He's forever reminding people of that old wartime slogan – "coughs and sneezes spread diseases".'

Now why did she have to mention that? The war was over long ago and she didn't want to be reminded of any of it. But to her annoyance, Stephen had noticed it, and she quickly realised he had her father's ear for choosing an interesting topic for a sermon.

'They had some sensible ideas during the war,' he agreed, 'and plenty of ideas for thrift, such as "make do and mend", which I'm sure many ladies were grateful to learn about. I think I might incorporate a few of those old wartime slogans into a future sermon, using some of Jesus's parables as comparisons.'

Ellen merely nodded as she cleared away the dirty plates from the table and took them to the kitchen, and Jessie hissed at Stephen.

'I'm not sure it would be a good idea to remind people too much about the war. It's over and done with, and we want to forget it.'

She hadn't meant to snap at him, and she flushed as she realised what she had done. Her father definitely wouldn't approve.

'I'm sorry, Jessie. I didn't mean to upset anybody,' he said. 'But your father and I had a good long talk about your brother the other day, and I can tell you it's released a good deal of his anxiety.'

'What are you, the original good Samaritan?' she muttered.

He smiled, not taking offence. 'Hardly. I've as

many faults as the next man, but I do what I can when I see somebody with a problem.'

'Oh really? And what's mine, then?' she challenged him.

He laughed, and if it wasn't such a boringly trite expression, she could see at once how he could charm the birds from the trees. His eyes seemed to become bluer when they got that sparkle in them, and his smile was open and honest.

'Oh no, lovely lady. You're not catching me out like that. I'm no clairvoyant. I don't ask people to tell me their problems. If they have them, they tell me if and when they're ready, that's all. So now that I've finished eating your mother's excellent Sunday dinner, I'm going to have half an hour to write some notes, and then, whenever you're ready, we'll go out for that ride.'

He left the room, and nice as he was, Jessie had the strangest feeling that she was somehow being manipulated. As if she was a puppet on a string, although she wasn't quite sure who was working the string – her parents or Stephen Daley. She shook herself, telling herself not to be so ridiculous, and went out to the kitchen to help her mother with the washing-up. And she had to ask her what was on her mind.

'Did Stephen bother you with that mention of the war, Mum?' she asked.

'Of course not. Why should he?' Ellen said in surprise.

'Oh, I don't know. We never talk about it, nor about Adam, and I wasn't sure what you might think about it. If he wrote that sermon and used it when Dad was back home to listen to it, I thought it might upset him too, that's all,' she added clumsily.

'I'm sure it wouldn't, but I also think Stephen's thoughtful enough to discuss it with your father beforehand. He knows the village better than Stephen, and would advise him on the reaction of other people. I think he'll be quite keen to come and listen to a younger man in the pulpit, especially one that he likes.'

'That's another thing that puzzles me. I was prepared for him to hate the very thought of somebody else muscling in on his preserve, but he doesn't seem to at all, does he? Is the man a magician?'

Ellen laughed. 'You say the silliest things some-times, Jessie. Stephen's just a very pleasant young man, that's all, and we should be thankful that your father isn't going to be ranting about him when he comes home.'

'How long is he going to stay?' Jessie said next, asking the question that had started to simmer in her mind.

'Why?' Ellen turned to her, her hands still steeped in soapy washing-up water. 'You've noth-ing against him, have you?'

'I just wondered, that's all. A month? Two months? Until Christmas?'

She hoped not. She really hoped not. It was her birthday at the beginning of December, and she didn't fancy having a stranger still living in the house. But by then, he wouldn't be a stranger, would he?

'He'll stay at least until your father's arm is out of plaster, and he can write his own sermons again and attend to his own parish business,' Ellen went on coolly. 'And until the doctors are satisfied with your father's heart condition and his blood pressure is stable, it will probably be a couple more weeks until they let him come home. There's no question of that, Jessie, and we have to make Stephen as welcome as we can. You go and enjoy the afternoon with him.'

She had to be satisfied with that, but all this talk of going to the old abbey ruins had also made her long to see Will again. She needed to know why he hadn't come to see her, nor even written to her. If he didn't want to see her anymore, she didn't think he was the kind of boy to just drop her without a word of explanation. She thought she knew him better than that.

She toyed with the idea of asking Stephen to take her over to Penzance on his motorbike, but how would that look? She could hardly turn up at the Tremayne house on the back of another good-looking bloke's bike. Will wouldn't take kindly to that at all, and besides, what could she do with Stephen then? Ask him to wait outside while she tried to sort things out with Will? Send him away and ask him to come back for her a little while later? No, it just wouldn't work, and she was just as frustrated and indecisive as ever.

An hour later she was sitting astride the powerful motorbike as it roared through the village on the quiet Sunday afternoon, feeling a burst of recklessness as she saw the startled, familiar faces of people pottering in cottage gardens, or taking their dogs for a walk. And especially meeting

Rita's outraged eyes as she waved gaily to her as they zoomed away from the village towards the open moors. Rita would have plenty to say about Jessie snatching the only eligible bachelor in the village away from all the other girls.

She giggled at the thought, never having considered Stephen in that way at all. Not for her, anyway.

'What's so funny?' he shouted back against the noise of the engine.

'Just my friend's face. She'll be jealous that I'm on the back of your motorbike.'

She couldn't catch what he said in return. It sounded like something about the fact that he wasn't here to escort everybody around the county, but the wind took his voice away and she couldn't be sure. In any case, she was too concerned with holding on to him as he opened up the throttle and let the bike rip away towards the moors and then slope down towards the abbey ruins. Whatever else he was, Jessie found herself thinking, he was just a big kid when it came to engines, like every other bloke.

She finally stepped off the bike, thankful to have her feet on the ground again. It wasn't a long ride from the village to the ruins, but it had felt like it today, especially as they had toured the moors first. Stephen stood in silence for a few moments, and remembering his calling, she wondered if he was praying for all those ancient lost souls, and if she should also stand in silent reverie.

'I bet this old place has seen a few trysts in its history, good and bad,' he suddenly said with a laugh, startling her.

She replied with a nervous giggle. 'It's been a general meeting place over the years for most of the younger folk in the village – and outsiders,' she added.

'And I suppose there were plenty of stories made up about what might have happened here in the past,' he asked, smiling as they began to walk forward among the pillars and arches, and the fallen, overgrown stones.

'Of course. Ghosts and ghoulies and things that go bump in the night and all that rot – but I suppose you'd disapprove of that, being a vicar.'

'I wasn't born a vicar, Jessie. When I was a child, growing up in Ireland, I had my share of family stories about ghosts and leprechauns and suchlike. The Irish are a fanciful people and all children like scary tales wherever they're born. Even now, there are plenty of folk who think the stories Jesus told are nothing short of magical fantasies.'

She shrugged, knowing her father wouldn't like that kind of talk. And besides, she didn't come here to be preached to. She was simply doing a kind act for a visitor, and if the truth be told, she didn't want to be here at all. It stirred up too many emotions, on her own account, and on Rita's.

'I expect you have special memories of your own here, don't you, Jessie?'

It was a casual remark, and she was about to brush it off just as casually, when she caught him looking at her steadily, and she gave an involuntary shiver. It was his eyes ... those very blue eyes that seemed to get bluer and more intense when he was looking into the sunlight, and could easily mesmerise someone into revealing secrets... She turned her gaze away from him and spoke almost angrily.

'Everyone has memories and secrets that are not meant for sharing, don't they?'

She bit her lip. He hadn't mentioned secrets, and she shouldn't have done so either. She might have known he'd notice the word.

'I'm sorry, I seem to have upset you and I didn't mean to. Perhaps we should take a walk around and then go back. I'm sure I can find some information about the abbey in your father's study later on. I'd like to know a bit more about it from an ecclesiastical viewpoint.'

He was efficient now, the interested vicar, and Jessie wondered if she had had a moment of madness, imagining that he'd been sent here to probe her feelings and find out all there was to know about her and Rita – and Will.

'I do have a young man,' she said abruptly. 'At least, I thought I did.'

'Ah, well,' said Stephen.

What did that mean? It was an expression that said nothing, and yet had such significance in the way he said it. He was pottering about among the stones now, not inviting intimacies, and yet she felt almost compelled to tell him more. The words almost tumbled out of her, sharp and forced.

'His name's Will Tremayne and he was going to come and meet my parents one afternoon, except that Dad had his accident and it never happened.

I've seen him since, though. I've even stayed at his house, but he hasn't been in touch with me since that day and I don't know why.'

She was trembling now, wishing she had said nothing, and hadn't felt obliged to confide in Stephen Daley at all. She hadn't wanted to do so. He'd undoubtedly trot out the old adage that confession was good for the soul, but she had nothing to confess, only the deep sense of hurt that Will was ignoring her.

'Why don't you go and ask him, then? If he means that much to you, then he owes you that much, Jessie. There might be a perfectly valid explanation. On the other hand, if neither of you is making the effort, perhaps it means that there was nothing worth saving in the first place.'

She didn't want to hear this. He spoke so calmly, as if he was talking to a child, and of course it all made so much sense. So much patently obvious sense. Even Rita had been urging her to do the same thing, and it was only her pride that was holding her back.

'I'll think about it,' she muttered. 'And I'd definitely like to go back now, please, if you've seen enough, that is.'

'More than enough for one day,' Stephen said, always ready to oblige, and with that all-knowing, beatific smile she was starting to dislike heartily.

CHAPTER SEVENTEEN

'Well, you're a sly one, aren't you?' Rita said, bristling all over.

They met at the cove after work the following day, and at her friend's words Jessie kept her temper in check with an effort.

'I know what you're going to say, so don't bother saying it.'

'What's happened to the great love affair, then? Or is Will yesterday's news now that golden boy has arrived in town?'

'Of course he isn't. And Stephen's no golden boy, either.'

Rita's eyes gleamed at once, scenting a bit of intrigue.

'Really? Everybody seems to think so, but don't tell me he tried it on. I didn't think a vicar was that way inclined. But you'll have to tell me everything now, Jess.'

'You are stupid. He didn't try anything on, and why shouldn't a vicar be *that* way inclined? He's still a man, isn't he? For your information, he just asked if I'd show him around the area, and the abbey ruins in particular.'

Rita stared. 'The abbey ruins?' she repeated, parrot-like.

'Why not? It's the only interesting thing around here. We're hardly in a big-city league for historic monuments, are we?'

'What did you tell him?'

Her voice had changed. It was hoarse and it dragged a little, and Jessie looked at her sharply.

'I didn't tell him anything. What do you take me for? He just wanted to see the place, that's all. He'd heard that it was haunted, and when he'd had a good look around he was going back to look up some of Dad's books about its history. I didn't go there as a kind of confessional, Rita.'

'That's all right, then,' Rita said, recovering quickly. 'It's just that I was talking to Fay Yendle at the shop and she said she and her cronies reckoned Vicar Stephen could wheedle anything out of anybody with those eyes and that smile. I think she's smitten,' she added.

'And you're not?'

'Not anymore. I think there's something a bit creepy about him.'

Jessie laughed out loud. 'Well, now I think you're off your head. He's all right. My dad seems to think so, and that's a miracle if you like. So why did you look so mad when you saw me on his motorbike yesterday?'

Rita shrugged. 'Just the association of old times, I suppose. And wondering if you'd forgotten Will so soon now that a new guy was in town.'

'Well, I haven't, and for your information I'm cycling over to his place after tea to find out what's gone wrong.'

'Well, it's about time!' Rita said, almost in relief. 'I'd hate to think you were falling for Vic. It's bad enough you having a vicar for a father without marrying one.'

'That's the last thing I'd ever do.'

She wished Rita hadn't put such a daft idea into her mind, but it was there now and she couldn't quite get it out. She could hardly miss the way her mother kept praising Stephen from time to time, or how much her father was looking forward to coming home and hearing how Stephen performed at the church. It was almost as though they were pushing her towards him – and that was ridiculous.

She told Ellen where she was going after tea that evening, and Stephen immediately offered to take her, saying he could call in at the hospital to see her father at the same time to discuss a few church matters with him.

'It's all right,' she said quickly. 'I need some fresh air after a day at the shop, and I'd rather ride my bike, then I won't have to wait around for you.'

'That's rather ungrateful when Stephen's been kind enough to offer, Jessie,' Ellen said.

'No it's not, it's practical,' she said. And she wasn't changing her mind, either. Imagine how Will would feel, seeing her turn up on some other chap's motorbike. She had pictured it once before, and no matter what had changed between them, it was simply not going to happen.

But later she couldn't deny that her heart was pounding when she had cycled the few miles to Will's house and saw his car standing outside. Now that she had come this far, she couldn't put it off any longer, but this could be a hideous mistake, and she might end up covered with embarrassment. Even as she stood hesitating, she saw the front door open, and heard him call out to his mother that he wouldn't be out for long. The next minute he had closed the door behind him, and they were face to face.

'Jessie,' was all he said.

'Hello, Will.'

It didn't sound like her voice. It was husky and strained, and oh God, she *knew* this had been a big mistake. She could see it by the expression on his face, which was about as unwelcoming as it could possibly be.

'I've been meaning to write to you,' he said at last, coming quickly down the path to where she leant on her bike, clinging on to it as if it was a lifeline.

'Why haven't you, then?' she asked inanely.

And what had happened that could have made it necessary for him to write to her, instead of talking in the old easy way they had had together? What had gone so very wrong? She felt like weeping to realise that for all that they were so close together now, they might have been oceans apart.

'Look, Jess, I was going to see Ronnie tonight – you remember him – but do you want to come for a drive instead? And then we can talk,' he said.

He was so stilted, so different from the boy she knew and loved. But she clung on to that one word – Ronnie. He'd said he was going to see Ronnie, so at least it wasn't another girl. She knew she was being pathetic to be so relieved, but she didn't care.

'All right,' she said huskily.

She leant her bike against the fence and got

into the car beside him. She wasn't sure whether this was so clever, either, as the interior of the vehicle enveloped her in the scent of soft warm leather. It felt far too nostalgic and reminiscent of the times when she was dreaming of being his girl for ever.

'We'll go over to Marazion, and then we can walk along the sands, if it's not too cold for you,' he said.

He was so polite, treating her like a stranger. But she was thankful he hadn't said they'd go back to the old abbey ruins – which would have been ridiculous in any case, since she'd just come from that direction. The long stretch of Marazion sands, with the fairy-like castle of St Michael's Mount rising out of the sea, would be a fitting place for him to say whatever it was he had to tell her. A perfect setting for having her heart broken...

'I've missed you, Will,' she said before she could stop herself.

'I know. I've missed you too,' he said, his voice tight. 'Is your father still in hospital? I'm sorry. I should have asked about him before.'

'He's still there, but he's getting on all right, and he'll probably be home soon. We've got a new vicar taking over for the time being.'

'Oh? What's he like? Some old bloke, is he?'

'Actually, no. He's quite presentable in a smooth sort of way, and half the village seems to have fallen for him.'

'Including you?'

'No, I'm one of the other half,' she said.

God, this was awful. They had been so close and now they were talking banalities. Well, not really banalities, since her father's health was hardly that. At least he'd remembered to ask after him, Jessie thought bitterly.

It didn't take long to reach the small, straggling village of Marazion that was almost an extension of Penzance, and once through the busy streets of the town they were driving along the long stretch of road bordering the sands. There was a smoky evening haze in the air now, and the ancient castle seemed to float, ghost-like, out of the sea. It was eerie and beautiful at the same time.

They left the car and began to walk along the sands. There was a cool breeze blowing, and as Jessie gave an involuntary shiver, Will tucked her hand inside his arm. It felt wonderful and comforting, and it encouraged her to blurt out what was in her heart.

'Will, what's gone wrong? Why haven't you contacted me all this time? If you've gone off me, I'd far rather you told me than left me in the dark.'

'Of course I haven't gone off you,' he said, squeezing her closer to him. 'It's just that something unexpected happened, and it knocked me for six. I didn't know how to deal with it, and Mum was so upset I couldn't think of anything else, especially when she got the crazy idea of going to France.'

'*What?*' Jessie stopped walking so fast she almost pulled him over. 'Why would she want to go to France, for goodness' sake?'

'To see where my dad was buried,' he said brutally.

They were standing quite still now, and Jessie's

heart was beating fast.

'You told me he'd left you and your mother years ago,' she whispered.

'So he did. I told you he'd gone off with his French tart, and we never heard another thing from him after that. Then a couple of weeks ago we had a parcel from France containing a letter from her, and a few of his things. We were also told that he was dead and that my mother was welcome to go and visit his grave if she wanted to. How cruel was that?'

'It was terrible,' Jessie breathed. 'I can't imagine how she must have felt. Nor you too, Will.'

He had started walking again, and she had no option but to walk with him. He didn't look at her, but she could hear the hurt in his voice.

'It made us both feel betrayed all over again. We'd never known anything about this woman, nor wanted to, but now she had a name and she was telling us about her feelings, and we learnt what had been happening to my father all this time, and it was a hell of a shock, I can tell you.'

'It must have been, and I'm so sorry. But Will, your mum wouldn't really consider going to France, would she? What good would it do?'

She bit her lip, because of course it would do her some good. It would be the closing of an important chapter in her life. Will gave a harsh laugh.

'Oh, don't worry, she's thought better of it now. But for a while I was really worried, because she kept going over the times she and my dad used to have, and it really sickened me to think he could have left her the way he did.'

'And that stopped you thinking about anything else,' Jessie stated.

'Well, what do you think?' he said angrily. 'You've met my mother, and you know what a well-balanced woman she normally is. You wouldn't have thought so if you'd seen her when that parcel arrived, though. It nearly broke her all over again.'

'I do understand, Will, truly I do,' Jessie whispered again, 'and I'm not condemning you.'

'It wasn't that I didn't want to see you, Jess. I felt somehow dirtied and ashamed by the whole thing. You had your own problems with your dad, and it just seemed better to have some distance between us for a little while.'

'And now?'

Suddenly his arms went around her, and he was holding her tight.

'*God*, but I've missed you so much, Jessie. I didn't realise how much until I saw you standing like a vision at my gate. In fact, I thought I was seeing things for a minute.'

She felt his mouth on hers in the sweetest kiss, and her heart soared with happiness at knowing he hadn't forgotten her, and he still wanted her. That much was very evident in every touch of his body against hers.

When they broke away he spoke softly to her.

'I'll never let you go again, Jess, but I promised Mum I wouldn't be out long. I meant to see Ronnie Hill tonight, as he's still so cut up over Des, but I can see him tomorrow, and I don't want to leave Mum on her own for too long. What do you say to coming back to say hello to her? I

299

know she'd like to see you.'

'Of course I will,' she said readily, even though her heart baulked at facing that lovely, confident woman in view of the way Will described her now. But how could she say no? She was a bit surprised to hear about Ronnie's feelings over Des Greenaway too, though she didn't know why she should be. Boys had feelings too, didn't they? And presumably they had been friends for a long time.

They walked back to the car with their arms around one another, and sitting inside it again, Jessie thought how different in terms of atmosphere was the short journey hack to Will's house. There were no more secrets between them now, and whatever mood she found Mrs Tremayne in, she would do her best to cheer her up.

As it happened, Doris was overjoyed to see her, exclaiming at once that she had kept on to Will to get in touch with her.

'He was too concerned for me, lately, Jessie, and I guess he's told you what's been happening,' she said, her face immediately becoming more pinched than it had been a moment ago.

'He has, and I don't know what I can say, Mrs Tremayne,' she said honestly. What could she say? She was not yet eighteen years old, and she had no concept of what it must be like for a woman who had been married all those years to suddenly lose her husband to another woman, and now to learn that he had died, still with that other woman.

'There's nothing anyone can say or do, dear,' Doris said with a heavy sigh. 'I have to get over it and so does Will, and the sooner he stops wrapping me in cotton wool the better. I didn't fall apart then, and I'm not going to do so now. So tell me how your dad's getting on instead, while I make us some tea.'

She was marvellous, Jessie told her mother several hours later, by which time she had promised to come and see Mrs Tremayne again, and she had cycled home, glowing with the knowledge that she was still Will's girl. She had called at Rita's to tell her what was going on, but her mother said she was out on an errand for her and wouldn't be back until later, so frustratingly, it had to wait.

'Mind you, I suspect Mrs Tremayne wilted a little after I left,' she continued to Ellen and Stephen, still involved in all that Will had told her. 'Will says she has these determined moods to make the best of things, and there are other times when she seems to be lost in the past.'

'I wonder if I could be of any help to her,' Stephen said thoughtfully. 'I dealt with many cases such as hers when I was stationed back in England. My work didn't only concern talking to wounded soldiers and helping them to accept their lot. Much of it involved helping the bereaved to understand what had happened as well as just listening to them talk. Some folk didn't want to hear any church teachings, but other bereaved folk found a great deal of comfort in it.'

'Mrs Tremayne wasn't bereaved because of any enemy action,' Jessie snapped. 'She was betrayed by a rat of a husband who went off with a French

301

tart. And those are Will's words, not mine.'

'Jessie, really!' Ellen said, outraged. 'Apologise to Stephen at once.'

'What for? I only spoke the truth. And I hardly think Mrs Tremayne would thank a stranger for butting in on her personal business, especially if she thought I'd been gossiping about her.'

'It's all right, Mrs Penwarden,' Stephen broke in quickly before a furious Ellen could say anything more. 'I understand Jessie's feelings, and it was thoughtless of me to think I could be the one to help. She's quite right in thinking I would be no more than an interfering stranger.'

'I didn't exactly say that,' Jessie muttered.

She thought it, though. The damn nerve of the man, thinking he'd be welcome to go to Will's house and speak to his mother about something that was no business of his. He was an insufferable prig, and the sooner he went back to his Irish bogs, the better. She felt her hands clenching, and she kept her eyes lowered, afraid that the unworthy thought might somehow transmit itself to him if she dared look at him right now. In fact, she could hardly bear to be in the same room as him anymore.

'I'm going out, Mum. I need to see Rita,' she said in a strangled voice.

'Well, I think you'd better, and perhaps you'll be in a less aggressive mood when you get back,' Ellen said.

She might be aggressive now, but she had been oh, so happy a short while ago, and remembering the sweet times on the sands at Marazion it didn't take long to get the feelings back. Rita was home

302

by now, and they went up to her bedroom to sprawl on her bed as they had done so many times as children, exchanging secrets.

'So it's all on again,' Rita said with a grin. 'Didn't I tell you so?'

'It was never off,' Jessie admitted. 'But I did feel so sorry for his mother when he explained it all to me, Rita.'

'I don't suppose the Frenchwoman could have done anything else really. I mean, she had to let them know Will's dad had died, didn't she? Supposing Will's mum had ever wanted to get married to somebody else? She needed to know that she was free, didn't she?'

'Good Lord, trust you to think of something like that!'

'Well, it's true, isn't it? Or do you think everybody only has one soulmate in this world?'

'Maybe I do.'

'And Will's yours?'

'Of course he is,' Jessie said dreamily.

'How do you explain second marriages then? They're not just taking second best. More like a second chance to get things right, if you ask me.'

'Well, I wasn't, and I think you're wrong, but I don't want to talk about it. What do you think your precious Vicar Stephen suggested?' Before Rita had a chance to surmise she rushed on. 'He only wanted to go and talk to Will's mother like some flipping guardian angel. He said he did a lot of it during the war – comforting bereaved women, I mean.'

'I bet some of them enjoyed being comforted too,' Rita said with a giggle, and then sobered as

303

she saw Jessie's face. 'Sorry, I didn't mean that, but you must admit he's got a way with words, and he's not exactly Frankenstein, is he?'

'You don't get it, do you, Rita? He's poking his nose in everywhere, making himself seem indispensable, and I reckon he wouldn't mind taking over permanently if my dad ever decided he'd had enough.'

Rita stared at her. 'You're mad. Your dad's years away from retiring. Vicars go on until they drop, don't they? Besides, it would take more than a pretty boy like Stephen to push him out!'

She was right, of course, and Jessie admitted it was just a crazy thought that had flipped into her mind for no reason. Of course her dad wasn't thinking of giving up, and Stephen Daley *was* no more than a pretty boy with a lot of Irish charm – even if he was more than ten years older than either her or Rita.

'Oh well, let's forget him,' she said with a shrug. 'Why don't we go to the dance on Saturday night? We haven't been for ages, and it's one place I doubt that we'll see Vicar Stephen, thank God!'

'What about Will? Will he be going?'

'He might,' Jessie said, blushing. 'Did I forget to mention that?'

The year might be drawing nearer to its close, but on Saturday night it still felt like a lingering breath of summer for Jessie and Rita to dress up in their best clothes and put on some make-up, to brush and curl their hair until it was bouncy bright, and then to arrive at the village hall for the dance. It was like old times. It was warm and noisy and exciting inside the hall, and they looked around eagerly for old friends. There was one in particular whom Jessie was looking for, but he wasn't there yet, and she ignored the little flip of uncertainty in her stomach, wondering if he was going to let her down again.

She and Rita were deep in conversation with several other girls, all of them asking after the good-looking Irish vicar and clearly envying the fact that he was living at the vicarage, when she saw Will. He was standing by the door of the hall, gazing around and looking for somebody, and then she saw his mouth widen into a smile as he found her. Her heart beat twice as fast as normal, and she pressed Rita's arm excitedly.

'He's here,' she whispered.

'And just look who's with him,' Rita said furiously.

Jessie allowed her gaze to move slightly away from Will for a second, and she gave a small gasp. Behind him, looking awkward and uncomfortable, was Ronnie Hill. In an instant, both girls were remembering the first time they had seen him with Will and Des, two months ago. It seemed like a lifetime.

'Give him a chance, Rita,' Jessie said. 'Remember that what happened between you and Des wasn't his fault, and don't forget how he must have felt when his friend was killed.'

'Did you know he was coming?'

'No, I didn't,' Jessie said honestly. 'But I'm not going to let him spoil my evening, and you shouldn't let him spoil yours either.'

She pushed past her friend and walked across to Will. Her heart was still pounding, and in a way, it was like stepping back in time, to the first time she had set eyes on him and thought he was the most beautiful young man she had ever met. She found herself blushing at the thought.

'I'm glad you came,' she said softly.

His eyes told her he was glad too. More than glad. He cleared his throat, and moved towards her while Ronnie still hovered near the door. He replied just as softly.

'So am I, and I hope Ronnie's appearance isn't going to cause a problem with your friend. He's been having a bad time lately.'

'Has he?' Jessie said in surprise. 'He looks tough enough to deal with anything that comes his way.'

'Not quite anything,' Will said. 'What happened to Des hit him pretty hard, and it took a bit of persuading to get him to come down here at all. You girls don't have the priority on feelings, Jess.'

He repeated her own thoughts, and she was still mulling over those words when she saw Rita coming their way, and from the look on her face it was obvious there was going to be trouble between her and Ronnie. She forestalled it by excusing herself from Will and whisking Rita off to the ladies' cloakroom where one of the Ladies' Committee was handing out raffle tickets for what she called a special prize later in the evening. Almost impatiently, the girls took one each, their minds on other things.

'You've got to give him a chance, Rita. Will says he's still cut up over what happened to Des, and anyway, it's not fair to blame Ronnie for the other thing,' she said meaningfully. 'It wasn't his fault, was it?'

'I know that, but I bet Des couldn't help crowing over how easy I was,' she said, her face flaming with humiliation. 'I never wanted to face either of them again, Jess.'

'Listen,' Jessie hissed, making sure no one else could overhear, 'Will says he's really changed since then. He's even sold his motorbike, according to Will, and he brought him here to cheer him up a bit. Couldn't you be a bit more charitable and do the same?'

'Why should I? I'm nobody's nursemaid.'

'You're not much of a friend, either, are you?' Jessie retorted. 'It wasn't Ronnie who did you know what, Rita, and you could spare him one dance, couldn't you? You know how bashful they all were about dancing when they came down here first of all, and he probably won't ask anybody else, and then I'll feel obliged to divide myself between the two of them.'

'God forbid that you should have to do that,' Rita muttered. 'All right. One dance, if I must.'

But as the evening wore on, Jessie was thankful to see that it had developed into more than one dance. Not that she could spare too much attention on what Rita was doing. It was blissful enough to know that there was only one partner for her, and that when she and Will weren't dancing, they were sitting out with glasses of lemonade, and making up for all the time they had lost. At one point, Rita and Ronnie came to join them, and Jessie didn't miss the way she was looking at her old adversary now.

'Ronnie's taking me to the flicks in Penzance next week,' she announced, her eyes daring Jessie to make any comment. 'We decided we might as well be friends as enemies.'

'Good for you,' Jessie said, not sure whether she felt more startled or more like laughing at the unexpectedness of it all. Ever fickle, that was Rita. But she realised it was just as Will had said. Ronnie Hill was not the same reckless biker who had come down to Abbot's Cove that first time looking for excitement and a few laughs. There was a serious side to him as well, and one that wouldn't do Rita any harm to copy. Stranger things had happened.

'I'm teaching Ronnie to quickstep,' Rita went on with a giggle as the music changed tempo. 'He's pretty hopeless at the moment, but with a bit of practice, we'll get there.'

Ronnie went off with her, smiling, and without too much protest.

Will laughed. 'I knew she'd come round, and what's the betting that once that little madam gets a project in her sights, she won't let go? I can see Ronnie will be wanting a lift to the next dance as well as this one.'

'Does that mean you're coming as well, then?'

'What do you think?'

She thought she had never been so happy. There had been troubles enough for all of them in these past few months, but somehow they had got through them all.

'I think the next dance will be on my birthday,' she said suddenly.

'That will make it extra special, then,' Will said.

She hoped he didn't think she had been fishing for a present. She had said it without thinking. Her birthday on 4th December was always a happy occasion at home, just as Adam's had been until three years ago, when it had turned into a source of sorrow because he was no longer there to celebrate it. But you couldn't live in the past for ever. It might be a trite saying, but life went on, and you had to go on with it. She wasn't sure how her dad would react to her spending the evening at a dance, though, and he would surely be home from hospital long before then, but as she swung around the hall in Will's arms to the music, worrying about that was the last thing on her mind.

Towards the end of the evening there was a little flurry of excitement among the older ladies on the Ladies' Committee, and even more among some of the younger girls who were still crowding on to the dance floor as the music came to a stop for a few moments. And then Jessie saw what the attraction was.

'I don't believe it,' she said furiously. 'What on earth does he think he's playing at, coming here?'

'Who is it?' Will asked.

Rita sidled up to them both. 'He's our dashing Irish vicar, Will, and this is a lark, isn't it, Jess? Is he going to ask you for a dance, do you think?'

Jessie didn't answer as Stephen Daley smiled benignly around the hall.

'I don't want to interrupt your evenings, boys and girls,' he said, 'but Mrs Price has invited me here to choose the winning raffle ticket, and to announce what the prize is going to be.'

'Oh no,' Jessie groaned.

As the ripples of anticipation grew, she watched as if in slow motion as Stephen dipped his hand into the bucket and pulled out a ticket.

Oh, please don't let it be mine...

'It's ticket number forty-three, and the prize is one dance with me, though I can't promise not to step on the lucky girl's feet – or should that be the unlucky girl!' he finished with a wide grin.

Was it her imagination or did he seem to look straight at her with an apologetic smile, as a screaming girl dashed forward to be claimed for the dance? If so, he needn't have bothered, Jessie thought, in relief. There was only one person here she wanted to dance with, and that was Will.

CHAPTER EIGHTEEN

Will said he would come down to Abbot's Cove again on Wednesday evening, and late on that same afternoon, Ellen came home from the hospital with cheering news. Providing Thomas's blood pressure remained steady between now and then, he would be allowed home at the weekend. He was advised to take moderate exercise and would remain under doctors' orders for a while yet. It would also be several more weeks before they could consider removing the plaster from his arm.

'And when that happens, I suppose Stephen will be leaving,' Jessie said, as she helped her mother clear away the tea things. He had already gone out on some mission or another, leaving them in peace for a change. Not that he was any bother in the house, but she never felt entirely free and easy with him around.

'I'm not sure when he'll leave,' Ellen replied. 'I think your father would prefer him to stay a while longer, and I'm sure the bishop will sanction it.'

'But there won't be any need, will there? Not once Dad can write his own sermons again, I mean. Knowing him, he'll want to get back in harness as quickly as possible.'

'Jessie, remember that your father's had a heart attack. I'll grant you it was only a small one, but all the same, it was a warning that he shouldn't go rushing about the way he used to do. The village can exist perfectly well without his finger in every pie, and I'm sure he'll be glad to have Stephen here as a sort of second in command for an extra month or two.'

'*Months?*' Jessie echoed.

Her mother looked at her sharply. 'Do you have any objection to that?'

Jessie turned away. Yes, she did, but it was hardly something she could explain in detail to her mother. She didn't want Stephen Daley in the house any longer than necessary. She wanted things to be the way they were. It may seem childish and un-Christian to resent his presence here, but she couldn't help it.

'I think it will be nice to have the house to ourselves again, with just our family and no outsiders,' she said lamely.

Ellen sounded annoyed now. 'Stephen has been helpful in so many ways, Jessie, I'm sure your father considers him almost one of the family. In any case, in the wider context, we're all one family in God's eyes.'

Oh Lord, now she was playing the church card, Jessie thought ungraciously. 'Well, he's no substitute for Adam if that's what Dad's thinking!'

She didn't know where the words came from. She didn't mean to upset her mother, especially when she was obviously pleased that Thomas was coming home. But Ellen's face went a dark red and Jessie could see how an angry pulse throbbed in her throat.

'Sorry, I didn't mean to say that,' she mumbled.

'But you said it, didn't you? So it's obviously

what you've been thinking and it was thoughtless and heartless, Jessie. Nobody could ever be a substitute for Adam, and you of all people should know that your father would never think such a thing.'

'I do know it! I'm sorry. I wish I could take the words back. Please forget it, Mum.'

Ellen looked at her thoughtfully. 'What do you really think about Stephen, then? You have nothing against him, do you? Everyone likes him and I see no reason for you to do otherwise.'

'He's all right, but I wouldn't want him around for ever.'

In the small silence that followed Jessie looked at her mother sharply.

'You and Dad haven't been doing a bit of wishful matchmaking on the quiet, have you?' she said with a laugh, since the idea was so absurd.

When Ellen still didn't say anything, she gasped. 'You have! You don't really think I could fancy Stephen in that way, do you, Mum? You know how I feel about Will, and I could never have those kinds of feelings about anybody else – even if he wanted me to, which I'm sure he wouldn't. He's never shown the slightest interest in me, and I wouldn't ever encourage it.'

She began to feel het up at the very thought, and the sound of Stephen's motorbike coming to a halt outside the house didn't improve her state of mind. She was never going to look at him in the same way now, wondering if he had given her parents the slightest hint that he had his eye on Jessie Penwarden as a future vicar's wife! The idea was more than unpalatable. It was repugnant.

'Calm down, my dear, he'll be indoors at any minute and he won't want to see you getting in a state. It was simply something your father said to me in passing, about what a very likeable young man Stephen is, and what an asset he'd be to any community, especially with a good wife behind him. You know we'd never force you into a marriage you didn't want.'

'I'm not thinking of getting married at all,' Jessie said, scrambling to her feet as she heard the front door open, 'but when I do, it will be to someone I love, not to someone who'll be an asset to the community!'

She was outraged that her parents might have been discussing her and Stephen Daley in this way. For all that her mother said they would never force her into marrying anyone – and she believed that – they had put the thought in her mind now, and she didn't want it there. She didn't want to be linked with Stephen in any way, however tenuously.

'I'm going upstairs to get ready to go out with Will,' she said, deliberately mentioning his name, and escaped before anything else was said.

She was trembling with rage by now. Had Stephen actually said anything to her father to put this idea into his head? He'd certainly never made any kind of overture towards her, and as far as she could tell, he treated her in exactly the same friendly way he treated every other female in the village. He was friendly to the point of nauseating, she had sometimes thought, and she had never really admitted it until now. Other girls might fall for his Irish charm, but she wasn't one

314

of them, and never would be.

By the time she heard Will's car arrive, her nerves were still jittery, and she was out of the house before he could walk up the path. Right now she didn't want him anywhere near her mother, and especially not near Stephen, having to make proper introductions and watching them assess one another. She was upset with her mother for putting such thoughts into her head at all, and she might have known that Will would pick up on her mood as she slid beside him in the car.

'What's up?' he said. 'And who does the motor-bike belong to?'

She started. As usual it was parked in the road outside the house and, of course, Will would have seen it for the first time. It was nothing like his old bike, serviceable and a bit ancient. Stephen's bike was shiny new, reflecting its angelic owner...

'It's the vicar's,' she muttered. 'Vicar Stephen. You saw him at the dance on Saturday night when he came to claim his dance with the raffle ticket winner.'

'I didn't know vicars rode motorbikes, and he's a lot younger than I expected too. I can see why all the girls fancied him.'

'Not all of them. I told you that. Look, are we going to sit here all night, or are we going some-where? And how's your mother?'

She knew she was speaking too quickly, and it was all Ellen's fault for putting such irritating thoughts into her head.

Will started up the engine and drove back through the village.

'Mum's fine, but she's still in two minds about

whether she ought to go and see where Dad's buried. My boss has been trying to advise her, and she always listens to his opinion. He's had an idea now that I hope she'll agree to. He suggested she writes back to this French woman and asks her to send a photograph of the grave instead. It makes sense, instead of travelling all that way for no real purpose except to upset herself more. She's gone to see Mrs Greenaway tonight, and I daresay they're chewing over the pros and cons. So what's got you all steamed up?' he finished, making her jump.

How could she tell him? And how could she not? Was it being tactless to talk about her own father's recovery, when his would never come home again? But he knew her well enough to know when something was wrong, and she knew he wouldn't let it go, so she drew a deep breath.

'My dad's coming home in a couple of days, which is good news, of course, and I thought Stephen would be leaving as soon as Dad's had his plaster off, but Mum seems to think he might be hanging on for a couple of months yet. It'll be ages before we have the house to ourselves again.'

'And that bothers you, does it?'

'Wouldn't it bother you to have a stranger always around? I dread to think what it will be like when Dad gets into his stride again too. He won't want to be second fiddle for long, and I can see trouble ahead, even though right now they seem to be closer than clams as far as I can tell.'

'Perhaps your dad sees him as a likely son-in-law,' Will said, his perception taking her so much by surprise that Jessie gasped out loud.

'Don't even think of such a thing!'

Will kept his eyes straight ahead as they drove towards the open moors and his voice was even.

'Well, I imagine a younger version of himself would be a far more attractive proposition as a son-in-law than a courier with no real prospects.'

'I think I'd have something to say about that,' Jessie said fiercely. 'I've lived with Dad being a vicar all my life, and I've no wish to take on another one, thank you. Besides, I'd have to love somebody before I thought of marrying them, and I certainly don't love Stephen Daley, nor ever could.'

The car slowly drew to a halt on the narrow road skirting the moors. They could look down on the ruined abbey from here, and the sight of it, gaunt and crumbling and long abandoned, could always make Jessie's heart skip a beat. As Will turned off the engine, the only sounds were the whine of the wind through the bracken and gorse, and the screeching of seabirds seeking their nests. In the distance behind them loomed the granite chimneys of long-disused tin mines. This was a lonely and desolate place now, so different from the sunlit expanse of moorland in summer, and she felt an odd sense of nostalgia for all the forgotten times of her childhood spent up here.

But childhood was far behind her now, and Jessie was also very aware of the different turn their conversation had taken. Was Will hinting that in due course he would want to be that son-in-law? And was she presuming too much in saying she would have to love somebody before she could think of marrying them? Where did all this talk of marriage come from? She wasn't yet eighteen years old, and she knew her father would have plenty to say about tying herself down, when in his opinion she was hardly out of the cradle.

'Jess,' she heard Will say softy. 'Jess, look at me.'

She turned her head towards him slowly, knowing her cheeks must be flushed and that her heart was beating fast. 'You know how much I think of you, don't you?'

'Do I? How much?' she echoed.

'Enough to want to spend the rest of my life with you,' he said simply. 'But some people would say it's far too soon, and that we haven't known one another long enough to be sure of our feelings. I only know that it took less than a moment for me to know you were the girl for me, but I need to know how you feel about me. If I have to wait for ever, I'd wait a lifetime for you.'

'You don't have to wait that long,' she said, her voice catching. 'Don't you know that I feel the same way about you, Will? I always have.'

She swayed into his arms, their closeness hindered by the mechanics of the car, but neither of them heeded them. It was a long while before they broke apart, and then he looked deep into her eyes.

'If this means we're engaged I'll have to ask your father formally.'

Jessie gave a nervous laugh. 'Not yet, please, Will! Let's just keep it to ourselves for the time being. Too many things have happened recently for us to give our families anything more to think

318

about. We have to consider my dad – and yours – and also your mother's feelings right now. I think we should wait. As long as we know what's in our hearts, that's all that matters.'

She felt ridiculously shy at saying all these things out loud. She had never spoken so freely before, but as long as he didn't think she was being too sentimental, it didn't matter. Nothing mattered, she thought, her spirits soaring, except that they had made a promise to one another. Keeping it a secret until the time was right only made the knowledge more magical.

He spoke more urgently. 'I have feelings too, sweetheart, and they're normal healthy feelings, if you know what I mean.'

She did know what he meant. She could feel the soft caress of his hand on her breast now, and she gave a small shudder that was part nervousness, part pleasure. Involuntarily, she covered his hand with her own, which only increased the gentle pressure he was exerting.

'I do know, Will,' she said huskily, 'and I'm not being a cissy about this, but I also remember what happened to Rita and all the worry it caused, and I couldn't bear to go through what she did.'

'But I'm not Des, and I'd never hurt you, Jessie. But engaged couples do have some privileges, don't they?'

'Is that why you want to be engaged? So you could have some privileges, as you call it?'

'Of course not,' he said with a small laugh. 'It's just my clumsy way of saying I love you and I want you as close to me as it's possible to be.'

She drew in her breath. He had never said he loved her before, and it was the sweetest thing to hear him say it now, when he was obviously restraining himself from being too passionate. But she was capable of passion too, she thought, remembering the dream she had had at his house, and with the memory came an over-whelming need of him. She *wanted* his passion, to know that she was loved and desired. But through it all, she had to remember who she was, and the way that passion could so quickly turn to regrets, to disgrace and scandal, and she couldn't do that to her parents.

'I do love you, Will, and I want you close to me too, but we have to be sensible, don't we?' she said in a cracked voice. 'One of us has to be, any-way.'

All the same, she wasn't removing his hand from her breast. She wanted it there, warm and pos-sessive. She wanted to feel the tingling sensations that ran through her at the small, involuntary movements he made. She wanted to feel her own response, reaching towards him, longing for more...

His kiss was gentle, and his mouth remained on hers as he spoke, just as though he could read her thoughts. 'You're so very right, my lovely vicar's daughter, and we've got all the time in the world to know one another.'

Providing some madman didn't decide to bomb half the world out of existence, taking too many young men with it. Taking Adam...

She buried her face in his shoulder, hugging him tight, and wishing the hateful thought hadn't swept into her mind. She had grown up through six years of war that had decimated the country of its young men, but you couldn't go through your life afraid that it was going to happen again. You had to live for the moment...the way so many couples had lived when they believed there would be no tomorrow, and for many of them, there hadn't been.

'Where have you gone now? Are you laying a few ghosts, Jessie?' she heard Will say quietly, and she realised he had removed his hand from its cosy resting place, and he was stroking her cheek as he looked into her eyes.

'I thought I was the one with intuition. Are you a thought-reader?'

'Not really, but I can always sense when your mood changes. I guess that's what happens when you're so much in tune with another person.'

'I guess it is,' she said, smiling provocatively into his eyes. 'So what am I thinking now?'

His answer was to gather her close again in a very satisfactory fashion that blotted out all other thoughts until the sun had long sunk low in the sky.

'Does this mean you're engaged?' Rita almost squeaked when they met at the cove the following evening after work.

'Sort of, but it's a secret at the moment, so I'm just telling you in private. I haven't got a ring or anything, and Will's going do the proper thing and speak to Dad first. But it'll all have to wait until Dad's home and back to normal again. We don't want to give him a relapse,' she added nervously.

'Why would it?'

Jessie shrugged. 'Well, for a start it would if he's got me all lined up to be a vicar's wife,' she said without thinking.

Rita looked blank for a moment and then shrieked. Thank God there was nobody else around at the cove on a Thursday evening, or the whole blessed world would be on to it by now, Jessie thought in annoyance.

'You're not serious, are you, Jess? You and Vicar Stephen haven't been getting up to anything on the quiet, have you? You know how the village girls fawned over him at the dance, and it'll put plenty of noses out of joint if you've nabbed him after all.'

'For pity's sake, I haven't nabbed him and I've got no intention of doing so. Aren't you listening to me? Will and I have got an understanding, and it just has to wait to be made public, that's all, so don't you go blabbing about it, Rita.'

'Of course I won't. What do you take me for? But why would your dad think Stephen's interested in you unless he's said something about it to him?'

'Well, of course he hasn't, and I wish I hadn't said anything to you now,' Jessie snapped.

All the same, her heart jolted as she watched Rita skim a pebble into the sea and saw the ripples spread outwards in ever widening circles. It was the way rumours spread. The way a word dropped here and there could sometimes turn into fact before you knew it. And the one thing she hadn't considered was that all this match-making might not have been solely on her parents' side. Supposing Stephen Daley had even hinted to Vicar Penwarden that he might be romantically interested in his daughter? Perhaps that was why Ellen was keen for him to stay on for a while, because it would be oh-so-suitable a match – from her parents' point of view, anyway. Imagine having a vicar for a son-in-law, with all the prestige and respect that went with it...

She was angry for letting her thoughts get so carried away. She and Stephen had hardly ever been alone together for any length of time, and he had certainly never made any kind of overture towards her. They had spent many hours at home in the evenings, but it was usually with Ellen present. They had talked of many things, and she acknowledged that Stephen was an intelligent and attractive man and very good conversation-alist, especially with his tales about his home in Ireland, which he obviously missed, but he wasn't a man she could love in a million years.

Rita spoke abruptly. 'I didn't mean it, Jess, and anybody could see that Will was the right one for you from the start. I'm just surprised it took you both so long to get around to it,' she added, unable to resist a last small barb.

'We're not rushing into anything, either,' Jessie muttered. 'We're going to get to know one an-other properly before ... well, before.'

The minute the careless words were out of her mouth she knew she shouldn't have said them.

'You mean you haven't done anything yet? He hasn't tried it on or anything?' Rita said, eyes full of teasing again.

Unfortunately it had the effect of making Jessie

feel inadequate and stupid, and she retaliated without thinking.

'No, he hasn't. I've got no intention of letting myself get in the same kind of mess that you did, either.'

'Well, thank you for that. I might have known I'd get that thrown back in my face eventually.'

'You were right, then, weren't you? And seeing as I got most of the flak from it, you might at least show some contrition about it.'

'Have you swallowed a dictionary now? Or is this the way your precious vicar talks? You may not think so, Jessie, but you're already beginning to sound like him, and Will Tremayne had better watch his manners if he's not going to be pipped at the post.'

She flounced away up the cove as fast as the sliding sand would let her. Jessie stayed exactly where she was for the moment, flinging pebble after pebble into the sea to let her temper cool down. She knew they had been behaving like schoolkids for the last five minutes, but knowing it didn't help to cool her emotions. She hated falling out with Rita, and even though their squabbles never lasted long, they always left a bitter taste in her mouth. Especially hearing Rita's last words. She hoped she wasn't starting to sound like Stephen Daley, and she certainly wasn't going to be charmed into wanting him over Will. She gave a small shudder at the thought and turned abruptly to walk back up the cove.

As she did so, her heart leapt. Standing at the footpath at the head of the cove was a tall figure, almost in silhouette as the sun's rays lengthened, but clear enough to be instantly recognisable. He began to walk towards her even as she scrambled back towards the road.

'What are you doing down here all alone?' he said with a smile. 'You look troubled, and like a woman with a lot of things on your mind, Jessie. If I can help, you know you only have to ask.'

'There's nothing on my mind, and I'm not alone, Stephen, at least I wasn't until a few minutes ago. My friend Rita was here with me, and she's just gone home, which is where I'm going now, so excuse me.'

She knew she sounded stilted and awkward, which was exactly how she felt. She wished she had the nerve to push past him, but good manners decreed that you didn't do that to someone with such a caring and compassionate look on his face. It was a look that made her teeth grate, and she wondered fleetingly if he was ever going to be the marrying kind, or if he was really destined to remain virginal white – if such a thing could be attributed to a man. She felt her face redden at the thought. In any case, he was never going to be marrying *her!*

His smile never altered and he didn't move. She realised that it was a habit he had, as if nothing that anybody said could really touch him. He was so blooming *perfect*... He waited until she reached him and then fell into step beside her. Well, this was going to look marvellous to any onlookers, she thought furiously. The last thing she wanted was for any gossip to be attributed to her and Stephen, even though she knew she was being unreasonably sensitive. Who would question the two of them walking through the village together?

'I can't help thinking you've been avoiding me lately, Jessie,' Stephen said at last. 'Have I done something to offend you?'

'Of course not, and I'm sure I haven't been avoiding you. I could hardly do so while we're living in the same house, could I?'

'You didn't look too pleased to see me at the dance on Saturday night.'

'It took me by surprise, that's all.'

To her horror he reached out and squeezed her arm gently.

'Oh well, providing that's all it was. I'd like to think we were friends, Jessie, despite the circumstances that brought us together, and good friends at that. When your father comes home from hospital at the weekend, I hope it will be to a harmonious household.'

Was that a threat? Or a hint? For a moment Jessie desperately wished she hadn't said she'd just been talking to Rita, then she could have made the excuse that she had to see her, and got away from him. But why shouldn't she say it, anyway? It was none of his business what she did. She moved away from him and spoke quickly.

'Look, I've just remembered something important I forgot to tell Rita. Will you let Mum know I'll be about another half an hour or so, please, Stephen?'

She turned and walked quickly in the other direction, knowing he could hardly refuse to give her message to her mother. She was aware of her heart still thumping uncomfortably and she almost ran the last few yards to Rita's house. Forgetting that they had parted in less than sociable circumstances she rushed into the house without knocking, and seeing Rita helping her mother set the table for their evening meal, she blurted out the first thing that came into her head.

'There's something I forgot to tell you if you can spare a few minutes.'

Seeing the way the two girls seemed to be almost on the verge of sparring with one another, Mrs Levant gave an indulgent chuckle.

'Well, whatever it is, you'd better go and sort it out and leave all this to me,' she said, waving Rita away.

Jessie grabbed her friend's hand and pulled her outside into the garden.

'I think you were right.'

'Well, that's a first. Right about what?'

Jessie gulped. It was going to sound so ludicrous once she put it into words, but when all was said and done, Stephen Daley was a man like any other, and why wouldn't he want a wife one day? And what better candidate than a vicar's daughter who already knew the ropes?

'About Vicar Stephen having his eye on me,' she said baldly.

CHAPTER NINETEEN

Thomas Penwarden arrived home in an ambulance on Friday afternoon. Although he had only been away from home for a few weeks, he couldn't help registering how different everything looked. It was as though the seasons had moved on without him noticing it, and there was already a chill of winter in the air. Or else he was too used to the stuffy atmosphere of the hospital, and was glad to be breathing in fresh air again.

Ellen fussed around him like a mother hen, filling him up with tea and cake, telling him to sit down with his feet up and not to dare to go inside his study just yet. After an hour of it he was obliged to tell her to stop.

'I'm perfectly all right, my dear,' he grumbled, 'and once I get this wretched plaster off my arm we can all get back to normal again. But please don't treat me like an invalid, because that's something I'm not.'

'You will concede that you've had a heart attack, though, and that you have to take it easy for a while.'

'I've also been told to take reasonable exercise, woman, so don't think you're going to wrap me up in cotton wool now that you've got me home again.'

But his face softened and he reached out with his one good arm and caught hold of her hand.

'It's so good to be home, Ellen. I never once thought I was never going to see it again, but it's good to have my own four walls around me again, all the same,' he said, more huskily than before.

She cleared her throat, not wanting to appear too emotional, or to confess that while he might have had complete faith in his own recovery, she had said more than a few fervent prayers for him to be returned whole to her and Jessie.

'I'm making your favourite meat and potato pie tonight to celebrate your homecoming,' she said instead.

Thomas smiled. 'That sounds good. You haven't been persuaded to create any strange Irish dishes while I've been away, then?'

For a moment she didn't understand what he meant and then she laughed.

'If you mean has Stephen had any such influence on the household, then no, he hasn't, my dear.'

'And how are things between you all?' Thomas said casually. 'I take it he's settled in very nicely, and I hope he and Jessie have been getting along.'

'Of course they have, but you know she's been seeing that boy over Penzance way, don't you? The one I told you about.'

Thomas almost brushed her words aside.

'Yes, you did mention him, but don't you think she'd be happier with a young man her parents approved of?'

'I approve of Will,' Ellen said, staring at him.

'He may be very nice, but Jessie's far too young to know her own mind, and she needs proper guidance in matters of the heart. Now, I think I'll take a slow stroll down to the church to give my thanks for my safe delivery. Don't worry, I won't overdo it.'

Ellen watched him go, knowing she couldn't stop him, and slightly affronted at the way he had glossed over any problem that couldn't be solved now that he was here to do it. She knew that many of his flock would be urging him not to overdo things, and she couldn't help feeling deflated that he hadn't wanted to stay home with her, or at least, asked her to go with him for a walk. But she also knew that when anything troubled him, he needed to be on his own to work things out. Despite his manner, she hoped it wasn't troubling over Jessie and Will Tremayne that was going to cause him any heart-searching.

Jessie had seen the ambulance go through the village from the window of the chemist's shop, and she felt a great sense of relief that her dad was safely home again. Although, guiltily, she knew that even if it was mostly relief that he was well enough to be sent home from the hospital, it was also partly relief that surely now they would soon see the back of Stephen Daley. She certainly didn't fancy the prospect of him staying on for a few more months in the house.

'So your dad's home again,' she heard Harold Price say behind her. 'He'll need to take things easy for a while,' he added with his pseudo-knowledge of all things medical.

'I doubt that he thinks the same way,' Jessie said. 'He'll want to get back to normal as soon as possible.'

Vera put her spoke in. 'Your mother will have something to say about that, Jessie, and besides, you've got that nice Vicar Stephen to take care of things now, haven't you? He's charmed most of the village since he's been here.'

'Well, he hasn't charmed me,' Jessie said crossly before she could stop herself.

Vera's eyebrows shot up. 'Really? My friend Fay Yendle said she saw you and he looking very pally the other day coming back from the cove, and I'm sure she's not the only one to think what a fine couple you look together.'

Jessie felt ready to explode. 'Honestly, you can't turn around without people noticing it in this village. We merely happened to meet, that was all, and we do live in the same house for now. We're not a *couple!*'

Harold gave a low chuckle. 'Methinks the lady doth protest too much!'

'I certainly do not,' Jessie snapped, uncaring whether or not her mother would think her rude, but the last thing she wanted was for the village to couple her name with Stephen Daley's! 'In any case, I've already got a young man.'

She knew it was a mistake the minute she said it. Harold Price was as big a gossip as anyone, and she saw his eyes light up with interest. Thankfully, Vera had already retreated to the back room or she would have been sure to put in her two-penn'orth.

'Who is it, then?'

'Nobody you know,' she retorted airily. 'He's just a friend, anyway...' despite the fact that her heart skipped a beat whenever she thought of him, and she felt her face flush, remembering the passion that had flared between them. Will was so much more than a friend, and there was so much more that she wanted him to be. She was still half-dreaming when she felt Harold Price's hand on her arm.

'Just be careful, Jessie love,' he said gently. 'I think you know what I mean, and I daresay you wouldn't get such words from your dad, so forgive me if I'm talking out of turn.'

Her eyes felt surprisingly moist at the fatherly concern in his voice.

'You don't need to worry, Mr Price, but thank you for the advice.'

She was glad when the shop door opened and some customers arrived for their medicines and customary chat with the chemist. He was a good old soul, thought Jessie, and it was true that her dad would probably never give her the same advice that Harold did. Not that he wouldn't want to, it was just that it wasn't in his nature to be so free with his speech. In his heart, he belonged to a more inhibited time, and there was nothing anyone could do about that.

'You can get off early today, Jessie,' Harold said when the last customer had gone and there was little else to do. 'You'll be wanting to see your dad, I'm sure. Give him my best wishes.'

'I'll do that, Mr Price. And thank you again.'

She felt awkward with him now and was keen to get out of the shop and be on her way home. She found her mother baking, and the house was filled with the succulent aroma of meat and potato pie. There was no sign of her father.

332

'Where is he, then?' she sang out.

Ellen sniffed. 'Where do you think? Gone to his beloved church to make sure it hasn't blown away during the time he's been away.'

Jessie's eyes opened wide. It was rare for her mother to make such comments, and she had imagined her to be full of joy that Thomas had come home after his experience.

Ellen caught her staring and gave a half-smile. 'Oh, take no notice of me, my dear. I daresay I expected your father to be a little more dependent on me when he came home. Even a bit weak, if you like, but that's not his way, is it? And I should be thankful he's the man he is. He's the man I married after all.'

To Jessie's horror, her mother suddenly fumbled for a handkerchief and began dabbing her eyes. In all her life, the only time she had seen her mother cry was when they got the news about Adam, and it unnerved her to see her like this.

'He does need you, Mum,' she said awkwardly. 'He just doesn't have an easy way of showing it, that's all. And I can understand his need to see that everything is the way it was before he had his heart attack. The church, the village – and us – and even his favourite meal!'

Ellen gave a watery smile. 'You're right, and I'm being a silly old woman. Besides, it's hardly right to be jealous of the church, is it? It's something I could never compete with even if I wanted to.'

Jessie had never heard her mother talk like this before, and she wasn't sure how to deal with it. But then Ellen gave a more normal laugh.

'Take no notice of me. I'm just having a bad moment, and it will soon pass. I suppose I expected to pamper your father, and it was a bit of a shock to find that pampering is the last thing he wants. I've known him long enough to have realised it. Now help me set the table, there's a love. The pie's nearly done and I'm sure he'll be home any minute.'

And when he was, he'd need help cutting up his food, since the plaster came halfway over his hand, and she was sure he wasn't going to like that! But she found that she was wrong. He seemed to find it amusing that he had to resort to having his food cut up into baby pieces, and once they were, at least he could eat with his left hand and his fork. Thankfully, Stephen Daley hadn't offered to do the cutting for him, and that role was left to Ellen, who had been cheered up immensely by the simple task of doing something for her husband, knowing the novelty for both of them would wear off soon enough!

'This is the best meal I've had for weeks,' Thomas declared when he had finished. 'You've no idea what the hospital food was like. They did their best, but it was always cold. I really missed your home cooking, Ellen.'

Jessie avoided her mother's eyes, but she knew this appreciation was exactly what she had needed. Stephen, too, was quick to praise Ellen's cooking, but his words meant less than nothing to Jessie.

After the meal the two men spent an hour or so in the study, presumably for Thomas to check on what had been happening since he had been away.

'He might as well not be home at all,' Jessie commented, anxious that her mother shouldn't feel left out. 'Doesn't it irritate you, Mum?'

'He needs to feel part of the community again,' Ellen said, shaking her head, 'and what better way than to read the sermon Stephen has prepared for Sunday, and probably to add his little additions to it,' she finished with a smile.

'He'll be wishing he was doing it himself, won't he?'

'Of course he will, but he wouldn't let anyone else write it for him, and it's impossible for him to do that with that wretched plaster still on his arm and most of his hand.'

'But once he can there'll really be no need for Stephen to stay, will there?'

She hoped she wasn't being too obvious, but remembering Vera Price's snide words, and the thought that other people in the village might have been coupling their names together, was setting her nerves on edge.

Ellen paused in clearing away the remnants of the meal.

'Jessie, when the time is right, I'm sure Stephen will want to go back to his old life, and until he does, I'll ask you not to show your resentment of him, which is becoming all too obvious, my dear. I can't think what you've got against him. He's a perfectly pleasant young man.'

Jessie tossed her head, annoyed that even her mother seemed to be so much on Stephen's side. Well, it was never going to happen, she vowed, even if the Vera Prices of this world thought it would be a very good idea for Jessie Penwarden to marry someone of her father's persuasion, to keep her on the straight and narrow after all the uproar that had happened previously...

She felt herself relax, because nothing had ever actually happened. She hadn't done anything wrong, and still hadn't, no matter how much she yearned to be all that Will wanted of her. It wasn't only boys who could feel the passion that made her flesh tingle and the rush of sensation inside whenever she thought of him – and she had better get the stars out of her eyes before her father came out of the study, or he might start to wonder about his angelic daughter!

When he did appear, both she and her mother noticed how fatigued he looked. Despite what he said, the excitement of coming home and all that it entailed had taken it out of him, and he was more than ready for an early night.

'I'm ready too,' Ellen said, to Jessie's surprise. Her mother stifled a yawn, even though the night was still relatively young, but with sudden insight Jessie realised, with his right arm in plaster and relatively immobilised, how difficult it would be for her father to prepare for bed. He would hate having to ask, but it was obviously necessary for him to have some help, and this was her mother's delicate way of saying she intended to do it.

'Goodnight then, Dad,' she said, and impulsively kissed him. 'It's good to have you home again.'

'It's good to be home, girl,' Thomas said gruffly, which was about all they knew he was going to say about the circumstances that had sent him away.

So then there were just the two of them left

downstairs, Jessie and Stephen, and she had no idea what to say to him. Did they make small talk about the weather or the price of fish? Did he expect a lively bit of conversation? After their last encounter at the cove, and the remarks Vera Price had made that afternoon, she began to feel hugely embarrassed at sitting so cosily in front of the fire with him. But if she got up to go to bed, it would just look rude at such an early hour. She knew she was avoiding saying anything at all, and the ball was in his court, as the saying went, but out of the corner of her eyes she realised he was smiling at her.

'What?' she said abruptly.

'Well, this is awkward, isn't it? You don't want to be here with me, and I'm not sure I particularly want to be here with you either.'

Jessie gasped. The damn cheek of the man! No, she *didn't* want to be here with him, but who was being rude now? And in her own house too. Furiously, she saw that his smile was turning into laughter.

'Oh Jessie, Jessie, my wee girl, did anyone ever tell you you've got a most expressive face? Your emotions are there for all to see.'

'Not all of them, I hope,' she muttered. 'And please don't call me your wee girl. I'm not yours, and I'm not a wee girl. I'm almost eighteen.'

'And I'm twenty-nine, which makes you far too young for me to ever think of you as anything but a child. I'm well aware that some of the village girls have had a bit of a crush on me, but it's only because I'm a novelty and my accent is different from theirs – and yours.'

She gasped again. 'You think a lot of yourself, don't you?'

Stephen shook his head. 'Not really. I'm just content within myself, and I'm certainly not looking for a wife just now. That time will come, I'm sure, but it will be a woman nearer my own age who shares my convictions and beliefs.'

'Well, I hope you don't think I'm one of the village girls who's had a crush on you,' Jessie said furiously, thankful that her parents couldn't hear this tirade.

'I don't, and considering your age, I think you've got a very sensible head on your shoulders, and if you'd only let me talk to you a bit more the other day, we might have sorted things out between us.'

'There's really nothing to sort out,' she muttered, feeling worse by the minute.

'But you do resent me being here, don't you?'

'Only because of the circumstances! I've never seen my father ill before, and I've never seen him miss a Sunday service before, not even when my brother died, and seeing you take his place in the pulpit every Sunday was more upsetting than I expected.'

She was shaking now, wondering just how they had ever got into this embarrassing conversation, but Stephen seemed the kind of man who could worm whatever he liked out of people. If it wasn't his soft Irish voice, it was his penetrating blue eyes that seemed to look into a person's very soul. Jessie shook off the thought angrily. Nobody was looking into her soul, least of all Stephen Daley! She forced herself to listen as he

338

went on talking calmly.

'I've enjoyed being here, Jessie, despite the reason for it, but Abbot's Cove constantly reminds me of my home in Ireland. I come from a small seaside village very much like this one, where everyone knows everyone else's business, or tries to,' he finished with a smile. 'I've a yearning to go back there to see my folks, and with luck I'll be there for Christmas. Contrary to what most people think, not every vicar is on duty over Christmas, and I've been promised that I can take some time off when I leave here, so that's what I shall do.'

'You'll be gone by Christmas, then?' she said, and then bit her lip immediately, realising how eager she sounded.

To her horror he leant forward and kissed her cheek. It wasn't a passionate kiss. There was no affection in it, and his lips were cold on her skin.

'I'll be gone before Christmas,' he promised. 'And probably by your birthday too, providing you father can write his own sermon by then. I've offered to do it for him, but he'll have none of it as you can probably guess. Will that please you?'

'You make me feel very ungracious now,' she muttered.

'There's no need. Just remember that all things come to an end, Jessie – even my stay here. And now I'm going to take a stroll through the village. I might even look in at a local hostelry for a jaw with the natives, so I'll bid you goodnight.'

As if half afraid he was going to kiss her again, Jessie jerked back, but he merely got up and took his coat from the peg behind the door, and

339

minutes later she was alone and contemplating the strangest half-hour she had spent with him. Maybe she had misunderstood him all this time, but her overriding feeling was one of relief that he was determined that his time here was coming to an end. And she wasn't going to be a hypocrite in denying the thought that she was mighty glad to hear it.

She told Rita about their strange conversation when she saw her on Saturday afternoon. Rita was seeing Ronnie that evening, but so far there had been no word from Will. She tried not to feel hurt after the wonderful time they had had on Wednesday evening, and their promises to one another, but all the same...

'I know he's still worried about his mum and what she intends to do, but it would be nice to hear something,' she sighed.

Rita was still goggle-eyed over the suddenness of her feelings for Ronnie, which were definitely reciprocated, and she couldn't take Jessie's worries too seriously.

'You don't need to be worried over Will. He was always mad about you, and you know it. I'm tickled pink over our dishy vicar saying you were too young for him, though. Didn't it make you feel like a naughty schoolgirl making eyes at a dirty old man?'

'Of course not, you idiot, because I never did that! I thought he had a damn cheek talking to me like that, if you must know, and he certainly has a great opinion of himself. He thinks half the village girls have got a crush on him.'

'Well, so they have. And the older ones too,' Rita sniggered. 'Miss Yendle thinks he could be a Hollywood film star.'

Jessie snorted. 'It's a pity he doesn't clear off there, then. But at least he says he's going back to Ireland before Christmas, so that's something to look forward to.'

'Your dad wouldn't think you were being very charitable about him, would he?'

'He'd hate it,' Jessie admitted. 'And I don't really think he's awful, it's just this feeling that my parents thought he'd make a suitable husband for me, and it's the last thing I wanted. Thankfully, it's the last thing he wants too,' she finished with a laugh.

'Aren't you the tiniest bit miffed about it?' Rita said.

'Good Lord, why should I be? Will's the one I want, not Stephen, thank you very much.'

'H'm. Well, I might have had a go at him myself if it wasn't for Ronnie. I might not be any older than you, but I think I'm a bit more worldly-wise,' Rita said idly, making Jessie burst out laughing.

'You're daft, that's what you are. And you seem pretty besotted with Ronnie if you ask me.'

Rita grinned. 'You're right, Jess. It's funny how somebody's right there under your nose and you don't really see them, do you? And then one day, it's like a rocket going off right in front of you, and there he is.'

'My God, that was practically poetic,' Jessie said. 'I hope he feels the same way about you, then.'

'Oh, he does,' Rita said dreamily. 'You never

341

know, we might end up having a double wedding. How fantastic would that be?'

'Fantastic,' Jessie echoed, at which Rita dug her in the ribs.

'Now who's being daft? I was kidding, you dope. Can you imagine your old man and mine giving the brides away? Yours would be all solemn and vicarish, and mine would probably be half-cut from the night before. They could drag in Vicar Stephen to perform the service, looking all mournful because he'd missed his chance with the beautiful vicar's daughter!'

'You should write a book. You've got a wild enough imagination,' Jessie mocked, but knowing she was right – at least about their two fathers.

And if she thought about it seriously, much as Rita was her very best friend, she didn't want a double wedding. Jealously, when she got married, she knew she would want it to be their own special day, hers and Will's, and nobody else's. And who had the wild imagination now?

'I'd better go back to another interesting evening with the old folks at home, since *I'm* not going to the flicks with my boy,' she went on reluctantly.

'Cheer up,' Rita said. 'Whatever's keeping him away, you know he loves you anyway.'

She did know it. It gave her a glow just to know that Will had told her he loved her, and to remember how sweet that last time together had been. She went home with a lighter heart to find her father in his study yet again, diligently practising the finger exercises the doctor recommended to keep them flexible.

'He'll be writing a sermon in no time,' Ellen said to Jessie. 'I've even heard the occasional mild curse when he dropped his pencil.'

This news cheered Jessie up still more. It meant he was determined to renew his old life as soon as possible, and that was good news for all of them.

'He'll have to let Stephen do the honours at church tomorrow, though,' she said.

'Yes, but he insists on giving a short word of thanks to the community from the pulpit. He won't let Stephen have all the glory.'

'Where is he, by the way? I didn't see his motorbike outside.'

'He's gone visiting for the afternoon and has been invited out for a meal this evening, so we've got the house to ourselves.'

Jessie found it hard to tell whether her mother was pleased about that or not. She was adept at hiding any such feelings. She had been schooled well in the art of being a vicar's wife, thought Jessie, and she admired her for her tact, knowing it was something she could never have mastered herself, and thankful it was something she would never need to do.

By the time Thomas came out of his study he was clearly still frustrated. It wasn't beyond him to write a few words, even though his fingers hadn't regained their suppleness yet, and the writing took more time than he wanted. Even so, he produced a paragraph of scribble with something like a child's elation.

'I think these few words will let the village know there's life in the old dog yet,' he said irreverently.

'They'll see that it won't take me long to get back to normal, and that the old ticker's still going strong.'

As he saw his daughter's astonished face, he laughed out loud.

'I can see what you're thinking. I mixed with all sorts in the hospital, Jess, and I think something of Stephen's easy way of talking has rubbed off on me too, but I'm sure it's not what Abbot's Cove expect of their resident vicar. I shall resume my parochial manner tomorrow.'

With every word, Jessie felt sure he felt as eager to be rid of Stephen as she was, although neither he nor her mother would ever say so. She wondered if Stephen had even said something to him about his plans to move on, and even more so, she thought suspiciously, if he'd hinted that he wasn't thinking of marriage just yet. It would be a great relief if he had done so.

It was also very pleasant to sit down at the meal table together that evening, and to enjoy normal family conversation. It was when the meal was over and Thomas had gone back to his study to try to perfect his paragraph still more, tinkering with it as always, that they heard the doorbell ring. Jessie had her hands deep in the washing-up bowl, and Ellen went swiftly to answer the door.

'It's probably someone for your father,' she commented as she left Jessie. 'I didn't think it would take long for people to want his help or advice once he returned home, especially the older ones who may not be so comfortable with a younger vicar, but I thought they might have left him a day or two to settle in again.'

It was almost the first time she had said anything remotely critical of Stephen or his parishioners, Jessie realised.

A few minutes later, Ellen came back to the scullery.

'There's a visitor for you, Jessie,' she said.

Jessie dried her hands quickly and went into the other room, curious as to who it might be. Not Rita, that was for sure, who would be on her way to Penzance to see Ronnie by now. Then she stopped dead, and her heart missed several beats before jolting on.

'*Will!* What's wrong?' she stammered, seeing his anxious face.

CHAPTER TWENTY

'Come and sit down, Will,' Ellen said at once, seeing the boy's pale face. 'You look as though you need to catch your breath.'

'I'm all right, Mrs Penwarden.'

'All the same, you've come all this way and it's not me you've come to see, so I'll finish the washing-up while you and Jessie talk, and then I'll bring in some tea for all of us.'

She left them to it, and Jessie turned at once to Will as he sat on the sofa beside her. Her heart was still pounding, knowing something must be wrong for him to come here so unexpectedly like this.

'Are you going to tell me or do I have to start guessing?' she said shakily.

He caught hold of her hands, and she registered how cold his were. She knew it was going to be bad news, but her head was in too much of a whirl to think what it might be.

'It's Mum,' he said abruptly, making her even more nervous. Then, seeing her face, he went on quickly. 'She's not ill or anything, but after agreeing with Mr Spencer that it was a wonderful idea to ask this Frenchwoman to send a photo of Dad's grave, she's decided it won't be enough, and she has to see it for herself.'

'Go to *France*, you mean?' Jessie said, after taking a moment to register what he was saying.

'It's not the end of the world, Jess.' He had an edge to his voice now. 'Plenty of our countrymen – and women – went there during the war.'

'I know that. But what good will it do for your mum to torture herself still more by seeing where your dad's buried – and presumably having to meet his … his … well, that woman.'

'She says it will underline everything. Put a finality to it all. And she wants to meet the woman now. She took care of my dad when he was ill, after all. I don't try to explain it, but it's the way Mum feels and I have to honour that. There's one more thing, of course.'

'What's that?' she said when he paused, and she felt his grip on her hands tighten.

'I'm going with her. I have to. I can't let her go all that way alone, and besides, it will mean something to me too.'

'What? When are you going, and how long will you be gone?' Jessie gasped. If this was being selfish she couldn't help it, but the thought of him going to France was somehow akin to losing Adam to the war all over again. She felt momentarily so disorientated by his news that, although her head told her there was no similarity, her heart said something different.

Thomas Penwarden came out of his study, his face like thunder with his continuing impatience at his inability to write the way he used to. He knew it would come, but he wasn't a man to take frustration quietly. He had always been in control of his life, and this one small thing was preventing that.

It didn't help to see his daughter with a young man he didn't know, sitting together on the sofa and holding hands, apparently so cosy together.

'What's going on here?' he snapped in a most un-vicarish manner.

Jessie and Will sprang apart, and they both stood up automatically.

'Dad, this is my friend, Will Tremayne,' Jessie said, still shaken by what he had been telling her.

Without thinking Will moved forward and held out his hand, without realising that it was impossible for the man to shake his hand, even if he had wanted to. And from the look on the face, Will was pretty sure it was the last thing he wanted. He dropped his arm and spoke nervously.

'I'm sorry to call unannounced, sir, and to make your acquaintance in such a way, but I had an important message for Jessie.'

'Did you indeed? And what might that message be?'

Knowing her father better than Will did, Jessie interrupted before he had a chance to speak. Her voice was shrill.

'Will's father has died in France, Dad, and he came here to tell me that he's taking his mother to visit the grave.'

There was silence in the room for a moment, and Ellen appeared with a tray of tea to find three people staring at one another, seemingly at a loss to know what to say next. She put the tray down heavily on the table and looked around in some exasperation.

'I was about to call you, Thomas,' she said to her husband. 'This is Will Tremayne, a friend of

Jessie's. You'll remember that I told you how his mother had made us both so welcome when you went into hospital.'

'I remember,' Thomas said without expression. 'Well, perhaps we had all better sit down, since you've made some tea, Ellen. And then Will Tremayne can tell me a little more about this proposed visit to France.'

It was Ellen's turn to gasp then, not having heard this latest news, and as she handed round the cups of tea, Will swiftly related what had happened.

Thomas was quickly calming down now and looking at the visitor with the same concern he would give to one of his parishioners who had come to him with a problem.

'I'm very sorry to hear this sad tale,' he went on, 'but I don't understand what your father was doing in France. Did he have business there?'

Jessie saw Will's face redden. How difficult was it going to be for him to tell a virtual stranger, and a vicar at that, that his father had been an adulterer? But as if anticipating that she was going to speak for him again, Will put his hand on her arm and took a deep breath.

'My father left my mother and me for a French-woman some years ago,' he said with barely concealed anger. 'He has been living in France with her all this time, and a short while ago we received a parcel of his belongings, together with a letter from the woman to tell us my father had died. You might imagine what a terrible shock that was.'

'To say nothing of cruel,' Thomas murmured.

'Go on, boy.'

'My mother had decided to ask the woman for a photo of Dad's grave, but now she's changed her mind, and has decided that she has to see it for herself, and obviously I can't let her travel there on her own. It would be too arduous and too painful, so we're setting out for France on Monday morning.'

Jessie swallowed, knowing how painful it would be for Will too, especially having to face the woman who had taken his father away from him.

'Then I commend you for agreeing to go with her, and for not trying to dissuade her. Clearly, she needs to do this, and it's only right that you should do it together,' she heard Thomas say.

Jessie hardly dared look at her mother. It seemed that because of the circumstances that had brought Will here tonight, her father had given him his blessing for being a good son – and hopefully, he would eventually give his blessing to something else as well. But now was not the time to be thinking of their own future.

'How long do you expect to be gone, Will?' she said nervously.

'No longer than possible,' he said, turning to her with something like relief in his eyes. 'Don't worry, I'm sure I shall be back before your birthday.'

Jessie caught her breath. Was this a comment too far? Would Thomas realise just how friendly the two of them had become if he knew her so personally? Before she could analyse it any further, Will had stood up and was preparing to leave.

'I'm sorry, but I must go. I promised Mum I

wouldn't be too long, and we've got a lot of preparations to make, and I've interrupted your evening for long enough.'

'Please give your mother my best wishes, Will,' Ellen said, 'and tell her I'd like to come and see her when she gets home again.'

'She'd like that,' he said, and looked directly at Thomas.

'My best wishes to you as well, Vicar.'

He merely nodded in response, and Jessie said quickly that she would see Will out. Once outside the front door, they breathed in the cool night air, and let out a collective sigh of relief.

'Well, you said you wanted to meet my father,' Jessie said jerkily. 'But not like this, Will. I'm so sorry for your poor mum, and oh, I'm going to miss you so much!'

He put his arms around her in the darkening evening, confident that no one could see them, and she nestled into him, breathing in the scent of his jacket.

'I'll be back just as soon as I can, sweetheart, and I'm sure Mum won't want to prolong the visit. I promise I won't miss your birthday.'

They clung together for a moment more, his mouth on hers, and then reluctantly broke apart. She watched him leave in his car, and then went quickly back indoors, already bereft at knowing he would soon be so far away from her.

'So that's the young man, is it?' her father greeted her as soon as she rejoined her parents.

Her chin lifted slightly. 'Yes, that's Will.'

'This journey will be quite an ordeal for his mother,' Thomas went on. 'From what I've heard

351

I daresay if the family split up some years ago she wouldn't be feeling the same amount of affection for her husband, but she'll be faced with another woman who has lived with him all this time, and will still be grieving. It won't be easy for either of them, nor for the boy.'

Since Jessie had been bracing herself for some discussion about Will and herself, she was staggered at hearing him speak with a certain amount of compassion. Of course, it was his job ... but while he could always dish it out to his parishioners when needed, she had hardly expected such words on Will's mother's behalf. It touched her more than she could say, and as he got up abruptly and went back to his study, she looked for support from her mother.

'What do you make of that, Mum? I thought he'd be angry that Will turned up like that,' she said, forgetting for the moment her own desolate feeling that her boy would be going away.

'I think it's done something unexpected,' Ellen said. 'It's the first time since coming out of hospital that your father has had someone else's problems to think about, other than his own.'

'I suppose so, but did you notice that he never addressed Will by his name? It was only Mrs Tremayne he was concerned about,' Jessie said slowly, trying not to feel resentful.

Ellen nodded. 'I noticed. And I think it's because it's also the first time a young man has been in the house since Adam, sitting and talking with us, and drinking tea. Didn't it occur to you that Will is about the same age that Adam would have been now, my dear?'

'No. It never occurred to me,' Jessie said, caught by her mother's perception. 'But you're right. Adam would have been the same age as Will by now. Do you think seeing him brought it all back to Dad? He sees plenty of young men at church and around the village.'

'I know he does, but not sitting in his own living room, and I'm sure he doesn't spend every moment of every day grieving,' Ellen said more briskly, seeing how they were descending into gloom. 'But there are moments when we all remember so sharply that the pain of it takes us by surprise. I suspect that was what your father was feeling when he saw Will, and that's why he couldn't bring himself to say his name.'

There was no reason on earth why Jessie should feel guilty on Will's behalf for not being Adam, but for a few moments she did so. And then she told herself not to be so stupid. If she and Will had a future together, her father would have to get used to seeing him.

'I'm not going to give Will up, Mum,' she said in a strangled voice.

Ellen's voice softened. 'Nobody's asking you to, Jessie, and if this was one more small hurdle your father had to face, then so be it. I'm sure he's feeling more vulnerable than he lets on after coming out of hospital, and every little thing is probably going to seem like an obstacle to him, especially being unable to write his own sermon for a while. He was never the most patient of men when it comes to feeling frustrated at every turn.'

'Amen to that,' Jessie muttered beneath her breath, and seeing the answering twinkle in her mother's eyes her face broke into a smile.

But worrying about her father's reaction to Will was soon farthest from her mind. More important was the fact that he was going away, and how much she was going to miss him. Even if they didn't see one another too often, he was always a few miles away, within reach, and now he was going to be an ocean away – well, the English Channel, but it might as well have been the Atlantic.

At any other time when she got some momentous news, she would have gone straight to Rita and shared it with her. Together, they could have diffused the anxiety of it all, and Rita's common sense would have been a blessing right now. But Rita wasn't at home tonight. She was in Penzance at the flicks with Ronnie Hill, and it left Jessie feeling more bereft than ever. It would have to wait until after church tomorrow before she could tell Rita what was happening, and she spent a restless night with intermittent and uneasy dreams, in which Will was being charmed by some seductive French mam'selle and deciding to do as his father did, and never come home.

Thomas had arranged to read a text in church the following day, his first Sunday back from hospital. There was no way he was going to stay out of the pulpit completely, and while he conceded that Stephen Daley gave a fine sermon, he was complacently aware that his parishioners looked forward to hearing his own few words, which he delivered with his usual gusto.

At the end of the service, he stood with Stephen

at the door and greeted every one of them, hearing how glad they were to see him back, and unable to resist a small glance at Stephen now and then to see how he was receiving it. Pride was one of the seven deadly sins, but there was no harm in having a little pride in knowing he was the vicar here, and that this younger man was just a temporary attraction, as fleeting as a summer breeze.

He watched as his daughter sped across the gravel to where Rita Levant was waiting for her father to join her and her mother. In her wheelchair, Mrs Levant looked pinched, and it was too cold for them to be waiting around. He was glad to see Zach Levant take hold of the wheelchair handles and start to wheel his wife away, as Rita turned to chat with Jessie. Then he promptly forgot them as several of the Ladies' Club members circled around him, gushingly saying how glad they were to see him back again. He was glad too, he preened, and the sooner he could get this damn plaster off his arm and resume his life properly, the better he would be.

As Jessie reached her, Rita could see that something was up, and forestalled her own enthusiastic report of last night at the flicks with Ronnie.

'Is he getting on your nerves already?' she joked, with a nod in Vicar Penwarden's direction. 'I see he had to get his oar in this morning.'

'Will came to see me last night,' Jessie said abruptly.

'What ... at the vicarage, you mean? Crikey, that didn't go down too well with his nibs, did it?'

Jessie felt a sudden anger. For heaven's sake,

she was on the brink of being eighteen years old, and if the time wasn't ripe for her to have a young man calling, she didn't know when it would be! But Will's own news overcame any other feeling, and she was bursting to tell Rita. The crowd of parishioners coming out of church now made her clutch her friend's arm.

'Not here,' she said. 'Let's go for a walk.'

'I can't be long. Mum's not feeling well, and Dad's actually flapping around her for once, and threatening to cook the dinner, though I doubt that he even knows where to find a saucepan.'

'It's nothing serious, is it?' Jessie said, deflected for a moment.

'I think it's the flu, but she's too stubborn to admit it, but if it gets too bad, she'll have to. She insisted on going to church, just to hear Vicar Stephen,' she snorted.

Jessie hid a smile, thinking that Stephen must be losing some of his appeal, if even Rita was getting fed up with him and his fancy Irish accent. But she couldn't be bothered to waste her thoughts on Stephen right now. They hurried away from the church and walked around the churchyard instead, and Jessie told her friend why Will had come to see her last night.

'Well, I think it's really a rather wonderful thing for his mum to do,' she said, to Jessie's surprise.

'Do you? Would you want to see the woman who stole your husband? I imagine you'd want to spit on his grave! Honestly, Rita, I think you're seeing the world through rose-coloured glasses since you've been going out with Ronnie Hill. Anyway, you're missing the point. Will is taking her to France, and I don't know when I'll see him again.'

To her annoyance, Rita started to laugh. 'You're such a drama queen sometimes, Jessie. He's not going to France for good, is he? He's got a job, for goodness' sake, and I don't suppose he'd be away for more than a week or so.'

'Well, he did say he'd be back for my birthday,' Jessie admitted, starting to feel foolish now. Trust Rita to cut things down to size.

'There you are, then. Stop worrying. Maybe he'll bring you back something French for a birthday present.'

'I don't care about that, just as long as he brings himself back.'

Rita wasn't prepared to stay very long to discuss the pros and cons of Will going to France. Jessie realised she was anxious about her mother too. She got little exercise in the wheelchair, and any small illness was apt to bring her down more than most people. And the thought of Zach wielding a saucepan or a frying pan, when his hands were more often than not on the shake from all the drink he imbibed, was a thought too much to bear.

So Jessie continued to walk around the church-yard on her own, her head down in thought, and with a little shock she came face to face with her father. Unwittingly, she had reached Adam's grave, and from the look of approval in Thomas's eyes, she realised he assumed it had been delib-erate.

'I often come here to contemplate,' he said. 'It's a good place for thinking, Jessie, and it makes me feel close to him.'

Her throat felt thick as she nodded.

'I still miss him too, Dad,' she said.

'I know you do, and I also had plenty of time for thinking in the hospital, especially over what might have been if my heart attack had been more serious. I decided then that we all have to look forward in this life, and just relish the memories of the past.'

She took a deep breath, knowing she had to say something about last night. 'I'm sorry Will turned up like he did last night, Dad, but you know the reason for it,' she said.

He didn't answer for a minute, and she wished she dared to ask what he thought of Will, but she couldn't go that far. Then he nodded.

'Suffice it to repeat that we all have to look forward in this life, and perhaps I've spent too long in looking backwards and forgotten that you're a young woman now. He's doing an admirable thing for his mother, and I applaud that. And they'll find, as we do here, that there's some comfort in seeing a loved one's final resting place.'

He wouldn't say anything more, and a few minutes later she tucked her hand in his good arm and they walked slowly back to the vicarage together.

It was the longest week she had ever known. She knew it was ridiculous. She didn't see Will every day, but she always knew where he was. Looking at the map of France in her atlas, and realising just how far away it was, was enough to send her heart plummeting. Also, her dad had quickly lost the feeling of largesse he'd had after church, and was now back to his most irascible self. Then, with his usual ear to the village grapevine, Harold Price could tell her a few days later that the doctor had been to see Rita's mother and had confined her to bed with the flu, as Rita had surmised, and in no uncertain terms, Doctor Charles had ordered Zach to look after his wife. It was amazing how much village gossip Harold gleaned without going anywhere, Jessie thought.

'I don't suppose the poor woman will get too much help from that old reprobate,' Harold said disapprovingly, after Rita had called at the chemist to get some aspirins and cough medicine for her mother, together with the prescription the doctor had written for her. 'That girl will be doing half the chores after work.'

'She won't let her dad get away with it,' Jessie told him, 'and he did look genuinely concerned about his wife after church on Sunday.'

Harold sniffed. 'A new broom sweeping clean, if you ask me, but if it keeps him out of the pub for a while it can do nothing but good.' He glanced at her. 'I must say you're not looking your usual self this week, either, Jessie. Are you sickening for something as well?'

'I'm all right, thank you, Mr Price,' she said. She certainly wasn't about to tell him she was heartsick over missing her young man.

But hearing about Rita's mother made her decide to go and visit her. Ellen agreed that it was a neighbourly thing to do, and on learning that Zach Levant was evidently in charge of household duties now, she insisted on Jessie taking one of her home-made fruitcakes with her.

'Whatever else he is or isn't doing, I doubt that Mrs Levant will be getting too many treats,' Ellen observed, with understated criticism.

Jessie put the cake tin in her bicycle basket and cycled down to Rita's house during the evening. To her surprise, the smell of cooking made her mouth water as soon as she went inside, but instead of seeing Rita at the stove, she nearly fell about to see Zach frying bacon, his shirtsleeves rolled up and one of Mrs Levant's aprons stretched ludicrously around his large bulk.

'Good evening, Mr Levant,' she almost stuttered. 'My goodness, something smells good.'

He gave a guttural chuckle. 'Now, don't you go telling folk you saw me dressed like this, my girl. My lady upstairs fancied something tasty, so this is what she's getting. Rita's upstairs with her now, so you can go on up and see her if you like, and tell her the feast will be coming shortly.'

She almost fled away from him, unable to keep the laughter at bay. What a joke Harold Price would make of this! But that was something he wasn't going to know, she vowed.

Upstairs, Rita was dusting the ornaments on the dressing table in her mother's room, and Mrs Levant was looking reasonably well, sitting up in bed and with her hair brushed and tidied, no doubt Rita's work. They both smiled a welcome as they saw Jessie appear.

'I've come to see how you are, Mrs Levant. Mum's sent you one of her fruitcakes, and your husband says that the feast will be coming shortly.'

'Thank you, my love. It's very good of your mother, and as you can see I'm feeling much better with my two helpers looking after me so well,' the woman said with a smile.

Rita laughed out loud at Jessie's expression.

'My dad's found a new role in life,' she giggled. 'I think he got a scare when Mum was so sick, and now he's vowing to turn over a new leaf and be a proper husband and keep off the beer. Lord knows how long it will last.'

'But it's very welcome while it does, so I'll hear nothing against him, Rita,' her mother put in.

She never did, Jessie realised. No matter what the village thought about Zach Levant, his wife had always championed him. With her love of romantic novels and the inevitable happy endings, Zach was obviously still her knight in shining armour, no matter what. And it was the sweetest thing Jessie had seen in ages when, a few minutes later, he appeared triumphant with a tray containing a plate of bacon and fried bread for his wife. He was still wearing her apron and the anxious, harassed look of a man unused to such chores and wanting approval.

'It looks marvellous, Zach,' Mary Levant said. 'Come and sit beside me while I eat it.'

Rita and Jessie left them to it and went downstairs, where Rita began clearing up the many kitchen utensils that had been used for such a simple task.

'Makes you sick, doesn't it?' she said with a grin. 'They're acting all lovey-dovey towards one another, and I can only stand so much of it.'

'I think it's lovely for two people of their age to

still think so much of one another – and I never thought your dad had it in him,' Jessie couldn't help saying.

'Neither did we! But thanks for coming, Jess. I know Mum will appreciate the thought. She's talking about getting up tomorrow, but I think Dad will be quite happy if she stays there another day or two.'

'But she is going to be all right, is she?'

'Oh yes. It was flu all right, but the doctor dosed her up and she's got over it quite quickly. It made Dad think twice about all the times he's neglected her, though, and I just hope he remembers it when she's downstairs again. And if he doesn't, I'll make darned sure I remind him,' she added. 'But how about you? Any news of Will?'

Jessie shook her head. 'I don't expect to hear anything until he gets back, and it's only been four days. I keep wondering what's happening, though. It must be very awkward for him and his mum to meet the other woman in his dad's life. I'm not sure I could do it.'

'Yes, you could. You could do anything if you had to, Jess.'

'If that's a compliment, I'm not sure I deserve it, but thanks.'

'It's a statement of fact, you ninny. You've got a lot of backbone, Jess, even if you don't always seem to know it. Who else could resist the charms of Vicar Stephen living in the same house, except you?' she finished teasingly.

Jessie flung a tea towel at her and they were both laughing when Zach brought the supper tray downstairs again. Rita sobered at once.

'If you want to go out for an hour or so, Dad, me and Jessie can stay here with Mum.'

He shook his head. 'That's all right, my girl. I promised your mum I'd read to her, though she knows I'm not much good at reading, and we might have a game of draughts later if I can lay my hands on the box. I think it's somewhere in the cupboard under the stairs.'

As he went off to find it, the two girls looked at each other in astonishment. Then Rita laughed, but her laugh was mixed with a kind of strangled emotion.

'It'll never last,' she whispered, 'but while it does, it's something like one of your dad's miracles.'

CHAPTER TWENTY-ONE

There was to be a christening in the village church on the second Sunday in December. The young Platt family came to see Vicar Penwarden, and were very anxious that he should conduct the service for the new baby as he had done for their first child.

'I'd be more than happy to oblige, but it may present some difficulty,' he said, seated across from the couple in his study that afternoon. 'With my arm still in plaster I couldn't hold the baby safely with such an encumbrance. If you insist on the date, Vicar Stephen could conduct the service for you and I would naturally be there to assist.'

The young man looked at his wife. 'We understand, Vicar, but we're both agreed that we want you to do it. No offence to Vicar Stephen, but you've christened all the babies in the village for who knows how long, and it's a tradition we don't want to break. We especially chose this date in memory of the day Gran died five years ago, and we'd be very unhappy to have to postpone it.'

'Well then, since it means so much to you, I shall have to see what I can do,' Thomas said decisively. 'Come back and see me tomorrow after I've had my doctor's appointment, and we'll see what can be arranged.'

'That's it, then,' he declared to Ellen, once he

had seen the visitors out. 'I don't intend to disap-point the Platts, so I shall see Doctor Charles and get him to arrange with the hospital for me to remove this plaster as soon as possible and then I can return to normal. I'm feeling perfectly fit now, and Stephen can have his marching orders,' he added.

'I'm sure you don't mean that to be as callous as it sounds,' Ellen said.

'Of course I don't, but he's given me plenty of hints that he's been here long enough, so I think it will be a mutual decision. And don't look at me like that, Ellen. I need to feel useful again, and right now I hardly feel like that in my own house. This christening gives me a goal to work towards.'

Jessie came home from work in time to hear the end of the discussion.

'What's happened? Is Stephen leaving?' she said, barely able to keep the eagerness out of her voice.

'Your father has a christening to arrange,' Ellen said shortly, 'and of course Stephen will be leav-ing eventually, but not until Thomas is perfectly fit.'

'I am fit, woman! Haven't I just been telling you that? I think the doctor will have more to say about it tomorrow, so when we hear what he thinks, there'll be no more arguing about it.'

He stormed out of the house and Ellen looked after him in annoyance. 'Just look at him. I can understand his eagerness to do the Platts' christ-ening, but I'm not sure a show of temper like that is good for his blood pressure.'

Stephen returned almost immediately afterwards, having met Thomas going the other way, and forestalled what Ellen might have been going to say.

'It's good news that Thomas feels so well, and I hope for his sake his arm will be in good stead for the christening in December. He'll hold the child in his left arm, and will only need his right hand to put the holy water on the baby's head, so all should be well. I don't think you need worry too much, Ellen, and it's also high time I moved on. You know what they say about two women in the same kitchen. I think the same could be said about two practising vicars in a household being one too many, wouldn't you say? Now then, if you'll excuse me, I'll be in the study for a while, ladies.'

Jessie was almost gasping for breath as he gave his usual lengthy spiel. He never seemed to say anything without making a speech about it, and although he had said it all with a smile on his face, there was a barb beneath it. And the remark about two practising vicars in one household being one too many was the most significant of all.

'Well, what do you make of that, Mum?' Jessie said when they were alone. 'Who's been getting on whose nerves, do you think?'

'I'd say it was six of one and half a dozen of the other,' Ellen said dryly. 'Nice as he is, Stephen's only been here as a temporary measure, but he's been in charge all this time, and now he's getting his nose pushed out of joint by your father. It was bound to happen. Abbot's Cove is a sleepy, old-fashioned community, Jessie, and I suspect that Stephen's youthful charm is also wearing a bit thin in certain quarters.'

Guiltily, Jessie couldn't help feeling cheered at the thought. It had only needed her father's return to be the catalyst for things to start changing back to the way they were, after all. There was never any chance of Stephen Daley being a permanent fixture in the village. Last Sunday had shown them how much affection her father was held in, and Stephen must have sensed it too. His day would come, but it wasn't now and it wasn't here.

The sound of the telephone from the office made her jump, and caused her mother to raise her eyebrows. It was a look that said *here we go again*. It was never very long before somebody in the village needed advice or an appointment for something, whether it was a christening, a wedding or a burial, or just to have someone to talk to. It was part of a vicar's role to be part of everything to do with the circle of life, and Ellen had always thought that one of the duties few people really appreciated was that a vicar was also something of a glorified counsellor.

Stephen came out of the study a minute later.

'It's for you, Jessie,' he said.

She started. She didn't know anyone who had a telephone, other than those in a more official capacity, such as the chemist, the doctor and the police station, and she had no idea who might be trying to contact her in such a way. During the war bad news had always come in the form of a yellow telegram, she thought, her heart turning over at the memory, but the thought of bad news was never far from anyone's mind as far as telephone calls to the vicarage went.

Her brain seemed to go to mush for a moment. Then she went quickly into the study and closed the door behind her before picking up the receiver that Stephen had placed on the desk.

'Hello,' she said huskily.

'Jessie, it's me,' she heard a familiar voice say, so close and so intimate that he might have been right there in the room beside her.

'*Will!*' she gasped, gripping the telephone cord tightly as if letting it go might take him away from her. The sound of his voice was so unexpected that she sat down heavily on her father's chair and blurted out the first words that came into her head. 'Where are you? What's happening? Is everything all right?'

'Calm down a minute. Of course I'm all right. And I'm home – well, I'm actually in Mr Spencer's office at the moment. I've come here to tell him we're back and he let me use the phone to call you.'

'And how-how did it go?' she stammered, knowing it sounded inane, but unable to think of anything else to say at that moment.

She was unused to talking to him this way, and more than anything she wished she could reach out and touch him. She wished she could see the expression on his face. His voice brought him close ... yet not really close at all. Not physically close...

'I'll tell you everything when I see you.' He sounded guarded now, and she realised how easy it was to notice the changing nuances in his voice. 'I'll just say it was the right thing for Mum to do, but I'd rather tell you more when I see you. I'll come down on Wednesday night if you think your dad won't object. Mum's going to see Mrs Greenaway then.'

'Of course he won't object,' she said quickly. 'He intends to go back to overseeing the junior Bible class then, anyway – and I can't wait to see you, Will.'

'I'll be down as early as I can. It's so good to hear your voice, Jess.'

'Yours too,' she almost croaked.

As the line went dead, she realised he had hung up the phone and she replaced the receiver carefully on its cradle. She sat there for a few moments before she went back to the living room, where Stephen and her mother were talking quietly. They looked up expectantly when she reappeared.

'It was Will. He and his mother are home, and he's coming down on Wednesday evening to tell me how it all went,' she said.

She couldn't explain why she felt uneasy. She was wildly relieved that he was back from France, and there was no reason for her to feel anything else. Unless it was the thought that Will had seen a different country, a different way of life, a different type of people, and somehow it had taken him away from her – living, as her mother called it, in this sleepy, old-fashioned community, which was the way they liked it. She shook off the feeling angrily. Will wouldn't have changed in so short a time, even though the week had seemed so endless to her. Will loved her as much as she loved him, and she clung to that belief steadfastly.

'You're being potty,' Rita told her. 'He was probably just tired after all the travelling, and of seeing his mum upset. He phoned you as soon as he could, didn't he?'

'I know you're right, but I can't help wondering what effect it all had on him, as well as his mother. In his heart I know he never wanted to see this other woman, nor to see where his father had been living all these years. Imagine looking around a strange living room and knowing this was your father's home, with his chair and his books, and maybe photos of himself and the other woman on the mantelpiece. It must have been an ordeal for them both.'

'Well then, you'll have to soothe his fevered brow, or whatever else you fancy, won't you?' Rita said, trying to cheer her up.

'Is that what your dad's doing for your mum, or has all the nursing worn off now?' Jessie said acidly.

'You'd be surprised. I didn't think it would last after Mum got up again, but he's been really nice to her and he's still keeping off the beer.' She shook her head slightly, as if wondering if this new side to her dad that she was seeing was the real thing or not.

Jessie shrugged. It wasn't Rita's dad she had come to discuss, but hearing about him reminded her of her own.

'Doctor Charles is arranging an appointment for my dad to go to the hospital to see about having his plaster off. It'll be a relief to everybody when it happens, I can tell you. And then it'll be bye-bye to Vicar Stephen, and we can all get back to the way we were before.'

'And how's that? With you sneaking around and meeting Will on the sly again?'

'Certainly not. He's coming to see me on Wednesday and he's coming to the house. There's no reason for him not to, now that Dad's met him, and that's the way it's going to be in future,' she added.

Thomas's hospital appointment was the next day, and he came home triumphant, saying the plaster would be coming off the following week.

'That gives me plenty of time to get my muscles working again in time to christen the Platt baby on 9th December without dropping it,' he joked to his family, in fine form now.

'And I shall be moving on soon afterwards,' Stephen told them. 'I've already informed the bishop, and he agrees that as soon as you feel able to take over completely, I may leave. I've written to my family in Ireland to expect me to spend Christmas with them, which will be a real treat for me.'

'It sounds like good news all round,' Ellen said with a smile.

'I think we should celebrate it all by a little drink of port, my dear,' Thomas went on expansively. 'What do you say, Jessie? You may join us in a glass now that you're nearly eighteen.'

For a moment she thought they had forgotten she was there at all. The sense of celebration seemed to be centred around her father's feeling of well-being, and their visitor's promised departure. Both of them were very welcome, of course, but nobody noticed that she wasn't completely in the mood for celebrating, and nor would she be until she had seen Will again and heard his news. But as her mother looked at her expectantly, she knew she couldn't bring the atmosphere down by her own misgivings, so she forced a smile instead.

By Wednesday evening she was a bag of nerves. As it happened, Will arrived before her father had gone out and the two men eyed one another warily before Thomas said archly that he supposed he had better get used to his daughter having a gentleman caller from now on. Jessie laughed out loud.

'Oh Dad, that's so old-fashioned!'

'Well, it's to be hoped that Will Tremayne *is* a gentleman. Can I count on that, young man?' he said.

'Of course you can, sir, and I will always treat Jessie as a lady,' Will said steadily, his face reddening, despite his efforts to stay calm.

'Then you'll always be welcome here,' Thomas told him. 'Now I must get on or I'll be late for my Bible class.'

'Let me help you into your coat, Dad,' Jessie said at once, knowing how difficult it was for him.

To her surprise his eyes suddenly misted as she did as she suggested.

'It seems hardly any time ago that I was buttoning you into your little coat and taking you and Adam out to Bible class, and now look at you, on the brink of being eighteen and a grown woman, and doing the same for me.'

He cleared his throat and shrugged away from her, aware that he had made the most unlikely remark, and countering it by telling Will shortly not to keep his daughter out too late.

'Where are we going?' she asked Will as she slid into the car beside him. She was nervous, not knowing what she might hear about his visit to France.

'I thought we'd go to the old abbey. I know it's a bit cold, but I feel the need to walk for a bit if it's all right with you.'

'Of course it is.' It was strange how it was sometimes easier to talk things out when two people were walking together, and she still didn't know exactly what things they had to talk out.

He said very little until they reached the road above the ruined abbey, and he had parked the car. Then she felt reassured by the way he tucked her arm in his as they walked down the slope towards the ruins. Late November wasn't the best time of year for walking. It was already dusk, and nor was it the kindest weather. There was a cool wind blowing in from the sea, whipping up the short grasses and sending fronds of bracken into their eyes. They must be slightly mad to think this was a good idea, thought Jessie desperately, as the silence seemed to lengthen between them.

But once inside the ruins, the air was calmer, and they found a flat slab of stone to sit on, much as they had done here once before when he had kissed her for the first time. She didn't feel that closeness between them yet. Even though his arm was around her shoulders, she still felt as if he was remote from her, as if he was still somewhere in that other country that she knew nothing about.

'Are you going to tell me how it went, Will?' she said huskily. 'Was it so much of an ordeal for your mother?'

He gave a troubled sigh. 'Mum found it much easier than me,' he said, to her surprise. 'She had got used to losing her husband all that time ago, and merely wanted to close a chapter in her life. But Madeleine Dupont was nothing like we had imagined. She was quite gentle and obviously brokenhearted, in a way that Mum wasn't anymore. I still resented her but I also felt quite sorry for her. Then it dawned on me that even though I always said I hated him, I'd still been seeing my dad through rose-coloured glasses all this time, thinking that some woman had stolen him away from us, and now I had to see the reality of it all. He had loved that woman, and she had really loved him, and it made me feel betrayed all over again. I know it's pathetic. I'm a man now, yet I still felt lost that my dad had gone away and left me.'

Jessie didn't know what to say. She had never heard him talk so long and so passionately, and she could see that he was still hurting. She put her hand in his, feeling how cold his was. She spoke very carefully, embarrassed at being so frank, and dreading saying the wrong thing when she could see that his feelings were still so raw.

'Will, I think it's time to put the past behind you, the way your mum has done. You'll never lose the memories of when your family was all together, but we all have to grow up eventually. If memories are all we have, we should cherish them. It's the same whenever I think about my brother, and – well, you heard what my dad said tonight. Fancy him remembering buttoning me into my little coat and taking Adam and me to Bible class. I'm sure these memories help him, and those are the things you should be remembering too.'

He was silent for so long she was sure she must have upset him by trying to sound so wise. Then she felt his hold tighten around her and he had caught her in his arms.

'You do me good, sweetheart,' he said shakily. 'In case I forget to tell you, you're the best thing that ever happened to me, and I love you.'

'I love you too, Will, so much,' she said breathlessly, sending up a silent prayer that he sounded more like himself, and that the lost look in his eyes had diminished. He was looking at her properly in the gathering darkness now, as if he was seeing only her, and no disturbing ghosts of the past.

But involuntarily, she gave a small shiver, remembering the many ghosts who were reputed to abide here in the ruined abbey, although none of them had ever really held any fears for her. She and Adam had always thought of them as benevolent ghosts, guarding the village that bore the abbey's name.

'You're cold, and we should get away from

here,' Will said at once. 'We'll sit in the car and look at the moonlight instead, which I've wanted to do with my girl ever since I got back.'

They walked back to the car with their arms entwined, and once inside it Will turned to her, holding her hands tightly.

'I'm sorry about blurting it all out like that, Jessie. I just had to get it off my chest, and I hope you don't think any less of me.'

'Don't be silly. It took a real man to do as you did and take your mother to meet that other woman. I'm proud of you, Will.'

They sat there for a long while, either talking quietly, or not talking at all, until the moon had risen high in the sky, and even inside the car it was getting too cold for comfort.

'I'd better take you home. Now that your father's more or less accepted that I'm not about to ravish his lovely daughter, I don't want to antagonise him by keeping you out late,' he said reluctantly, finishing with a kiss.

She could hardly explain the rush of emotion that she felt then. A vicar's daughter was no more a saint than anyone else, and she didn't feel shocked to know that she wanted more than anything for him to ravish her and love her, love her, love her... But knowing where that might lead, she was also too full of common sense to let the feelings out, and instead she merely clung to him and kissed him back with all the passion in her soul.

'You're the best thing that ever happened to me too, Will,' she whispered.

Thomas's plaster was finally removed and he was learning to use the muscles in his right arm again. By then, Ellen had been to visit Doris Tremayne and was glad to see that the sorrow she had felt about her husband's betrayal was now well and truly in the past. Doris also mentioned that on going through some of her old papers, there was a small life insurance policy which Will insisted should be honoured. It was the least his father could do for his mother, and she finally agreed to it. It was a small enough legacy, but she knew it gave Will the sense of finality he needed.

In the week before Jessie's birthday Stephen Daley left the village to a small fanfare of parishioners at the church hall.

'You know, I'm not sorry he's gone,' Jessie told Rita. 'He was never any bother in the house, and at first I think Dad liked having him around. I suppose it was because of having another young man in the house, the way Adam would have been. But all that palled when they started to clash over church matters. It's far better to be just the three of us again.'

'Or four, when Will comes to call,' Rita said with a grin. 'I'm still surprised he didn't bring you anything back from France.'

'Well, I'm not as mercenary as you, and it's not why he went, is it?'

In any case, he had hinted more than once that he might have something special for her on her birthday, and she tried not to be over-impatient.

It was accepted in the village, now, that Jessie Penwarden had a young man. He was a frequent visitor to the vicarage, and more often than not, he brought Ronnie Hill with him to see Rita. They sometimes went out together, but the best times were always those that Jessie and Will spent on their own. And on Saturday it was going to be her birthday, and she couldn't deny a huge sense of anticipation, especially when Ellen said she could invite Will for tea before they went to the dance that evening.

They didn't go in for parties, even on such an important occasion as an eighteenth birthday. Being frugal was still something of a legacy of the war years, when food was in such short supply and it seemed extravagant for one family to enjoy luxuries when others went without. All the same, Ellen had baked a special cake and decorated it with hundreds and thousands, and there was ham for tea, followed by one of Ellen's special trifles, lavishly filled with tinned fruit.

There were presents too. Harold and Vera Price had given her a bottle of lavender water, taken from stock, no doubt, but still enough to make Jessie blink and stammer her thanks. Rita had bought her a book of poetry, and Rita's mum had sent her a small box of chocolates. From her parents, there was money in a money box that had been saved for her ever since she was a little girl, and the sum in the box brought a lump to Jessie's throat.

'I never expected this,' she said, swallowing hard.

'You're to think of it as your nest egg for whatever you want to do in the future, my love,' Ellen said.

Jessie hugged them both, knowing very well exactly what she wanted to do with her future, and was hardly able to wait for when Will would arrive that afternoon. When he did, after leaving Ronnie at Rita's house, he brought a card and a bunch of flowers from his mother, and told her she had to wait for his gift until after the dance that evening.

'Do you know how frustrating that is?' she said with a small pout.

Thomas put in a word, expansive with the pleasure of this day.

'Exercising patience was never one of Jessie's strong points, Will, but I'm sure she'll manage it somehow.'

She laughed at his teasing, thinking how good it was to see him whole and happy again. Adam wasn't here to share this day with them, but Will was, and she thought that in a small way, her dad was finding comfort in that. There was nothing to beat having a loving family and good friends around you, and tonight her best friend, Rita, and their two boys, were going to the dance together. She thought she had never felt happier.

The dance hall was crowded as usual that evening, and although Jessie would have preferred to keep quiet about it being her birthday, some of her old school friends remembered, and had mentioned it to the Ladies' Committee. So, during the interval in the middle of the evening, to her embarrassment one of the organisers announced that it was Jessie's birthday, and encouraged everyone to sing 'Happy Birthday' to her.

'It's a nice gesture, but I wish she hadn't done it,' Jessie said, pink-faced as Will and Ronnie went to fetch the girls a drink of lemonade.

'Well, you're only eighteen once, so enjoy it, for goodness' sake – and you haven't told me what Will's bought you yet.'

Jessie laughed. 'That's because I don't know. He's making me wait until after the dance and it's driving me crazy! My dad says patience was never one of my strong points, and he's right!'

But there was also something rather sweet in the anticipation. She knew there was going to be a surprise from Will later on, and nothing was going to dim the happiness of this day. By the time the last waltz was being played and couples were drifting around the room, lulled by the romance of the music, she leant her head against Will's shoulder, and thought that only something very special could surpass these moments.

'It's time for your present now,' he said against her cheek. 'We'll run these two back to Rita's house in the car and then it will just be ourselves.'

Jessie felt a small twist of envy at his words. Rita's parents were so accommodating towards Ronnie, and she knew he would be able to spend as much time as he liked drinking cocoa and exchanging motorbike yarns with Zach Levant. She wished her own father could be as unbending as the newly domesticated Zach – and it was one of life's mysteries to even think like that!

As they drove back to Rita's house, Rita was still trying to persuade Will to tell her what Jessie's present might be, but she finally gave up, knowing she would get nothing more out of Will and would have to wait until she saw Jessie the following day. They parted amid much laughter and plenty of guesswork.

Then at last Will and Jessie were alone, and by common assent Will drove to the top of the cliffs overlooking the abbey and the cove, with the village some distance behind them. From up high it resembled fairyland now, with lights twinkling from every house, and looking so different from when the wartime blackout had turned it into a shrouded and impersonal place. Now, it was alive again, despite those who would never come home. Jessie pushed that last remnant of sadness out of her mind as the car stopped, and turned to Will.

'If you make me wait one minute longer for my birthday present, I swear I shall burst,' she said.

He laughed, reaching underneath his seat to bring out a large flat packet wrapped in a bright sheet of paper. He turned on the interior light in the car and handed the packet to her.

'This is the first part of your birthday present, Jess,' he said. 'I don't have the words to say all that I want to say, but this should tell you some of it.'

She unwrapped it quickly, and drew in her breath as she saw the sleeve of the gramophone record and recognised her favourite song of the moment. At once, the first lines of the song were running through her head...

You sigh, the song begins; you speak and I hear violins; It's magic...

Nobody could sing 'It's Magic' the way Doris Day could, and since she knew by heart all the lovely sentiments it conveyed and realised what Will was trying to tell her through the words of the song, it sent a lump to her throat. He couldn't

381

have chosen anything better.

She leant forward and threw her arms around him. 'Thank you, Will. It's lovely.'

'Well, like I told you, that's just the first part. This is the most important part, and I hope you're going to like this even more.'

He drew out the small box from his pocket, and handed it to her. His voice was thicker now.

'I'm really not much good with words, Jessie, but I'd give you the world if I could, so this is just a token of the real thing.'

She opened the box, and nestling inside was a thin necklet on which hung a small golden heart locket. She gasped, and took it out with trembling fingers.

'Oh Will, this is the loveliest thing anyone has ever given me. I shall wear it always. Will you fasten it for me?'

As he did so, with awkward, clumsy fingers, she felt the coolness of the gold against her neck, and then he bent to kiss the point where the locket met her skin. She was in his arms properly then, and he held her so tight she thought he was never going to let her go. But when he did so, he had a serious question to ask her, and she could sense that he was nervous about asking it.

'Do you think tonight would be the right time for me to ask your father if we could become officially engaged at Christmas, Jessie?'

Her heart soared at his words, and her voice was as husky as his.

'I think there could never be a better time, Will darling,' she said.

The publishers hope that this book has given you enjoyable reading. Large Print Books are especially designed to be as easy to see and hold as possible. If you wish a complete list of our books please ask at your local library or write directly to:

Magna Large Print Books
Magna House, Long Preston,
Skipton, North Yorkshire.
BD23 4ND

This Large Print Book for the partially sighted, who cannot read normal print, is published under the auspices of

THE ULVERSCROFT FOUNDATION